The Academy of Love

Ida Duque

Domiveni Publishing LLC

To my daughters for inspiring me every day. For laughing with
me and at me.
To my husband for always making me laugh.
To our parents.
To romance readers everywhere. Especially those that love
romantic comedy.

Contents

Olivia

"*Botany?* You want to take botany?" I ask again.

He squares his shoulders as he says with certainty, "Yes."

I purse my lips and will my eyebrows not to move. "Already then."

Since the moment they walked in, the mismatched couple in front of me has been holding hands. The well-mannered woman in front of my desk screams class in her crisp and tailored black business suit. The man sitting next to her might be the same age, but with his backward baseball cap, baggy shirt, and seriously oversized pants that fall under his waist, I'm reminded of a 1990s movie.

His poised wife gazes at him, nodding with adoration when he speaks. Earlier she explained they were high-school sweethearts. "Ms. Campbell, he's smart," she says, looking at me again.

"Please, call me Olivia." I'm inclined to believe her after looking at his stellar, albeit old, SAT scores on the screen, and the outstanding placement test scores he recently took after six years out of high school.

"I want him to do something with his life, go to college and get an education, a better job, you know?" she says, sending him a sideways glance.

I'm beginning to think coming here might not have been his idea.

I turn to him again. "What classes would you like to try?"

"I'm not sure," he mumbles.

"Why do you want to do botany specifically?" I wait a few seconds. "Look, John, I just met you and unless you share something you like, like a topic or a hobby, I can't help you. I could register you, but you might end up in classes that you'll hate."

I ask the same questions, phrasing them differently. "Do you like plants? Are you good with plants?" He gives me a blank look. "We have a program in architecture and landscape design. Does that sound interesting?"

"I don't think so," he says. "I *just* want to learn about plants. Do you think they cover all types of plants in botany class?" I raise my eyebrows. *Wow. A full sentence.*

I honestly have no idea what kinds of plants they talk about in botany class. Besides biology and science students, and the occasional art student who wants to learn how to draw nature, botany is not a popular class, but now I'm intrigued. I go with it and start firing off questions. "What kinds of plants are you into? Which ones do you want to learn about? Flowers? Trees? *Bonsai?*"

His wife squirms in her seat, her face turning every shade of red known to man. *Why is she uncomfortable?*

"Here's the thing." He pauses to look at his wife, then looks straight at me. "You asked me if there was something I liked or that I was good at, and there is one thing."

"Okay! Awesome, what is it?" I lean forward, thrilled we may finally be getting somewhere.

"I want to learn about plants because I want to sell plants. I want to see if I can plant and sell marijuana plants—I think..."

Annnd there it is. For a second, I'm tempted to slap my forehead. He keeps going, explaining *allll* the reasons why he loves selling *this* particular plant and how good he is at doing it.

Crap. I need to find a polite way to steer the conversation back to academics *pronto* before he gets too excited. A few of my students look like they *might* be drug dealers, but so far nobody has ever admitted to *being* a drug dealer. No student has ever acknowledged they like selling illegal substances. *EVER.* At least not to my face.

Should I tell a student to pursue or not to pursue his illegal enterprise? With "illegal" being the operative word. I make a mental note to ask Judith, my supervisor, about laws on encouraging a student in illicit enterprises. While I'm at it, I should also ask if I could go to jail for promoting this.

I look over at the wife. She's regained her color but squeezes her lips together and raises her eyebrows. Her shoulders tense and she takes a deep breath. I wonder how many times he's told her about his love of the *plant*, and if she's given up on persuading him otherwise. I can't help but try to guess how lucrative his enterprise is... *or not.*

I notice he's stopped talking and they are both looking at me. I refocus on them. "Okay," I say after a moment, searching for words. "Let's forget for a few minutes that you like selling... *plants.* Have you considered that maybe you just like selling?"

I can see the wheels turning. His eyebrows squish together, and his fingers rub over his chin.

After a full minute he says, "I don't think so. I don't want to work for a company. A company will use me for profits while they get rich. I'll be stuck working for a supervisor I'll hate, and I don't want to be a work-slave to corporate America."

Work-slave? Is he serious? A few of my students don't believe in the power of a college degree. They only enroll in college to please their parents or because they don't know what else to do *but* go to college. I have a few students who see going to college as a waste of time. Many want to be entrepreneurs and dream of starting a business and becoming wealthy overnight like Mark Zuckerberg. A select few even think they're smarter than a professor with a Ph.D. who has field *and* career experience.

Let's try something else. I search for a way to get the information I need from this man. "Can I ask you a personal question?"

He looks at his watch before answering, "Sure."

"Do you work now? What do you do for a living? Selling the plants doesn't count." I add quickly, before he can reiterate how his sales currently generate an income stream.

"I do jobs here and there," he reluctantly admits as he shakes his head sideways, giving away nothing. Honestly, at this point, I don't even want to know.

"Look, John..." I hesitate, taking care to place my clasped hands just so on the desk in front of us to get his full attention. "The fact of the matter is you're married to a beautiful woman. A woman who went to college and obviously works. As she gains more experience, chances are she'll start making a lot more money. At some point, she just *might* get tired of supporting you. And besides, don't you want to support *her* and help *her*?" I can't help but point at her with my hand while she says nothing. This comment hits a nerve. He looks down, crumpling in his seat.

Appealing to the protective macho-man in my students always works. "The best thing you can do is get your degree. You don't have to work for a company and be a 'work-slave,'" I say, making air quotes. "You could start your own company and sell whatever you want. There are a lot of salespeople out there who make a ton of money. You can have a successful career and a wonderful life with your wife. Besides, medicinal marijuana is now legal in Florida. You can open a shop, get approved by the state, and sell it *legally*. If you study business, you can learn about accounting, managing a business, and marketing your... *product*, you know?"

He stays quiet before meeting his wife's eyes. "Okay, you're right," he murmurs while her lips slowly turn upward and she smiles at me.

Yes! Mental fist bump! Thank God that worked!

After I print out his schedule and give him a copy, I tell them where they can pay his fees, get a student ID, and a parking decal. I remind him when classes start while he nods. His wife thanks me and gives me a big smile as they walk out, leaving me alone in my office.

Yep. Coming here was definitely her idea.

I rest my head on my desk, thankful for a minute of peace and quiet before reaching for my coffee that's now stone cold.

As an academic advisor I help students register for classes and resolve academic issues, sometimes *brainwashing* some of them into picking a major that will potentially lead to a career while also dealing with helicopter parents who might or might not agree with said choice. Nobody told me when I started this job five years ago that occasionally, I would also have to be their personal psychologist.

From time to time, I'm even pressed to give relationship advice, not that I'm necessarily qualified to do so. When I became an advisor, I convinced myself that I would make a difference in the lives of my students. My ultimate goal is for them to choose a major that will lead to a paying career and fulfilling professional lives...one student at a time. *Now that I think about it, no one told me I'd also have to be a therapist when I took this job. Should I ask for a raise?*

I set my coffee back on my desk. Ugh, unintentionally iced coffee is terrible. Some days my job is crazy and overwhelming, but I love organized chaos. Besides advising duties, I'm expected to take part in no less than ten committees, anything from event planning to staff hiring. Sometimes said committees will all insist on meeting at either the exact same day and time or at random times during the week. I also have to tame the wild beast called email. I answer over seventy-five emails a day from students who all want to know what class to take next semester or tell me again why they hate math and why I need to change their math class before the semester starts *and the world implodes.*

My life would be so much easier if they all followed my advice. Unfortunately, some of my students are clueless. On the other hand, the new fall semester will bring endless possibilities. I can still be positive, right?

I quickly open my personal email and find an email from a potential roommate. She wants to know if I mind exotic pets. *How exotic?* A blue macaw? I loved the movie *Rio.* Excitement builds and I can picture myself with it on my shoulder walking through downtown Miami. Until the words *iguana* and *boa constrictor* appear in the following sentence.

Cue the record scratch. Yeah, not happening.

"Olivia?" One of the student assistants, Lucy, materializes at my door as I type a quick reply and then look up.

"Yes, what's up?"

Her eyes widen and she slides forward, stepping inside my office. "Did you hear?"

"What?"

"HR removed the advisor position from the website. They're going to bring in somebody from the central campus instead."

One advisor quit recently and another one is on medical leave. The position was *just* posted. Now they're transferring a person in? "What? Why?"

"I don't know," she says, shrugging. "Oh, also, Judith wants to talk to you."

"Okay. Thank you." I love the student assistants. They provide an endless source of entertainment and useful gossip.

"You're welcome," she says before she walks away. When my computer screen darkens, I quickly check my reflection and stand up.

Our long rectangular office is decorated with motivational messages along its white walls. I love reading them. '*You can do it!*' says one; a picture of men scaling a mountain reads '*Aim High*,' and it honestly seems fitting. *Yes, I will.* As I walk along the hallway, I wonder if the students ever read them. I can't be the only one, can I? *Focus.*

My boss, Judith, has been at the university for over twenty-five years and at her current job for ten. It's been rumored she'll be retiring soon as our department director. At the last staff meeting, she talked about wanting to pursue other interests, such as teaching at the university and having more free time to spoil her new grandkids. Judith is very Zen, always having the perfect response and advice for any situation, all the time. It's like having a wise grandparent constantly present to give you wisdom. I tap on her door and get her attention. "Judith? You wanted to see me?"

"Yes, come in, Olivia. Sit. Close the door, please."

I look at her and imagine Katie Couric sitting behind a huge dark mahogany desk interviewing me... if Katie Couric had brown eyes and salt and pepper hair. I force myself out of the mental picture, because the second my butt hits the seat, she jumps right in. "I had a lengthy conversation with a parent yesterday. She said you were trying to undermine her in front of her son. She was upset."

Oh, crap.

The second she says this, I immediately know who it is. "No, I wasn't. She wants her son to be a doctor, and he bombed basic chemistry *five* times. All I said was its perhaps not going to happen, and she needs to let it go. If she's in denial, that's her problem."

"Olivia, you can't tell a parent that."

"I didn't say it in those *exact* words." The *exact* words I wanted to use would have *definitely* gotten me fired.

"No, but when we have challenging students or parents, we must listen to them."

"I did listen to her. She expressed her opinion, then I expressed mine."

She leans forward in her seat, and her fingers interlace on top of her desk. "Olivia, let me be blunt. I will be retiring soon. As a matter of fact, I don't think I'll be here by spring. You have potential. Your peers respect you and your students love you, *but* if you want to move up and have a career in higher ed, you need to be more diplomatic with the parents."

I know Judith's right and that she wants me to succeed, but *this* parent needed to hear the truth. "Thank you, I appreciate that, but I'm not here to advise parents. You pay me to help students."

"Parents pay tuition."

Touché.

She lets out a long breath of air and looks at me. "Look, I agree with you. He probably won't get into med school, but next time try to be more sympathetic to the parents. When you talk to a parent, listen to their concerns, don't contradict them, just listen. *Then* I want you to direct them to the website and tell them to do further research. Have them read about the major or the career they want their son or daughter to pursue *and* the requirements of that major. Let them realize it on their own terms. Remember, it's a mourning process. The parents have to let go of their dreams, too. Okay?"

"You want me to lie to them?"

"No. That is not what I'm saying. I want you to... redirect them," she says while her hands turn sideways.

"Okay."

"Olivia, let me tell you a story about a boy and a martial arts master. One time, when the pupil was upset, they walked into the woods and stared at a stream. When the boy didn't understand what they were doing there, the master told the boy to look at the water. He explained even though the rocks are in its way, the river doesn't just slam into them out of frustration, it simply *flows* over and around them and moves on."

Am I supposed to be the boy, the rock or the stream in this scenario? Should I ask?

"O-kaaay."

"That'll be all. Thank you." She nods and turns to her computer while I force a smile and stand up. *Still confused.*

As I rush back to my office, I raise my chin and straighten my back. I can't help but wonder how many people she's told that she's retiring. It doesn't matter, because for the next few months, I vow to be like Judith and be Zen. To start, I will strive to be as calm as a cucumber. I will not, under any circumstance freak out, no matter what a student or their parents tell me. I will keep it together, all the time, and will help everybody around the office with my wisdom and listening skills. I will work on harnessing my wild energy and only focus on being a leader. The best leader. I will show Judith I can do this. I will impress her and the dean and when the time comes, they'll have no choice but to make me director. *How can I possibly fail?*

Olivia

S ummer in Miami has two settings. First, summer is wet season AKA hurricane season, which could mean daily rains, soaked and dark, with miserable traffic. The alternative is sunny with clouds, nice, tolerable, or hot with different levels of humidity. Essentially, beach weather. We all complain about the heat, but the beaches and parks are full. The truth is, we don't care about the heat and humidity; we avoid both at all costs by being in air-conditioned offices. We measure the humidity by the levels of hair frizz and how much you end up looking like the Lion King. Frizz, as it happens, is a great predictor of rain. Who needs the weatherman? The more frizz, the higher the chances of rain.

Every couple of weeks I meet my friends for lunch. Since we all work at the university, it's a brilliant way to catch up on all the gossip from our various departments. I park my car and start walking. By the time I arrive at the restaurant, my skin gleams and my hair is sticking to my forehead. *It's not sexy at all.*

Today we're meeting at a nearby burger place. The smell of meat and spices is mouthwatering. The place is full, possibly because it's payday for everyone at the university and I have a feeling we'll be forced to sit outside. Sunny with clouds beats rain and hurricanes—unless the thermometer reads two hundred degrees, hair is sticking to your face, and you're forced to wait outside.

I hug and kiss my friends, Bianca, Nicole, and Valentina. "Nice boots," I tell Bianca while we're standing, waiting for a table. She looks down at them. Bianca is the reason I have my job. We've been friends since undergrad, and after a brief stint at a public elementary school failed, she suggested I apply at the university.

"Thanks," she replies, smiling.

"How many inches? Like three? Four? Aren't you afraid of falling?" I would.

"No. I'm used to them. I'm small. These put me at 5'5"."

I can't help but correct her. "You're 'vertically challenged', not 'small'."

"Technically, I'm short. You're like 5'10. You're tall."

"I'm only 5'8". Not tall," I say as we spot and rush toward a table under a ceiling fan. *Jackpot!* "And I don't wear heels. Besides, you spend less time shaving your legs."

My friend throws her head back and laughs. "Oh my God. You're crazy but that's actually true," she says, grinning as we sit. "Hey, I meant to ask you— what's going on with the new advisor search?" Bianca works in the Student Life Department. She works with student organizations and has what you would call "the fun" job, which suits her fun-loving personality. She's a petite blonde, super friendly, has the warmest smile and students love her.

As we're settling, I take a couple of seconds to reply. "I have no idea. This morning I found out HR took the position down from the website. They're going to interview a few people from the central campus and two of *those* people will meet with our dean next week."

"Wow, they're moving fast," Nicole says, glancing at me as she grabs her napkin. "You know, that probably means they had somebody in mind." Nicole is the Honors program coordinator. Her students are what I would call "high-achievers/overachievers," times three. They are 4.0+ GPA students whose sole mission in life is to transfer to an Ivy League school, get a master's followed by a Ph.D. and discover another planet. She's way too nice, which is why she puts up with them. Incredibly, she tells all of them what to do, and they do it. It's like she's the overachiever whisperer or something.

A server materializes from the crowd and we order. "I don't know. I didn't think about it, to be honest, but you're right, it's going a little fast." I shrug after the server leaves. "I had a meeting with Judith today."

"What happened? Did she announce her retirement?" Bianca asks, leaning forward.

"No, *but* she told me I had to work on how I talk to parents."

"Why?"

"A parent complained."

"Why? What did you do?" Bianca asks, cocking her head.

"I did nothing. The point is, she told me she's not going to be here by spring."

"Does she want you to take over?"

"She didn't say, but I think she does. At least I hope she does. Which also makes me a bit apprehensive. If I'm the director and a parent complains to Dean Lozano, I'm gone. He'll fire me. I'm not Zen like Judith."

"He won't fire you. You'd be an amazing director."

"You guys think so?"

"I think so," Bianca says, smiling. I'm touched by her faith in me. If all fails, I know that my friends have my back.

"How's the roommate search?" Nicole says, interrupting my thoughts. "Any luck finding one?"

"I interviewed someone a couple of days ago. It was interesting to say the least."

"How so? What happened?" Nicole stops playing with the straw in her Coke and leans towards me, conspiratorially.

"She was kind, seemed normal, and well-adjusted. She has an expensive education, a good job, and after I showed her the house we went to eat. To be honest, I liked her a lot. She seemed perfect. The only odd thing was her cell phone rang quite a few times, but I didn't think it was a problem at first."

"Who was it?" Valentina piped up.

"Well, her phone kept flashing "Happy Happy Joy Joy," and after the twentieth time, I asked her if she needed to answer it. She told me not to worry about it, that it wasn't a big deal and she would call the person back later. Later on, she admitted she was a dealer. She sells prescription medication on the black market."

Valentina's mouth falls open. She recuperates quickly and with a high-pitched voice manages to say, "Oh. My. God! On the black market? She *admitted* to that?"

"Yes, she did. Like I said, it was interesting."

"How many people have you interviewed so far?" Valentina asks.

"Let's see, I interviewed a pleasant lady that offered to bless my home with a Wiccan spell. There was the sex operator who answered her phone in weird sexy voices. Another was a casino dealer that works at night and sleeps all day. *She* wanted me to play poker with her and bet me that if she won, she would live six months in my house, rent-free. Still, yet another asked me my thoughts on her being a dominatrix and bringing people over. And today somebody emailed me asking how I felt about iguanas and boa constrictor snakes."

Bianca's eyes bulge out in a horrified look, as she shakes her head. "I draw the line at *snakes*. I don't even know what to say to that. At least people are answering your ad?"

"They are, but you know—."

Valentina narrows her eyes at me; she knows me so well. "Stop being so picky. You said you need the money!"

I know she's right, but I have no control over who answers the ad. I don't want to be murdered in my own home, so I'm being extra cautious. "I do, but it's not working out as I hoped it would. I don't want to push it. Haven't you guys seen the movie *Single White Female?*"

"Olivia, you're being a *tad* dramatic. This isn't a movie," she says. Well, Ted Bundy was real. *We all know how that turned out.*

"I wish I could break my lease, then I could be your roommate," Nicole says, regretfully.

Ugh, that makes two of us. At the same time, I know if she could, she would.

"I saw Bran at a restaurant the other day. I almost didn't recognize him," Bianca says out of the blue as our food arrives. "He asked for you, wanted to know how you were doing, and said to tell you 'hi.' I told him you were great and up for a promotion. He looked a little scruffy. He said he lost a major account or lost money in a bad deal due to a computer error? I don't quite remember now."

Bran is my idiot ex. A *bad deal?* For a few seconds, I picture Bran or "Brandon," as he likes to be called, living homeless in Miami after a *few* bad deals. We bought a house together, but we're not together anymore because he's a cheating bastard.

Who breaks up with their girlfriend on her birthday and the day they have the keys to a new house? *A cheating bastard, that's who.*

"Olivia, what are you thinking?"

"Oh, nothing. I don't know what his problem is but something's going on because lately he's been liking all my Facebook posts. Is that supposed to get my attention? Remind me to block him."

"He's a cheating bastard, screw him," Valentina says. If she had her way, she would have run him over. With a bus. Twice.

Nicole glances at me from her burger. "Is it working?"

"Didn't he unfriend you?" Bianca asks casually.

"One, yes, he's a cheater. Two, no, we've had no contact for over five months because he was a cheating bastard. And three, yes, he did unfriend me, right after I unfriended him, for *being* a cheating bastard." I look at each of them as I answer their questions.

"You really need to block him. Better yet, have one of your brothers *talk* to him," Valentina says as she makes air quotes.

"Absolutely not. Are you crazy? Do you want them to go to jail? I had to hold them back from beating the crap out of him the last time."

Bianca looks at me. Her eyes sparkle and I can see the wheels turning. "Maybe you should start dating again. Let Bran see that you've moved on."

"It's been over six months. I have moved on."

"Forget about him. He's a dick anyway. He doesn't understand our jobs. At the very least, you should have somebody who supports your career," Valentina says as she sips her Coke.

"He's still dating that girl. Cheater Girl. Josh told me he put a recent picture of them together as his profile pic. I am so sorry, Olivia," Bianca continues, wrinkling her nose.

Josh is one of Bianca's best friends. They also work together in the student life department. We suspect he's in love with her, but she's too busy looking for the love of her life. *Tunnel vision* are the words that come to mind. I don't think she realizes her love might be right in front of her.

"You know what? If he's dating, you should be dating too." Bianca says. "My friend Wendy asked if I had any single friends. Her second cousin's single and I thought about you." Her upbeat tone signals she's gaining enthusiasm. *Oh boy, here we go.*

"Like a blind date? No."

"You haven't been on a date for a long time. Don't you think it is time?"

"This from the girl who has a new date every week and whose relationships don't last over three months? You're not qualified to give me dating advice." I say as I give Bianca a warning glance. I love her to death, but I swear to God, she's two dates away from me making her talk to a psychologist.

"Hey! I resent that. My relationships last more than three months. They usually last four."

"Are you serious right now?"

"Besides, how else are you going to meet somebody unless you date?" she asks, raising her eyebrows.

"You *should* go on a date," Valentina joins in.

"Can you not encourage her? Plus, you go on even fewer dates than I do. How many men have asked you on dates lately?"

Valentina narrows her eyes and takes a deep breath. "Who cares about dating? Have you seen the divorce rates? Besides, I'm too busy coordinating, teaching music, advising students, crushing dreams and getting a masters. I don't have time to date." She huffs like it's beyond obvious, and I roll my eyes. She's a 5'6" Latina with a curvaceous figure, lush brown hair, and a sultry voice. Men always want to date her.

"Ugh. I hate dating. Dating will lead to a relationship and I hate the word relation-*ship*. It makes me think of a ship. Ships leave *and* sink." Boy, I hate that word. In case you're wondering, my dad left on a ship. Why couldn't he take a plane like normal people?

"Don't start with that. Go on a cruise and get over it. Besides, when was the last time you went on a date? Since before Bran? At this rate your va-jay-jay is going to go on strike," Bianca warns, and I fight the heat going to my face.

"That was wrong on so many levels. We're eating! Can we leave my va-jay-jay out of this conversation? Let me think about it, Bianca. I'll get back to you over the weekend."

"You have until Monday. I took the liberty of giving him your number and told him to call you on Monday. His name is Dan." She is unable to hide her smile as she bites into her burger.

I narrow my eyes at her. "I hate you."

"No, you don't. You love me," she replies sweetly, her smile dimming so she can chew.

I can't help but ask, "Why don't you go out with him?"

"I tried, but we could never coordinate our times and I moved on."

"Come on, what's the worst that can happen?" Valentina chimes in.

"I suck at dating, so your guess is as good as mine." *No pressure.*

My friends let the subject drop, finding a new topic of conversation. When I finally bite into my burger, I sigh contentedly. *Can burgers be classified as comfort food?*

Before I know it, lunch is over and we have to go back to work. As I walk back to my car, I contemplate how to gracefully back out of this blind date. Ugh, I hate dating. I get anxious just thinking about it.

Why do people have to ask if I need a date? I know they mean well, but who cares if I'm single or not? Instead of asking single people if they're single or why they're single, why not just let it go? Nobody asks married people, "Why are you still married?" At least I don't think they do. I need to find a married person and ask them ASAP.

A glance out my office window reveals it's another gorgeous August day. It's a new week and at least I can count on the days to be sunny, barring unforeseen hurricanes. We are in hurricane season but if you think about it, hurricanes are actually not too bad. You know they're coming days in advance, and you have time to board up your house and gather supplies.

If you prepare "Miami style" you can buy enough water and tuna to feed a small army of people or cats, unlike say an earthquake that gives you no notice. If given a choice, I'll take the hurricane any day.

A knock on my door breaks up my natural disasters discussion with myself and I look up at a handsome student. He walks into my office as I address him. "Hi, Erick. How are you?" He's one of my regulars, good-looking *and* polite, a rare gem these days. He's tall, muscular, and has intense blue eyes with dark blond wavy hair that falls across his forehead. He looks like a movie star and every time I see him, I wonder how he keeps the girls off him.

"Hi, Miss Olivia," he says politely and extends a hand.

"How are you? What can we do for you today?"

"I'm about to register for a summer class but I thought about our last conversation, and I don't want to pursue theater as a major anymore," he announces, not wasting any time. I have several students that like two or three majors and can't make up their minds and pick one. Erick keeps going back and forth between theater and business.

"Are you sure you want to do finance?" We've had this conversation many times. At some point, he has to make up his mind, *right?*

"For now, can I leave my classes and major as they are? Just in case I change my mind." We talk a bit more about classes and he leaves my office. *Why do I have a feeling he's going to change his mind again?*

A few minutes later, a student assistant materializes at my door. "Leo's on the phone."

"What does he need?"

"He told me he's applying for an internship and wants to know if you can give him a recommendation letter."

Leo is another one of my regular students. He comes in every semester for me to help him register because he's always afraid of picking the wrong classes. All academic advisors have at least a few students like him. Students who can't make up their minds or are afraid of making a mistake and ruining their lives for eternity. However, he seems to be very needy lately. I have to find the time to speak to him and see what's going on. "Tell him to email me the details. He can come by later and pick it up. Tell him I want to talk to him when he does."

As the student assistant leaves, my cell phone buzzes. It's a number I don't recognize, but since I'm waiting for Bianca's mystery date to call me, I pick up. He confirms his name is Dan, and after a brief chat, we agree to meet. As a reference point, he tells me he'll be easy to spot because he's tall and very muscular. *Very muscular?* I make a mental note to ask Bianca for a picture *ASAP*!

How do I get myself in these situations? It's going to be a long week.

Olivia

<hr>

His choice of restaurant near the Miami River is not what you would call a popular one for a first date, but I've been to the area and know there are few hidden gems there. Besides, you can't beat the spectacular Miami River views and relaxed vibe in some of those restaurants.

As I walk towards the restaurant, my cell phone is vibrating and pinging. A myriad of emails and texts are coming in about the two people that were chosen to meet with Judith in the upcoming days. I turn off my phone and resolve not to think about it. *Not right now, anyway.*

It's my first date in a long time and I decided to put a little bit of effort into it. To start, I put on green eyeshadow, which brings out the green in my hazel eyes, and my medium-brown hair is softly loose around my face. I swapped my work blouse for a colorful pink polka-dot sleeveless top, but I kept my knee-length black pencil skirt. Shiny black ballet flats complete my ensemble. As I walk in, I adjust my shirt and fight the urge to keep pulling it down. *Deep breath.*

I head toward the bar and based on his description of "muscular," I spot him easily. "Hi, I'm Olivia. Are you Dan?"

"Yes. Hi, Olivia," he says while stretching out a massive hand yet staying in his chair. "Muscular" is clearly an understatement. He's huge and *muscular* times ten. A WWE pro-wrestler is the first thing that comes to mind. He has light brown eyes, short dark blond hair, and a receding hairline. His short-sleeved, white shirt is so tight I can see his nipples. I wonder if he's about to rip his shirt off at any moment, jump on top of the bar and cup his ear while patrons cheer him on. My imagination is running wild (and not in a good way), but you get the idea.

He informs the bartender that we're ready for our table and stands up. He's at least 6'6" and at 5'8", I feel like a middle schooler. It takes me only a nanosecond to realize this will not work. Physically it's just not going to happen, if you get my drift, but then again maybe he trains so hard at the gym to overcompensate for something... *else?*

Well, I'm here so I'll make the best of it. Besides, who knows, we could turn out to be best friends. *Positive thinking.*

A waitress arrives to escort us. We quietly leave the bar and I can see the Miami River ahead as we walk through an open room. The floor-to-ceiling windows have beautiful white and blue sheer drapes that billow softly. It only takes a few seconds to cross through it. Finally, she stops at a quiet table on the outside deck. The surrounding tables have pristine white tablecloths and candles that flicker gently with the breeze. Small round lights glow along the length of the deck. *Nice and romantic.* From the table, I can see the river and the buildings of downtown Miami and I'm pleasantly surprised. I make a mental note to bring my friends here one of these days.

After we sit, the waitress hands us menus. "This is very nice. Have you been here before?" I ask before I glance at the list of options.

"Yeah, I've been here a few times. They have a lot of healthy choices and the prices aren't too bad," he says in a flat voice, never taking his eyes off the menu.

Okay, so far so good. Let's hope he'll surprise me and be more than just muscle. Not that muscles are a bad thing... especially in the right location. He's silently looking at the menu and I *have* to ask, "Do you work out a lot?"

I have a feeling he does, but I'm trying to make conversation, plus I'm curious about the muscles.

"Yeah, I work out four to five hours a day, a combination of weight training and cardio. Based on my height and weight, I need to consume about 3700 calories per day. How many calories do you eat a day?" he asks, looking at me for the first time, his eyes narrowing.

Excuse me? "I have no idea, to be honest."

"Do you work out?"

Work out? "No, not really. I live next to a golf course, and I walk or jog around it sometimes, but it's not a daily thing. Sometimes I just stand on my porch and watch people," I realized too late I shouldn't have added that last part.

He shoots me an unsympathetic look and raises an eyebrow. "Walking and jogging are healthy habits but to make any impact on your body you need to walk or jog at least 30 to 90 minutes a day, at least five or six days a week."

Five to six days a week? Is he serious? "I will think about it."

I focus on the menu but when I glance at him over it, Dan is shaking his head. "You should think about it, it's your health. If you don't take care of your body, your body won't take care of you." *Really?* If that's the case, should *he* be bulging at odd places?

Our waitress materializes out of nowhere and asks if we are ready to order. "Yes, we are," he answers without looking at me.

"Actually, I need a few more minutes."

She nods at me. "Would you like something to drink in the meantime?"

"Yes, we'll have water. No bubbles," Dan says.

Is wine not part of his diet? *Should I tell him I love Coca-Cola?*

After a few minutes, the waitress returns with our waters and bread. "Your eyes are beautiful," she says to me and I can't help but smile. "Ready to order?"

"Yes, I am." Dan looks at the waitress again without glancing at me. "I'll have the wild salmon, no sauce, no butter. Broccoli and green beans, no sauce in them either, and the garden salad, no croutons, no dressing. And can you tell the chef to not use too much oil?"

Holy crap, is he anti-liquids? I hope he doesn't pass out when I order. "Can I please have the garden salad with extra croutons and extra ranch dressing? I'll have the lemon-grilled chicken with extra sauce on the side and the broccoli with ranch dressing on the side too." This is actually a healthy meal for me, as I usually go for something filled with carbs or topped with pasta (more carbs), but my date need not know that.

After she leaves, Dan goes back to health. "Do you know how unhealthy ranch dressing is? It's super bad for you. A little bit of ranch is packed with calories. It's also super high in fat, it has carbohydrates with no vitamins, no minerals, And then, there's the sodium." He's counting each evil element with his huge fingers.

In case there was any doubt in my mind that he's the anti-carb czar, when I absently grab a piece of white bread from the basket, the lecture continues. "White flour is *super* bad for you. It has no fiber, is super processed, and super unhealthy. The brown bread is only a little better because it has fiber."

I'm tempted to say "*super*" but I don't think he would be too amused. Instead, I take a deep breath and change my white bread for a brown piece. I debate adding butter but I wonder what he'll say so I skip it to avoid the continued sermon. Have you ever noticed that sometimes brown bread without butter tastes like cardboard? *Le sigh*. Thankfully, at that moment the server arrives with our salads. "So, what do you do for a living?" I ask, trying to derail his health conversation while absently adding the extra ranch dressing to my salad.

He glances at my salad and quirks an eyebrow, "Right now, I'm working on becoming a pro-wrestler. I'm currently taking acting classes because wrestlers have to memorize lines and talk in front of hundreds of people and do promos. I'm also working with an acting coach on developing a character and trying to come up with a catchphrase. And I'm saving money to move to Orlando, where the WWE has a facility and operations. I've been checking and waiting for a job opening so I can apply and move up there."

Shocking. He wants to be a pro-wrestler. I have a sudden vision of watching a promotion for the WWE Smackdown on TV and the voiceover guy saying something like "and heereee is DANNN the MANNN!" I obviously have an active imagination but instead, I say, "Wow, that's so cool, you're following your dream. I always encourage my students to follow their dreams and be prepared so that they're ready when the opportunity presents itself."

"Yeah, that's why I have to keep eating healthy and working out. Did you know the US is one of the top ten fattest countries in the world? Over seventy percent of people in this country are fat or obese. It's an epidemic..." Is there anything else he's obsessed with? I mean interested in, besides health and healthy *things*? Slowly my mind starts drifting off. By the end of the meal, I'm ready to go home and watch a Disney movie. I love Disney movies. Everybody gets their happy ending.

The food is amazing and my foodie heart is happy, but after dinner is over and the waitress asks if we want coffee, we both answer no. I guess I'm too unhealthy for him. While we wait for the check, he goes on about coffee, caffeine, and white sugar and – you guessed it – how unhealthy they are. He tells me I should change to brown sugar ASAP. *Brown sugar? Are we really having this conversation on a first date?* After we settle the bill and I've thanked him, I bolt out of the restaurant before he has a chance to ask something like "Can I walk you to your car?" or worse "How much do you weigh?"

Why would my friends think for one minute that I'd date a guy whose arms are bigger than my thigh?

It's safe to say my first date in a long time did not go as I expected, but it could have been worse. I could have set a napkin on fire with one of the votive candles or set my date on fire and have him end up in the Miami River trying to extinguish the flames. Okay, maybe not, but you never know.

Olivia

It's been more than a week since my date and I'm meeting with my friends at another restaurant. This hip place is family-owned, and since they know we work at the university, they always serve us quickly. The décor is simple with pictures of food on the walls. Square and round tables mixed with booths near the windows make the setting interesting. I concentrate on the black chalkboard with the specials for the day. Today everything looks scrumptious, *yum*. Turkey with brie or maybe with fresh mozzarella or chicken with avocado. Ummm, no contest: avocado wins every time. Chocolate croissants for dessert and boom, it's a meal.

"What are you drinking?" I vaguely hear Bianca ask next to me. "The mango smoothie, right?"

Leaving the chalkboard, I look at her and we exchange smiles, "Yep, definitely the mango smoothie." Behind her, Valentina's sharing a story with Nicole about the new crop of incoming music students. She's excited about them. I have a mental image of Simon Cowell telling her that one, or several of them suck, and have to purse my lips to suppress a smile.

A cute guy walks in. I try to focus on my friend, but I feel a magnetic pull. *Wowzah.* I watch in slow motion as he walks in, peels his sunglasses away from his face, and tucks them in his shirt. Perhaps it *seems* like slow motion because I've been watching way too many Disney movies lately.

He's at least six feet tall. He's wearing blue jeans, a white button-down shirt, sleeves rolled up, and black loafers. I try looking away, but every time I turn back to talk to my friends, he's always somehow in my line of vision and we keep locking eyes.

After we order and sit, I spot the hottie sitting at a few tables away from us, glancing our way. I barely register when Bianca talks about an idea for her students. She asks for my opinion, but I'm too busy trying *not* to look at the hottie to pay attention to her. "Do you want me to go and say 'hi' to that guy? Should I bring him over?" she asks. "Maybe *he* can be your next date."

"Can you give me a break?" I'm mortified but a second later go back to *not* looking at the guy.

"Talking about dates, how was Dan?" she asks after a few minutes.

Here we go. I forget about the hottie and turn my attention to her, "My date? Let me ask you, did you *see* this guy before you set me up with him?"

"No, Wendy was going to send me a picture, which I was going to forward to you, but I never got it."

"Ahhh, no wonder." *Of course, that would happen to me.*

"Why? What did he look like?"

"Picture a seven-foot-tall, WWE wrestler, skintight clothes and everything...with a fitness obsession."

"Seven foot tall? Are you sure? You have a wild imagination and you do tend to exaggerate."

"Bianca, I know I exaggerate, but he was huge!"

"I have a question, are we talking *lucha* libre clothes?" Valentina asks with a bark of laughter, and I shoot her a look.

"That bad? Or that big?" Bianca uses her hands to make a foot distance in the air while Nicole and Valentina start giggling at the gesture.

"That is not funny. This is *not* funny. I got lectured on ranch dressing. Do you know what that was like? Out of all the things to be lectured on? War? World peace? The economy? Religion? Immigration? He went for *ranch dressing*?! I didn't even order pasta. I think if I had mentioned pasta, he would have passed out from shock. It was unbelievable." My friends start laughing at this and I join. "And did you know he wants to be a pro-wrestler? Not that there's anything wrong with that, but a pro-wrestler? Come on, can you guys picture me living in Orlando with a seven-foot-tall wrestler? With bulging muscles everywhere?" I motion on top of my shoulders with cupped hands.

Bianca seems to think about this and shakes her head while twisting her face in disgust. "I am so sorry. I didn't think he would be that terrible."

"He wasn't terrible. He just wasn't for me."

Oh well, at least I have friends that support me and love me. You can't have it all, right?

"Olivia, would this be a bad time to tell you that *I* have a date for you?" Nicole asks.

A waiter appears with a giant tray and places piping hot plates in front of us. After he leaves, I frown at her. "Yeah, forget it. Not happening."

"Come on, I told my friend you would go on a date with her cousin."

"I know this is Miami, but why are you guys setting me up with other people's cousins? And why me? Bianca and Valentina are single too," I respond pointing at them.

To this Valentina quickly declares no. "*No puedo*. I'm too busy, but maybe next time." She shrugs and goes back to her sandwich.

"Please? I already told her you would." She looks at me with sad puppy eyes and pouts her mouth "Pretty please?"

"Fine. I will go on a date with him, but only because *you* went through the trouble. While we're on the subject, no more blind dates. Okay? I don't want a *ship*."

"I'll let him know you said yes. Hey, did you guys hire an advisor yet?" She changes the subject, probably afraid I'll back out of this date.

"Well, the rumor is we finally did and he's starting next week, but nobody knows exactly who or when. The only thing we know is that he's some hotshot from New York," I grumble while taking a sip of my smoothie.

"It only took a week? That was fast. I'm telling you, something's not right," Nicole counters.

Valentina cocks her head. "Nicole, not everything is a conspiracy."

"It *is* a conspiracy when you work at a university."

At this, Valentina rolls her eyes and focuses on her seasoned French fries. After a pause she states dramatically, "Olivia, I swear to God, if that guy gets the job over you, we're going to riot."

I pause. "We're not going to riot. Relax."

"Fine, then we'll picket or protest or do whatever people in higher ed do to complain about injustices. I don't care."

"Do you care to get fired?" When she doesn't respond I counter, "See, that's what I thought. Let's relax. We'll stay Zen and wait it out." She doesn't seem convinced but doesn't argue. We keep eating and talking animatedly until I drop sauce... on my *white* blouse. It leaves a small green stain right on top of my breast. I try wiping it off with a napkin and of course, I make it worse. Now I have a colossally round green stain covering half my breast. *Ack*! I have to go back to work!

I excuse myself and head to the bathroom. I pull the door but it's surprisingly light and I almost fall back from the force. I make a mental note to push *slowly* when I leave. I try carefully to clean the stain but after a few minutes I give up. I decide once it dries, it won't be too bad, plus, I have a jacket in my office that'll cover it.

As I leave, I push the door with more force than I intended to, forgetting my previous experience, and... WHACK.

Oh. My. God!

Did I kill somebody?! Is it a kid?! My hands automatically go to my mouth while I try not to panic. *Shit*! I go around the door in search of the victim when I see the hottie. *Double shit*!

"Ow," he mutters, rubbing his forehead with his palm, "motherf..." When he realizes who has smacked him in the head, his eyebrows relax. He fixes his gaze on me while he lowers his hand. Somebody else comes out of the bathroom and pushes me from behind, causing me to stumble into him. He takes a step back while I lose my balance. He instinctively grabs my upper arms as my hands rest against his chest. I can feel his heart beating through his shirt, and we lock eyes. I can't help but feel his body. He's rock-solid and electricity shoots through me. I'm rooted on the spot.

His eyes are still on mine as he moves us to the side of the narrow hallway, so that we don't get hit again, then he lets me go. He's even more handsome up close. He smells of soap, leather, and sun. The stranger has dark hair, an athletic frame, and captivating green eyes. His eyes are a shade of green that distracts from everything around you. They are a unique hue with tinges of gold in them and I have to force myself to break contact.

"I am so sorry," says a voice from behind me. "Are you guys okay?"

"Yeah, don't worry about it," he tells the woman, his eyes still on me.

I turn away from the man with the amazing eyes and reply to the newcomer, "We're fine, thank you," before returning my gaze to a pair of bright green eyes. I tear my eyes away again, glance at the floor, and notice his cell on the ground.

I bend to retrieve it, keenly aware of his eyes following my movements. "Are you okay?" I ask as I hand him his phone.

"I'm okay. I might have a baseball-size bump tomorrow, *but* it's my fault for walking and texting. I'm Tom, by the way," he says quickly and extends a hand.

"Olivia," I answer, feeling light-headed and warm. "I'm sorry about the door." I can't seem to let go of his hand. *Can I keep him?*

"It's fine, I wasn't paying attention. They warn you about texting and driving, but apparently texting and walking are equally dangerous." His lips quirk into a side smile and I can't help but return it. He lets go of my hand but leans forward a little, narrowing the space between us, and his eyes focus on me for a few seconds until he looks down to focus on his phone.

I know it's rude to stare but I can't seem to stop myself from watching him tinker with it. After several seconds, his phone beeps, and he looks up from it. His phone comes back to life like a symphony. He's very popular. *How many girls are sending him texts or trying to call him?*

"It works. That's great. Again, I am so sorry...Ummm, I have to go. My friends are waiting, and I have eager students waiting to tell me they hate math."

"Wait, you work at the university?" he slowly takes a step back.

I can't help but nod, "Yes, I do."

"I'll be working there too. Maybe I'll see you and your friends around campus sometime."

My friends? Because he noticed us staring at him like a bunch of horny teenagers? Perfect.

"That would be cool. It was nice to meet you," I answer as we shake hands again. *That would be cool? Ack! What am I, sixteen? What is wrong with me?*

I turn towards my friends with him close behind me. They say nothing at all as I walk in their direction and sit down, then we all watch him walk out of the restaurant. The second the door closes, and he disappears from view, they all turn their attention to me, excitedly talking over each other.

"Did you ask him for his name? His number?" Bianca asks. Of course, she would ask that.

"I got his name, not his number, but he will be working at the university so there's hope I'll see him again."

"What department?" Nicole asks.

"I don't know but if any of you see him around the campus, please call me so I can go and *properly* introduce myself. Minus the green chest stain." We all burst into laughter.

After a few minutes, I happily refocus on my avocado.

Olivia

I'm back at the office, and ready to help students succeed and graduate. *Positive thinking, right?* I wish I could apply this positive thinking mentality to my love life, but that's another story. This week I had a date with a guy named Manny. It was a semi-disaster. At the same time, you can't really blame me, he was a Neanderthal. Besides, I haven't been on too many dates in quite a while, (current dates notwithstanding), and I'm just out of practice. I'm *sure* I'll get better at this... *eventually.*

In any case, I can't worry about the state of my love life right now. Time to focus on my career. Coffee at my side, check. Settled into my chair, yep. Time to go through my emails. I notice one from my boss and open it first, only to find myself reading a mass email regarding the new advisor.

I am pleased to announce that Mr. Thomas Williams has accepted the position of Academic Advisor. Mr. Williams joined the university a couple of months ago and has been advising our students at the central campus. Previously Thomas worked at NYU where he was an Academic Advisor and

Advising Program Coordinator, among other jobs. He has a wealth of experience advising college students, facilitating workshops, and working with international students over the span of his career.

Mr. Williams completed his undergraduate studies at Penn State University. He earned his Master's degree in Higher Education and Student Affairs from NYU University. He is originally from Miami and is familiar with our student population. We are lucky to have him join our team.

Please take some time to welcome him to our department.
Regards,
Judith

Are we lucky? Or he's lucky he got a job? Maybe Nicole was right. That *was* fast. I try not to worry about it or think it's a conspiracy, but all throughout the morning advisors are going in and out of each other's offices. Everyone's talking about the new advisor and how fast they transferred him. Gossip is proliferating like wildfire. This is worse than working for the FBI because they *all* want to investigate the poor guy. It's difficult to concentrate when somebody interrupts me yet again. How can we work like this? It's insanity!

Andrea, a fellow advisor, tells me she's already looked him up on Google *and* LinkedIn and that he's in fact very cute. He graduated from a very prestigious and *costly* university, so she assumes he's wealthy. He also has a lot of experience, great credentials, and is probably single. *All of that from a LinkedIn profile?* I would hate to think what she'd find if she searched public records. On the other hand, if I ever need a private investigator, I know who to call.

I resolve to look him up myself, *just* for information purposes. A girl needs to be prepared. God only knows if he's here to replace Judith. I'm debating research strategies and thinking that LinkedIn is probably the best way to start when one of my regular visiting students walks into my office.

This student wants to be a teacher but had difficulties passing the only required math class. The last time she was here, I advised her to find a tutor and visit the math lab. She failed the class the first time and wasn't doing any better the second time around. "I went to the lab and I passed," she says with a satisfied smile once she sits.

I pull up the results on the screen. She *barely* passed. *Thank God.* "Well, the good thing is that you did, and you don't have to do any more math classes. For next semester, I think you should try the Intro to Teaching class to see if you like it."

"Okay. Cool," she says with a relieved smile and flopping back on the chair.

"Maybe you can try the psychology class, too."

"Sure. Psychology's interesting." I suggest a few other classes: sociology, science, art history, then we talk a little bit about her life. Before she leaves, she gives me a hug and promises to return. She's one of those students that will do meticulous research on professors while trying to find a perfect match. Armed with class suggestions, she's off to create her flawless schedule.

Investigation seems to be the theme of the day. Come registration time, some of our students will turn into police detectives. They'll ask their professors, friends, and classmates for suggestions on who teaches what better and who to stay away from. They'll visit rating sites like *Rate my professor*, and will schedule their classes around the highest-rated instructors. Some, even go as far as postponing taking a class if the only professor teaching it has bad reviews. When all else fails, they'll stalk professors and beg for overrides if the class they want closes before they have a chance to register.

After she leaves, I see students back-to-back; I get into an advising rhythm and before I know it, the day is over and I forget to research the new hire.

Yesterday was crazy, but with the mysterious new advisor joining us today, I'm not expecting much improvement. I grab my coffee and try to relax and appear professional. I'm wearing a long-sleeved blouse and black pants, even though it's the middle of summer in Miami. *Ack! What was I thinking? Thank God for air-conditioning.*

It's still early in the morning, but a couple of advisors have already told me Judith is making the rounds and introducing him to the staff before it gets too hectic. Again, somebody tells me he's handsome, and after what seems like an eternity, but is less than an hour, I hear them coming my way. They're finally at my door and... *Oh. My. God!* It's the guy from the restaurant! *It's the hottie!*

They're standing outside my office and I can't seem to formulate the words to say. *Hi, nice to meet you. Welcome.* Instead, we lock eyes and I'm frozen in place.

He pauses at my door momentarily, giving me an unreadable look, then walks in and reaches out to shake my hand. "Hi, I'm Thomas Williams."

My arm raises robotically. "Olivia. Olivia Campbell." I stammer like a starstruck dork while I shake his hand. I can't stop looking at him and his green eyes are focused on me. I struggle to keep my mouth from falling open and my heart is ready to pump itself out of a job. *Oh, Jesus.*

Judith turns her attention to me. "Olivia, what are you working on?... Olivia?" *Shiiit.* Katie Couric would be appalled by my lack of professionalism. I whip my head to her and my eyebrows, refusing my commands, decide to point upwards.

And cue the awkward pause.

I must be in shock or something because I've lost all ability to speak and form sentences. Somebody *please* kill me now. She looks at me, looks at him then back at me and keeps pressing on. "I heard from IT, and they said it'll be a couple of days before he has access to this campus's systems. Since we know how these things are and it'll most likely be more than that, I was thinking in the meantime he can shadow a few advisors." She turns to look at him with a wide smile. "Olivia is very popular with our students— she gets a lot of requests. I was thinking to start you can train with her for a couple of days, then afterward you can shadow other people."

"Sure," he answers, looking at her. He glances at me then turns back to her.I wonder if he remembers me or if he's so popular with women, he has no clue we've already met.

She turns to me again. *At this rate, her neck is going to fracture.* "You guys can work out a schedule that works for both of you based on student appointments," I manage to nod. "Okay! Let's keep going, Thomas. Bye, Olivia."

She smiles at me before she walks out of my office.

He says, "It was nice to meet you," and follows her out. I notice the way his broad shoulders and muscled back stretches his suit as he turns towards the door. He looks back at me and I smile nervously and nod *again* as they disappear from my view. I'm speechless while trying to control my heart palpitations. As my head hits my desk, I wonder what the odds are. This doesn't happen to regular people. You just don't meet super cute guys with amazing-unnatural-green eyes at restaurants, and then they turn out to be your new coworker.

You have *got* to be kidding me.

When it's lunchtime I head over to the campus cafeteria. I usually bring lunch and sit outside but today I'm waiting to meet with a potential roommate, *again*. I figured this is the best meeting place; everybody knows where the cafeteria is. At least in my mind, the potential for being murdered is low.

Safety first, right? I probably should have asked one of my friends to join me. *Too late now.*

While I'm waiting, I start thinking about the hottie. I mean, Tom. *I have to train him?* This could be very good or very bad. He might be handsome, but maybe he's here because he wants to be the director, too. Advisors are a chatty bunch and I'm certain that by now, everyone who works in Higher Ed in the South Florida tri-county area has heard that Judith wants to retire. This could be terrible for *my* chances of becoming a manager. At the same time, if I want to be viewed as a potential administrator, I have to take the lead. I'll be a complete professional. This is the perfect opportunity to show I *can* be the director. I have nothing to worry about. What could possibly go wrong?

Actually, don't answer that.

I notice a woman and a man approaching me and sit up straighter. *Is that whom I'm meeting?* She seemed normal enough over the phone so I agreed to meet with her. From our brief call, she's older than I would have wanted, but beggars can't be choosers.

"So, before we start, do you got any money? I'm hungry," she says. *Ooookay.*

Sadly, it's another bust. Potential druggie, with an even sketchier boyfriend and no bank account or credit card and who only wanted to pay cash when she was there—no thank you.

Will I ever find a roommate?

Tom

- -

I lower my car's windows and rest my elbow on the door. The warm air reminds me I'm back in Florida. Yesterday I spent all day stuck in a crazy Human Resources workshop for new employees. Three months ago, I was able to bypass it, but this time HR came after me and I didn't have a choice. If I'm honest, the retirement benefits part was interesting, but other than that, it was a complete waste of time. I grew up on a university campus. Dinner at my house always included lengthy discussions by my parents or grandparents on the state of the university, university politics, and its inner workings. It was, and sometimes still is, like having an annoying uninvited guest sitting at the table every night, one who wants to share everything about themselves, and although you find him irritating and can't stand him, you can't help but want to listen to the stories, too.

It was an endless day at work and as I drive home, it occurs to me it's actually great to be back. I'm right where I belong. I'm ready to take my career to the next level. I have to admit, not counting my family and cycling, the university is the only other thing I'm really passionate about. The campus holds a strange familiarity I need. The university is home. After being away from Miami and after giving this move a lot of thought, I decided the best course of action would be to come home. In fact, it was the most logical decision.

Today was my first day in the new office. My new co-workers seem cool. One, in particular, comes to mind.

I noticed her while we were in line at that restaurant near the campus and *obviously,* she caught my eye. She was wearing a short-sleeve white blouse with a form-fitting, black-and-white striped skirt. It was hard not to look at her flawless sun-kissed skin and long legs. When she crashed into me, it was even harder not to check her out. I debated over asking her for her number until she mentioned she worked here. Getting involved with a coworker? *Pass.*

Once upon a time, I was a testosterone-filled college graduate that decided it would be a great idea to date a coworker. You can guess how that went. In all fairness, it was my first professional job and I didn't know any better. On the other hand, I'm a quick learner. I haven't repeated the stupidity ever since.

I have to admit, it was a complete surprise today when I walked into her office. I'd be lying if I said the sight of her didn't catch me off guard. Out of all the people in Miami? In her defense, she seemed to be just as shocked. She was actually speechless, with her thin smile frozen on her smooth, very kissable lips. I was not expecting that. At all. Her big hazel eyes were pointed in my direction while her brown hair flowed around her face. Her office was warm and welcoming, with pictures of students all over. It smelled of vanilla, like her, and I had to make an effort to look into her eyes and *not* other parts of her anatomy. When Judith mentioned she was popular with students and we would train together, she blushed and looked adorable. All I could do was try not to fixate on her pink lips. *Train with her? Shadow her? This should be interesting.*

I recently moved off from my parents' house to be closer to this campus. My new roommate, Keith, has been my friend forever. Our parents are friends, and we've known each other our whole lives. Since I moved in, I haven't had a chance to try the nearby golf course.

I arrive home and change into cycling gear. With a nod to Keith, who is already home, changed, and pre-hydrating in the kitchen, we head out to the garage for our evening ride. After we perform a ritualistic check of our bikes and spend a few minutes stretching, we make our way out to the course.

As we warm up, we catch up. We talk about our families, any movies currently playing or cool new restaurants we've visited recently. We also talk about our jobs, and particularly our bikes. Since we're best friends, sometimes, it could also be a girl we're into... *or not.*

Cycling demands extreme effort and concentration. Once we get going, there won't be much talking. The only sounds will be the purr of the bikes, the wind, and the random revving of passing cars.

"How's it going at work?" Keith asks from next to me.

"Yesterday was annoying. I spent all day in a useless HR training. Today was my first day in the office and it was... interesting"

"*Interesting?* That's the word you're using to describe it?" He glances at me with a quizzical expression, raises an eyebrow, then turns back to the street.

"What do you want me to say? I made friends and we sang 'Kumbaya'?"

"Dude, I know you. Did you meet somebody?"

"Somebody?"

"A girl? Or maybe a boy?"

"Very funny, you're hilarious." At this he laughs. I keep going. "Even if I met a girl, which I haven't, I have no intention whatsoever of getting to know anybody on that level at work." That would be a half-truth, but he doesn't need to know that.

I can't deny the attraction, but I really have no intention of going there with a coworker. *At all.*

A car on the side of the road catches my attention. Doors are a hazard on a bike. Luckily the driver notices us, quickly hops out, and waves. We nod and keep going. "Are there any hot girls in your office?" he says, trying a fresh angle. I glance at him, resisting the urge to punch him on the shoulder or call him out on his frat-minded remarks.

"Most of my new coworkers are female."

"That wasn't the question."

"I guess a few are hot, but who cares, it doesn't matter. You better than anyone knows why I won't go there."

"Knowing you? You probably had five women approach you and ask for your numbers since you moved to this side of town. How are you going to be able to resist them?" he says and grins like an idiot.

"Resist them? What am I, fifteen? I'm sure I can manage."

"If you're not going to date anybody at work, can you at least introduce me to somebody?"

"Not happening."

"Why not?"

I can't help shaking my head. "Because something's seriously wrong with you. I have no intention of making *my job* your dating pool."

"Dude, relax."

"Right. Let's talk about your love life. How's that going?"

"It's great. I'm a popular guy."

"Sure, you are."

"I have a date Saturday, so at least I can say I'm more popular than you."

"You lucky bastard," is all I can think to say before we burst out laughing. A few hours later while we cool down, it occurs to me this is what I needed, to sweat it out. By the time we're on our last lap, I'm exhausted and clearly out of shape. Thank God for exercise. Going to the gym and riding my bike, help me keep my sanity. Now all I have to do is focus on my career and kick ass. *Piece of cake.*

Olivia

Today, I start training Tom. I have to keep reminding myself to be Zen and keep it professional. When he stops by and says hello, he looks gorgeous. I have second thoughts that I can actually keep it together, let alone professional.

To start, his eyes are a lighter green color than I remember, most likely playing off the light blue shirt he's wearing, and black pants that fit him *perfectly*. His hair is dark and cut neatly, short on the sides but longer on top. His strong jaw is clean-shaven, and he has an air about him that suggests confidence and self-control. My Zen thoughts are immediately replaced by not so Zen thoughts.

O-kay, I admit it, I'm screwed.

After a few minutes of pleasantries, he grabs a chair and places it next to me, near the corner of my desk, where he can see the computer. *Does he have to be that close?* I take a few deep calming breaths. *Think Zen and be professional.*

He looks at me and raises an eyebrow but says nothing.

Aaaand now he probably thinks I'm weird or crazy, possibly bly both. Perfect.

I look away and resolve to avoid all eye contact and keep my head forward. When he clears his throat, I glance at him and start talking. "So, you're the new transfer everybody's been talking about these last couple of weeks."

"I guess that's me, but I had no idea people were already talking about me."

"You'd be surprised."

"I think I'd rather *not* be surprised."

"Right. And I met you last week... at a restaurant."

"Yes, you did."

"What are the odds?" I look at him and chuckle. "I was surprised. Were you surprised?" *Ack.* Stop using that word.

"I was surprised. It was a nice surprise, though."

A nice surprise? Can he expand on that, please?

He rests back on the chair and I glance at him. "Well, we're working together, anything you need, let me know, you know." Oh my God. *What is wrong with me.*

"Likewise," he says.

I should focus on the job before I say something embarrassing, although I'm pretty sure it's too late for that. Since my next appointment is not for another thirty minutes, I spend time going through our online system. I show him where to find the grades, a student's current schedule, and their degree inventory, which shows every class the student has taken and what she or he needs to graduate. Tom listens quietly. I suspect he probably knows all this already, but he never says otherwise, so I keep going. After my first appointment walks in, I introduce Tom as an advisor-in-training.

This student recently found out one of her professors gave her an F in a class. Yet, she was under the impression that she passed it with an A. Although she has been emailing the professor, she has been unable to communicate with him. "Let me call the department and see if the professor's around," I say. Several calls later, we learn the professor has been out since the end of the spring term and will not be back until the fall semester. After I explain the problem and somebody from the department promises me they'll help her, I tell her where to go and who to speak to. All the while, Tom just nods quietly. I don't have time to dwell on his silence because another student appears out of nowhere.

Leo's at my door. He's here to double-check the classes he registered for fall term are okay with me. He stops for a few seconds at my door and glances at Tom. Finally, he comes in and sits across from us. "Hi Leo, how are you?"

"I'm good, Miss Olivia," he says, glancing at Tom again. *Maybe my gaydar is off?*

"Leo, this is Tom, an advisor who's in training. He's going to be sitting in our meeting today. Okay?"

Leo's a senior who's also a business major. We clicked during our first meeting and while they have faculty advisors in the School of Business, he still comes to me for help. I can't help but notice he seems tense and his posture stiffens a little. "Fine," he says finally.

I share with Tom a sheet from the business department that details all the classes their students need to take. It's a super handy guide broken down by concentration. Leo looks back and forth between Tom and me while we talk about the sequence of classes. Tom finally says, "At the central campus, all those were in the front, but I haven't seen them here anywhere. Where do you guys keep the program sheets?" This is the most he's spoken at a single time today, and because I'm still getting used to his modulated voice, I can't help but glance at his mouth.

"They're online and we print them for the students, as needed. I'll email you the links so that you have them, too." We go over Leo's classes, but he's quieter than usual and hardly speaks. To be fair, students are frequently intimidated by new advisors. After the student leaves, we talk about where to put notes in the system. I enjoy writing meticulous notes, while some advisors don't put any notes at all. Writing notes helps me remember what I talked about with the student and protects me from future disagreements with challenging undergrads.

"How long have you been working at the university?" he asks suddenly. *Are we getting personal now? Oh boy.*

"Right out of college, I worked in an elementary school because I like kids but then I discovered that while kids were cool, the parents were not so cool. A friend told me about this job, and I replaced little students with bigger students and no parents. What about you?"

"After college, I went to work for a famous company in New York and hated every second of it. Then... I got fired." He shakes his head at a memory. "At the same time, my parents worked all their lives at a university. I thought I wanted to do something different but then I don't know, I guess I missed it. So, I searched for the closest campus to me and got a job there, trying different jobs throughout the years."

"Why did you come down to Miami?"

He pauses for a second before answering, "My mom got sick. I got a call and I took the first flight out."

"Oh, I'm sorry to hear that. Is she okay?"

"Yes. She's okay. She's actually great now. But then shortly after, my dad got into a minor accident. It was one of those things you don't think about, then you realize your folks are getting older and you need to be around. You know?" I nod. "The icing on the cake was when one of my sisters was having boyfriend issues. I don't know, it's difficult for a creep to take you seriously when you're two thousand miles away and in another state."

"Did you want to strangle the guy?" I feel myself relax as we both smile.

"Oh, did I ever..." he says, shaking his head again. He gives me a playful grin before his smile fades a little. "After that episode, I decided it was time to come home, at least for a while. I got a job at the central campus and came on down," he declares, before a knock on the door interrupts our conversation.

The next student in front of us needs help with a hold. After we remove it and quickly go over the student's degree requirements, he leaves, and we go back to our chat. "How many siblings do you have?" I ask.

"I have one brother and two sisters. You?"

"No sisters. I have two brothers though. I'm the middle child," I answer without thinking.

"You must be very diplomatic. I'll bet you had to be the peacemaker between those two," he jokes with a lopsided smile.

I can't help but grin at this remark. "Does that mean you had to do the same thing with your sisters?"

"*Maybe*. It takes one to know one. Actually, it would explain why we're great advisors."

Interesting observation. "I never thought about it like that, to be honest."

Our next student is at my door. After I introduce Tom, immediately and wasting no time, this student tells us he needs us to give him a class and a major ASAP. *Hmm, super advisor to the rescue, again?*

"I have AP credits, SATs from three or four years ago, and I took a bunch of tests yesterday.
He flops on the chair.

As I look at the computer, I wonder if the information is accurate. "I see that they gave you credit for AP English I and II, Calculus I, Biology I and II, Chemistry, Physics, History, and Economics. You have over thirty AP credits. Wow, you were busy."

"We had AP classes at my high school and I had a college near my house. They had a dual enrollment program and I took advantage. After I graduated high school, I wanted to work to buy a car and move out. I don't know," he admits, shrugging.

While I look at the screen and double-check the information, I have a sudden mental picture of the movie *Good Will Hunting.* Is he an orphan? Would it be rude to ask? "What do your... *parents* think?"

"They're happy I want to go to college. Here's the thing. I have a job but there's an opening on my team and the pay increase is substantial. The problem is my boss won't give it to me unless I get a degree or at least show him I'm registered for classes."

Okay. Not an orphan.

"Got it. You have most of the basic requirements, and at this point you would have to be admitted into a program and officially start a major."

"I don't care, put me in whatever you want, just give me a class. I'll take any class."

He looks desperate and I'm starting to feel bad. I guess he likes his job and really wants a promotion, but since this is not typical, I'm not sure what to do with him. I look at Tom. "Any ideas?"

"Have you done linear algebra? Discrete math? Organic Chemistry?" Tom says, confidently.

"Some of it."

"Tell you what—head over to the math department, then check out physics, engineering, computer science, and talk to the academic chairs or faculty advisors. Ask them about their programs, see who you'd like to work with, and we'll take it from there."

"Do you think they'll help me?" he asks, and for the first time looks like the distressed young guy he is.

"I think if you go and level with them and ask for help, *nicely*, they'll give it to you. Once they see how brilliant you are, if you're polite, they'll help you out." This student seems satisfied with this answer. He shakes our hands and leaves. After we see a few more students we take a break for lunch, separately. By the time I come back, Tom's sitting on the side chair waiting for me. The hours fly by with more students that need class suggestions, holds removed, and help deciding what to major in. At some point, we switch seats and I let Tom take over.

Our last appointment of the day is a philosophy and English major who *just* decided he wants to be a lawyer. Tom talks to the student about the classes he should enroll in the next few semesters if he wants to go to law school, then answers the student's questions on what extracurricular activities he could do. "You know, choosing classes is somewhat like... having a good lunch. Make sure you have a balanced meal, or course load, eat your vegetables or requirements, and leave room for *dessert*."

After a few seconds, the student looks at Tom like Tom just told him the secret to making gold. His eyes slowly start going wide. He then takes Tom's hand in a firm handshake, shaking both their arms up and down, and says, "Thank you, man, thank you," before rushing away.

Tom freezes and stares at the door with wide eyes, then looks at me. I'm dumbfounded and take a few seconds to process the conversation. "Tom. I love food but I'm going to be honest and say I've never seen anybody use a food analogy in an advising session before or a student react so... *enthusiastically*. That was... interesting."

"He looked confused. I was trying to help. The way to a man's brain is through food or sex. I wasn't going to pull a sex analogy, of course, so I went to the next best thing, but he didn't let me finish," he notes, pointing towards the door.

"Except for how his eyes went wild at the end, it was not too bad. You and I were thinking *elective classes* but he may have had *other* things in mind." For the first time, Tom looks a bit stressed. His hand rubs his neck before it casually runs through his hair causing a few strands of hair to stick up.

Would it be unprofessional if I fixed them? Yeah. Okay.

"That was terrible," he groans, "I promise you, I do know how to advise students," he hastily adds, looking at me with brows furrowing.

"It's not a big deal. That was a good try, but he might have interpreted the word *dessert* a bit differently."

"I was talking about advising. He's the one with a dirty mind," Tom complains.

The words leave my mouth before I have time to filter them, "He's a college student. Of course, that's where his mind would go— to the gutter." But after a few seconds, I burst into laughter.

"That's not funny."

"It is a little funny." I'm trying not to laugh, but I can't help grinning. "Don't worry about it. We have his email in the system, just send him an email."

He takes a deep breath, releases it, and looks at me. "You're right. You're right. I can do that," he says, relaxing visibly.

I'm smiling as I say, "It's time to go home. Come back tomorrow and we'll do it again. Maybe with no food analogies, though." I stand and stretch my hand. "Welcome to the team." He takes my hand and I feel a jolt of electricity. He walks away from me, but my pulse speeds up when he turns at the door and gives me a full smile.

Oh boy. I am so screwed.

Olivia

The next day, Tom comes in and right off the bat, tells me he emailed the student. He talked about *safe activities* and gave him suggestions on balancing his schedule *and* his social life, including a link to Student Life.

'Safe activities'? Do I even want to know?

As we're sitting, I make a mental note to warn my friend Bianca about that particular student now heading her way. A few seconds later, Jackson, one of the student assistants, turns up at my door. With him is another student in need of an advisor.

I address the recent arrival. "Hi, how are you? My name is Olivia, and this is Tom. He's an advisor-in-training, and he will be sitting in our meeting today. Okay?"

"Sure," the student blithely agrees, after he sits.

"What's going on? How can we help you?"

"I'm a senior. I need help to figure out a major or a program that'll get me out of here."

Usually, by the time my students are juniors most of them have a major. I go into the system and read off the screen. "Why are you looking for a new major if your major is sociology?" I'm curious. This is not a normal occurrence for a senior student.

"I had a meeting with the chair yesterday, and he told me he was going over all the senior students' classes and noticed mine. Then he said I didn't belong in sociology and told me to come and talk to you because he was dismissing me from the program." I focus on the screen again. In general, all his core classes are As and Bs. However, all his sociology classes are Cs and Ds and even one F.

Tom also stares at the screen. He absently leans the chair a little towards me. "Why did you take these art classes?" he inquires, glancing at the student. A second later, he raises his arm to point at the computer screen, touching with his index finger where some As are listed and moving his finger across the screen. I take a whiff of his cologne and for unknown reasons, my libido decides *this* is the time to wake up.

Gah, does it realize I'm working?

I think Tom notices something about my reaction because he instinctively pulls his arm back. All I can do is nod and try to focus on the student who's talking. "... and I took art as electives, for fun, you know."

Tom glances at me before turning back to the student, "You did well in them. Why don't you major in art and minor in sociology?"

"I never thought about it, to be honest. Art was a creative outlet."

As Tom's talking, he's getting into the conversation. He rests his forearms on the desk and leans forward, his shoulders drop and he starts to relax. "Here's the thing, right now, as a senior you don't have a lot of room to start a program from scratch. You're close to one-hundred twenty credits. Since you have a lot of art classes, we can graduate you faster as an art major."

The student lowers his head, deep in thought. "I see." After a few seconds, he simply says, "Okay. Let's do it," and we both listen to Tom confidently walk the student over the different classes he needs to complete the art program.

After the student leaves, Tom sits back on the chair and looks at me. "That was great, Tom."

"Thank you." He gives me an unintentionally sexy closed-lip smile and holds eye contact. I'm speechless and let me tell you, that doesn't happen frequently. I've been doing this long enough that I know my job inside and out. Majors and minors, check. Academic departments, no problem, requirements for limited-access-programs, easy. I can send a student to get any services they might need. Coming up with an answer is painless when you've been here a while. Yet *speechless* is turning into a new normal every time Tom's around. My brain frantically looks for words to break off this spell. Thankfully, a knock by a new student does the trick.

Another student, another major selection issue to fix. This student also needs help to figure out what to major in. I try to focus on her while wondering what the problem is. She's beautiful, has a slender body, beautiful almond-shaped eyes, gorgeous long dark hair, and surprisingly huuuge boobs. I unconsciously start to wonder about those, while I ask the basic questions. "When you were a kid, what did you think you were going to be?"

"I always thought I would be a dancer but then these grew up," she says while pointing at her huge boobs. "I had to quit the team. I mean, I still dance. I go to the studio and help with kids' classes, but they bounce too much. The coach and I decided my dance career was pretty much over at that point."

She talks with sadness and I can't help but sympathize. Not with the huge boobs, for the record, I have regular boobs, but it sucks she won't get to realize her childhood dreams of being a dancer. "I'm sorry you had to end your dance career. I'm sure it was a tough decision. Is there something else you like?"

"I don't know. I'm undeclared because there's nothing else." She produces a long heavy sigh and stares at her hands. She looks sad *and* deflated and I instantly feel worse for her. *Should I hug her?*

I look over at Tom, who's looking at me and not at the student.

Concentrate on the student, #badadvisor.

"You mentioned you go to the studio and teach kids. Do you like it?"

"To be honest, I enjoy working with the little kids but I don't know if I could be a teacher."

"Would you be willing to try a few of the teaching classes? You can teach dance or art. There are performing arts schools all over this area, and in other cities, and you have studio experience."

I ask Tom if he has any suggestions or ideas. I can't help but also wonder if he likes big boobs or regular-size ones. *Ack, what's wrong with me?*

"Look, you never know, what you thought was the worst thing could end up being the best thing to happen to you. It could be your calling to teach the next generation of artists and dancers. It'll be your legacy. Don't think about it as giving up on your dreams... Think about it as modifying your dream." Tom adds and looks at her.

She perks up, her face brightens, and I think she's warming up to the idea of being a teacher. "Okay," she tentatively agrees, her smile widening more while looking at him. Tom talks to her about the classes in the program and recommends a few for the fall semester. When he finishes, he sends her off to the School of Education to get more information on their majors.

After she goes on her merry way, I look at Tom. "I know she's going to be fine but I'm sure she's feeling much better now, thanks to you."

"I feel vindicated after yesterday. See, I can give good advice to students," he grins.

I have to admit after he leaves to shadow somebody else, half of me wanted him to stick around. At the same time, I'm relieved. I enjoyed having Tom in my office but you can't be yourself when you're training a new employee in the "proper" ways of the office. Not to mention, I still don't know if he was brought to this campus to take Judith's position.

A few days later, I grab my lunch, head outside and find a table next to one of the campus's natural lakes. This area is full of tiny lakes and I'm lucky to live and work in a place like this and to have access to these little gems. Because it's summer and there are much fewer students on campus, it is easy to find a quiet spot near our building. I sit and eat while I look for a book on my ebook app. After a few minutes, I instinctively raise my head at the sound of footsteps to see Tom walking towards me. "Hi," he says warmly, raising a hand as he approaches.

"Hey, what's going on?"

"Are you waiting for somebody or can I join you?"

I swallow quickly and clear my throat, "No, not at all. Please join away."

He smiles and takes the seat across from me, then starts to unpack his lunch. I can't help but look at his eyes. This is the first time I'm looking at them outside and I'm enthralled at how his green eyes glimmer with the sunlight highlighting the gold specks in them.

He's shaking a bottle of iced tea and glances at me. "Is this where you hide?" he asks, opening the bottle. I try hard to concentrate on my food and not on his mouth.

"Ha, this is not hiding. Trust me, when fall classes start you won't be able to find me."

The second I say this, his eyebrows go up. "*Yeah?* Is that a challenge?"

Crap. "I didn't say that."

"Remind me again, why do you hide?"

"Because otherwise my students won't let me eat. Not all, but some will see me at a table eating, and will approach me and ask me questions. I love my students, *but* we all need a break and a few of our students have no boundaries. Case in point— the other day I was at the supermarket and a student saw my university shirt, then she, the bagboy next to us *and* the cashier behind us started asking advising questions."

"In the middle of the supermarket?"

I take a sip of my soda before answering. "Yes, at the cashier's line."

"Did you answer them?" he asks while pointing a fork in my direction.

"Yeah?" *Ummm. Why do I suddenly feel like a loser?*

"Olivia, you should have said no. Told them to make an appointment."

"I know, but I feel bad."

He cocks his head and after a brief pause says, "Next time that happens, tell them that your ice cream's melting or that you have a date," as he looks at me through thick eyelashes and I almost choke on my Sprite.

"Are you alright?"

"Yeah, yeah, I'm fine," I stammer. After I recover, I attempt a smile. He grabs a forkful of food and keeps his eyes on me. "Yeah, my dating life hasn't been so hot lately. It's more like a tundra."

"I find that hard to believe," he says with a smirk.

"Well, believe it. I mean, I go on dates, don't get me wrong. But lately, for some reason, I can't seem to go past the first date."

I know I shouldn't, but I can't help but ask about *his* dating life while pointing my fork in *his* direction. "What about *your* dating life? With those green eyes, I'm sure you're busy."

Ummm, this conversation's getting *highly* inappropriate. This fraternization with the enemy is bad, *very bad.*

He smiles and looks down. "My dating life has been non-existent lately. I just moved from my parents' house near downtown, to a friend's house. My parents want me to stay in Miami. My friend's a little crazy. I have way too many things on my plate right now to worry about dating—Wait, does a hot date with my bike count?" he asks, raising an eyebrow.

"A hot date with your bike? Well, it's hot and sweaty, that's for sure." The words leave my mouth before I can stop them. *Gah! Stop flirting with this man.* Remember the goal. Focus on your career, be Zen, and avoid temptation at all cost. Keep all dirty thoughts away from your head and focus on non-naked-in-bed-thoughts.

"Very hot and sweaty," he says evenly but with mischief in his eyes.

Wait, are we still talking about his bike?

After a very interesting, but very platonic, co-worker lunch (flirting notwithstanding), I head back to the office.

Olivia

Today is Saturday night, and for a change, I have a date. I know I said no more dates, but once again I was reminded that I need to date more. I probably shouldn't be following her advice, but Bianca can be very convincing. Something about kissing a few frogs before we find our prince. *Positive thinking.*

I'm meeting George, who's a friend of a friend, or is it somebody's cousin? I can't remember, but we agreed to meet up at a hotel in the Financial District of downtown Miami. On weekends, the "financial" part is non-existent, but there are many restaurants and cool places with live music and a vibrant nightlife. I'm wearing a white blouse with colorful geometric shapes, jeans, and black pointed-toe ballet flats. Finding a parking spot is relatively easy, but it's downtown Miami and a little bit of walking is expected.

I meet George in front of a hotel and after some very basic introductions, he takes me gently by the elbow and leads me inside. He's tall, fit and very cute. He sports a groomed goatee, thick eyebrows, and dark eyes. His gorgeous black hair moves with the wind. He keeps pushing it back and it keeps flopping over his forehead. I can't help but wonder how many girls meet him and get the urge to run their fingers through it, not that I'm tempted or anything. *Not at all.*

The Langford Hotel was a bank in the 1920s. It's a classic and majestic building that's had the inside renovated and modernized. As a matter of fact, you can see the old columns and the original façade on the inside and outside. Besides being a gorgeous building, it has a very cool vibe. I have a sudden vision of coming back one of these days dressed as a 1920s flapper girl. *Okay, maybe not, but there's always Halloween.*

The rooftop restaurant has one of the best views of downtown Miami and the Miami skyline, day or night. A few minutes later, we're sitting in big comfy lounge chairs, the speakers are belting out hip music and we start looking at the menus. When drinks arrive, we get into casual conversation. As we talk, he keeps glancing at my...*front.* It's less than five minutes before his lips curl and he casually asks, "What's that print supposed to mean?"

Print? "My shirt? Why? Do you like it?" My lips turn up. *It's so great that he noticed.*

"No, I hate it," he says indifferently and turns away, only to turn back for a swig of beer.

My stomach clenches, and I swallow hard. "Oh," I mumble, deflated. I'm thinking about something witty to say when he keeps on.

"I like how your jeans are tight and sexy, though." He makes a round gesture with his hand, then winks at me.

Okaaay. Time to prepare an exit strategy.

After some awkward chat the food arrives, and we start an animated exchange again. Thankfully, there are no questions about politics or religion. I have to admit the conversation is pretty decent over dinner...until we talk about our jobs. I tell him about my students at the university while he shares that, he works as a salesperson in one of the bigger local furniture stores. "The store is so big and I hate walking back and forth... people make me walk, then change their minds and buy nothing... my feet *and* my back hurt all the time... clients that return furniture are the worst... don't get me started on kids *and* elderly, they walk so slow!... They're very annoying and such a waste of time... my coworkers are not team player. They keep stealing my clients... I hate working weekends *and* holidays... working on commissions sucks..." Finally, he complains about his bosses and how they boss him around. *Is he serious?* Is there anything he *won't* complain about? Wait. Can *I* complain to the dating gods about *his* complaining?

When the bill comes, he tells the waiter he has a Groupon. *A Groupon?!*

I feel this is one of those slap-my-forehead-moments.

The waiter takes the Groupon and comes back with the remainder of the bill. She puts it in the middle of the table and he makes no attempt to grab it. "I left my wallet at home," he says after a few minutes, but his eyes are darting back and forth. After I settle the bill, and we walk out of the hotel, he offers to walk me to my car.

I noticed an ice cream shop on the way and now, as we walk in front of it, he opens the door for me. I'm always up for a sugary treat. As we walk in, the aroma of sugar and waffle cones is simply intoxicating. We stand in line looking at the long glass case with dozens of ice cream buckets and I try to relax. *Does he have cash? Has he suddenly found his wallet in his pants?* After we both order, he stops by the register, turns to me and nods. In shock, I take out my credit card and pay. This is un-freaking-believable.

After walking a little more, we finally arrive to my car. He opens the door for me but when he lowers his head, I kiss his cheek quickly and leave. I make a mental note: date somebody that likes his job. P.S. Also date somebody that remembers to carry a wallet.

Thank God I love my job. My dating life seems to be going from bad to worse, but at least I can take comfort in the fact that I love my job and I'm good at it.

I'm in the break room preparing a cup of coffee when Tom walks in and my heart flutters. "Good morning," he says cordially as he reaches for the coffee pot.

"Good morning," I reply casually, temporarily distracted. I grab my cup and taste the black liquid. Yuck! I instinctively open my mouth and my tongue pushes forward while I shake my head like an idiot. *Crap! I forgot the sugar.*

My reaction causes him to chuckle. That chuckle and those green eyes directed at me, threaten to turn my legs to gelatin. Without saying a word, he narrows the space between us and hands me the sugar. I try not to react to his touch. After I put in a couple of spoonsful, I taste the coffee again for the second time then take a step back. I can't help but look at him over the rim of the cup. *No ring.* I have a feeling he's also surveying me. My heart races and I feel my skin flush. *What would it be like to kiss him? Focus.* Remember, he's the frenemy. I still don't know his game plan.

After a few minutes, he breaks the silence. "Do you have a lot of students today?"

"I have a ton of freshmen today," I reply while trying to concentrate on my hot coffee and not on my hot coworker. "What about you? How's training going?"

He rests on the counter and lowers his cup. "It's going well. I met Sandra, now I'm training with Ralph. I think Andrea is the last one." His eyebrows knit together, and he frowns in confusion and looks adorable. "Or was it Andrea, then Sandra? I don't know. It's too early in the morning and I'm just now having coffee. Ask me again in an hour," he says, bringing the cup back to his lips.

"Sandra's great. You'll like her."

"I'll let you know."

Sandra's my friend, she's older and married. However, I can't help but groan inwardly knowing Andrea's young like us *and* single. Not to mention she always looks amazing. But then again, I just met the man. Why do I feel so possessive? *Gah. Disengage.* Must not fraternize with the hot-new-coworker/potential rival. Must focus on future career promotion instead. "Well, I have to go. I have an appointment but it was nice chatting with you," I say as I head towards the door.

"Sure. Likewise."

That was awkward. I need to work on my disengaging techniques or maybe it's not a good idea to be alone in confined spaces with him, period.

I finally make it to the front counter and call in Kevin, another of my regular students. He's into music and plays the piano, guitar and sings beautifully. Music students usually go to the music department for academic advising, but his grades were not the best in high school. Since he started, he's been concentrating on academics and trying other things. He's planning to audition for the music program, but he won't say *when*.

Maybe I can call Valentina and arrange an academic intervention. What am I saying? I've never done an academic intervention, that is not a thing and if it is, I bet Dean Lozano is involved and he's so serious. Better to stay away from him.

"Hi, Miss Olivia. How are you?", he greets me as he sits in front of me. He gives me a bright smile and continues, "You're looking very nice today." Did I mention he's a flirt? *Yeah.*

"Thank you, Kevin. How are you? What brings you here today?"

"You mean besides the pleasure of your company?"

"*Yes*, besides that. You should have meet with me *before* you left on vacation. Do you know what classes you want next semester? Any ideas?"

"I want to do Music Theory II and Music Business. I also want to try psychology and oceanography or astronomy or *maybe* philosophy," he says, enthusiastically.

"Philosophy and astronomy? Are you sure?" *Yikes*. That sounds so different from what he usually goes for, mostly music. Maybe I've given him too much rope, but he can't just keep taking random classes, can he?

"Yeah, my friend recommended this teacher and I want to try it and see if I like it."

"Are you ready to audition?" I ask, point-blank.

"Maybe next semester. Hey, by the way, I'm playing this weekend. You should totally come to see me."

"Thanks for the invitation, but I have plans," I lie.

"Did I tell you my last girl was your age?"

Here we go. "Yeah, you've mentioned it."

"You look pretty today. Just go on a date with me," he says casually, like it's not a big deal.

And get fired? No thanks.

"You never know, it might be worth it, you might like it," he says and winks at me again.

Okay then.

"I have other students waiting to see me. What do you want to do? Audition?" I say gently.

"No. Not yet, next semester."

Clearly, this is not working.

I have a sudden vision of a TV set playing "Sesame Street." Elmo comes out and says: "The words of the day are *next semester!*" For a second, I'm tempted to laugh out loud at the image but manage to hold it in. "Okay. Here's a question for you. You're a music man. Since I met you that's all you've talked about. Why are you trying to deny it?" When I ask this, he's silent. He's stands up, his eyes fixed on the window for a few seconds but doesn't say anything. "Kevin?" He sits down again and shrugs but doesn't say anything. I can't help wonder why he's resisting. "Okay. Tell you what, think about it. Think about what you want out of your education. You can't keep wasting time and credits, not to mention money, when at the end of the day you're out there looking for gigs. You'll be better off studying music, getting better at it, and connecting with music faculty and students." I lean back in my chair and my body relaxes as I look at my student.

"If I declare a major, will you go out with me?"

Yeah, the fact that I can't go out with him is not registering.

"Kevin, go register. Pick a science class, a math, and two or three music classes. I'll lift your advising hold so that you can register. If you have any questions, send me an email or make another appointment."

"If I have a question, I'll definitely come back," he extends a hand and I do the same. When he has it, he turns my hand over and kisses it.

I have a sudden need to pull back and rescue my hand. "Bye Kevin, see you *next* semester." As he walks out, I start thinking about what to write my notes. My male students are not usually like him. In fact, he's the only one. Most are very respectful and want to play it cool in front of a "girl" advisor. I can't put half of the conversation on my official notes, but then Tom walks by my office and nods. I feel my stomach do cartwheels and forget about Kevin and his sexual drive and start wondering about Tom's sex drive instead. *Oh, lord.*

Olivia

I t's the first day of fall classes. Every space, table in and around any food establishment or body of water has students on it or around it. Call it the invasion of the college students. Over five thousand of them to be exact, all descending on a college campus during the same week, like a horde of hungry locusts.

The line in advising is endless but we advisors must eat or pass out, so I head to the Horticulture building for lunch. I guess not many people want to major in agronomy, but it's perfect for peace and quiet. On my way there, I say hello to no less than ten students and give at least five hugs to eager undergraduates thrilled to see me. They're happy to be free and back on campus. *I'm feeling the love.* I can't stop smiling. When I *finally* make it, I actually find empty tables under massive shade.

"Hey."

I jerk my head back and see Tom walking my way. "Hey," I reply.

"I can't believe I found you," Tom admits, sounding pleased with himself.

Did he mean to find me? "How did you know where I'd be?"

"I didn't. The campus is insane today. I asked Ralph for a quiet spot and he mentioned here, then I saw you and kind of followed you here. I have a very serious question to ask you," he intones as he sits beside me and starts opening a can of Coke.

"What?"

He's serious as he asks, "What's up with Ralph and the Hawaiian shirts?" Upon hearing that, I grin and his lips turn upwards.

"Yeah, I don't know. He likes to be unique and memorable so that students don't forget him and come back to see him."

"Well, he's certainly memorable, I'll give him that," Tom says with a bemused smile.

"The fascinating thing is, they do remember him. They'll stand at the front counter and ask for 'Hawaiian man.' Maybe there's a method to his madness." Ralph is the cool advisor, always making the students and the staff laugh. His daily "uniform," if we can call it that, consists of loud Hawaiian print shirts.

Clearing his throat, Tom adds, "I saw you hugging students on your way here. You're pretty popular."

"I guess. But then again, this *is* Miami. Everybody hugs and kisses."

"Should I be taking notes? Do I need to start wearing Hawaiian print shirts or go around hugging students to be popular around here?"

I pause for a second before answering. "Yeah, I don't know about that strategy. People would freak out if you start hugging them. Judith might fire you, and I don't know if a Hawaiian shirt would suit you." I have a mental picture of Tom in a Hawaiian shirt and have to pinch my lips to avoid laughing.

"I would look ridiculous in a Hawaiian shirt. That's probably what you're thinking."

I glance at him. "I said nothing."

"You didn't have to. Your face says it all."

I burst into laughter. When I get myself under control, I look at him. "Sorry."

"Sure you are. I'll have to hatch a plan to become popular around here. One that doesn't involve hugging people at random and wearing questionable fashion pieces," he says he starts in on his lunch.

"Okay. Let me know how that works out for you."

"I definitely will."

I start pulling things out of my own lunch bag and glance at him as I do. "I didn't peg you for a plotter. Should I be afraid of your evil plan... hatching?"

"I'm not planning world domination. I would settle for university domination, even campus domination. There's nothing to worry about."

"Says the evil plotter. Let me know when you cross over to the other side." The moment I say this, his lips turn upward and he chuckles.

"You're funny. Maybe I'll convince you to come over to the dark side. You never know. You might like it." He winks at me and I smile.

"I'm going to plead the fifth on that one."

"You're no fun."

"I think you just might be too much fun for me."

"Maybe, maybe not..." he says, taking a forkful of food.

"*Some* people might think you're coming out of left field or that you're not qualified to lead a bunch of strangers."

When he's done chewing, he quickly says, "Trust me. I'm qualified."

"For what it's worth, I think you are. Then again, there's a *slight* problem with your plan."

He's preparing to eat another forkful, but pauses to ask, "What?"

"You need a Ph.D. if you want to proceed with a hostile takeover."

"I never said it was hostile, and FYI I'm working on the Ph.D. I'm halfway there. As soon as I get settled, I'll go back to class."

"Good to know. I'm going to have to watch what I say around you. In case you do become campus president, I wouldn't want to give you a reason to fire me," I say.

"I would never do that. Not to you, anyway. I think my first rule will be to ban questionable fashion pieces."

"Oh my God, you're mean."

He grins. "I'm kidding, I'm kidding. You know I'm kidding. I couldn't care less what people wear."

"Should I start calling you Darth Vader?"

"Maybe you can call me Luke Skywalker."

I'm serious as I say, "Maybe I'll call you Chewbacca." I look at him deadpan and after a few seconds we burst into laughter. Lunch goes by in the blink of an eye while we share stories and laugh.

Olivia

<hr>

After a long day at work advising students, including an advising session where the student spent pretty much the whole session looking at my computer screen and never made eye contact, another student who started and ended every sentence or statement with "you know" and another one involving a bouncy and gurgling baby, I finally arrive home. Actually, the baby was adorable, I can't complain. Once home, I change into yoga pants, an old t-shirt, and have a debate... tea or wine? *Hey, it's five o'clock somewhere. You know.*

I head outside for my amazing golf course view and stand on my porch for a few minutes. There's a narrow two-way street with a median in the middle that surrounds the course. There are so many flowering trees. Large Banyan and Royal Poinciana trees bloom red in the spring and paint this part of town red and green. Also, this area has tons of smaller Tabebuia trees that have gorgeous yellow blooms during spring and make the golf course surroundings more beautiful.

I take a deep breath, grab my cup of warm peppermint tea, sit on a rocking chair and watch a squirrel on a nearby tree. The sun is setting and I can't help but admire it. The August sunset has painted the sky yellow around a huge sun. The clouds closest to the sun have a glow of light-orange and pink. The sky opens up to a cloudless blue with a nearby lake reflecting it all.

I sit there content, remembering why I kept this house. To be honest, in my current situation I could have made a nice profit selling it, but I would have never found another one like it and that I could afford. I have to admit I got lucky with real estate. Too bad that luck didn't extend to the relationship department.

When I get promoted and become director, the first order of business is debt management. The second is to give the house a little love... not necessarily in that order. *Maybe a couple of cool art pieces.* Definitely, a new patio set with one of those cool cantilever umbrellas and a chrome BBQ set for my backyard. A distant third is dating. *Maybe.* Regardless, I'll be back on track and everything will fall into place. Valentina's right; for my next relationship I have to find somebody who supports my career and understands how important our jobs as advisors are. We're shaping future generations and satisfy-ing the workforce. It's very important stuff.

A group of cyclists is heading towards me and I focus on them instead of my terrible love life. Maybe I should take up cycling. Bianca might approve of that. I mean, it's cycling, you just hop on a bike and pedal. *How difficult can it be?* I scan the group as it passes in front of my house. I can appreciate their fitness and coordination. *Hmmm. Are the shorts Lycra or spandex?* Maybe I do need to take a look into it.

After an hour of contemplation, I stand up, glance at my mailbox, and try to remember the last time I picked up the mail. I put my cup on a little side table and head that way instead. Once at my mailbox, I glance through the envelopes.

Utilities, several credit card bills, junk mail, ugh. Now I remember why I don't like my mailbox. It is so depressing, a gloomy reminder of how much my financial situation sucks. As I'm standing there, I see the cycling group of men coming my way again. I keep pretending to look through my mail then shift my eyes to them. Since I'm here, I might as well take a closer look.

The large group zooms by me going at least eighteen to twenty miles per hour in rows of two. As the last couple of cyclists approach me...I think I see *Tom*. For a few seconds, I wonder if I'm imagining him and maybe it's just somebody who looks like him. But then he breaks away from the group and crashes about a hundred feet away from me. My mail flies through the air as my hand flies to my mouth. I instinctively run towards the Tom-look-alike as he's getting up.

"Oh my God! Are you okay?" I ask breathlessly while yes, *the* Tom, "my" Tom, stares at me with wide eyes, his jaw clenching and grimacing in pain. The rest of the group moves on. "Why aren't they stopping? Why is no one stopping to see if you're okay?" I glance back as the group disappears around the golf course.

"No," he says calmly as I turn and focus on him, "they don't stop." He takes a deep breath and bends at the waist then looks at me, still hunching over, "Olivia, if I didn't know any better, I would think you're trying to kill me. First a door and now this. Is this your idea of 'killing the competition'?"

"What?! No! I didn't do anything. I mean, I admit it, I pushed the door too hard, but I had nothing to do with this." I feel a flush creeping on my cheeks. *Gah!*

"I know." He stretches to his full height and I'm rewarded with a slight smile. I start to grin back and then notice he has scraped his knee and has a tiny bleed.

"Why don't you come inside. We'll clean that up and put on a Band-Aid." Tom grabs his bike and follows me. Obviously, he's wearing a cycling outfit and as we head back to my house,

I find myself noticing the snug fit of his clothes and his very noticeable *assets*.

What am I thinking?! What's wrong with me? Focus.

I pick up my discarded mail from the ground as he sets his bike on my porch. While Tom takes off his helmet and gloves, I see that his palms are red and raw from the impact. I feelbad that he's hurt and I ask again if he's okay. "Yep, I'm good," he replies as he cleans his sweaty brow with his yellow, spandexy-looking shirt and I get a peek at his well-defined abdominal muscles. *Oh my.*

"Is your bike okay?" I ask, looking at it as I close the door.

"Yeah, she'll be fine."

"She?"

"*She* is an expensive piece of equipment who gets a lot of love." Once inside my house, he stops and stands in the foyer.

"Come on, let me give you a tour," I walk towards the hallway on the left. "I have a first aid kit around here somewhere." I can't remember *exactly* where it is, but he doesn't need to know that.

"To my left, we have a room/office, followed by a bathroom." I walk into the beige and green-palm-tree-themed bathroom, I open the medicine cabinet, then kneel to look through under the sink. As I stand up, I accidentally glance at his... *package. Dear Jesus.*

No Band-Aids, so I keep going. "Here we have another room." I raise my arm and wave it dramatically and he chuckles. The second bedroom has minimal furniture. The curtains are open, which highlight the big windows and views of the golf course. He immediately notices it and walks over.

"Nice view you have here," he says as he admires it, glancing back at me. I nod, walk into my bedroom across the hall, and head in. He walks after me but stops at my door. The doors of the closet are open and I pray he's not paying attention and doesn't notice the mess or the shoes all over the place. *Today, it looks like a bomb went off. Sigh. Of course.*

I make a mental note, always leave Band-Aids in one of the bathrooms so I can *find* Band-Aids when I need them. After I rummage through my bathroom, I head back to the living room and kitchen area with Tom trailing behind me. "Have a seat," I gesture towards a nearby plush, soothingly neutral cream chair and he complies. "Would you like something to drink? Water? Tea?"

"Sure, water's fine. This is a nice house. Have you lived here long?"

I hand him a glass of water and go back to the kitchen and start opening cabinets at random. "Not too long. I moved in about six or seven months ago." He takes a sip of water but his eyes are on me, so I keep going. "It belonged to the parents of a college friend. Her dad passed away a few years back and her mom was living here alone. Kate finally convinced her to move with her to Ft. Lauderdale and sell it. At the time, we were looking for a house and she offered it to us well below market value. It's close to the university, so it was a no-brainer." I don't know why I'm sharing all this, but I can't seem to stop myself from spilling my guts.

"We?"

"Yep, my ex. After a couple of years together, we started talking about getting *our* place, then this house became available."

"If you don't mind me asking, why did you break up?" I stop opening cabinets while I debate for a few seconds if I should answer such a personal question from my *co-worker/frenemy.*

When we lock eyes, I absently think about the old shirt I'm wearing and my messy bun. "Ummm, we bought it and started remodeling it. We gutted the bathrooms and the kitchen, added brand-new appliances, and new paint in and out. A day before my birthday the contractor gave us the keys, and we went to dinner to celebrate. I was politely informed he was not *in love* with me. I was also informed that he was seeing somebody else. I guess he liked her bed more and…you know…"

When he doesn't say anything, I go back to searching cabinets, "Anyway, the following day I went back to his house and pretty much left with only my clothes. I then proceeded to fill what was left of my credit cards with furniture. I'm currently paying for the remodel, the mortgage… and pretty much everything you see here, by myself… you know…" I pause and look at him. "Wow, sorry about the long rant. That was way too much information." I take a deep breath.

"No, not at all. I'm sorry to hear that, Olivia. It sucks and nobody deserves that." He comforts me in a soothing tone, with kind eyes and concern; he never breaks eye contact.

"Thank you." I open a high cabinet and a couple of plastic containers land on my head and my kitchen floor. When I step on one and it slides, I lose my balance and make contact with the floor. Whoomph.

Ow. "I'm okay." I quickly get up and look at him. He's up from his seat but when I raise a hand, sits back down.

"Are you sure you're okay?"

No. "Yes." *My assets hurt.* I look up, *finally* I spot the first aid kit on the top shelf, grab it, and start walking in his direction.

His eyes follow me as I walk towards him. "Do you live here by yourself?"

"Yeah. I'm looking for a roommate and I've interviewed a few people, so we'll see. I've met a few *fascinating* people."

"I bet." I sit on the coffee table in front of him, point to his leg, and saying nothing, he raises his leg on top of my lap. I grab gauze and antiseptic and clean the red line going down his leg. He's still silent but looking straight at me. Deep breath. *Be Zen. You've already fell on your butt and had the verbal diarrhea, what else could happen?*

I dab a cotton ball with some alcohol and put it over his knee without warning. He winces and closes his eyes for a second. "Sorry, sorry." His brows are knit together and there's a tic in his jaw, like he's grinding his teeth, trying to hold back. I wonder if he's holding back a curse word. *What is his favorite curse word?*

"Next time how about a little warning?"

"Come on, don't be a baby. Ready?" When he nods, I dab again, except this time, afterward, I hold his knee gently and blow softly onto it. Touching his knees with my fingertips causes a weird energy to go through me. After a few seconds, his brow relaxes. When his jaw eases, his lips open slightly.

I turn to rummage through the first aid kit, grab a tube of Neosporin, put a tiny bit on another cotton ball, and apply it lightly. "We have three choices for Band-Aids. We have regular Band-Aids, very boring," I say playfully, "then we have *Frozen* or *Star Wars* Band-Aids." When he raises an eyebrow, I explain. "I have nieces and nephews and these are way cooler. At least, that's what they tell me."

"*Star Wars* it is. May the force be with me, right?" There's a twinkle in his eyes and after a couple of seconds, a lopsided smile forms on his lips.

That gorgeous smile causes the butterflies in my stomach to go crazy and my heart starts to beat a mile a minute. My stomach is tussling so hard, for a few seconds the fear that I'll fart right here, right now is overwhelming. *What the hell's wrong with me?* I think the cycling outfit is doing weird things to my brain. A knock on the door interrupts... *whatever this is.*

A cute guy is at my door. He's about our age, sweaty, and wearing a cyclist outfit similar to Tom's. "Hi, I'm Keith," he says, out of breath. "Is Tom here?"

"Yeah. He's right here." I look back at Tom, who's coming our way.

"Hey, man," Tom greets the stranger, as he grabs his helmet and gloves.

"Hey, are you all right?" the stranger asks.

"Yeah, I'm good. Let me introduce you to Olivia, my coworker," he says as Keith extends a hand. "Olivia, this is my best friend, Keith. We live nearby."

"Oh, cool."

"Yep, very close. We bike around here and even play golf sometimes," his friend adds.

"Really? In the few months since I've moved here, I've been *dying* to try golf."

"Hey, next time we come out to play, you're welcome to join us," Keith says in a deep voice. His lips turn up and his pearly whites are on full display.

"Thanks for the invitation. One of these days I might take you up on that." I reply, looking at both of them, but mostly at Tom, and grinning like an idiot.

"We both suck at it, but sure," Tom replies.

"Don't listen to him He sucks, but you're welcome to join me anytime." Keith grins.

At this, Tom literally pushes his friend out the door. "We're going to get out of here before this one embarrasses me further but thank you for everything." He strokes my arm as they walk out, and I freeze.

I clear my throat and manage a reply, "You're welcome," then watch them hop on their bikes and ride off.

Sex on a stick. What am I thinking... again? This is not like me. *At all.* I need to control my physical impulses.

I'll start tomorrow.

Olivia

T oday the campus is electric. Everywhere we go, there are students. They're talking, laughing, smiling, flirting, playing, making plans and being loud. Very loud. Today, there's music in at least three locations around campus and at least half the students seem... lost. *How many of them will pass out from the heat?*

On the other hand, the energy's amazing. I love working on a campus.

Once again, a few students stop me to say hello. When they do, I introduce them to our new advisor. A couple of the girls give him a quick glance over; if he notices it, he takes it all in stride.

Tom and I finally make it to a quiet table on the far end of the university and I'm relieved to avoid a sensory overload. Tom is quiet. From time to time, he glances my way as we eat but doesn't say anything. Come to think about it, since the day he crashed in front of my house, he's been quiet and his office door's been closed. Not that I've gone by it or anything...like every day. *Not at all.*

Should I leave him alone or poke the bear? In this case, poke the cyclist? Hmmm. I'm poking, don't judge me. "How's your knee?"

"It's fine."

"How's your bike?"

At this question, he chuckles and tries to hold a smile from forming. "She's fine, too."

"How far away from the golf course do you live?"

"Around the block from your house."

"So now that you know where I live, should I be expecting you to come by and borrow a cup of sugar?"

"I don't know. Do you have any bike oil?"

Bike oil? Are we still talking about the bike? "I don't have any bike oil, but I can tell you a funny story."

"Okay. Shoot."

"I had a student today, who moved into the dorms. Since he didn't know anybody, they paired him at random with a student who's from Papua, Indonesia. Now he's freaking out because he found out his roommates' from a region where tribes are known to practice cannibalism. Basically, he's afraid his roommate will chop him off into little pieces and eat him in his sleep. Obviously, he's overreacting. First week nerves...or something."

"Did you read about that student in Maryland who admitted to eating his roommate's brain?"

"Do you think that's true?"

"Yes, it is. You can Google it. Did your student contact housing?"

"Yeah, but he has to wait a couple of days because they're swamped with requests from students trying to change rooms for different reasons." I sip my Coke and look at him through my eyelashes, and he does the same. "Change of subject. Do you have any hidden talent I should know about?"

"Besides cycling? Maybe..." He slyly pauses, then shakes his head and looks at me, "Not really, no. You?"

"Does cooking count?"

"Do you like to cook?"

I squirm like a schoolgirl at his gaze. *Why can't I be cool or at least pretend to be cool?* "Yes, I do."

"Are you good at it?"

"My friends think so."

"How come you're not a chef?"

"I don't know. Right now, I guess cooking is a fun hobby with the added bonus of healthy eating. I don't think I would want to spend ten hours in a kitchen, though. My hair would be a mess."

"Yeah, we wouldn't want your hair to be messed up," he says chuckling, nodding his head and pressing his lips together to keep from smiling, but smiling with his eyes nonetheless.

"Are you making fun of me?"

"I'm not, I swear. I agree with you. You have nice hair."

"Okay, fine. Whatever."

He clears his throat. "I think you should let me try your food and be the judge of your culinary abilities."

"You want to judge my culinary abilities?" When he nods, I share a piece of my chicken and wait for his reaction.

"Wow, that's actually fantastic."

"You seem surprised."

"I am. I mean everybody thinks they're a top chef, but you could actually be on 'Top Chef'."

"Not really, but thank you."

"You're welcome. Let's rewind. Forget bike oil, next time I'm hungry, can I drop by to see if you have any food?"

I can't help but chuckle, "Ha, you're funny."

"I'm just saying. If you have leftovers, you can call me. I'm always up for a home-cooked meal."

I smile and say, "I will keep that in mind," then try to concentrate on my food. Every few minutes, we glance at each other... *It's going to be a looong semester.*

I meet with my mom and brothers over the weekend for a family lunch at my brother's home. Not that I'm looking forward to being grilled, but I have to show my face at some point so that they know I'm alive, otherwise, they send search parties after me. I arrive and immediately go around saying "hi" to everybody with hugs and kisses. Inevitably, I end up in the kitchen, only to be kicked out.

When we finally get called to eat, I find my awesome sister-in-law and sit next to her. After a very satisfying meal, I decide to look for the tiny humans and hang out with them.

I spot the group of kids and stand nearby and watch them play. Emma, who's five, notices me and comes over. "Do you like horses or unicorns?" she asks, peering up at me. *Is this a trick question?*

I kneel down to her level and grab on to her little hand. *She's so soft.* "I love horses!"

"Unicorns are better."

"You think so?"

"Yes. First is unicorns, then flying horses, then ponies and theeennn horses," *Wow, she's really thought about this. A whole hierarchy of taxonomic animals.* Sadly, after a few minutes of conversation, her attention is captured by music coming from a nearby iPad and she runs off. I notice my brothers when they surround me, which they think is the funniest thing ever. A "sister sandwich."

"What's up, sis?" my older brother William asks as I stretch to my full height while taking the hand he offers.

"What's up? The sky," I answer amusingly and point up.

"Ha-ha, funny," he replies with a serious expression. Unable to hold it any longer, his lips turn up and he downright laughs.

"You're so annoying. I don't know how you convinced Julie to marry you."

"I didn't have to do anything. Once I kissed her it was game over…"

"Ego much?"

"I'm confident. We'll come back to that," he grins. "We're here to warn you," he says, turning more serious. "Mom has been asking about our single friends and I have a feeling she might try to set you up."

Michael, my younger brother, is chewing popcorn but pauses to talk. "She's taking matters into her own hands," he says in-between loud bites.

I take some of his popcorn and contemplate this…actually, there's nothing to contemplate. This is a terrible idea; I don't need my mother meddling in my already disastrous love life. Her blind date set-ups are worse than my friends'. It's either old guys she knows or her friends' kids, who are all divorced, commitment-phobic, and have at least two and a half kids. "Can you close your mouth when you chew? Why are you still hungry? We just ate!"

"I have the metabolism of a hummingbird."

"Maybe you have worms?" He pauses mid-bite, then shrugs and keeps chewing. I shake my head. "Can one of you guys talk to Mom? I don't need her playing matchmaker. I already have Bianca for that."

Michael grabs the popcorn and I roll my eyes, "We told her to relax, but she said we didn't know what we're talking about. Apparently, since you're not dating, it's mathematically impossible for you to find a guy."

William grabs Emma mid-air as she runs toward us. She looks at her dad adoringly, grabs his cheeks with her little hands and smiles as he focuses on her. *Awww, can I take her home?*

"Ugh. For the record, I am dating." Glancing back at me, Will narrows his eyes and I shrug, "What?"

"Since when?" he asks.

"Since…a few weeks ago."

"Good for you, sis," he says as Emma giggles sweetly at us. "Make sure he doesn't do anything stupid where we have to go after him. I'm married with kids and I would hate to go to jail."

"I'm not married. If I go to jail, you can come and bail me out." Michael interjects.

I look at my brothers. "There will be no jail involved in this scenario. Are we really having this conversation about my nonexistent, pseudo-boyfriend?"

"Hey, it's never too early to start," Will says, and winks at me.

Perfect. Let's now add overprotective siblings to the list of things to worry about when dating. "Tell you what guys, if and when I find a 'mate,'" I say, using air quotes, "you'll be the first to know." I go in search of the matchmaker— I mean, my mother— but not before stealing Mike's popcorn bag. They will not be the first people I tell about my dates, not even close, but they don't need to know that.

Is it crazy that my mother has an easier time getting dates and getting married than I do? In case you're wondering, Mom is now married to husband number four. Even though I'm withholding judgment, she just might have found a good one this time around. *Finally.* To be honest, the idea of *her* getting married again is exhausting. Having had no children with them, she has no contact with husbands number two and three. Husband number four has four kids of his own. I honestly don't have the energy to try and figure out my place in this modern family. At least I have my brothers. They are and have always been my unit.

Mom is friendly and flirty and loves to dance. Miami's the perfect city for her. Growing up, weekends were fun, with family and *friends* always around. To be honest, not counting a particularly embarrassing episode of singlehood that resulted in repeated flirting with one of my male teachers and an admission of a "mom-crush," it was not too bad. We were taken care of and managed to grow up as happy well-adjusted individuals with a strong love for family. Well, except for a mild aversion to relationships and dating, but we can't all be perfect.

I find her in the kitchen, and we catch up on family matters and work before she jumps right in. She casually mentions that her friend's son just became single, and she's been wanting me to meet him. *Ummm. Why does she want me to meet him?* The topic of my dating life is always trending with my family. Since I am a woman, I should be married and breeding kids like my brother by now. I sit on a stool and wait.

"She wants him to settle down with a nice girl. He works as a partner for one of the Big Five. He has a great job and he's handsome, but he's single again, and she wants *nietos* like me." I'm assuming she's referring to the Big Five Accounting firms in Miami, which is nice but tells me nothing besides the fact he has a decent job. And what it is with moms' and grandkids? *Is this a competition?*

"Have you met him?" I ask as I chew on some popcorn. "Why is he single *again*? What's wrong with him?"

"*Cierra la boca.*" *Don't talk with your mouth full*, she says shaking her head. "Yes, I've met him a few times... and why are you asking what's wrong with him? *Por que* do you think there's something wrong with him? This is why you're single," she says exasperatedly. "*Nunca te vas a casar.*" *You're never going to marry*, she's saying.

"Unbelievable. It's a fair question. If he's handsome and has a great job, why is he single?" I can't help but roll my eyes, which she ignores and keeps going.

"I've met him. *Es buena gente, de buena familia.* Polite, and that's all you need to know for now," she says while she sprays something on the counter. *I disagree, I don't think that's all I need to know.*

The aerosol mist reaches me and I cough. *What in the world is she doing with that thing?* Before I can say anything, she attacks the already clean counter with a sponge.

Why is everybody trying to set me up on dates? Ugh, it seems when it rains, it pours, and yet I somehow agree to a date with John, the "Big Five" wonderboy. *Sigh.*

Olivia

A couple of days after meeting my family, I got a call from John. Because he does seem polite over the phone, I agree to go on a date with him. Since he works in downtown Miami, we meet for drinks in Brickell. It's a weekday, but I travel against traffic and it doesn't take too long to arrive there. Besides, I'm familiar with the location and I have a feeling it'll be awesome. It's in an area with many hotels and great restaurants that face the bay and have stunning water views. The truth is, the food in this part of town is just simply, *amazing*.

I valet my car at one of the bigger hotel chains and ask for directions. When I finally get to the restaurant, the hostess informs me that my date's already there and I follow a waiter to the back deck. This particular spot is a hotel that has a marina behind it.

As step out, I can see small boats moored right behind the restaurant. There are dozens of yachts of different sizes bobbing gently at their respective docks. On the very far end is one of the bridges that connects to downtown. The view of the bay is spectacular. Because it's a weekday and the bar's relatively deserted, I spot him easily as he's the only one sitting by himself. He seems to be in his forties and as I approach him, I notice he's talking with the young female bartender. When I finally reach him, he stands up, shakes my hand, and pulls up a chair for me. Even though it's early evening, his white shirt is still perfectly starched and his expensive suit jacket sits on the chair next to him like a trophy.

Everything looks good... except for his hair. It's unnaturally dark, and maybe a tad too black? *Ummm, is it supposed to look like a rug?*

Thankfully, we get into an easy chat about the bay and the yachts sitting nearby.

After the waiter takes our drink and food order, we settle back into an effortless conversation. He's very intelligent and a skilled conversationalist. Although I'm not feeling a physical attraction, this is nice. It feels like we could talk forever.

As we share appetizers, he asks about my job and listens graciously. He also talks about his job. *A lot.* He loves accounting and math and I'm surprised by how passionate he is about it and how much he enjoys it and his clients. "I'm a junior partner at an accounting firm. I work with brilliant people. We work really hard, and they're great," he says, then spends the next *hour* talking about what they do in his company. "General accounting, general ledger maintenance, fixed assets, leases, inventory and accounts payables and receivables..." He drones on and on and on about accounting things with names I can't seem to remember. Have I mentioned that I hate math? *Ugh, now I sound like one of my students.*

During our lengthy pro-accounting conversation, I notice he looks at anything with legs that moves. I'm tempted to ask if he's a fan of Don Juan.

By the time dessert arrives, he shares he's been thinking a lot lately about starting a family. "*La verdad* is that I usually go for younger women." *The truth,* he confesses in between bites, "but it never works out. I'm not sure why... but my mom knows your mom, who told my mom you were single, and they both agreed I should date somebody older." *Older? Is he serious? I'm only twenty-eight, did she tell him that?*

After another hour of conversation, I tell him I have to go. He tells me he'll stick around and refuses to let me pay. We both stand up and he gives me a light hug, then casually grabs my ass. When I jump in surprise, he has the audacity to wink at me. *Seriously, dude?* He gives me a soft kiss on the cheek and tells me he'll call me. When I glance back awkwardly, he's focusing all of his attention on the bartender.

To be honest, I hope he doesn't call me. To be cheated on once is more than enough for a lifetime. As I walk away, I begin to wonder what I'm doing wrong and how do I get myself in these situations? *I can't be that bad at dating. Can I?*

I have a ridiculous mental picture of being interviewed by Dr. Phil. Right before going to commercials, he talks to the camera. *"Join us in a few minutes as we try to figure out what's wrong with this poor girl who just can't seem to get a second date."* Fadeout.

Oookay. That does it.

No more dates, I'm done. Besides, I don't want a relationship. Who has time to go on dates? Or spend money on gas traveling all over the city of Miami? Not me. Dating is bankrupting me even more; you have to be rich to date in Miami and I'm not. *Not even close.* Dating is more depressing when none of my dates has resulted in sex. Now that I think about it, I've been nowhere near. Not even a single kiss? Or a second date? *Should I be worried that there IS something wrong with me?*

Tom

I walk into a restaurant and I have no idea what to expect. Ralph told me our co-workers were getting together and somehow, I agreed to join him. I'm still questioning his choice of Hawaiian print shirts, but he's a cool guy and I trust his judgment. *Mostly.*

A waiter leads me to a long table and without intending to, I end up sitting at the head and now everybody will spend all night staring at the new guy. *AKA me. Great.*

I get a beer and start trivial conversations with my co-workers. After a while, I start to wonder who else is coming. *What was I thinking? I should have gone cycling instead.*

Then I see her.

Olivia waves shyly and I nod instinctively. Her top shows off her nice collarbone and her jeans highlight her figure. I have to force myself to look away and concentrate on my drink.

As more people *and* drinks are arriving, the conversations are going from fascinating, to interesting to downright stupid. There's a discussion about relationships going on and I can only hope nobody asks me, as I have absolutely no intention of going there. A conversation on HR and dating is in full swing in the middle of the table. *Is it true all relationships have to be reported to HR?* I obviously wasn't paying attention when they covered that at the training. I'll have to ask my parents about this. But then again, why the hell would I care? I have no intentions of getting involved with somebody at work.

"Hey," I hear Ralph say next to me.

I glance her way as I answer. "Yeah."

"Not that it's any of my business, but she's pretty cool."

I look at him. "Who?"

"You know who. I can see your wheels turning. Don't do anything stupid."

Crap. Is it that obvious? "Are you telling me to date her or not?"

He shrugs. "Neither. I'm just saying she's a nice girl." He takes a swig of beer but doesn't expand.

"And you know this because?"

"I've been working with her for a few years, and she's friends with my girlfriend." The beer in my hand stops mid-way. I pause and focus on Ralph but again he doesn't elaborate. "What?" he asks.

"Wait a second, let's rewind. *You* have a girlfriend?"

"Of course, I have a girlfriend. Why do you seem surprised?" After a second, pointing the bottle my way and smiling he says, "I'm not a loser like you."

"Give me a break. You dress like an old tropical vacationer...or something." I pause. "You're right, I am a loser. Wait a minute, you have a girlfriend? But you have no pictures in your office."

"I had a couple but knocked them down. Then I figured I would just change them all and I haven't gotten around to it."

"Wow. I mean, don't get me wrong, you're a cool guy, but those Hawaiian shirts. How?"

"Hey, don't hate on my clothes. They're comfortable and I look cool in them." He pauses. After a few seconds, we both burst into laughter. "Okay, fine, but I wear them for a reason.

The students might not remember my name, but they always remember the shirts. I think about it as my uniform."

I raise an eyebrow. "Sure, buddy. Keep telling yourself that." At this, he laughs and I can't help but chuckle.

"In all fairness, during weekends. I wear regular clothes. My girlfriend's not complaining. She thinks it's funny, so..." he trails off shrugging.

"I'm glad somebody appreciates your sense of humor. What does she do?"

"She's the social media assistant manager at the college."

"Nice. How did you meet her?" I ask.

"Olivia introduced us. She thought we would hit it off and we did."

"That's awesome man. I'm happy for you."

"Thanks, man."

"Are Olivia and your girlfriend close?"

"Close enough. All I'm saying is don't be a dick. If you're not interested in something serious, walk away. She's had a rough year and there are plenty of women out there."

"I don't know if I want something serious with her, or with anyone else for that matter, but I will take your advice into consideration."

"Cool." And because we're guys, that's the end of the conversation. On the other hand, if I have any questions about Olivia, now I'll know who to ask.

I take another swig of beer and glance her way again, then turn and listen to Ralph make stupid jokes about advising. The last one has him asking how many student affairs professionals it takes to change a light bulb and the answers have me laughing out loud. I catch her, yet again, looking at me. Her eyes sparkle, and it completely breaks my train of thought.

"She's here," Ralph says and a huge smile breaks on his face. Whoever she is, she has his attention. That's when I notice a pretty girl with short brown hair talking to Olivia. A few seconds later, as she approaches, Ralph stands up to greet her.

After they hug, he introduces her as Gabby, and she extends a friendly hand. Her smile seems genuine and I instantly like her.After a few seconds and against my better judgment, I offer to move so that they can sit next to each other. Without thinking, I gravitate to *her*.

I sit between Olivia and Sandra. It takes less than five minutes before Sandra starts talking about her brother being a lawyer and offers *his* help if needed. *Why the fuck would I need a lawyer? Do I look like a guy that would get in trouble with the law? My Cuban parents would kill me.*

I turn my attention to more interesting things... *Olivia*. Her exposed shoulder is distracting me, and she's so close, I can't help but glance at it. She smells of vanilla and fruits and it's both calming and intoxicating. It's driving me crazy and I'm starting to question if sitting next to her was a good idea. She asks how I feel about advising, clearly a safe subject.

"You know it's the same, the principle is the same, what changes are the policies and procedures of the university you're in but the students have the same hopes and dreams and issues. We can only hope to give them the best advice and help them graduate so that they can become useful members of society. The health of a society is measured by how educated its citizens are. Our job is to give them the tools so that they can be successful," I say without thinking.

As soon as the words leave my mouth, I regret them. *What the fuck's wrong with me?* That might have been a little too philosophical. *Yep.* That was a little too much. *And now she's looking at me with funny eyes and probably thinks I'm gay.* Not that there's anything wrong with that, but oh my God.

After a few minutes of conversation, I make a stupid joke about her getting drunk. She blushes and gives me another smile. She's gorgeous. I wonder what she'll say when she finds out who I really am and who my parents are... actually, I think I'll keep my anonymity for now. Besides, nothing will happen between us, so it doesn't matter. This will stay strictly a professional relationship. There'll be no more flirting and certainly no kissing or sex.

"How did you get into cycling?" she asks.

Cycling, *another* safe subject. Except now, she'll think I'm obsessed with it because I can't seem to shut up. *Oh, Jesus.* I have no self-control when she's around.

I make a joke about my dad in boxers and we both burst into laughter. She returns my smile with sparkling hazel eyes and full dimples that are adorable. She's focused on me until she gets pulled into a side conversation. She has that girl-next-door sex appeal, a good sense of humor, *and* she's smart. When she's with students she's professional and assertive. It's sexy as hell to watch her interact with them, take over a conversation and tell them what to do. More than that, every time I eat with her I feel we have a connection.

Maybe the solution to this dilemma is to stop having lunch with her or looking for her during our lunch break. But then again, if I have to eat, I might as well eat with her. I enjoy her company and she's not bad on the eyes; the alternative is to eat alone or eat with Ralph. *I don't think so.* Besides, I take pleasure in watching her eat, which I admit is a first for me. She's not one of those girls that never seems to eat or that only eats arugula salad and dressing; she has a healthy appetite and can cook to boot.

To be honest though, right now she seems nervous and it's cute to watch. She keeps making animated gestures and fidgeting with her hair, putting it behind her ears and our shoulders keep bumping. Men as a whole appreciate feminine beauty in any shape or form but some of us have preferences for certain areas or features. Have I mentioned she has great hair? Yeah, she does. She has long brown locks and as it happens, I'm into hair. I can't help but wonder what it would feel like to touch it, run my fingers through it or have those silky strands on top of me... to have that whole body on top of me would be nice.

After a few minutes of staring at each other, while pretending we're not, we both quietly concentrate on our plates. I look up when I hear the sound of glasses against the table and take a minute to look around. Utensils clinking, hums of conversation and the easiness of it all, the laughs. I have to admit this is a great group. They really like each other; they're having fun and it's contagious. I can't help but feel great, relaxed. I smile at somebody and take a deep breath because this *is* great. I can do this all night.

Then I hear her giggle.

I turn to look at her. She's talking to people and *still* eating cheesecake. Her tongue dances across her plump bottom lip but when she notices me staring at her, a slow smile spreads. I'm three seconds away from lifting my index finger and cleaning off the cheesecake on the corner of her lips but I manage to stop myself. Instead, I motion to it and she uses a napkin.

When she sighs, I picture myself running my hands through her hair, then going down...*oh for God's sake.* I need to remind myself *again* that I need to have a one-track-mind and my focus should be *only* on my career. The last thing I need is to get involved with a woman who works with me. *That* alone makes her off-limits.

When one of the student assistants starts a conversation, which ends up being more like a debate about kissing with the eyes open or closed, the discussion is fascinating and the answers are riveting. She looks at me with heat in her eyes. Her pupils dilate, and I can't help but glance at her mouth. *Why do I have a sudden urge to kiss her and see if her eyes will close?*

I'm not supposed to like her, much less want her. The stress of the move, combined with the lack of free time to cycle or hit the gym is clearly affecting me. *Clearly.*

Olivia

The next morning, I get to the office and immerse myself in my job. I tune out all distractions, including the male variety. By the time it's mid-morning I have a rhythm going. I have appointments with continuing students and new incoming freshmen, mixed with random walk-ins. The day is flying by. Before lunch, I advise a student that spends half our session complaining about Miami traffic. Another made me think of the artist Salvador Dalí with his spiky mustache. And a third one started every sentence with "My mom thinks..." I was about to ask if his mom was an academic advisor, but I had a feeling he wouldn't have appreciated it.

After lunch with Bianca under a gorgeous South Florida sun, I return to my office and get back to my flow. The semester is moving along and life is good. I have to admit, I shared nothing about our office dinner or talking to Tom or anything at all with Bianca. I'm a terrible friend, but I kept the whole thing to myself and spent any free time reliving my conversation with Tom in the privacy of my own head.

Once I'm back at the office, I go to work on my advising notes. When a knock interrupts me, I look up to see a familiar student. "Hi, Piper, how are you?" I advise Piper from time to time, and I think she likes me, but she has no allegiance to me or any other advisor. If she has a question or needs something and I'm busy, she won't hesitate to see whoever's available.

"Remember how we spoke about me repeating statistics?"

"Yes, I remember." I also remember she wants to be a nurse and needs statistics. Unfortunately, so far, she hasn't been able to pass it. We agreed that the third time's the charm and if she can't do it this next time around, she's going to move on to another major. I know there's a high likelihood she will not, but for her peace of mind, I'll let her try one more time.

"I came because I needed an advisor to remove a hold but they told me you were busy. So, then the new advisor told me I couldn't do statistics and then told me he was going to block me from registering for it." Her eyes water. Instead of letting the tears flow, she dabs her eyes with her fingers and holds them in. "I want to be a nurse. It's the only thing I've ever wanted to do. I'm paying for the class — why can't I take it? I don't understand."

As she speaks, I look through the system and see Tom has indeed placed a hold on her to prevent her from registering. I understand why he would block her, but at the same time, he doesn't have the whole picture. I'm certain once I talk to him, he'll remove the hold. No big deal. "Hey, Piper, will you give me a minute? Have a seat and I'll be right back."

I go in search of Tom and find him in his office talking to Janine, our office administrator, and Judith's assistant. They're engrossed in a conversation about office supplies and I patiently wait for them to finish. As she walks out, I walk in. "Hey."

He stops moving and gives me his full attention. "Hey, what's going on?"

He looks gorgeous and I want to ask about if he liked hanging out with us outside of work, but instead I focus on the situation. "Quick question, did you put a hold on my student to prevent her from registering for stats?"

"Piper? The student I just saw?"

"Yes. Her," I say.

He stands up, comes around and leans in front of his desk. "She has no advisor listed. Is she your student?"

"Not officially, but if you can please take the hold off, that'd be great. Thanks." I smile, turn around, and start walking out.

"I don't think so. I don't think she should be retaking that class at all."

And cue the record scratch.

I freeze, then turn back around to face him. "She needs it if she's going to get into nursing and we're going to give it to her."

"No. *We* are not."

He folds his arms slowly but doesn't say anything else. *O-kay. Do I want to get into an argument with him?* Well, right now I have a strong need to stick up for my student and I don't really care. "Look, she's had some personal issues, but we made a plan. We both agreed this would be her last chance and if she doesn't do well, she's changing her major."

"I disagree with this plan. If she fails it again, her GPA is going to drop. Forget about a nursing program, she could be dismissed from the university. Keeping her in is more important."

"Don't you think I know that? But she wants to give it one more try so that she doesn't spend the rest of her life wondering. I think we should give her a chance." I take a couple of steps forward, smell him and my brain short-circuits.

"I don't think so, Olivia. I'm not removing the hold," he says, unbending and putting his hand near his chest as he says it.

Wait, what?! Who the hell does he think he is, coming here and telling me and my student what to do and changing our plans!? As if reading my mind he says, "Look, it's in her best interest. You know she's not going to pass. Why put her through it if we can help it?"

"First of all, you don't know that. Second, her GPA is over 3.0. She could still do it and third, we're not 'putting' her through that," I say, making air quotes and trying to stay calm. "*She* has chosen to retake a class after it was explained to her the consequences of not passing it. After *I* explained the consequences."

"I'd rather she keep her GPA up, then she can go to grad school later."

Here we go. "Fine. Let's ask Judith what she thinks." Without waiting for an answer, I turn and walk over to Judith's office with him trailing behind me. We're like two little kids searching for a teacher. Luckily, she's free. We both walk in and present our arguments while Judith listens quietly with her Zen demeanor. "Judith, she's my student. I've known her for quite a while. She understands this is her last chance. We've spoken about it in length. She had personal issues but now she's focused, and determined and she doesn't want to give up on her dreams yet." As I talk, I have a sudden vision of us in a court of law with Judith dressed in judge's robes about to give a verdict.

I'm trying to explain things calmly, Zen-like, but Tom's shaking his head and jumps in unexpectedly. "Nursing is way too competitive, meanwhile her GPA is tanking, and the lower it goes, the lower her chances. I don't think math is her thing — she did great in everything else — let's redirect her to another major in the health field and move on," he concludes, looking at Judith.

For a second, rage flows through me like lava. I force myself to stay Zen and remember I'm at work. *Or not.* I turn my body to face him and can't help but raise my voice a little. "I'm not moving on, it's her life. If she wants to try one more time, why can't we let her? This is not your decision to make. It should be up to her to decide and own up to her own choices."

He turns to me and shakes his head, clearly not buying it, which oddly infuriates me more. "Actually, as her advisor, it *is* my decision," he says, steadily.

What the actual f... "You met her *five* seconds ago!" I can't help glaring at him and moving my hands.

"It doesn't matter. Part of our job is to protect the students from themselves. Math is not her friend. Find her something else."

"Okay. Okay," Judith interjects, raising her hand like a referee, which immediately shuts us both down. We both turn to look at her in unison and hear the verdict. For a second, I half expect her to pull out a gavel and bang it against her desk. "This is what we'll do...the hold stays."

What?! "*Come on.* That's not fair, he doesn't even know—" But she doesn't let me finish, as she lifts an arm up again and I stop. *I can't believe this!*

"The hold stays...for now. Tom's right, if her GPA keeps dropping, it'll be harder for her to get into *any* grad program. *For now,* focus on non-math classes and recommend that she gets a math tutor. In a couple of semesters, we'll meet and *maybe* I'll remove the hold and let her try again. Thank you," she finishes and turns back to her computer. *Shit.*

We both nod and walk out, but as I walk back to my office, a thought occurs to me. This is why co-workers shouldn't date. I can't argue with him about students, then go home as if it's nothing. I can't. Right now I want to wring his neck. This is further confirmation that dating at work is a very, very bad idea. *I must stop thinking about him naked and focus on boring-work-related thoughts.* "Do you want me to go and talk to her?" I hear him ask as we walk.

"No, I got it. You've done more than enough for today. *Thanks.*"

"Come on. It's not personal. You're too emotional."

I feel a flash of irritation, and for a second, I want to punch him. *What would Rocky do?*

Instead, I stop and turn around so suddenly my hair slaps my face, "Too emotional?! Are you freaking serious right now?" I snap as I absently push my hair behind my ear. A few hairs are still sticking to my face and Tom detaches them while his expression softens.

Gah! Does have to touch me? Why is he looking at me like that?!

"I apologize. Wrong choice of words. That sounded different in my head." He raises his palms in defeat and lowers his voice. "What I mean is, maybe, just maybe you're too close to the situation. Let's be honest, you know third and fourth attempts never end well. Look at the statistics. Why let her tank her GPA if we can help it?"

"I'm not debating this with you. You're new here. The student wants another chance. It's our job to also provide learning opportunities that will help her build character. If she fails, she's done, and she understands it and is ready to take responsibility."

His brow knits together. He looks at me like he doesn't know how to placate me. *Shit.* "You know what? I don't have time for this. *My* student is waiting. Bye." I'm feeling slightly possessive of my student and I don't really care what he thinks right now. I walk into my office and try to explain to my student that her dreams are on hold, thanks to my colleague, but they will come through. For now, we'll focus on keeping her GPA up, get her math tutoring and when the time comes, I know she'll be ready. *Hell, yeah.*

After an exhausting afternoon, half of it spent advising, the other half avoiding Tom, I finally make it home. I change into yoga pants and a tank top, put in a load of clothes and head on out to the supermarket. I get the essentials and cheap ice cream. It's a brand I've never tried before, but it was on clearance. Unless it's awful, it should definitely improve my night. Plus, I got a bottle of discounted wine, in case it sucks.

After I park my car and debate if I should have wine on my porch or the patio, I walk into my house and turn the lights on. *Wait. Why is the floor so shiny?*

It takes me a few seconds to realize it's not that the floor is shiny but that my house is flooded.

Olivia

<hr>

Since the door is now open, water is flowing out freely through the door. I stand there motionless, like a statue. *Are you kidding me?*

A sense of urgency kicks in and I run in, throw the grocery bags on the sofa and immediately find the culprit. My washer has been possessed by a demon; it's shaking violently and spewing water non-stop. I have a sudden vision of the lights shutting off and the washer coming after me like a Stephen King horror movie. Which is obviously *not* helping my current predicament. I try turning it on and off and press random buttons, but nothing's working. Meanwhile, my pants are getting soaked from the water gushing out of it. After a few minutes of battling buttons, I desperately climb on top of it. Slippery surface and threat of electrocution notwithstanding, when I pull the plug, it finally stops.

I go back to the sofa, pick up the bags and put away what needs to be refrigerated, then wade to my room. Thankfully, the water has only come halfway down the hallway; most of the water traveled to the living room and kitchen. *Thank God for tile floors*. I run in the opposite direction and grab the broom and mop. I push as much water out as I can before putting towels in all the doorways to prevent the water from coming in, then I vaguely remember the front door's still open.

As I near the main door, I slide on the water and fall flat on my ass. *Ow*. I stay under my door frame, let my head gently lean against it, and close my eyes for a couple of minutes, while my pants and my ass get drenched. I take a deep calming breath and think *Zen. Whatever that means.* When I open my eyes and raise my head, Tom's coming up my driveway. *Crap*.

He's walking in my direction, half-panting, then stops to catch his breath. "Hey, stranger." When he pauses, his hands go to his hips, and he looks at me while water runs out of my house.

My arm raises in a limp wave from the floor, but I don't move. "Hey."

"Are you okay?"

Is that a trick question? "Yep, I'm great." *Obviously*. I take another deep breath and focus on my hands.

"I was out for a run and I wanted to make sure you were okay."

He was out for a run? Of course, he was.

"I'm peachy." I look up to him and give him a thumbs up. I get the feeling he doesn't believe me when he strides purposely toward me.

"No, you're not peachy. I can see the water. Where's it coming from?"

"It's coming from my possessed washer. I just unplugged it." Because I don't have the energy to explain or argue, I leave it at that and focus on the golf course and the few cars going by.

He takes a deep breath, exuding calm and focus. "Do you need help?"

I look up at him. *Yes? Maybe?* "No. I got it." His hair is wild, and he's wearing shorts and a sleeveless shirt that shows off his upper arms and forearms. I'm temporarily distracted by the contours of his muscles before I go back to sulking on my floor. "Where's your bike?"

"Home. She's resting," he says, giving me a lopsided smile. "Are you still mad at me because of the student today?"

He's clearly not wasting any time addressing the elephant in the room *or the pool.* "No. It's fine. Don't worry about it."

"Olivia, come on, let me help you."

"Why?"

He pauses for a few seconds and his eyebrows dip in the middle. "Because we're coworkers."

"You do realize I don't usually call my coworkers when my house floods."

"Oooo-kay. We're neighbors."

I look in his direction. "Barely. You don't live on this street."

"I'm around the block," he says, pointing back with his hand. He pauses. "We're friends?"

Ummm, are we though? My eyebrow shoots up.

"Sure, we are. You, me, my bike. We're all friends." He gives me a slow smile and winks at me. I can't help the smile that forms on my face while he takes the last few steps toward me and offers a hand. I debate for a few seconds if this is a good idea, but then I take it and let him lift me effortlessly off the floor. *Holy cow.* The skin-to-skin contact feels amazing against the warmth of our connected palms and my body electrifies.

Either my feet are not working or my shoes aren't, because I slip again but this time, he manages to hold on to me. I instinctively hold on to his biceps while he grabs my waist to steady me. Our palms are still connected and I'm acutely aware of his heart racing. He glances at my mouth then looks at my eyes with an unreadable expression. I know it sounds like a Disney movie, but when I look into his eyes for a second, time stops. *Oh, boy.*

I glance at his very kissable and very lickable mouth and I'm torn in half as the little angel on my right shoulder tells me to be a good girl and the little demon on my left tells me to kiss him. I'm frozen in place, unable to listen to either of them. *Can they both shut up now?*

"Hi," he says casually, lowering his voice to a sexy-as-hell-hypnotizing hum. "Are you sure you're okay?"

I'm trying to keep it together, but it's clearly not working. *Actually, something else is working.* "Yeah—yes. My shoes aren't working," I manage to stutter.

His hand shifts and his fingers hug my waist a tiny bit tighter. He has a strong arm around me and our faces are inches away from each other, while we're still connected via our palms. His eyes glance at my mouth again but after a few seconds, he slowly lets go of my hand and takes a step back. He slides his other arm from behind me but doesn't completely let go of my waist, anchoring me in place with both hands.

I stand there speechless, until the sound of him clearing his throat pulls me out of my libido-induced-haze. "You should go and get changed," he says sharply in a voice that almost sounds like it's an order, and if it's possible, I'm even more turned on. *What is wrong with me?* I've turned into a depraved nymphomaniac since I met him. Whenever he's around all I can think of are sex and dirty thoughts. This is ridiculous, I'm a grown woman. *What happened to my self-control?*

Nonetheless, all I can do is nod and march to my room. After a quick debate on clothing, I settle on another set of yoga pants and change my underwear to a matching set, *just in case.* By the time I come out, he's opened the glass double doors in my kitchen, has a broom in hand, and is pushing water out. I find the mop and work my way from the bedrooms to the front. As I get closer to him, I can see his eyes dancing playfully. "Is your possessed washer under warranty?" he asks with a wicked smile while stopping to look at me.

"Yeah. I bought it six or seven months ago. I have the receipt somewhere."

"Tell me a story. Tell me something I don't know about you."

"A story?" I repeat. *A PG story? An X-rated story?* "I've got nothing," I reply diplomatically then look at him and wait a beat. "Fine. I hate pistachio ice cream...Actually, I hate pistachios in general."

"Pistachios? Okay, good to know... Did you know that the mango and pistachio trees are related?" he adds, stopping to look at me, half-smiling.

"That is very random information... and you're smiling. Are you making that up?"

"I'm not. You can look it up." He's trying not to laugh, but the twinkle in his eyes and the soft crow's feet around them betray him.

"You're laughing. I don't believe you."

"It's true! I swear! Okay, fine. Tell you what, Google it, and if I'm right, you can buy me ice cream."

"Pistachio ice cream?"

"No, I like plain vanilla."

"Okay. But if you're wrong, I like chocolate chip."

"Chocolate chip? Good to know *but* I'm not wrong, you'll see."

I look at him and tilt my head at a thought. "How come you're not on the bike today?"

"I don't know, I needed a run. I also go to the gym with Keith sometimes. I like to mix it up, you know." When I nod, he asks, "How come, living so close to the golf course, you haven't taken up cycling or golfing?"

"I haven't lived here that long, and I don't know anybody who golfs or has a bike." I shrug.

"Now you know me."

"I do, but I also heard that the bikes are expensive."

"I guess they are... a little."

"What do you consider a little? How much are we talking about?"

"I would say about $3,000 for a basic model," he guesses, as his open palm shakes.

I can't help but cough dramatically. "That seems like 'a little' to you? For a *bike*?"

"I mean it's not really a bike, it's a sophisticated piece of equipment. It has special speed cranks, chain guides, a carbon fiber frame..." *I must visit a bike shop ASAP.*

When he's done, I reply, "Or I can go to Walmart and buy one for fifty bucks."

"You did *not* just say that."

"I did, actually."

"One of these days we'll have to have a real conversation about bikes."

That sounds promising. "Sure."

"Are those guys in the pictures your siblings?" he says motioning to a picture nearby.

"Yes, they are."

"You guys and your mom? Where's your dad?"

"He was never around. Apparently, he and my mom weren't compatible. Since then, she's been searching for someone who is. What about your parents?"

"They're together. Going on thirty years."

"Wow. They're lucky. That's so hard to find these days." I pause. "So, have you done anything exciting lately?"

"You mean besides cycling?" he asks, grinning, "Not really, no. I lead a boring life."

"Sure, you do."

"At the risk of this sounding like a line or a cliché...has anybody ever told you your dimples are adorable?"

"A few people have. Yes."

"Okay, just wanted to throw that out there." He stops to look at me and smiles.

I feel my cheeks getting warm and I fight the temptation to fan myself. Instead, I nod and concentrate on the floor and the water. For the next couple of hours, we push water, laugh, and exchange stories.

Tom

All things considered, I have to admit the last couple of weeks have been great. I'm enjoying my new job and the challenge of helping my students. I met my coworkers outside of the office and appreciated getting to know them better. I've also been getting to know Oliva more, can't complain about that. Not that I was purposely *trying* to get to know her, but we've had some great conversations lately. It's nice to talk with somebody in the same field of work that *gets* it and even more so when that person is so easy to talk to.

I couldn't help it when I was out on a run, saw her fall, and being the gentleman I am, I offered to help her. *Then came within seconds of kissing her.* Not a good idea because we work together, and we could both be fired if it became something more, but when we're together it's like Fourth of July chemistry-infused fireworks. I can't help myself from teasing her or flirting with her. Not only that, but those sexy dimples are getting to me. Every time they appear my resolve crumbles just that much more.

I'd be lying to myself if I said I wasn't attracted to her because I think about her *a lot.* The fact is, something's different this time. She's smart, passionate, and has a way of looking at people, at her students, like they matter. When she looks at me I can see the genuineness in her eyes.

As much as I enjoy the easy banter between us, I should stay far away from her and stop this.

Boundaries. I need to establish boundaries.

To top it off, today is shaping up to be a slow day, which leaves a lot of time to think. In case you didn't know, at most universities there's a lull during the months of September and October. Starting in mid-September and ending right before spring registration starts in November, students are busy going to classes and studying for midterms or completing projects. Only those who are desperate or have problems they can't fix on their own, come by and our office slows to a depressingly slow crawl.

I get up from my quiet office to walk by the front counter to see if there are any students that need help. I see the student assistants talking animatedly, playing computer games, and catching up on TV episodes online between homework, studying, working the counter, and overall displaying serious multitasking skills.

Besides the gossip the office staff engages in, we all have to find ways to entertain ourselves. We try to keep the shenanigans to a minimum but since it's mid-October and both basketball and football season are underway, Ralph and I engage in public displays of sportsmanship. To start, we prominently hang Miami Dolphins team posters on our doors—this is the year they'll win the Super Bowl. *We know it.* Besides having a golf putter in his office for days like this, Ralph has a football. Since we don't have any appointments and there are no walk-ins, we take ourselves to the empty conference room and start throwing it around.

An hour and a fun conversation later, we're still at it. I throw it at him, but his cell phone rings right at the wrong moment, distracting him. He not only *doesn't* catch it, but inadvertently directs it to the wall with his foot where it bounces, hitting the floor, and then flies out of the room. *"Ouch!"*

Uh-oh. "Ralph, who did we hit?" I ask while his attention is focused on the door.

He whips his head to me, then back to the door. "Crap. You hit Olivia."

Fuck. "Me? You should have caught it, not kick it like a soccer ball." I jog over to his side and notice her outside the door, bending midway and holding her calf. I can't help but cock my head sideways and admire her... *assets* until the irritation in her voice brings me back.

"What in the world are you two doing?"

"Sorry, Olivia, the ball bounced on the floor," Ralph says before he looks at me. When his cell phone rings again, he answers it. "Gabby?" Looking at me, he mouths *sorry* and walks away. *Traitor.*

I glance at her. She tries walking but instead discovers she can't put any weight on her leg and stays in place.

"Come on." I saunter towards her and instinctively put my hand on the small of her back then lead her into the conference room before she has a chance to argue. When I pull up a chair, she sits down and narrows sharp hazel eyes at me in a mostly pissed-off way. "Are you okay?" I inquire as I kneel in front of her, acutely aware of my own heartbeat. All I can do is clench my jaw and breathe.

"Yeah, I'm great, *obviously.*" Why do I get a feeling if she had something in her hands, she would probably throw it at my head?

"Don't be a baby." I glance up at her and her eyes narrow even farther. Her mouth opens, but no words come out. She gives me another angry glare while I fold her pants leg up and gently massage her calf myself from the cramp the football gave her. Her skin is warm and smooth. For a few seconds, I consider running my hand higher up her leg.

Breathe, dude.

After several minutes of rubs, the look is gone. Instead, she produces a slight, involuntary sigh. As her eyes half-close, her breath hitches. Her expression changes when she realizes this, and she turns a pleasant shade of pink. "Thank you," she says in a throaty voice while she looks at me. "I have to go... to my office... right now." She bolts out of the room with one pant leg up and the other one down.

I stay in place and wait a few minutes for the blood to go back to my brain before I head back to my office. When I walk by hers, she looks at me with enormous eyes and a sheepish expression. *Fuck.* I need to stay away from her. This is going to be a disaster. At the rate this is going, my family will disown me, or worse, we'll both lose our jobs. *Boundaries.* For now, it'll be best to avoid her. *Completely* avoid her, I mean... *Woof... woof.*

Wait. That can't be a dog. *Woof... woof.*

I look out my door and sure enough, I see a dog running down the hallway. From time to time, we have service dogs in the office and occasionally students will bring puppies in, but service dogs are supposed to be on a leash. *Right?*

This dog runs in front of my door again, this time with a lady's shoe hanging from his mouth. I watch with amusement as a few seconds later a young woman runs after him, with our fellow advisor Andrea close behind... without shoes. I get up and stand under the door frame and for a few minutes watch as the dog gives his owners and a couple of advisors a run for their money running up and down the long hallway. The scene is so comical I have to hold back from laughing out loud. A few minutes later, I watch the dog run by with a sandwich in his mouth and yet another advisor following him. *Probably the sandwich's owner.* Andrea stops by my office, shoeless, and slightly out of breath. I can't help but ask if everything all right. "Everything's *not* great," she retorts.

"Why does a dog have your shoe?"

"Because I was advising his owner and my shoes were off and I guess he decided they were toys and ran away with one. But he dropped it somewhere and replaced it with a sandwich."

"So, he's a runway and a thief. Where is he now?"

"He disappeared... with my shoe!" she cries, pouting like a kid.

"He can't be far. We only have one outside door. Did you look under all the desks?" She nods and walks away. For the record, we have several doors that lead outside but only one main door where students come in... *unless this dog can read signs*, but we all have to agree it's unlikely.

I go back to my desk and after a few minutes, the dog walks in and lays in the middle of my office. He's a gorgeous golden retriever and I can't help but approach him and pet him. That's when I notice he has the shoe again. "Hey, Houdini." I look up when I hear Olivia; she's standing in front of my door. The dog looks up at me and goes back to his original position.

I glance at her and raise an eyebrow. "Houdini? It says *Rocky* on the tag."

"Oh," she blurts as her cheeks redden but she recovers quickly. She kneels next to us and starts petting the dog herself. "Andrea's looking for her shoe."

"You mean this shoe?" I ask, producing a cream-colored, half-chewed shoe. It's full of tiny holes.

"Yep. That's the one." Her eyebrows go up and her lips pinch together.

"How's your calf?" I ask with strong eye contact as we continue petting this dog. Memories of my hands on her calf overrun my brain, leaving no room for thought processes. All I can think of is how much I wanted to slide my hand up.

I'm so wrapped up in her gaze, I don't notice someone else at my door.

"There you are, you goofball." Upon hearing his owner's voice, Rocky stands up, tail wagging happily to greet her. She stoops to his level and when they embrace, he looks so happy. I can't help but smile. "I am so sorry guys. We're training him to be a service dog, but he just wants to have fun."

"Maybe he's not cut out for this," Andrea says from the door and we all turn towards her. After a few silent seconds, I stand and hand her the shoe.

"Andrea, I believe this is yours," I say with an exaggerated flourish. Her eyes bug out and the horrified look on her face is priceless. She grabs her shoe, inspects it, then growls. *Yikes.* She takes a deep breath, and walks out, with the student and her dog behind her. I look down at Olivia, who crinkles her nose and shakes her head but says nothing. I offer a hand and help her up. "That student's brave to go after Andrea," I say to no one in particular. Once we're at eye level, I look at her but don't let go of her hand, "I'm sorry about earlier. I didn't mean to make you uncomfortable."

She slowly slides her hand out of mine and takes a step back. I want to reach out and hold her again. "It's fine. Don't worry about it," she quietly states and before I have a chance to say anything else, she rushes out of my office. For the rest of the day, I stay in my office and avoid all distractions.

Another slow day in advising. I stay in my office and try to focus on paperwork, no more playing around or wasting time. From now on, I will focus on my job and only my job. Except I haven't seen Olivia for a few days and now I want to go find her for lunch. Maybe catch up with her. *Nothing wrong with that.* After I order food, at lunchtime, I can't help but wonder if she's eating alone. *Only one way to find out.*

"Hey," she says as she sees me walking towards her. A smile slowly starts to form on her lips and by the end, her dimples are on full display and my heart skips a beat. *Oh fuck. That smile is going to get me in trouble.*

The truth is, her smile is captivating. It's hard for me to look away. I can't stop thinking about it and get lost in it. Another one of those smiles and I might actually do something stupid... like ask her out.

Today she's wearing a sleeveless shirt that shows her lean arms and her knee-length skirt rises a little as she moves her foot. Her thighs are exposed on the sides and as I walk in her direction, I can't help but look at her legs. I suddenly remember touching her calf and how soft her skin felt. "Hey. How are you? How's your day going?" I ask, trying to sound casual but it's lunchtime and instead of thinking about food, I'm thinking she looks good enough to eat.

"Okay and yours?" she answers contentedly. She gives me another smile while moving her hair to the side of her head where it all gets pooled over her right shoulder. Sunlight is striking it, making it shine and turning it lighter somehow, reminding me of honey and hypnotizing me.

"Not bad. Did you eat?" She tilts her head, gives me a perplexed look and one of her eyebrows rise. *Crap.* "Never mind. You're obviously eating now." She grins at me and I smile back at her. "Yep, it's one of those days," I admit.

I'm about to sit next to her, then wonder if it's better to keep my distance. "What's in the bag?" she asks casually as I sit next to her on a backless bench. "That smells wonderful."

I remember she's a foodie and half of me wants to impress her. "I went to this restaurant with Keith the other night. The food was amazing. I just ordered from there. Here, you have to try this." I open a container and wait eagerly to hear her opinion on the dish.

As the strong aroma wafts over us, she looks at me expectantly. "Oh my God, yes." I can't help but grin and watch her as she enthusiastically grabs a forkful. When her mouth closes around the fork, her eyes close gently, and she hums in appreciation. It's the sexiest thing ever. Her mouth is mesmerizing. "Wow, this is excellent. You have to tell me where it is so I can take my friends there."

For a few seconds, I forget she's talking. I'm spellbound by her cat-like eyes. Sunshine is striking her hazel eyes making them seem yellowish-brown, like two gold coins. "Yeah, yeah, we should go there one of these days," I say without thinking. *What. The. Fuck.* I really, really need to stop flirting with this woman.

"I'd like that," she says with another disarming smile.

What am I supposed to do now? Should I block her out? Stay away from her? The more time I spend with her, the less I want to do that and now I have indirectly asked her out. *Great. Way to go, Tom.*

Back to my plan of avoidance... at least until I think of a new plan.

Tom

<hr>

You know how sometimes your just day starts out wrong? You want to go back to bed and not come out until you hope the day just ends. In my case, I wish I would have stayed home and gone cycling instead because today is shaping up as one of those. It must be a full moon because the entire student population seems to be up here complaining about something. *They should be studying.*

After avoiding Olivia, for pretty much the rest of the week after that lunch where I indirectly asked her out, I spent all weekend contemplating my next move... and fighting my brain on the useless fantasies it was coming up with every time I thought about her. The worst thing is, cycling with a group has now become a health hazard. At this rate, I'll crash and break my neck. *Not good.*

This is so far off the mark of where I want to be. I moved back home, not only to be with family but also to advance my career and take it to the next level. I should focus on that, not thinking of ways to flirt with the woman or make her laugh so I can see those cute dimples of hers, or worse, ponder about the myriad ways to get her into bed. I cannot mix business and pleasure. I don't want to.

Today, however, is not a good day to have this existential dilemma.

To start my day, a student complained to Judith that I didn't give her the class she wanted and said I was sexist because I didn't help her. Even though, in reality, she didn't have the minimum math required for said class. *Enough said.* Another advisor, namely Andrea, was mad at me because I took the time to advise her student; although, in my defense, I didn't know that was her student or that she was so territorial. *Duly noted. Moving forward, I will not be advising ANY of her students.* A third student got into a loud, heated argument with his girlfriend outside of my door and I had to get involved and pull the guy away. *"Bodyguard" was not on my job description.* And yet another student didn't understand why she couldn't see her advisor without an appointment and was threatening to complain to the dean about our "lack of customer service." What is it today? *Complain about the advisor day?*

The craziest thing is, it's not even lunchtime yet— *perfect.*

I keep debating if I should take the rest of the day off and hit the pavement with my bike. If it weren't for the fact that I have a staff meeting later and Olivia will be there, I might have left. Except when I hear about still yet another situation with Olivia and a student, all I want to do is find her.

She's in her office, the lights are off and I don't know why, but I immediately want to comfort her. I walk in, close the door halfway and stand in front of her desk, my hands on top of a chair. "Hey. Are you okay?" She looks at me and nods. "Sandra just told me that one of your students died." Olivia looks absolutely miserable and I have a crazy desire to kiss her and make her smile. "Is there anything I can do?"

"I'm okay, just sad. He was one of my regular students. He died of a heart attack. Fifty years old. I know he was an older student but still, it's just so weird to have a student just die.

Death is not something we deal with around here. It's surreal." She pauses. "He was so close to finishing too. He worked so hard. He'll never get to walk the stage at graduation. It's just so unfair." There's vulnerability there and I want to take the pain away for her. She stares into space, nodding wistfully, while I debate if I should hug her.

"I'm so sorry to hear that, Olivia. She looks at me but says nothing. "Will you let me know if you need anything?" She nods. "Are you going to the meeting?"

"I have to call Dean Lozano's office. They had me write something for the communications department about my student so that they can write a press release. Then I have to call the provost office and the academic dean and talk to some other people about his grades and his current classes, but yeah, I think I'll be at the meeting later."

I nod, then I go ahead and leave her alone, but when it's lunchtime I go around the campus searching for her in her usual hiding places. When I can't find her, I give up and decide she doesn't want to see anybody, not even me.

After lunch, I sit in my office and wait for the staff meeting. I can't seem to stop my foot from bouncing and I can't help but glance at my watch every few seconds. Ten minutes before the meeting, I'm up from my chair.

When she *finally* walks into the conference room, she looks better. She's not smiling, but is chatting graciously with our co-workers and at least seems at peace. I take a deep breath, relieved for now that she appears to be okay. I know I said I needed to get her out of my mind but instead I have a fierce need to protect her.

For the first time, I notice her shirt.

She's wearing a blouse with a V-neck but keeps tugging on it upward subconsciously as she talks to the group, and it's a complete turn-on. I'm already wired, but I try to keep it together throughout the meeting. At one point she concentrates on the paper in front of her. Her lips are pursed, her hair framing her face. Every so often, she lifts her hand and pushes her hair behind her ear and it's super sexy. *She's sexy.* When the meeting's over, and the rest of our coworkers have left the conference room, against my better judgment, I offer to join her at her office.

She gets comfortable in her chair and starts working on a standard advising form. When her arm comes down, her blouse slides with it, showing the lines of her breast with it and giving me a new side peek of her lace bra. *I wonder if it's a matching set.* She pulls it up yet *again*, and after half an hour of this, I can't take it anymore. "Olivia? Is there something wrong with your blouse?" I ask. I try to sound casual, but I can't stop looking at her.

She gives me a perplexed look, then looks down. She takes a few seconds to answer. "What do you mean?"

"Your shirt. You've been pulling it for the last hour. It's distracting." I rub my face, my stiff neck with my palms, then turn to her and give her my full attention, causing her to blush a little.

"Sorry for distracting you but my new washer is off or something. I'm still trying to get used to it," she says with a worried face.

"Ahh, the spawn of the demonic washer." I joke. At this, she chuckles. "Olivia, your shirt is too big."

"I guess so, but it keeps sliding off. Is this a problem?" she says casually, wringing her hands and fidgeting.

I keep my eyes on her and she seems self-conscious. "Do you want me to be honest?" I say, as I lean forward, put my forearms on the desk and start playing with a pencil.

She turns to look at me as she narrows her eyes and stares at me. A smile curves her mouth. "How honest are we talking about? 'Appropriate' honest or 'inappropriate' honest?"

"Probably inappropriate," I say, not denying it, then I see her blush and I feel my smile creeping up. *Okay, maybe I'm enjoying this too much.*

"Yeah, let's not get carried away. Better if you lie to me." She pretends to go back to the paper but then looks up at me through her long eyelashes.

Is she expecting me to keep my comment appropriate or inappropriate? "Okay. Here we go." I pause for a moment for dramatic purposes. "The color looks great on you... it just seems to be two sizes too big... maybe three?"

A slow smile returns on her face that reach her eyes. She tilts her head. "It is not two sizes too big."

"Olivia."

"Okay. Fine, maybe it is."

She shifts in her seat, causing the shirt to slide down and my eyes automatically glance to the V-neck and back to her eyes. This time she doesn't pull the shirt up. She goes back to a paper on her desk. I lower my head and go back to my own paper and wonder if she knows what's she's doing to me. Should I tell her that what I really want to say is, *"I'm seconds away from taking you to a storage closet so I can take that shirt off myself and have my way with your lacy bra."* How *appropriate* would that be?

Olivia

After a crazy few weeks that included one of my students dying, arguing with Andrea over a student, getting involved in a young couple's squabble inside our office, and dogs running wild, I can safely say the highlight of my week was Tom telling me my blouse was distracting him... and looking at me like he wanted to eat me. Actually, I think I need somebody to slap me. He's my co-worker. Not only that, a co-worker who could potentially be my competition and even worse, he could be my boss. *Crap*. This has the potential to be a disaster. Why does he have to be so gorgeous and nice? Why couldn't he be fat and annoying?

I know I only met him a few months ago, but is it weird that I look forward to eating with him and sharing stories? I feel like I've known him for much longer than I have and that I can tell him anything. It's so easy to laugh with him... and if I'm honest, sometimes *at* him. At the same time, I've worked too hard on my career to just throw it all away now. If I want to be department director, I have to make decisions with my head, not my heart... or my ever-betraying body. From now on, any decision being influenced by lower body parts need to take a backseat to my loftier (and more *noble*) ambitions.

It's not Friday, but I asked my friends for lunch. Somebody needs to tell me what to do. Tom has indirectly asked me out, (*I think*), then avoided me for a week, only to blatantly flirt with me at the office yesterday.

Maybe we're just not communicating properly.

Today I carpool with my friends and arrive at a new restaurant near the university. The owners reached out to Bianca's department — Student Life — and offered coupons for the students and staff to try it out. Bianca's been handing out coupons to everybody and their cousins all semester.

As a thank you for her help, they personally gave Bianca a gift certificate, and we shouldn't say no to free food, especially if we're kind of on the edge of broke thanks to credit card debt. Talking about which, why hasn't anybody invented a registry for people that are suddenly single? When you get married you get showered with nice homey gifts. When you go through a breakup, you still have to fill out a home, albeit alone. In addition to big things like beds and tables, there are hundreds of tiny boring things like potato peelers and pasta strainers, plates and cups and before you know it, you've spent a small fortune with your already-maxed-out credit card.

Near the hostess stand we greet Gabby, who works in downtown Miami. Let's say she's taking an *extended* lunch today.

Once in, the hostess directs us to the bar, and we wait and wait and wait. After an indeterminately looooong time (good thing we were enjoying yummy pre-lunch cocktails), the hostess takes us to a table and a young man, who could be one of our students, appears. He fumbles with a small notepad until he *finally* finds his desired page; Valentina just shakes her head. He sounds uncertain as he reads the specials of the day. When he clears his throat, no less than fifteen times, I wonder if he's sick and if it's contagious. Just in case, after he's gone, I'll share a bottle of hand sanitizer.

To continue our culinary expedition, we order more drinks, appetizers, soups, and salads. *Hey, with a free certificate, gotta' try the entire menu, right?* He writes something on his little pad and takes a few steps back. We watch our server walk away and almost fall into a table which he manages to avoid, only to crash into another server holding a tray full of empty glasses. *Okay, he's a little clumsy.* It is a new restaurant, let's hope he's just nervous and doesn't mix up our orders and kill us all. *Positive thinking.*

"Did you find a roommate yet?" Nicole asks, pulling my attention away from the hopeless waiter.

"The roommate search is going... So. Damn. Slow. I mean, I don't know what to say. I was sure I would have a roommate by now. Can you believe *I* was disqualified as a roommate by a potential roommate? She was an agnostic/atheist and said that because I'm Catholic she couldn't be my roommate."

"Wait, can you even *be* both?" Nicole asks, confused.

"Apparently you can. They're not mutually exclusive. One has to do with knowledge and the other with beliefs. Apparently, *my* beliefs are too much for her to handle or something, not that super I'm religious, but as I said, *she* disqualified me."

A different waiter drops off our drinks and warm bread. As we dig into it, Bianca casually asks, "So what else is going on with you—any more hot dates?"

"Let's see, my last date? My mother tried to set me up with a womanizer who may or may not have hair. She's now conspiring with her friends to get grandkids."

"Ugh, don't get me started on that one," Valentina says. "My mother is driving me crazy with that too. She's desperate for me to have kids. *Me tiene loca.*"

"Was he cute at least?" Bianca says undeterred, as she puts more butter on her piece of bread.

I take a deep breath. "He was nice. Brilliant, actually, with a great job. He was a gentleman, to be honest. Except for the part where he looked at anything with legs that moved, grabbed my ass, and would probably be a serial cheater, I would say he's a *great* catch."

"Try to be more positive, please, sweetie? It's a numbers game," Bianca pleads.

"Bianca, it's not easy. Not everybody is as charming as you. Some people just suck at dating," I sigh, and I mean it. Dating is unquestionably *not* working for me.

"If it makes you feel better, *I* agree with you," Valentina says and we elbow bump.

"Of course, you do. Are you for real? Do you guys *want* to be single your entire lives? Your eggs will rot and you won't be able to have children," Bianca says melodramatically.

At Bianca's comment, Valentina raises an eyebrow. "*Que dramática.* Bianca, maybe we don't care about our 'precious' eggs. Maybe we're perfectly happy as single, independent women. I think you're obsessed with your reproductive health. Do you realize you're not even thirty? You should relax, your eggs are not going anywhere."

"We're all close to thirty. The eggs will deplete and by the time we do get pregnant, we'll be officially considered geriatric."

"The new term is 'Advanced Maternal Age,'" Nicole says chirping in.

"Still doesn't change the fact our eggs will die a slow and untimely death," Bianca says before she takes a bite of her bread.

Okay, now we're on to death. "Bianca, what is it with you and the va-jay-jays or the eggs while we eat? At a *public* place? These are not the kind of eggs anyone wants to hear about during lunchtime... at a restaurant."

"Fine," she rolls her eyes but after a beat Bianca casually adds, "I meant to ask you something. I heard the advising group went out to dinner. Is that true?"

She glances at me. I glance at Gabby. *What?* Gabby mouths. She's dating Ralph, so technically she has insider information. I narrow my eyes at her but turn my attention back to Bianca. "Do I want to know how you know this?"

"I have my sources. Now spill, otherwise, I'll make Gabby tell us."

"*Yo no se nada.*" I know nothing, Gabriela says.

Never mind. I wish we were still discussing the eggs.

The truth is, I'm not ready to discuss Tom with my friends yet. "Yes. One of our student assistants got his first real job, and we all went out to celebrate."

As our appetizers and soups arrive, Nicole asks, "Was Tom there?"

"Yes, he was," I say calmly and find myself nodding. The mere mention of his name makes me nervous. "Most advisors and student assistants were there."

"Aaaannd? Can we get details?"

"We had dinner as a group. Had a great conversation about advising and cycling. The food was great. I went home—*alone*. The end."

Bianca looks at me and one of her eyebrows shoots up so high, I think about The Rock. "That was it? No kissing?"

"Nope."

"Did you give him your number?"

"I'm assuming by *him* you mean Tom—why would I? If he was interested, he could have asked me for my number. Newsflash, he didn't."

"Why? Oh, I don't know—because he's single, he's hot, he's nice *and* has a job? What more could you possibly want?"

"Bianca, first of all, it was a work thing. The whole team was there. Second, did you guys know we're supposed to report any relationships within the university to HR?" I announce, looking at my friends while eating another piece of pretty awesome bread if I say so myself. I grab a spoon and go for the soup.

Bianca looks at Gabriela, who replies, "What? I have no idea. I only had a couple of dates with Ralph, then I left town. I work at the college now, remember?"

"I heard that there is a non-fraternization policy in place," Nicole says, "but I don't remember the specifics from the HR training. I can call HR and let you guys know."

As I talk, I start to feel weird; my throat is itchy. I take a deep breath and keep eating. "Something did happen the other day," I say. "He indirectly asked me out, I think." For some reason, I'm struggling to talk and have to pause to breathe.

"He either did or he didn't. You can't be half pregnant," Valentina says, because everything is black or white to her. I'm in the middle of explaining my conversations with Tom and our interactions these past weeks when I start to feel even more out of breath. I pause again and take another deep breath.

Bianca pauses eating to look at me. "Hey, are you okay? Your face's a little flushed," Bianca says, touching my arm.

I'm struggling to breathe but manage to gasp out, "Something's wrong."

"Aren't you allergic to fish?" Valentina asks and all I can do is nod.

Valentina and Gabriela are looking at me concerned. Nicole grabs a phone, while Bianca calls our waiter. "Excuse me, what was in the soup?" Bianca asks the waiter as he approaches, her voice rising with every word.

He's shifting in place and his eyes are huge, "Whyyyy?"

"What was in the soup?" She demands again, this time standing up. "Was that the Chicken Stir-Fry soup? Are you positive?"

"I think so, but I can check with the kitchen." He almost runs over a couple as he rushes to the kitchen. He's clearly a disaster and has no business being a waiter.

A few minutes later the manager, a chef, and other strangers materialize out of nowhere. "That was a fish and shellfish soup," a kitchen person says.

"Our waiter grabbed it by mistake, it was meant for another client. We're so sorry," the chef adds, while he rubs his hands down his apron.

Outstanding. Why don't you just kill me now?

"Are you guys okay?" one of them asks, but his gaze keeps going all over and patrons keep looking at us.

As my chest tightens, I start to feel lightheaded and dizzy. From the corner of my eye, I see Valentina stand. "We're not okay. Your dumb waiter messed up the order. My friend could die. This is not okay. What kind of restaurant is this? *Estúpido!...*" She's roaring while Gabby holds her hand back in an attempt to pacify her.

Nicole's on the phone and I really, *really* hope she's calling an ambulance or a doctor. At this point, I would even settle for one of our pre-med students.

Bianca looks slightly pale. She looks at me with huge eyes and gives me an apprehensive smile before she bites her lips. She never let go of my forearm and her thumb keeps rubbing me maniacally. Her eyes are dancing to every corner.

Is this it?! Killed by soup? Out of all the things to die by? Are you kidding me?

My stomach shifts uneasily and I'm so overwhelmed, I can't talk. Not being able to talk is the last nail in the coffin and I start to panic. My hands are tingling and my heartbeat's speeding and everything's moving in slow motion, like a movie. It is then I remember I have an Epi-Pen in my purse and search for it frantically. My friends look at me with panicked expressions on their faces, but before anybody can say anything, I inject my thigh.

A few minutes later everything goes black and I hope to go to heaven.

Tom

I 'm alone in my office, the door closed, when Judith knocks and walks in. She looks distressed and she's speaking a mile a minute. Immediately the energy in the room shifts. "Hey, Tom, do you have any scheduled appointments? Any students? Can you see students?"

"I don't have many but I'm helping with walk-ins."

"I need you to take care of Olivia's students. She had an emergency and won't be coming back to the office. I'll tell the front counter you'll be seeing her students. One of them is waiting outside."

"No problem, I'll take care of them."

"Thanks, Tom," she says before walking out. As she leaves, I wonder what the emergency is. I know I'm supposed to keep my distance from Olivia, but I can't help it.

As I approach the front counter to retrieve her student, I notice the student assistants chattering wildly. As soon as I reach them, the chatter dies. As we walk back to my office, I notice a group of advisors huddled. Her friend Sandra is among them. She's biting her lip and somebody else is wringing their hands. My mind immediately goes to Olivia.

Something's not right. I take care of the student as fast and as efficiently as I can, then go in search of Sandra. Without waiting, I invite myself to her office. Me not having a good excuse, or any excuse at all to talk to her, is not a deterrent. All I want is information. I just need to know she's okay. "Hey, Sandra."

"Hi Tom," she says, looking up at me from her computer.

"I was wondering if you'd heard from Olivia? I wanted to ask her a question about a student," I lie.

"She had an emergency and is at the hospital," her friend responds without missing a beat.

"Oh, I'm sorry. I didn't know she had somebody in the hospital."

"She doesn't. *She's* in the hospital. She had an allergic reaction to food at a restaurant."

Fear prickles my scalp and I feel the blood leave my face. I take a few seconds to articulate a response. "Is she okay?"

"We don't know. We're waiting to hear back from one of her friends."

"I see. Could you let me know when you hear something? *Please?*"

"Sure."

For the next few hours, all I can do is wait. I advise students on automatic, but my mind

is not there. The hours are going by agonizingly slow and a few times it occurs to me that I'm such an idiot. If she died, I'll spend the rest of my life wondering about the what-ifs and kicking myself in the ass. Between my students, Olivia's students, and the occasional walk-in, I don't have time to question her friend further. The couple of times that I manage to finally make it to Sandra's office, she has a student with her. *Damn it!*

It's almost the end of the day when Sandra finally comes in and tells me Olivia's okay. She'll be at the hospital overnight, but she's okay. Immediately a sense of relief overcomes me.

I release the breath I didn't realize I had been holding and finally calm down but can't help the overwhelming sense of urgency. I thought dating her would be a bad idea but the fact is, I could have lost her without having her at all. *Fuck avoidance.*

Olivia

I wake up in a strange bed, squinting at a light directed right in my face and surrounded by the concerned faces of my friends. The last thing I remember is being at a restaurant. I hear doctors getting called over an intercom and I instinctively know we're in a hospital. After a couple of minutes, a cute doctor comes in. He wants to keep me in observation overnight as a precaution but tells me I should be okay. *Thanks, Epi-Pen.*

My friends are talking about our restaurant adventure when somebody from Patient Services comes in and asks if I have health coverage. I give the gentleman my insurance card and answer at least fifty questions. *I'm dying and you need to know all that? Right now?*

After he leaves, I look for my phone. It's then I realize my phone has been lost or stolen. I guess somebody felt I needed a new challenge.

A few minutes later, my mom arrives with her new husband. After a while, I send my friends home. And later, when my brothers arrive, I send my mom and her husband home.

"How do you feel?" my big brother William asks.

"A little dazed but otherwise okay. Where's Julie?"

"She's at home with the kids. I texted her, and she's happy you're okay." He pauses as he sits on a nearby chair. "Let me tell you, that was scary," he confesses, rubbing his face.

"I agree. Maybe next time you should go to a restaurant where there's no fish on the menu." The bed squawks as Michael sits at end of the bed and puts his hands over my feet.

"Agreed. It would suck if something happened to you. You're irreplaceable. Emma would be left without an aunt."

"Awww, were you guys worried? I'm okay, you won't be able to get rid of me that easy... wait, back it up. Do you just want me around because your wife has no sisters?"

"Are you seriously asking that? You're obviously drugged. Moving on, how was the date with the accountant?" William asks.

Who? "Wait, how do you know about that?"

"Mom mentioned it," Will elaborates, shrugging and sitting back in the chair.

At his comment, Mike perks up. "Wait, the accountant? John? Isn't he like fifty? Why would you go out with that old guy?"

"I have no idea how old he is, he didn't say. How do guys know him?"

"He came to Mom's house one day to pick up *his* mom, and we happened to be there. I can't believe he went out with you. He likes them young. The girl he was with that day barely looked twenty-one."

"Wait, are you saying I'm old?"

"I didn't say that. You're not old, but you know, he likes *fresh meat*," Mike smirks.

"What does that mean?" *Fresh meat? Does that make me old meat? Expired meat? Hmmm.*

"Don't make that face. You're not *that* old and you can do better than an old skirt-chasing-narcissist womanizer," William pontificates, as usual.

"Thank you?" *I think.*

"You're clueless," Mike adds.

My brothers look at each other. Will shakes his head. Stopping to look at me he asks, "Why is Mom getting you dates? I don't understand what the problem is. *We* don't understand. You're smart and attractive. You work at a university. It's a huge campus. Males work there, don't they?"

People assume the dating pool is gigantic, but that is not the case. When you remove the married, the career-obsessed, the eternal students, and the non-heterosexual, the pool narrows. Throw in the fear of getting fired, and it's a non-existent dating pool. "I guess."

"You guess? Are you telling me there are no single guys?"

One comes to mind. "Yeah, there are. It's complicated, though. Not everybody is looking to date, and we have to report relationships within the university to HR. If they find out, it's grounds for dismissal and that turns people off from dating each other."

"A no-fraternization rule?"

I nod. "Yes. I mean don't get me wrong, from time to time we do hear about people dating and getting married. But nobody wants to get fired unless they're sure it'll lead to something."

"When you know, you know," Will says cryptically.

In response, Mike rubs his chin and frowns. "How do you know?"

"I don't know. You just do," William says, nonchalantly.

"Thanks, Captain Obvious. That wasn't helpful at all," Mike retorts.

"What do you want me to tell you? You fall for someone and... you know."

"Will, no offense but that's the stupidest explanation ever."

"You're an idiot—that's why you're single," William concludes. Upon hearing their exchange, I shake my head. Michael rolls his eyes and ignores our big brother.

After a few minutes, William turns serious and looks at me. "I told Mom to stop trying to get you dates."

"What did she say?"

"That you needed help. I told her you're perfectly capable of getting dates on your own. Unlike this one, you're pretty smart."

I take a deep breath and sit straighter. At least I can count on my brothers to play interference occasionally. "Thank you."

"You're welcome."

When you know, you know. Do you? Is it really that easy?

After they leave, a nurse comes in to check on me. While I observe her fussing with the pressure cuff and putting it on me, she tells me I look familiar. When I tell her I work at the university doing academic advising, she tells me she remembers I advised her. Even when she successfully transferred to a very competitive nursing program, she came back a few times to see me. She credits me with helping her graduate as a nurse. My heart swells with joy upon hearing her talk about being a nurse and how much she loves her job. This is one of the reasons why I love *my* job. What I do means something and can truly make a difference in people's lives.

I wake up to yet another nurse checking my vitals.

Again.

For the thirtieth time since I arrived, somebody's pulling or pushing something in or out, or in this case, placing a finger clip to my index finger, while I'm sleeping. *Doesn't she even realize I'm sleeping?* I wake up more tired than when I came in due to a lack of sleep. How can they expect you to get better if you can't sleep? This is why people hate the ER and hospitals in general. You can't get any freaking sleep.

I'm relieved when a couple of hours later they tell me I'm clear to go home. *Thank God!* I call work from the hospital and update Judith, then I go home and go straight to bed.

After a few hours, I wake up feeling much better. I don't have a cellphone, but luckily, thanks to my trustworthy land-line phone, I can make a few phone calls and catch up with my friends. I also call campus security and check on my car. Except for the fact that I have to pay for a new cell phone, it's nice to be cell phone-free at home and to enjoy peace and quiet. In case you're wondering why I have a landline, I live in Miami and hurricanes cause power outages which translates to — ta-da, no cell phones. At least with my trusty house phone, I'll be able to call if I need to be rescued someday.

After I shower, and as I sit by myself, I'm forced to contemplate what would have happened if I didn't have my EPI pen. To start, I would have missed out on my family's future milestones, like getting to see my niece and nephews grow. I would have missed out on anything with Tom, and possibly any promotions — maybe or maybe not. What the hell am I thinking, who cares about a promotion?

My stomach grumbles and I'm forced to table this discussion with myself and think about food. I open the door to the refrigerator and stand there like a zombie, debating what to do about dinner when there's a knock on my door. I casually open it expecting family or one of my friends, but it's my handsome co-worker.

Tom's at my door.

Olivia

"Hi," I say in a higher-than-normal voice. *WTF?* I clear my voice and try again. "Hi." Okay. *Better.* I run my hands through my hair, grab my hairband and pull it through so fast that it flies through the air, like a sling shot, and lands on the floor. I whip my head to him and pause. He raises an eyebrow, and we both burst out into laughter.

"Hi," he says with a grin and my eyes get lost in his sparkling green eyes. Today they're a shade of greenish-blue that completely disarms me. I take a deep breath and try to contain myself. He's wearing jeans and a light blue buttoned-up shirt with the sleeves rolled up to his elbows. At work, he always wears long-sleeved shirts; without intending to, my eyes travel to the *expensive* silver watch latched around his wrist, which is holding a small box of beers. His other hand grips a pizza box with flowers and pint of ice cream on top.

I silently thank God I took a bath and have a nice set of PJs on. Actually, I don't have any makeup on. *Why didn't I put some on?* Maybe I should run to my room to at least apply lipstick and mascara.

"Wow, you look beautiful. Nice PJs," Tom grins.

I glance down, then look at him. "Thank you. What are you doing here?" I ask casually.

"Well, I heard that a waiter tried to kill you with soup and I wanted to make sure that you were okay."

"Thanks, that's very nice of you. I'm feeling much better."

"I'm glad to hear. I also thought, since we're neighbors, I could bring food around. I wasn't about to bake a casserole, but everybody eats pizza, right? I mean, you do eat pizza?"

"*Yes neighbor*, I eat pizza."

"Okay. Good, this is good."

"Pizza and beer? What else do you have there?" I take a step back, open the door and allow him access to my home. While I grab the wayward hairband from the floor, he walks in like he owns the place, heads straight toward the open floor kitchen and starts unloading things.

"No beer for you. Besides, if I remember correctly from the restaurant, you're a martini drinker. But I did get you some chocolate chip ice cream, even though you still owe *me* ice cream because *I'm* still right and pistachios and mango trees are related." He stops to look at me and hands me flowers. "I also got you some flowers to cheer you up."

I'm standing close to him and looking up at him. When he looks at me, I try to fight the heat from taking over my face. When he grins at me, a smile forms on my lips.

I take the flowers and without thinking, smell them. They are a beautiful arrangement of white and pink roses, white lilies, carnations, and other white and pink flowers. I'm smitten and I barely manage to say, "Thank you," before I break eye contact to walk around the kitchen counter. I arrange the flowers in a vase while he settles down on a stool across from me and opens one of the beer bottles. "So, what happened? Why didn't you have time to bake a casserole?" I tease as I work on the bouquet.

"I thought about it, but I needed the time to get ready." He gives me a half-smile and winks at me before taking a swig of beer.

"Ahhh, yes, that explains it." I try not to laugh, but I can't help snickering. *Yep. He's being charming and I'm behaving like a horny teenager... then you wonder why I'm single.*

"I had a student that had a financial aid issue, they had put a hold on him by mistake. I had to take it all the way to the financial aid director, and it took me much longer than expected."

This comment immediately grabs my attention, and I stare at him across the counter. "Wait, wait, you spoke with the financial aid director? Like, you actually *spoke* to him?"

"Yeah. I did."

"On the phone?"

"Yes?"

"Wow. Now I'm impressed. He's never taken any of my phone calls."

"I have ways with people."

"Sure you do." *Why would the financial aid director pick up his call and not mine?*

"Back to the point. You don't have a casserole because a student kept me over," he says, derailing my questions regarding the financial aid director. Who, by the way, is like a mythical creature who's sooo busy, he only talks to Judith when it's absolutely necessary.

"Yeah, blame the student. Excuses, excuses. Why do advisors always want to blame the students for everything?" I ask, half-joking.

"Many times, it *is* the students' fault... Actually, I take it back, in this case, it was the *department's* fault."

I open a few cabinets, get cups, plates and napkins and walk towards the couch. He follows me as I set everything on the coffee table, then sits right smack in the middle of the sofa. I'm forced to squeeze next to him. I can feel his warmth.The

TV is on, and we talk about work while eating pizza. He shares stories about a couple of students he advised while I was out, and updates me on my own students. I relax, and turn to sit facing towards him, my legs curled under me.

We get into a conversation about bad dates and I tell him about the guy who used a Groupon, the wrestler and the ranch dressing debacle, and the *probably* hair-less accountant. He bursts into laughter and his gorgeous eyes crinkle with his cute crow's feet appearing. He also shares a couple of bad dates and makes me laugh. For once, it's nice to know I'm not the only one suffering from dating catastrophes.

An hour later, we're quietly watching TV.

I'm sitting sideways, with my back resting partly on the couch and slightly on his chest. One of his arms is curled behind me and his long legs stretch out relaxed in front of him. Strong fingers are caressing my exposed arm, lazily. Un-expectedly, he stops touching me. "What happened at the restaurant?"

The question catches me off-guard. I'm forced to stretch my neck and strain back to meet his eyes. "Um, a waiter tried to kill me? Not intentionally though, but you know."

"Are you okay?" he asks, while he looks at me with a serious expression.

"I am. I'm allergic to shellfish, but it's not a big deal. It won't stop me from going out to eat and enjoying food."

"Has this happened before?"

"Once, when I was a kid. It's how we discovered it."

"Were you scared?"

"I was. I panicked and passed out."

I can feel his chest rise as he takes a deep breath. "I was scared, too. I kept thinking I wasn't going to see you again." He's nodding to himself, glances at the TV, then back at me.

"I thought that, too." My heart races, a low hum warming my blood. I look into his eyes, his sharp and clear gaze, but before I can think about what's happening, he raises a hand

and gently caresses my face with the back of his fingers until his thumb rests on my bottom lip. His other arm gently pulls me towards him, but when we're only inches away, he pauses. I move an inch toward him, and he softly presses his mouth against mine and tentatively kisses me. His lips are full and smooth. It's a slow, deep, passionate kiss that gives me goose-bumps and is unlike anything I've ever felt before. When he opens his eyes and looks at me, I know he's feeling it too. I feel his warm hand slide down and cradle my neck gently, before his fingers intertwine with my hair.

Ohmygod, ohmygod, ohmygod. Eeekk!

After a few seconds pass, he kisses me again, more fervently. His breath is as fast as mine and this kiss turns more passionate. I wrap my arms around his shoulders. My hands move up on their own accord and caress the back of his neck as his long fingers travel down my back to hug my waist. "I love your hair," he whispers and kisses me again while his hand embraces my stomach and my back.

This is really happening. What would Dr. Phil say now?

His hand pauses. He stops to play with the waistband of my PJ's, fingers meet skin and move sideways, back and forth. Desire is pooling at an alarming pace. Until the phone rings... and rings and rings... *Now? Really?!*

"I think you better pick it up," he says, in that soft husky voice of his, his eyes closed, as he rests his forehead against mine. *Jesus, that voice is going to be the end of me.*

"Do I have to?" I manage to say, breathlessly, against his mouth.

"You should. You were in the hospital." He opens his eyes just as I open mine, then lets me go but keeps one hand on my back as his thumb rubs against the base of my spine.

"You're right." I reach for the phone sitting on a side table only to find out it's my mother. I look back towards Tom, and mouth *sorry*. After she confirms that I am, in fact, very much alive, I'm forced to promise to call her back before she'll let me get back to my... *business*.

As I hang up, Tom takes a deep breath then leans forward, resting his elbows on his knees and lacing his fingers together. He lowers his head, but doesn't say anything. "I think it's going to be better if I leave now." He glances at me, then turns forward again.

I'm fighting the powerful urge to kiss him. Actually, I want to do more than kiss him, *way more.* "You don't have to go."

"Shit," he sighs. "Don't look at me like that."

"How?"

"We work together, and this could get complicated."

"How complicated?"

"We could both be fired complicated."

I don't know what to say, because it's the same argument I keep having with myself. "Why does that sound familiar?"

"Does it? Is that an argument you're having with yourself, too?" His brow furrows.

"I would say it is. "

When I say this, his lips turn down slowly. "Okay. Tell you what, maybe in a couple of days we can meet and talk about it together. Today, it's getting late. Besides, I hate to keep reminding you, but you *were* just in the hospital. You should be resting."

I attempt to smile and try to hide my disappointment. "Okay."

"Not to mention, I need my beauty sleep." He half smiles, stands up to his full height, then offers me a hand. I take it and let him lead me to the door. He stops under the frame.

While I debate what to say, *Bye? Night? See you at work?* he surprises me with another kiss and walks out.

That was hands-down, *the best kiss of my entire life.*

Olivia

S ince I don't have a cell phone at the moment, I set an old alarm clock leftover from my college days. I guess it's too old because it doesn't work and I sleep well into the morning. I wake up, get ready in record time, and run out of the house like a maniac. It is only then I realize I don't have a car. I carpooled to the restaurant with my friends and my brothers dropped me off from the hospital. *Mental forehead slap.* Not to mention, I have a tight budget and public transportation is not on it. By the time the Uber comes, I'm both behind schedule *and* over budget. *Crap.*

I had woken up with a slight headache… only to have to deal with Miami traffic, if only by proxy. I wish I could take the bus to work instead, but service outside of downtown Miami is spotty at best. For some reason, Miami people refuse to leave their house without their car and refuse to use public transportation. I do have to admit, for once, I'm glad I can just walk straight into the building. I *finally* get to my office and start advising.

As I power up my PC it occurs to me that I hardly slept thinking about Tom. I can't believe I'm contemplating getting involved in an office romance. *What is wrong with me?* Judith *and* the dean will think I'm unprofessional, or that I lack judgment. This whole thing will derail my promotion and career aspirations. Ugh, and once people start talking, it'll be never-ending. *This is such a terrible idea.*

By mid-morning and even though I should be working, I text Bianca and ask her if she can meet me. I tell the front desk I'm taking a break and walk out.

One of Bianca's student groups is holding an event in one of the courtyards, and she's standing next to a table handing out flyers. After we greet each other, I can't help but wonder where the other coordinators are. "Are you here by yourself?"

"No, Josh just went inside to get more copies of the flyers. Hey, I tried calling you at home last night. When is your cell phone coming?"

"Tomorrow, I think. The company said two days at most, and I'm still waiting," I say gloomily.

"Are you feeling better?"

"I feel okay. I was home all day yesterday resting." I pause. "To be honest, I hardly slept. Tom kissed me last night." I blubber it out before I can stop myself.

"What? How?" She looks at me, her eyes widening.

"He went to my house last night, brought pizza, ice cream, and flowers and we... talked."

"Ice cream? That's nice," she says after a student walks by.

"It was... aaaaaand then we kissed."

"And?"

"And it was nice?"

"Annnnd?"

"It was wonderful, amazing, earth-shattering."

My friends pause to look at me. "Really? Are you lying to me? Is that why you have your freaking-out face?"

I stop for a second and look at her. "What exactly is my 'freaking-out' face, Bianca?"

"Your eyes are huge, you're staring into space, and you keep twisting your watch."

"What?!"

"What? I've known you for like a decade. I know your tells. Take it one step at a time. Maybe he'll be bad in bed, who knows? Don't think about the ship. It'll be fine."

I have a feeling he won't be bad in bed, but I don't need to share that. She hands out a flyer to a passing student and when I don't answer, she keeps going. "Don't you want somebody special? I know deep down you do."

"I do, but I'm afraid it won't work out and I'll be heartbro-ken. This would be ten times worse — heartbroken and fired? I'm already broke. How would I pay for my house?"

"You won't get fired, you're too good at your job."

"I think HR *might* disagree with you."

"Look, all we can do is try. You don't know unless you try. Besides, if it works out, your ovaries will thank you and your kids will be gorgeous." She smiles brightly. When I gape at her and tilt my head, we both burst into laughter.

Olivia

I get back to the office and spend the day advising and catching up on paperwork and emails. Since I don't leave my office at all, I don't see Tom. I keep wondering all day if I should go by his office, or just wait for him to come by, but he never does. By the time it's finally time to go home, I'm exhausted. I walk like a zombie around the staff parking lot until I finally find my car. I make a mental note: Google apps or car-finding-type-devices. I settle in my car and turn the ignition.

Except it won't start.

I'm tempted to Google why, then remember I don't have a cell phone. I keep trying the ignition, over and over, while my head rests on the steering wheel. *Clearly, this isn't working.*

"Come on! Pleeeease? I promise I'll give you premium gas!" *Annnd now I'm talking to the car.*

At that moment a knock on my window startles me, causing me to jump. My hand flies over my heart. *Tom.* "You scared the shit out of me," I say after I recover. I open the door and get out while he takes a step back; his palms go up.

"Sorry, sorry, I didn't mean to scare you. I noticed your car wasn't starting so came over to see if you needed help."

"Riiight. Are you stalking me?"

One of his eyebrows goes up, but he says nothing. While I give him space, he put his things on the roof of my car. Before he opens the door, he stops to look at me. "You're having a busy month, aren't you? Footballs attacking you, demonic washers, poisoned by soup, and now your car?" He opens the door to my car and keeps talking as he gets in. "You know, you should let me know if we should have a schedule so that I can plan my calendar around rescuing you from disasters."

"I don't need to be rescued. Thank you very much. I'm totally capable." *Most times, anyway.* Lately, I don't know what the heck is going on, but he does seem to be rescuing me a lot. *Hmmm, can he rescue me from bad dating?*

"Sure you are. Let's try it," he says as he tries the ignition a few times. "Okay, good news and bad news."

"What's the bad one?"

"Your battery is dead."

"And you figured it out in three seconds flat by trying the ignition?!" I blurt in surprise.

"No, I figured it out by trying the ignition *and* reading your panel."

"Oh." *Great. Why do I now feel less capable?*

"Here's the good news... it's a very easy fix. We'll try a boost. If that doesn't work, I'll take you to a store, we'll buy a battery, and I'll put it in. Within the hour you should be home." He gets out and leans on the car.

"Oh, okay, that seems easy." *And I get to be in a car with him.*

"There's, uh, a condition, though."

My eyebrow raises on its own accord. "A condition? Are you bribing me? To help me? Are you serious?"

"Yes, kind of," he says, moving his head sideways. "I will fix your car if you agree to go to Bike Day with me this Saturday."

"Bike Day? What's that, what are we talking about here?"

"Nothing too crazy, just riding bikes around Coral Gables."

"Why?"

"Because Keith and I are part of the cycling community. We'll go out there and support our friends. They have scheduled tours every hour. We'll bike around, check out a few points of interest. It'll be fun. Afterward we could grab a bite. I mean, if you want to."

"How safe would this be? Are the tours are led by professionals who know what they're doing and the streets closed?" I know I'm asking too many questions, but with my luck, a car would probably run me over.

"Yes, these people are trained and I'll be with you. I promise you'll be safe."

When he puts it like that, how can I say no? "Okay. Fine, I'll go with you."

A contagious smile breaks on his face, "Yeah? Great! Pick you up at ten a.m.?

"Ten a.m. on a Saturday? Ugh, you're killing me."

"It'll be worth it, I promise. Will you have a cellphone by Saturday? Here, give me your number. I need it in case we get lost in Coral Gables and I have to come rescue you again," he says handing me his phone.

I take it and start inputting my cell number. "I'm excellent with directions. You never know, *you* could get lost and need rescuing."

As I hand him back his cell and he looks up from it and takes a step forward, closer to me. "Is that right? Are you sure?" he says slowly, with his sexy-husky voice, and looks at me before glancing at my mouth. *Nope. Not sure at all.* That voice causes my heart to speed up in a way that would cause any eighty-year-old to have a heart attack. His eyes go from playful to hot and when our hands touch, I feel an electric shock. I clear my throat. "Although to be honest, I wouldn't be opposed to a girl rescuing me at all." *Deep breath. Be Zen.* He backs away with a smirk, seeming pleased with the reaction he caused.

What exactly was he expecting?

He lifts his chin and gives me a throaty laugh. "Come on."

"Fine." I grudgingly follow him across the parking lot to an expensive black sports car. What is it with men and sports cars? What does that say about him? I hope he's not overcompensating for something. *That would suck.*

We drive to a nearby store to buy a battery and I spent money I don't have. I mean, *$130 for a battery? Is that normal? Should I have asked for a discount?* There goes my budget. He offered to pay, but I declined. After we return to campus and he installs the new battery, he offers to take the old one back to the store. Before saying goodbye, he deposits me safely into my car and gives me a light kiss on the cheek. He doesn't mention anything about our previous night. Since I don't want to appear too eager, I don't say anything either.

I wake up before eight a.m. on Saturday, both out of habit and because I have no idea what to wear. I should have bought an outfit or borrowed one from one of my friends. *Too late now.*

After an hour spent shaving, trimming, blow-drying and changing six times, in the end, I settle for a light blue short-sleeved shirt and a pair of new-ish white shorts. Not before wondering at least a dozen times how short is too short.

Crap. It's almost ten a.m. and I'm chickening out. What was I thinking? This is such a terrible idea. Somebody from HR will hear about this, we'll both be fired and I'll be homeless. *Breathe, Olivia. Breathe.* When my doorbell finally rings, I jump in place.

Opening the door, I'm startled to see that Tom's *not* wearing a cycling outfit. Instead, he has on a polo shirt and short cargo pants, a baseball cap, and cool sunglasses. The shiny watch, back on display. As I take him in, freshly shaven and handsome and smiling back at me, my internal debate about being fired goes right out the window. "Good morning, Olivia," he says cheerfully, removing his sunglasses. His eyes scan me from top to bottom. "Are you ready?"

My heart skips a beat at the sound of my name on his lips. "Good morning," I try to contain my excitement at being with him on a weekend, but I can't help the answering grin that forms on my lips. I grab my keys and after I close the door. I put them in a fanny pack. I know they're old-fashioned, but I have to put my things somewhere. As we walk towards the car, I notice Keith's in the driver's seat. "Hi, Olivia," Keith says, smiling and I reciprocate it.

Once we get to Coral Gables and park, I watch them carefully take the bikes down from the car's rack. As we walk towards registration, I notice that there's a stage, with dozens of tents on each side, and the park itself is filling up fast with people. There are swarms of kids and families with and without bikes all over the area. Everybody's talking and enjoying the outdoors. This is, surprisingly, very nice. We complete the registration and sign up for one of the tours.

Tom and Keith are very popular. They seem to be saying hello to everybody, and many people know them by name. As we make our way through the event, men friends are getting man-hugs, while women friends are getting hugs and kisses on the cheeks. Plenty of gorgeous, *tanned* women are batting eyelashes at them left and right. A few blatantly whisper in Tom's and Keith's ears as they pass. How many of them do you think are possibly *propositioning* them? *Slow down, Olivia. Don't jump to conclusions.*

While we wait for our tour to start, we stop to hang out in a tent with some of the guys' friends. Eighty percent of the conversation centers on cycling or cycling-related issues. Tom, Keith and their friends talk about what stores to buy from, who's having a sale or discount, when is the next race, and who's competing against who. Who's healthy or had an injury. They talk stats, miles per hour, and who's going faster or slower. The latest food trend and on and on. The remaining twenty percent of the discussion is about jobs and families.

I don't have much to contribute, but it's fun to see Tom and Keith interacting together. They spend the morning joking around and teasing each other. Tom laughs more than usual while Keith is entertaining to be around. He's handsome and has a relaxed personality. He's also very popular with the opposite sex. From time to time, he walks away to meet, greet or flirt, while Tom stays close to me, occasionally placing his hand on the small of my back to guide me or push me closer. Tom keeps giving me panty-melting smiles and teasing me throughout the conversations. I already have a crazy imagination, I don't need any further encouragement, but at the rate this is going...

The tour takes us around the City of Coral Gables, and it truly is beautiful and relaxing. The city has historic houses on quiet streets, where massive old trees intersect and form cool canopies. The houses are lovely and immaculate due to strict zoning restrictions and city ordinances. After a couple of hours of biking, we return to the park. In the end, we hit at least four food trucks and I can honestly say I'm in food heaven. After the afternoon comes and goes, we say goodbye to their cycling friends and head home.

Olivia

<hr>

When we arrive, Keith offers a goodbye but stays in the car while Tom walks me to my door. "Thank you for coming with us," Tom says gratefully as we approach.

"Thanks for inviting me." I grin.

"Did you have fun?"

"I did, it was perfect."

"Good. I aim to please." He gives me a lopsided smile as we stop at my door and I search for my keys. "I'm going to get going now, but see you at work on Monday?" He beams at me as I lean in to kiss him on the cheek, but when I go to take a step back, he takes a hold of my hips to keep me in place and kisses me, *really* kisses me, and my knees get weak.He pulls back a little, but stays inches away from my face and looks at me heatedly. "I'll see you at work."

I laugh, holding on to his waist. "You already said that."

"I know," he says as he grins again and shakes his head. "My brain's not working too well. Don't forget to lock the door." I nod and as soon as I close the door, I immediately do as he says.

Oh. My. God. *Swoon*. I rest my back against the door for a second, but then I can't help but want to see him leave through my living room window. He jauntily waves and I quickly duck back behind the door. After a few minutes, I go to the kitchen for a cool glass of water before calling it a night. I'm finally on my way to my room when there's a loud knock on my door. I open it, only to see Tom standing there. He looks at me with intense eyes. His pupils are dark and luminous in the moonlight, and he's breathless. "Hey," I say surprised while my heart goes wild and starts thumping in my chest.

"Hey."

I'm half expecting him to say something, but when he looks at me, I can see the storm brewing behind those beautiful eyes, so I wait and wait. *Ooo-kay.* "Back so soon?" I finally ask. "Is everything–"

Before I realize what's going on, his hand is instantly on the back of my neck. His fingers intertwine with my hair and pull me towards him. My hands intuitively hold on to his waist. He deftly maneuvers us in, spins, and turns into the house, while closing the door, and I lose all sense of direction. I feel the sofa behind me when one of his arms pulls my body close to him and... *oh sweet lord.*

His lips travel down my neck while my hand moves to his shoulder. I cup the base of his neck in my right hand, then move my other hand to his chest and feel his rapid heartbeat. After a few minutes of better-than-Chunky-Monkey-dripped-in-hot-chocolate-sauce passionate kissing, I gently nudge him away. "What are we doing?" I ask, looking up at him as I stroke his neck with my thumb and try to catch my breath.

"Do you want the long version or the short version?"

"*Short* version? Ummm, random question: did you ever read *Dr. Jekyll and Mr. Hyde?*"

His eyebrows go up and his mouth opens and closes, but no sound comes out for a few seconds. "Let's pause that thought.

Who am I supposed to be in this scenario? Dr. Jekyll or Mr. Hyde?"

Shit shit shit!

"Oh, my God. I'm sorry. I didn't mean it in a murdering-other-people kind of way." I moan and my forehead hits his shoulder. I look up again. "Like, I know you're not trying to murder me. At least I hope you're not. It's just that sometimes it seems like you're two different people. Like Jekyll and Hyde... bad, terrible example... not really, but you get the idea," I exclaim in one long, rambling, embarrassing, mumble.

"For the record, I'm not trying to murder you. I don't mean to give you mixed signals, or maybe I do. I don't even know anymore. The thing is... people expect me to act a certain way at work, but on the other hand, 'not-office' me is crazy about you," he clarifies without missing a beat as his mouth crashes against mine.

"Not-office you?" I question as he moves to my neck. My amused grin is interrupted by the tickle of his stubble as he kisses me again.

His lips slowly form into a matching smile. "Yep, 'not-office' me was going out of his mind today looking at your legs. He could not *wait* to have you alone to do a more thorough inspection."

"How thorough are we talking about?"

"Extremely," he says and winks. "Let's go." And before I can protest, with one swift move he lifts me up and carries me across his shoulder, caveman style. I can't help but laugh and squeal in secret delight.

Admit it, you probably saw that one coming.

Olivia

A sound I don't recognize wakes me up. After a few seconds, I realize the sound is an alarm that isn't mine. Also, there's a big, warm body here *and* we're tangled up together *and* we're naked.

"Are you awake?" the big, warm body asks in a low, sultry, sexy-as-hell morning voice that breaks through my musing thoughts. It instantly turns me on.

I look up to see him fondly looking down at me. His eyes catch mine as he gently removes strands of wayward hair from my face. "Was that your phone?" I ask, dazedly.

"It's just a reminder. I had plans to go cycling with Keith and a group of friends."

"On a *Sunday* morning? Wow, you guys are really committed."

He laughs and goes for his cellphone. "You have no idea. He knows there was a change of plans, though."

"Is that so?"

"Yeah, I'm a little busy with a pretty advisor who needs some advisement on how to *not* get fired," he jokes, grinning as he turns off the blaring sound.

I can't help but smirk back. "Hey, that's not funny. I love my job. I don't want to get fired."

His phone disappears from sight and his hand is on me once again, on me, roving lower and lower on my body.

"I know, I like my job too. Let's have an advising session and talk it out," he seductively murmurs right before his mouth crashes on mine. My hand travels to his neck as I close my eyes.

He seems to savor every second with an intensity that matches mine. This man is causing emotions I never even knew existed. It's like being trapped in a bubble of time and space, where nothing else exists, only this bed and him kissing me. I realize I've never wanted anyone like this before. He pauses, and when I open my eyes, he's looking at me as if I'm more precious than gold. I can feel his heart beating next to mine. The back of his hand lightly caresses my face and the pad of his thumb settles on my cheek, and he takes a deep breath. It is as if he too is struggling to express all the feelings he can't say.

I'm actually feeling many things. Excited, vulnerable and terrified come to mind. To be honest, it's overwhelming to have him look at me as if he wants to burn my face or this moment to his memory. After a few seconds, his eyelids droop slowly closed and he kisses me again.

When he kisses me, all thoughts disappear and I'm a goner.

This is the moment I know. *Life will never be the same.*

After a thoroughly enjoyable "advising session," we have the longest shower I have ever had in my life — massage included— followed by breakfast and more... *advising.*

A while later, we're in bed and my stomach grumbles, followed by his. We look at each other and burst into laughter.

I let my head crash on my pillow as we laugh. "Come on. I'll feed you," I say after we've calmed down.

I put on shorts and a t-shirt and pile up my hair on top of my head. Hairs are sticking out in odd places, and I adjust the bun as I walk. He's wearing his jeans and t-shirt but unlike me, he looks so damn sexy. "You're cooking for me?" he asks as we arrive in the kitchen. He sounds amused and I nod. "I feel special. I never got to come by and borrow a cup of sugar," he winks.

"Well, I guess now you *can* come and borrow a cup of sugar any time you want."

"I officially have permission? Interesting." He pauses. "Are we still talking about sugar?" When he gives me a crooked smile, I giggle.

I grab things out of the pantry as he sits on the stool facing the counter and watches me. His elbow on the counter, propping up his chin. He looks relaxed and without thinking, I start humming.

When I glance at him again, he's grinning at me. "Can you sing?" he asks.

I grin back. "I wish. Sadly, I can't sing. I can cook, but I can't sing for shit." At my confession, his lips turn up.

"Can I just say, I find you endlessly fascinating," he confesses.

"Thank you. Likewise."

"How's the roommate search going?" he asks casually.

"Honestly? It's a disaster. I'm stuck in a vortex of never-ending roommate interviews... but I'm hopeful. I mean, logic tells me it's only a matter of time before I find the perfect roommate. Hopefully sooner rather than later. I have to be patient. It's math, probabilities or statistics or something."

"Do you like math?"

I snort, "Not at all. Math is like a medieval torture device."

He shakes his head and chuckles. "Okay then."

"Do *you* like math?"

"I don't love it, but I'm not bad at it. My brother's much better at it, though."

"What does your brother do? Is he an accountant or an engineer?"

"Neither. He's a cop, actually."

"A cop who's good with math. Interesting." I smile. After a few minutes, while I cook he stands up, finds plates and utensils, fills two glasses with drinks and sets them up on the counter, right next to each other.

It's crazy how comfortable he seems in my kitchen. For a few more minutes, I imagine what would happen if this situation was... permanent. If we really dated. *Would he want that too?*

I've cooked roasted chicken with lemon, and a salad. After I serve it on the plates, I sit next to him and we eat silently. "What?" I ask when I catch him glancing at me too many times.

"Nothing."

"Now you have to tell me. Come on! Tell me. Tell me what you're thinking." I know I sound like a kid but he's grinning at me.

"I was thinking... that you're beautiful."

"Thank you?"

"Why do you say it like that? Do you not think you're beautiful?"

I cover my face with my face and shake my head. "I'm normal? I don't know. I'm just a regular girl, you know what I mean? I don't feel like I have it together at all sometimes... I'm still working on this adulting thing, my budget is out of control, and I mean, I can't even find a roommate, something so simple... aaaand I'm rambling."

"I don't think those things are mutually exclusive. Many people don't have it together. Adulting is hard, and I'm happy to hear you ramble." He shrugs. I nod and we eat in silence.

When we finish eating, I wash the dishes and he puts them away. I'm almost done and he's standing nearby. Quiet. Arms crossed, looking at nothing. Glancing at him, I ask, "Has anybody told you that sometimes you're very intense?"

"Nah." He shakes his head. His lips turn down and I try not to laugh. "I like to think about it as... focused."

"Sure, buddy. Keep telling yourself that." At this, his lips slowly turn up and his arms loosen next to him.

He shakes his head. "I think you're hilarious."

"I'm just pretending to be funny." I wink at him.

"Sure you are." After a pause, he asks, "Should we talk?" He's resting on one side of the counter, as I wipe a small puddle of water on it.

I finish and glance his way. "About?" I dry my hands with a paper towel and toss it away. This might be the moment he tells me he had a great time... *but.* I stand still and face him. I can't help but grip the counter behind me and wait. The past twenty-eight hours have been surreal. The truth is, he's not like anyone I've ever been with before. Alarms are going off somewhere in my brain. It knows this has the potential to be a monumental disaster in my life, in more ways than one, but my heart can't (or won't) deny the undeniable pull.

"Sleepovers? Or not?" He asks, his jaw tensing a little. I watch as it ticks a couple of times.

I don't know what I was expecting, but *that* was definitely not it. "Sleepovers?"

He takes three slow steps towards me, puts an arm on each side of me, and literally cages me in. Dark green eyes look at me and I melt on the spot when his mouth crashes against mine. Our tongues wrestle each other for control before he gives up and moves down to my neck. My hands hold on to his waist for dear life. "You're so soft," he says.

"You need to stop being so nice to me. A girl might get the wrong idea."

"I'm a nice guy. Deal with it," he says, now looking at me. Turning more serious, he continues, "Olivia, I really like you." He waits.

I feel spellbound and woozy. His eyes roam my face intently and wait for an answer. Finally, I admit it. To him as much as to myself. "I really like you too."

"Can I be honest?" *More honest? Oh boy.* I nod. "You're driving me crazy," he says with a murmur.

"I am?" He's kissing my neck again but answers *yes* in a muffled voice.

"It's good to know I'm not alone in the you're-driving-me-crazy department," I say honestly.

When I say this, he pauses and looks at me. "You're not alone. I'm done fighting this."

He is? "You are?"

"I'll figure something out, but for now, can we keep this between us?"

When I say "I won't tell if you don't," he gives me a smoldering smile, then kisses me. After a few minutes of intense make out, his arm hugs my waist tighter and he pulls me closer. My breast is flush against his toned chest and I can feel his heart racing. He pulls me up and I wrap my legs around him and hug his shoulders. Still holding on to me, he walks towards my room. Once there, he sets me down gently and in one swift movement, he takes off his shirt, then mine and he's on top of me. *How did he...?*

I pull him closer, feeling the delicious heat in our connected bodies. After a few minutes... actually, that's all you're getting. *Use your imagination.*

Olivia

Halloween's here and several advisors collectively dressed up as lovable, yet goofy minions. As always, Ralph is the ringleader. As if Hawaiian print shirts are not enough. To be honest, I usually go along with the fun/wacky ideas, but this year, I just didn't feel the whole minion vibe. Some of us are randomly dressed, others are not dressed at all. Most of us are handing out candy from our offices. Since this is a college campus, half the student body is also dressed up, a few more creatively than others. Throughout the day I look at the students and marvel. There are no words to describe what some of my students have come up with. On the other hand, it does make for a fun day. We basically spend all day laughing and smiling at them and with them.

In the afternoon, I have a meeting with Tom. To be honest, I wanted to make an impression, hence my lack of minion costume. Instead, I pulled an old costume from my closet. It's a fairy costume I bought to help Bianca in a student life Halloween event; it's at least a couple of years old. It's also a little tight and I can only hope my breasts don't go all magical on me and explode right out of it... *at least not right this second.*

After I see a few students back-to-back, including one with Leonardo da Vinci's beard which gave me the feeling his beard may not have been a costume but a daily fashion statement, a student who complained about having to go to class because his professor took daily attendance and a student who's worried about graduating on time because her scholarship's running out, Tom finally drops by.

Tom's eyes get big as he takes a double look. He stops at the door for a few seconds to rap on the door frame, then lets himself in and takes a seat quietly in front of me. I'm slightly worried I overdid it while I simultaneously pray the dean doesn't walk into my office. The dean might fire me on the spot for indecent exposure.

Tom is still speechless. I can't help but ask if everything's okay.

"Yeah, everything's fine," he answers, nodding with his still wide eyes. His Adam's apple moves, and he glances at my breasts. "They're beautiful. I mean, you're beautiful." When he shakes his head and gives me a sheepish smile, I smile back. *And score!*

We have a productive meeting and have started wrapping it up when Angela comes in and tells me I have an emergency call from one of my brothers. Tom's eyebrows squish together and he gives me a concerned look. My heart races and I feel dizzy. When I pick it up, it's my *ex*.

"Bran? Why are you calling me at work and saying it's an emergency? Are you out of your mind?" When he screams at me in response, I immediately say, "Good bye, Brandon," and before he says anything else I hang up on him. Turning to Tom, I say, "Sorry about that."

"Is everything okay?"

"Yeah, everything's fine. Just a friend's idea of a stupid joke on Halloween."

His eyebrows relax but he says nothing. "Sooo, do you have plans tonight?"

"Yeah, I'm going treat-or-treating with my niece and nephews, early though. You?"

"Keith invited me to a Halloween party, but I'm scrapping that idea. As a matter of fact, I think I'm scrapping everything and coming up with something new," he says, nodding again, then pausing mid-nod. "Yep, I'm definitely coming up with a plan... maybe go in search of some fairy dust," he says with a roguish smile and a twinkle in his eye. I can see the mischievous wheels turning. Is he thinking what I'm thinking? *Oh my.*

After a *very magical* Halloween night, I wake up early and head into the office. I also magically avoid Miami traffic *and* nab a parking spot right in front of our building. As I walk into the office it occurs to me, all things considered, my morning's off to a brilliant start. At this point, the only thing that can make it better is Tom. *And maybe some coffee.*

Cue the record scratch. I might have spoken too soon and jinxed myself.

As I stand in front of my office door, there are two guys and a ladder smack in the middle of it. I stand there speechless, wondering if I want to know what's going on when one of the two guys notices me.

"Hello," a tall guy at the bottom of the ladder says, glancing my way. "Is this your office?" He looks up at the ceiling momentarily, then re-fixes his gaze on me.

"Hi. Yeah. What's going on?"

"We're from IT and we're replacing the wires."

The wires? Oh boy. I'm stunned and stay frozen in place, wondering what my next step should be. "Do you know how long this is going to take?" I ask.

"It's going to be a day or two, shouldn't be more than that." He looks at me then back at his partner who's up at the top of the ladder, head obscured by a hole in the ceiling and doing God knows what.

I nod and march straight to Judith's office. Thankfully, she's at her desk. "Good morning, boss. Do you know anything about my office?"

"No. What's going on with your office?" She stops to look up at me.

"Can you come with me? Please?" She narrows her eyes and gives me a confused look, but joins me in the hallway, her assistant trailing behind. We walk together back to my office where the IT guy repeats what he told me, then apologizes for his department's secretary who obviously did not inform our department. She thanks them and addresses me as we walk back to her office. "For the next couple of days you can work out of one of the cubicles close to my office. Come with me."

After she gives instructions to her assistant, she leaves us.

"Don't worry. We have six cubicles, I use one and the student assistants use the rest. Just go around and pick one," Janine says and smiles.

"Thank you." I'm grateful as I walk around the cubicles. This is a solvable problem, and she solved it in ten seconds flat. I'm feeling better about this. I'm a professional, all I need is a desk and a computer. It'll be a great way to show my boss that I'm adaptable, a necessary quality of a leader. *Brownie points for my future promotion.* Besides, it's a day or two. What could possibly go wrong?

I keep walking around while looking at the cubicles. I pause. The two cubicles in front of me are *busy*. One has a couple of white foam boxes on top *and* a few more on the garbage can. *Is this the lunch cubicle?* The next one has a lot of books and scattered papers on top. *Let me guess, this is the homework cubicle.* A third one has a ton of papers and printouts for... *research?*

I take that back. Maybe it won't be as easy as I thought to take over one of the cubes, as the students have completely monopolized these. I resume my walk to the other side and inspect the last two. They have phones *and* computers, and... ummm, actually, these two look spotless.

It's only then that I notice *Tom* standing at *his* office door.

My head automatically turns his way without asking for permission. *Oh crap.* There's my answer. The female student assistants are trying to impress Tom, or at the very least, not look like total slobs.

"Good morning, Olivia." He looks at me, folding his arms and resting ever-so-nonchalantly on one side of his door frame. He looks gorgeous and I'm unsuccessfully trying to ignore him because we're surrounded by people. *A lot of people.*

"Good morning," I echo. I force my brain to focus and be professional. Too bad *both* cubicles are smack dab in front of his office. *Of course, they are.*

"Are you deciding between door number one or door number two?" he asks, casually.

After a couple of quick seconds, I grab the corner one and open the biggest drawer to put my purse in. "Door number one it is," I say out loud and look at him. His eyebrows dip in amusement.

"Why are you in a cubicle in front of my office?"

"Because IT took over my office to replace *the wires* or some such and I'm office-less for a while," I answer as I slump onto the chair.

"*The wires?*" I nod. "What does that even mean?" I shrug. "I see. For how long?"

"They said one or two days."

"Well, since we're going to be neighbors, if you need anything, let me know."

If I need anything? Anything? Can he be more specific? Because I can think of something... no... bad Olivia! I clear my throat. "Thanks, but I'm okay for now," I reply, trying to sound cool and professional.

"For now? Okay. I'll check with you later and see if there's anything you need help with." He gives me one last knowing look and disappears into his office. I feel my face flush warm and I suppress the urge to look back immediately. Instead, I wait a few minutes, then very stealthily take out my compact mirror and watch him watching me. He's looking at his computer but every few seconds looks my way through his eyelashes. This keeps going for a few minutes until his phone rings and Lucy simultaneously walks up to tell me my first appointment has just arrived.

At the counter, I say hello to a young, cute redhead who follows me back to the cubicle. The computer's slow and as I log into the system we chat about her major and her classes.

"Have you gone to the math lab?" I ask, as I look at her math grades on my screen.

"I've been there, but one tutor was weirding me out so I stopped going."

"I'm sorry to hear that. I can see how that could be a problem."

"It's fine. Whatever. I don't need any more math."

We chat some more and after she's gone, Tom comes out of his office. "I'm sorry, but I couldn't help but overhear – what's going on with the math lab?"

"A math tutor with a high libido?"

"This is not the first time I've heard about this. I think it may be more than that. Did anybody ever talk to Judith about it?"

"Yes, she didn't want to get into a turf war with Academics. Besides, I heard he's somebody's cousin. It's unlikely they'll fire him just for being young and horny."

"Want to bet?" he says cryptically and goes back to his office.

Later in the day, one of the student assistants tells me my student Leo is here to see me. Since I don't currently have any students and my next appointment is not for another hour, I agree to see him. It turns out to be a minor issue: getting my opinion on the classes the last advisor suggested. The last advisor of course being Tom, who's now sitting less than fifteen feet away from me with a very open door. *Oh boy.* Well, I need to pick this kid's brain and there's no time like the present.

Quickly looking up from his file I start. "So, I noticed you've been coming a lot to advising lately and I wanted to make sure that everything is okay with you. Is everything okay?"

"Yeah, everything's fine. Did I get you in trouble? I don't want to get you in trouble," he blurts.

"No, you're not getting me in trouble. It's just that most of my students only come around once a semester for help picking out classes. They rarely come back unless they have a problem, and I wanted to make sure you were okay."

"Yeah, I'm fine. It's very nice of you to worry about me." He gives me a look, a lost puppy-in-love look that makes me pause. *I think it may be best if I don't mention this to Tom.*

Tom, by the way, is also with a student. Not a second after both our students leave, he comes over. "Is anything going on with him? Anything we should know about?" he says quickly as he sits next to me.

"Were you listening in?" I ask.

"Maybe. What did he say?" he asks pertly.

"He said, 'Everything's fine,' and he thanked me for being concerned."

Tom shakes his head, and his body stiffens a little. I'm about to ask what the problem is when he says flatly, "He's wasting your time. You need to do something about it."

The fact that he's questioning how I do my job is infuriating, "Why would you say that? How is he wasting my time? This is our job."

"Yes, it is our job and you're very good at it, but this is different."

"How is this different? He's a student. This is what we do."

"I think there's something else going on."

I cock my head and look at him. "What could possibly be going on with him? Enlighten me, oh, wise one, please."

"I don't know. I have a feeling."

"A *feeling*? O-kay, Freud. You know what, let's stick to academic advising and leave the personality psychoanalysis to the pros."

He looks like he has something else to say but then doesn't. Instead, he abruptly stands up and heads back to his office.

Except for the fact that we keep looking at each other like we're back in middle school, the rest of the day is uneventful.

When it's time to go, from the corner of my eye, I see Tom getting up, backpack in hand. He walks in my direction, and I stall by clearing up my workspace. "So," he starts when he reaches me, "I made a few calls and the overly 'enthusiastic' math tutor has been... *relocated.*"

I turn off the computer and stop to look at him. "*Relocated?* What do you mean?"

"There was an opening. He's now processing invoices in the accounting department with a bunch of oldies, where I'm sure he'll be thrilled... or maybe not, but at least he got a pay raise. Maybe now he can get a girlfriend and... take her out to dinner?"

Processing invoices? What? I can't help it and laugh out loud, then cover my mouth with my hand and shake my head. "How did you..."

He smiles back at me, eyes bright and mischievous. "I have many talents," he says casually with a shrug, then turns to leave. He slings the backpack over one shoulder as he walks away. As I watch him, I make a mental note to ask him about this. *Who did he call to make that happen so fast?*

As I gather the rest of my things and get up, I get a text from him telling me he's coming over later. My inner girl squeals. I'm thrilled and about to burst with anticipation. I run home, dash into the shower and quickly put on a bit of makeup. I chose a loose-fitting rose-colored tank-top with tight (and hopefully slimming) black leggings. I pair them up with matching cute black booties. I leave my hair down and loose and head towards the kitchen, where I debate if I should grab tea or wine. *Definitely wine.*

Finally, there's a knock on my door and I jog to open it, excited.

Except it's not Tom. *It's Bran.*

Olivia

S hit. Shit. Shit.

He waves awkwardly with one hand, and my heart pumps wildly in my chest. *Oh. My. God.* I need to use all of my Zen and calm down if I want to avoid having a heart attack.

"Olivia, how have you been?" Bran asks, staying in place.

"Hiii... Braaaannn." For a few seconds, I've temporarily forgotten that I ever dated him. Even with these booties, my ex towers over me at over six feet tall. As usual, his brown hair is flawless. His blue eyes are too blue and cold and his face is too square. When he's not harassing me, he can be very charming. Did I mention he's always well put together and half the time I'm trying to avert some kind of disaster? Come to think about it, I honestly don't know why I dated him at all.

"What a surprise! I'm okay and you?" I'm in shock and hoping to prevent my eyes from popping out of their sockets. *Obviously,* I was not expecting him. *What does he want?* Tom will be here any minute. *How the hell do I get rid of him?*

"I've been better, but life goes on." I nod... and nod and keep on nodding. After a full minute passes by he asks, "Are you going to let me in?"

Should I let him in or not? I'm leaning towards a *no.*

Finally, I say, "Sure," and step out of the way. I close the door after him but stay a couple of feet away near the entrance. My hands settle to rest on my stomach, in what I hope looks like a relaxed way. "What's up?" I ask, trying to keep it casual.

"Wow, the place looks amazing," he says, stopping to look around. When he's satisfied, he turns back to me and looks at me from head to toe. His eyes grow huge and scan me again, making me slightly uncomfortable. "You look great, too."

"Thank you. You don't look bad yourself." I lie. He needs to shave, though. *Would it be rude if I told him?*

He chuckles creepily and the movie *Chucky* comes to mind. I have an image of the lights turning off and his face illuminated from the bottom with a flashlight. *What the... Get a grip, Olivia.* I take a deep breath and force myself to stay calm.

He turns away from me, looks around my house again, and starts walking in, slowly.

"Heh, I look like crap, but the house looks really great," he repeats as he explores the living room and the dining room taking in the large double room with an open floor plan. Then he walks into the kitchen and stands directly in front of the double glass doors that overlook the backyard. He folds his arms and looks out. After a few minutes, he walks back in my direction, "How was work today? Did you save any students from a career as a DJ or a taxi driver?" he says disparagingly, pointing at me with his index finger.

Here we go. See what I mean?

I look down at my floor for strength and then look up at him. "Ha-ha hilarious. Is there anything you want, or need, or did you come all the way here just to make a joke and insult my students?" I can't help folding my arms as well, while I wait for his mostly unwelcome revelation.

"Actually, no," he replies. He goes to sit on the sofa, but when he notices I'm not moving, he gets back up and stands less than three feet in front of me. *So much for personal space.*

I'm waiting for him to tell me the reason why he's here, but at this very moment there's another knock and we both turn our heads to the door. Bran frowns and gives me a blank look but stays in the same spot, waiting.

I open the door, and of course, it's Tom. *This just keeps getting better and better.*

I hesitate. Should I even introduce them? Before I can say anything, Bran takes a step forward and introduces himself. "Hi, I'm Brandon Lloyd, her ex," and points towards me with a thumb.

Shiiiit! I feel my face growing warm and I want the ground to open up and swallow me. "Thomas Williams," Tom replies as they shake hands. I can see them sizing each other up.

"Brandon, can you give us a few minutes?" I glare at him but before he can answer, I turn and push Tom out the door then close it behind me, "Tom, I am so sorry. I know we made plans, but I had no idea he was coming over. He just showed up and—."

"It's fine." He says, his jaw clenching. He's quiet for a few seconds, then says, "You know what, I should go. You're busy. We'll talk another day."

Before I can reply, he walks away. "Tom, wait," I call after him, but he doesn't stop. Half of me wants to follow him, but the other half is afraid that Bran is alone in my house. I quickly go back inside to face my exasperating ex. "Why are you here? What do you want?" I ask without preamble.

He's resting his body on the back of my couch. "Is that your boyfriend? Are you dating him?" He motions to the door with his head.

"That is none of your business."

"Fine. Listen, I came because I'm tired of calling you and emailing you. I don't know why you're completely ignoring me, but I'm having some issues and I need your help. We bought this house together, and I was thinking I never got my half."

Is he serious? For a second, I'm so angry it takes everything I have not to slap him or throw something at him. "You were *thinking*? Are you fucking serious? Half of *what*? You never lived here." I want to kill him for showing up here and because Tom left. Instead, I have to force myself to take deep breaths and try to stay calm.

"Yeah, but *we* bought it. We remodeled *together*. I was here, remember? I spent a shit ton of money. I even paid the first few months of the mortgage while the renovations were going on. I figured you owe me." He looks at me and I don't think he's kidding. He is in fact very serious.

"You're a jerk. I'm not paying you *anything*." My heart's racing and I take shallow breaths.

At this comment, he takes a step toward me. All six feet muscle of him. "Okay, then we'll need to get the law involved. I can sue you for unjust enrichment," he says cockily and crosses his arms, barely a couple of feet away from me.

"Sue me? Are you kidding me right now? You left. You walked out on this house and this relationship." I can't help but point at his chest with *my* index finger. "*You* are entitled to *nothing*."

"Look, I'm not debating our relationship right now." He raises his voice, unfolds his arms, and moves his hands in a sideways negating motion as he speaks. "We broke up and I admit it, I could have handled it better, but this house was partly a financial transaction."

"We broke up because you're a cheating bastard. This was not a financial transaction for me. We agreed I would keep the house because you already owned one."

"That was before we broke up," he counters quickly.

"That is *not* my problem. You should have thought about *that* before you cheated. The title and the loan are under my name, which means it's mine. End of story."

"Enough!" he roars. I take half a step back and for a few seconds, I'm rooted on the spot. "All I'm saying is I spent a lot of money too and you kept the house and since we broke up, I deserve to be compensated. It is as simple as that."

My heart accelerates, and it takes me a minute to find my voice. I clear my throat and look up at him again. "You know what, do whatever you want. Call the police, a lawyer or a judge— I don't care." I turn to the door, open it and wait.

For a few seconds, he doesn't say anything. His head drops, he lowers his voice with a sigh. "Please don't be like this, I don't want to do that. Let's try to figure out how much we spent, and talk about it like normal people."

"Like normal people? Right, because it's *normal* that you showed up here after months and months to scream at me. Which, by the way, you've never done before. It's *normal* that the guy who cheats wants to make his ex sell a house *she* bought and paid for. Not to mention, the person that kept allll of the furniture and left me with nothing. Sure, it's all *normal*."

"Olivia—"

"As far as talking, you know what? Maybe not. Talking is overrated. Goodbye Brandon." I gesture towards the door.

"This house is worth a lot of money. It's in a great location, next to a golf course, close to the university and the remodeling came out great. How about this? We'll sell it. I'll keep half and give you half. You can buy yourself a nice apartment somewhere."

"You've completely lost your mind. Please leave."

"Olivia, I can prove with checks and credit card statements that I contributed to the purchase and remodel. I have receipts of materials. The realtor's my witness that I was involved in the buy from the beginning."

"*Your witness?* Are you insane!? You can't do this. This is my home, you jerk!"

"You're irrational and I can't talk to you. I'll be in touch and when you've calmed down, we can have a conversation like two adults. You do look great. I mean it." When he finally walks out, I slam the door behind him.

Shit. I'm *irrational? Are you kidding me?* This is the last thing I need, either to pay him or to spend money on lawyers. *Doesn't he realize that I'm broke?* I absently wipe a runaway tear and think about Tom. *Double shit.*

Olivia

I wake up to a rainy day, which I know will automatically make traffic worse. Rain will also translate to no parking left near the buildings because nobody will want to get wet, even though getting wet is inevitable.

Because I want to get to the office and talk to Tom, I leave my house extra early. I still end up parking a mile away and getting soaked. By the time I arrive at the office, Tom's already at his desk. I put my things in the cubicle and walk to his office, forgetting that I look like a wet dog but not really caring. I skip the formalities, walk in and close the door quietly. "I'm sorry about last night and my ex. The truth is, we're having a disagreement. Which is ridiculous, because it's my home but he wants—"

He raises his hand and effectively stops me. "Look Olivia, you don't owe me an explanation. We're not official and I understand that you had a life before you met me but, as a rule, I like to avoid drama at work if I can." He goes back to glaring at the papers in front of him. His jaw is tight.

"I don't want drama either but I want to explain. He's my ex and there's nothing going on between us. As a matter of fact, until yesterday, I hadn't seen him in over six months, he—"

He raises the hand again and my heart drops. "I'm going to stop you right there. I don't want to get in the middle of whatever it is you guys have going on. Maybe we need to take a step back while you take care of your *disagreements* with whoever that guy is."

I hate the way he says the word *disagreements*, but I can't argue. He's right. I need to deal with Brandon. I have two choices: one, have a potential gossip-inducing-argument at the office with Tom and *make* him listen to me or two, walk away. Reluctantly and having no other real choice, I walk out.

Since then, he's barely talked to me or looked at me. Lunch comes and goes and by mid-afternoon, I don't know what to do so I walk into Sandra's office and sit in front of her desk quietly. She's working on the computer but starts glancing my way. "What's wrong?"

"Last night I was home waiting for Tom. Brandon showed up. Then Tom showed up."

"That's not good. What did Brandon want?"

"He needs money and wants to make me sell my house."

"Wait, he can't do that. Can he?"

"I don't know. He was talking about lawsuits and something called unjust enrichment. I don't even know what that means. I need a lawyer."

Her brother's a lawyer. I know this because she mentions it any chance she gets. "My brother's a lawyer but his thing is usually traffic tickets. I can ask to see if he can help you or if he can give you a referral to somebody who can."

I can't help but sigh, relieved. "Thank you so much."

"Don't worry about it. Did you tell Tom what Brandon wanted?"

"I tried, but he said I didn't have to explain. I don't know. Maybe I should leave it alone, forget Tom and focus on my career and try not to get sued."

"Olivia, having a career is great, but it's also lonely if you don't have somebody to share it with."

"Yeah, easy for you to say when you're married with kids. Men are unreliable and relationships are like ships... they sail away."

"Ships? Again with that?" She cocks her head confused, then continues, "Olivia, you can't decide against a relationship based on one unpleasant experience. Just because the last one didn't work out, it doesn't mean the next one will fail too."

"True, but look at my mom. She keeps getting married trying to get it right. I don't want to do that."

"I've met your mom. I don't think she looks at it as 'trying to get it right.' Maybe she's hopeful that the next one will work out and every time she gets closer and closer to true happiness because she's learned something from the previous relationship that makes the next one better."

Ummm, I never thought about it like that.

After a few more minutes of talking, I go back to my cubicle.

Every other minute I want to knock on Tom's closed door. It takes all my willpower to stop myself from knocking it down or saying something... anything. *If only I had a good excuse.* But I don't, and by the end of the day, I'm forced to leave without saying a word. I walk by my own office and the IT guys inform me that I can have my office back tomorrow.

Olivia

It's the first week of November and there's a hurricane coming. Let's add natural disasters to the circus that's become my life. Technically Mother Nature isn't wrong, she still has a few more weeks to inflict pain as hurricane season doesn't officially end until the end of November.

Tom's barely talked to me these last couple of days, but I can't worry about him. I need to prioritize. A hurricane trumps love, even more so if said love is a platonic-slash-secret relationship with a handsome coworker that mostly comprises great sex and conversation and that could potentially derail an awesome career.

I wake up early and go around the backyard cleaning, picking up anything that might become a projectile with hurricane-force' wind. I bring the furniture in and try closing the hurricane shutters. *Try* being the operative word. Since I don't have the time or the strength to fight them, I call for reinforcements. I go to the front of the house and repeat the process, picking up and cleaning. It's mid-morning when I get a text from Tom.

Tom: What's going on? Are you hurricane-ready?
Olivia: Ready as I'll ever be.
Tom: I'm coming over.
Olivia: No need.
Tom: Too late.

Oh, come on! I'm dirty, sweaty and wearing shorts with an old shirt, topped with hair in a disheveled-messy-sideway bun and no makeup. As I'm typing a response, he pulls into my driveway. I quickly put my phone in my mouth, pull my hair band out and try to tame my wild hair with my hands while simultaneously pulling it into a ponytail. *How the hell did he arrive so fast?*

His windows are down, and I watch as he parks on my driveway. He removes his sunglasses and throws them on the dashboard. I can't help but walk in his direction then stop a few feet away to look at him. "Tom. What are you doing here?"

"I told you, I came to see if you were hurricane ready," he says, getting out and resting on his car. He's wearing a t-shirt, cargo shorts, full of pockets and zippers, and a baseball cap. His eyes are dark; he looks hot as hell in more ways than one.

Brooding male alert, check.

"Actually, you *didn't* tell me. I'm fine, you need not worry. Besides, aren't you mad at me or something?" He lets out a sigh while he adjusts his cap in place with both hands. When he moves his head from side to side, I hear a few cracks. *Yikes.*

Tense male alert, double-check.

He crosses his legs at his ankles, then crosses his arms. "Yeah, well, a hurricane's coming. Priorities," he says, his jaw tense. "I would hate to see you or your house get blown by a storm," he looks down at his feet, then looks up at me, "What's going on with your shutters? Why haven't you closed them?" He sounds bossy, annoyed and pissed off all rolled into one.

I'm already getting shit from Brandon. I don't need it from Tom. I don't like his tone and I'm tempted to say something rude, but that would probably make things worse. *Cooler heads must prevail, or should anyway.* I take a deep breath and try to stay Zen. "These don't want to close. The ones on the back are stuck too."

"You bought this house less than a year ago, didn't you check them?" he says, giving me a look. After a few seconds, he walks towards my house. As he walks, he pulls out his cap and puts it on backward.

"Yeah, ten months ago was spring, right in the middle of *dry* season. Plus, I had a contractor. I assumed he or my ex checked them."

"You're pretty capable. You could have checked... or asked." He pulls and pushes one of the shutters. It makes a huge metal-scraping sound but barely moves.

Here we go. "Okay, that's enough. Did you come here to berate me or help me?" I glare at him and put my hands on my hips.

"Both," he says, grunting. Since it's clear the shutter's not moving, he lets go of the shutter-pulling and turns to face me. After a second, he puts his hands on his hips and lets out a breath. His breathing slows but he says nothing.

Ooookay. Staring contest in the middle of the day. *Got it.* "You know what, I don't have time for this. There's a hurricane coming. You should go home." Since he *still* won't talk, after a few seconds, I roll my eyes and walk away from him.

I can hear him grunting behind me. "*Fuck.* Wait, wait. Jesus, can you please hold on?"

"You don't need to worry about me. I'm closing my house and heading to my brother's. Bye Tom."

"Wait. *Please.*"

I stop a couple of feet from my door and turn back to look at him, "Tom, *you* came here. What the hell do you want from me?" Without saying anything else, he crosses the few feet between us and grabs the back of my neck with one hand. His thumb brushes against my cheek and his other arm pulls me towards him by the waist while he gives me an electrifying kiss. My hand immediately reaches for the back of his head, while my other arm wraps around his waist. *Wow.*

He pauses, rests his forehead on mine and takes a deep breath. "I'm sorry. I know I'm behaving like a lunatic, but I didn't like meeting your ex. I know you said there's nothing between you and him and I believe you, but he rubs me wrong and I don't like it. I don't like him. I want him far away from you."

I take a step back and look up at him. His anger has gone down a few notches and mine's dropping by the seconds. "There's nothing going on. He wants me to sell this house and give him money. Which I have no intention of doing. He has a girlfriend, the girl he cheated with. He's still with her."

"Still. I want him far away from you."

"What was that Mr. Hyde?" I joke.

"You know what, whatever, I don't want to talk about him. I came to make sure *you* were okay. Do you have a toolbox?" I do, and after he rummages through it, he tries using a hammer on the shutter. It doesn't move at all. Instead, it's making a lot of noise. He keeps hitting it to no avail. When a car turns into my driveway, he pauses. "Are you expecting someone?" Tom asks, looking over his shoulder.

"Yes, my brother."

His head whips around and the hammer stops midair. "What?" he says flustered, but after a few seconds he recovers.

Is he nervous? Is it time for a panic attack?

"*Shit.* I just realized I haven't told any of my family members about you. You and I... we're... this is supposed to be a fling!" I'm whispering maniacally.

"So you keep saying."

"Hi sis," my brother says from a few feet away. He embraces me with a hug and kisses the side of my head.

"Tom, this is my brother Mike. Mike, this is Tom... my... neighbor."

I know, I'm lame, don't judge me.

Tom mouths, *neighbor?* glancing at me, while Mikes raises an eyebrow.

"Hi Tom. I'm Michael," Mike says while stretching a hand. "What's going on with the... shutters?" he says, looking at both of us.

"They won't close... or move at all," Tom answers. They spend the next few minutes pulling, pushing, and hammering at it to no avail. "Okay, this is not working. Plan B. Let's find blocks of wood and line them up next to the shutters. Then we'll put plywood over the blocks to cover the windows, then we'll deal with the shutters," Tom says, looking at Mike while he motions where the blocks would be with his hands.

Mike is silent but nodding his head. "That's a great idea, the only thing is... it's too late, there's no plywood anywhere. All the stores have sold out."

"I know a guy," Tom says, and we both look at him as he grabs his cell from a pocket in his shorts and makes a call. Two hours later, plywood is delivered to my house. I have no idea how, but I'm grateful. I'm also glad they seem to like each other. Between nailing plywood and drinking beer, they have a friendly conversation going.

Beer and hurricanes... is Florida, that's a thing. *Don't ask.*

"I've gotta' get going sis, I think you got it from here. I have to take care of a couple of things before we hunker down but call me if you need me. See you tonight. Tom, it was great to meet you," my brother says as they shake hands. He winks at me and drives away. *Jesus.* I give it a week before my mother calls me and asks about my dress size.

"Your brother's pretty cool," Tom says as we walk towards my front door.

"Yeah. He is."

"You know, to be honest, this wasn't how I pictured my first meeting with a member of your family."

"No? What did you have in mind?"

"Well, after we figured out this whole HR situation and this whole relationship thing, I mean. I would have liked to have met them at your house over a nice home-cooked meal or in a nice restaurant or something... down the line, I mean... if it came to that..."

"Oh." I pause. The confession throws me off. It's been a long time since I allowed myself to stop and think about a relationship. The truth is I suck at dating and sometimes wondered if Brandon was a fluke, if maybe I'm meant to be alone. On the other hand, when I look at Tom, there's something in his eyes that's safe and warm. It doesn't feel like dating; with him everything just feels natural and effortless.

Does that mean he wants more? He's seeing the potential between us? *Should I allow myself to want more too?*

"Are you staying with him?" Tom asks, pulling me out of my head.

"Yeah. With him and our older brother William and his family."

He takes a step forward and pauses in front of me. "When are you leaving?"

"I'm going to take a shower and get going soon."

"A shower?" His voice drops an octave and I pause. "I need a shower too. We could save water," he says as his eyes darken and his lips slowly turn up.

"Water conservation. *Riiight,*" I can't help but grin. When I open the door, he interlocks his fingers with mine and pulls me inside for a long... *shower.*

Tom

----

*E*xhausted.

Three days cooped up in a house. I can't even describe how I feel right now. I survived three days with my mom, dad, and sisters. Not to mention, my brother coming in and out. I survived three days of parental *and* sisterly interrogation. *Enough said.*

I endured my sister Elizabeth's endless stories about her job as a teacher, her students and coworkers I've never met and probably never will. She actually made it through another school year. This is interesting coming from her, who seemed to have a new job every single week and changed her major at least a dozen times. I also heard everything about my other sister Laura's job as a lawyer *and* her love life or lack thereof. Sidebar, she talked a lot about Kyle, Keith's brother. I need to find out what the deal is with them; more like find out if I need to kick his ass.

I also evaded more questions than I could keep track of from my mother about the state of *my* love life. Which, truth be told, I came close to sharing. Finally, I was not sure I would survive another comment or question from my dad about the state of my 401K. How much he *thinks* I should save if I want to retire before I'm ninety. Not to mention his *insights* on South Florida real estate. If I hear about one more building in Brickell or a house for sale in the greater Miami area, I might just really leave the state.

During the hurricane, I kept myself busy by searching for a company to replace Olivia's shutters. The fact that neither her contractor nor the idiot ex-boyfriend noticed or bothered to check them is disturbing. At the same time, it should have come up on the home inspection. The alternative is they did check, and ignored it, which frankly is even worse. I should probably have somebody go there and inspect her entire house, just to be safe. At least she'll have all the information and she'll know what she's up against.

Thankfully, nothing happened during the hurricane besides a lot of rain and wind. On the upside, the weekend is coming and we have two more days off. As I'm finally driving home though, there's only one thing on my mind. *Olivia*. I track her down and make plans to meet with her before the end of the day.

I can't wait to see her. Something about her inexplicably draws me to her, which I realized makes no sense, but I digress. The truth is, I love being around her, she just has a great vibe. She makes me laugh, she's authentic and confident in who she is and I love how she handles things to the best of her abilities and with a positive attitude. She's had a rough year and instead of being bitter or spiteful, she's upbeat, and she's handling everything with grace.

It's early evening by the time I go searching for her. She waits for me at the door, barefooted, wearing a simple white t-shirt and a knee-length pink polka dot skirt. She looks *so* pretty. She's radiant. Her smile is like the sun, casting a bright light on everything around her.

I get out of my car and go straight to her. When I reach her, I immediately kiss her. Her lips are full and soft and I can't stop kissing them. I run my fingers through her hair and inhale her scent. I stroke her cheeks with the pad of my thumbs and when we break contact and I stop kissing her, she sighs and smiles at me. Her smile is intoxicating. I love her dimples. I run my thumbs over them and her hand clasps to my wrist, but she doesn't say anything. After a few seconds, I hug her and bury my face in her neck. She hugs me back and cradles my neck with her soft fingers, and traps me in her never-ending warmth. I'm suddenly hit with an "I never want to let go," feeling.

This is the moment it hits me. *I'm falling hard for this woman.*

"By the way, a guy's coming tomorrow to measure the shutters and replace them. I also have another guy coming to do a home inspection," I tell her from the kitchen counter as she's cooking us dinner.

She stops chopping to look at me with narrowed eyes. "I'm sorry, but what are you talking about?"

"We're replacing the shutters and inspecting the house to make sure there's nothing wrong with it. You said you never saw the home inspection report. Since we have no idea what they found, I figured we should start there."

"I heard, but I don't remember having a conversation about this. How am I going to pay for it?" After a beat, she goes back to chopping vegetables.

"Don't worry about it."

"I do worry about it. Do you think, I don't know, that maybe you should run things by me *before* you call people at random?"

"You're right. I apologize for not talking to you about it, but I won't apologize for worrying about your safety. I want to make sure that when the next hurricane rolls around, you're going to be okay."

"I appreciate the gesture but I'm not taking your money. I'm not with you for your money."

"I know."

"Okay, then."

"If you were my girlfriend we wouldn't be having this discussion."

"I disagree. We would *definitely* be having this conversation." She stops chopping and looks at me. "Also, for the record, I hate the word relation*ship*. It always makes me think of a ship that sailed. It's very depressing."

"I don't know how to respond to that."

She shakes her head, then goes back to chopping. "Never mind. I just have a thing against ships."

I run my hands through my hair and look at her. "Let's back it up. When I met you, you were actively dating. Olivia, I hate to break it to you, but this is a relationship." I say, motioning between us with my hand.

"Sex and great conversations do not a relationship make."

"Let's circle back to that. Can we at least get an estimate for the shutters? I want to know how much it'll cost to replace them before next hurricane season."

"Fine. And the house inspection?"

"Wanna go half and half?" Thankfully, she seems pleased with this arrangement and smiles at me. When she nods, I angle my body towards her. "Deal?"

When she says, "Deal," I lean down and kiss her. When our lips meet, I feel her smile and I smile too.

Now if I could only change her mind about the ship...

Olivia

"Are you hungry? I'm starving. Let's get some food," Tom says, glancing at me. He gets off the bed and puts on his t-shirt and jeans. "How do you feel about pizza?"

"Sure," I say while I grab a shirt and a comfy pair of pants, then add, "Before this gets too crazy, I was thinking we should have rules."

"Rules? Now? Isn't it too late for that?"

I throw a pillow at him and he laughs. "Shut up," I say as I walk out of the room, with him trailing behind me.

He sounds intrigued when he asks, "Just out of curiosity, what kinds of rules are we talking about?"

"Can we agree to keep *this* a secret?" I say, moving my hand back and forth between us. "At least until the end of spring semester."

"Let me guess. That's when Judith's retiring."

I try not to react to the fact that he already knows it, but I can't help wondering how long he's known and if he's interested in the job. "First question, how do you know about that?"

"We work in a very gossipy department."

"Right. I was thinking, we should always arrive at work and leave at separate times and no more talking at work." While I grab a couple of glasses and some iced tea, he sits on a stool on the kitchen island and turns on his phone.

"Okay, James Bond." He throws me a glance. I give him a few minutes to order the pizza and wait. "Done." He says, putting the phone down and walking around the kitchen island.

I look up to him. "Ummm, should we have a code name? Maybe a secret meeting place?"

"A secret meeting place?" he repeats. I nod. "What, like a private place to do kinky stuff? You want to turn the guest room into a playroom?"

Oh my God. "What?! No!" I can feel my cheeks burning.

"I mean, I don't know. Why do we need a secret meeting place? Don't you own this house? Are you expecting your husband to walk in? Should I be worried?"

"Last time I checked, I was single..."

I hear him mumble, "Not for long..." but when I look at him, he says nothing else. His eyebrows go up, but he's silent. "What?" He leans his hips on the kitchen counter and waits. After a bit, he asks, "Are you sidelining me because I hired those guys and talked about a relationship?"

"No. Besides, this is a fling, not a relationship. You don't have to help me with my house."

"Ummm, here's a word for you... denial." I throw a towel at him and he catches it in midair with a grin. "These rules, how are you planning to implement them? You realize we work together. If we completely avoid each other, people wouldbesuspicious," he says.

"True, good point. Amendment to that rule, at work we can talk about students."

Once the pizza arrives, we grab plates, drinks, and sit in the family room. Again, he sits on the middle of the sofa and stretches his legs, looking comfortable on my couch. *It's almost like he belongs there.* "Remind me again why you're having a secret fling with me?" I ask, a short while later as he's changing TV channels.

"As opposed to what? A non-secret-affair? Which is what I think I want." There's an amused tone in his voice.

"As opposed to having an affair with a supermodel or a Miami Heat cheerleader." *Maybe a Miami Housewife from that show?*

His head is resting on the couch and he turns it sideways to look at me but says nothing for a few minutes. "Are we having a serious conversation now?"

"We're having *a* conversation."

"I'm with you because I love your vibe. You're nice, I like nice people." He shrugs.

"Are people not nice to you?" I ask.

"Yes and no. It's complicated. Also, you're smart, you can cook, you're great with people, funny and I love your dimples," he says without missing a beat. "Plus, you have great hair." He gently tugs the ends of it but after a few seconds, he lets go and turns back to the TV.

My heart's hammering in my chest, but I press on. "Okay. Fine, let's have a serious conversation." He focuses on me, watching me intently, and I keep going. "I'm sorry that people aren't always nice to you and I'm glad you like my hair but I'm not interesting at all. There's something wrong with my energy, or the aura, or the chakra, the Zen... something's not working."

"First of all, nothing's wrong with you. You're perfect. You just hadn't met the right person. *I* find you very interesting. Second, if there was something wrong, I'm pretty handy and more than eager to help you fix anything that breaks and if I can't fix it, I'm smart enough to hire somebody who can."

Is this a metaphorical handiness we're talking about?

"Why do you want to be with me? You're... you're you."

He frowns. "Huh? Who am I supposed to be?"

I let my head drop, then look up. "What I mean is... you can carry a conversation, you're handsome and athletic. You're nice. You have a job."

He's wide-eyed when he says, "I have a job? What kind of guys have you been going out with?"

"I don't know... you know what I mean. You cycle, you're healthy and... tall." Oh my God. Why can't I stop talking? *Somebody please kill me now.*

"Olivia, no offense, but I think you've set your bar too low."

"You have green eyes?" This last comment causes a slow smile to form on his lips and I can't help but get all soft inside.

"Hey, look at me, don't sell yourself short. You're amazing too. I know the whole relationship thing scares you. We'll take it slow."

"What about the advising director's job?"

He pauses for a moment. "Why don't we cross that bridge when we get there?"

I take a deep breath and look at him and let my head fall on his shoulder, "You don't understand, I suck at dating. I never make it past a first date. I'm going to fuck it up."

He kisses the side of my head. "You're not. Trust me, okay?" I nod and he presses on. "Can I ask you a question?" When I nod again, he asks, "Why do you have a problem with ships?"

I lift my head and look at him. "Because my dad left on one. I was about five years old. He didn't like to fly so he took a cruise ship to see family and never came back. *A cruise.* I mean, I've always wondered, why a ship? Why not a car or a train?" I pause. "My last memory of him is a ship. We haven't heard from him since."

That right there is the crux of it. How do you reconcile with the fact that the second most important person in your life, the person tasked with protecting you, actually abandoned you? How do you stop yourself from self-sabotaging long enough to see that not all men (or women) will abandon you?

"I'm sorry, Olivia," Tom says softly.

"It's fine. It was a long time ago." I pause. "Actually, I've never told anybody that," I confess. I take a deep breath, feeling somewhat lighter after sharing that with him.

"Thank you for telling me." He kisses the side of my head again. After he waits a beat, he says, "Sooo, you like my eyes?" I try not to smile but when he pulls me for a real kiss, my insides turn to jelly. I take another deep breath and look at him, "What now?" he asks, tilting his head.

"I don't understand how you're single. I was just thinking women probably take one look at you and line up to marry you and have your babies." I pause. "You're not a serial killer, are you?"

After a second he bursts into laughter. "Olivia, look at me. That's not how it works at all. Nobody's lining up to date me. To be honest, it's been a long time since anybody challenged me intellectually and made me laugh... you're keeping me on my toes. I like being with you. Actually, there's nobody like you. Nobody has ever asked if I'm a serial killer."

"I'm sorry. I know you're not and for what it's worth, I like being with you too."

"Okay, then turn off your brain." He presses the space between my eyes. "I need you to turn this off and turn something else on."

"Ummm..."

"That's *not* what I was thinking, at all, but I like where this is going." We grin at each other and he kisses me. *Something else is definitely getting turned on.*

Olivia

"**C**an we talk?" I look up and see Tom standing at my door. Work has been crazy, and we have spoken little this week. Our time alone together has been spent in more interesting ways than talking, since it's a secret fling and all.

Registration for spring term starts mid-November and students need help trying to figure out what to register for and getting holds removed. By now, many students have figured out if they'll pass a class or not, and need alternatives. Add to that, the new students who delayed admission until Spring, and we've had students back-to-back.

Today he looks so handsome, I want to say, "Yes, come in, sit and tell me everything." Instead, I'm forced to reply, "I'm swamped, I have students waiting and over fifty emails to reply to. What's up?"

He takes a few steps inside. "There's something I want to talk to you about," he says before a student assistant appears behind him.

"Your one-thirty is asking if it's going to be a long time because she has class in one hour," the student says looking at me.

"Tom, can we talk later?"

He nods but looks disappointed and I can't help but wonder what he wants to tell me. "Sure," he finally says.

I make a mental note to find him as soon as I have a chance. I also want to ask him if he's going to the upcoming advising workshop. The day goes by fast and by the time five p.m. rolls around, I'm famished. After my last student leaves, I wrap up as much as I can and walk out quietly before somebody notices or stops me for help. Unfortunately, in my rush, I forget to check in with Tom.

Tonight, I'm interviewing a potential roommate. Around seven p.m., a girl with a radiant smile is at my door. We spoke on the phone and she seemed normal. I could feel her smile and invited her over. Her name is Leyla and she's a Miami native who has spent the last decade traveling the world and might be ready to come home. After a tour, she tells me she likes the house. I tell her I have to check her references and will let her know. One of her contacts is our student dean, Dean Lozano. Apparently, he gave her my information. I bet there's a story there.

The truth is, I'm grateful. I might have *finally* found a roommate.

Things are finally looking up.

It's Friday and all advisors must go to a mandatory training on Advising and Customer Service. Some advisors were mean to students this semester and students complained. Dean Lozano is making everybody go to a meeting. Our training includes advisors from all three campuses and the downtown campus is more central, so the meeting is located here. I wake up a little early, meet Sandra and Ralph, and we carpool.

Traffic is miraculously light, and we arrive with plenty of time to spare, which is a blessing. We enter at a small auditorium and I notice several advisors are already there. People are striking up random conversations and mingling around.

I need caffeine and something to eat *pronto* before we start this thing. I won't survive five hours without food. After asking around, we're directed to a food establishment inside the campus. On our way there, we run into Tom. He's wearing a gray suit with a blue shirt and looks amazing.

Oddly enough, we can't seem to walk over twenty feet without running into people. This is Miami, the land of the late. Why the heck are we all early?

Everybody we see says hello to Tom. I recall he worked at this campus for a few months, yet he's uncommonly popular. People that have never said hello to me are saying hello to us. We finally make it to the food court, have a substantial and carb-filled breakfast, and head back. It's a repeat, with everybody stopping us to say hi to Tom.

A few times Tom asks if he can talk to me in private, but every time we get a chance, someone interrupts us. We are almost back in the auditorium when we run into a group of campus administrators chatting. Tom knows all of them by name and makes the introductions. It gets strange when one of them shares a story about Tom and his brother running around the campus as kids. Tom smiles, embarrassed, and gives me a sideways glance but continues his conversation. By the time we return to the auditorium, it's packed.

I soon realize, this meeting is starting and I don't have time to ask him what's going on. At the same time, I keep thinking about all of the things he's been able to do since he arrived at our campus. He can talk to people that have never taken my calls and he can influence staff changes in less than a day. I can't help it but I have a bad feeling about this and my breakfast is threatening to come back up.

During the lunch break, groups start forming by osmosis. Tom's only a few feet away from me when Judith calls him. He turns back to join her, and the deans from all three campuses and my heart sinks. I end up having lunch with Sandra and Ralph. Alan and Peter from the downtown campus join us, as well as my friend Gabby, who works in downtown Miami.

We arrive at a restaurant near campus, order, and start an informal conversation about students and student issues. We exchange war stories and laughs. It's very pleasant until Tom's name comes up. "How do you guys like working with Tom?" Alan asks.

"He's a great guy, we all like him. He's an excellent advisor," Ralph says casually before he takes a bite.

"How long do you guys think it'll be before he's director or a VP?" Alan asks, glancing at all of us.

While I process the comment, Sandra addresses him. "What do you mean? What are you talking about?"

"He was an advisor here for like three months before they moved him to your campus."

"Yeah, because we needed an advisor and Judith was desperate," Sandra counters.

"Oh wait, don't you guys know who his parents are?" Sandra and I shake our heads, while Ralph and Gabby shrug.

"His parents are the Whiteford's. They were both VPs here. They recently retired and now they're adjuncts. His grandparents were VPs and deans and donated money that funded one of the colleges at the campus. They are well known in the higher ed community," he states, as if that's common knowledge. *Wait, is it?*

"But that's impossible. He doesn't have their last name," I say naively.

"That's because Tom and his brother were toddlers when their dad passed away in an accident. Their mom remarried a few years after that. Many people here know the family. As kids, the campus was literally their playground."

"Oh. We had no idea," Sandra says and looks at me, but I'm too stunned to speak. When she asks if I'm okay, I nod, then imagine myself at Kennedy Space Center. The words, *Houston, we have a problem* blares out over a loudspeaker and a rocket takes off right behind me. I don't touch my food. For the rest of the lunch, I don't speak and listen politely as my coworkers tell stories about Tom and his family.

By the time we come back to the meeting room, I can't think straight but I notice Tom coming in a beeline towards me. His face is giving nothing away but when we lock eyes, without asking, he grabs my hand and leads me out of the room and down a side corridor. As we walk, I can't help but notice a broken light panel and flashing light. *Creepy empty corridor, check.*

I'm about to ask if he knows where he's going when he opens the door to a small meeting room. The door creaks as he leads me in; it is eerily quiet. There are no windows but there's a lonely laptop on top of a small conference table and I can hear the hum of the air conditioner. I turn around and face him. My heart starts hammering against my chest while he's breathing fast and I wait, hoping he has a good explanation, but he doesn't say anything.

After a few seconds, I can't hold it any longer. "Is it true? Are you a Whiteford?"

"Olivia, I am so sorry you had to find out from somebody else. I wanted to tell you."

"Why didn't you tell me?" I ask calmly. "You had a lot of opportunities to come clean, we've been seeing each other for months now. *Months.* I mean, wow. Apparently, you're higher ed royalty."

"I'm not."

"Well, everybody knows your family. Everywhere we go people are telling stories about *your* parents and *your* grandparents. Don't you think that was something you needed to share?"

"Olivia..."

"What, Tom? What?" I move my hands.

"Calm down."

"Don't tell me to calm down." I point at him. "*You* let me assume you were a regular guy."

"I am a regular guy!"

"No. You're not. At all!"

"Why are you freaking out!?"

"Because I can't believe I'm in this position. I trusted you!"

"I didn't mean to break your trust. I was trying to protect my fam—"

"Oh my God, I'm so fucking stupid," I whisper almost to myself and stop moving. I drop my head for a few seconds, then look at him. "This is why you can call anybody on campus and they always answer."

"Olivia—"

"You knew she was retiring in the spring. Didn't you?"

"Does it matter?"

"Cut the bullshit. Did you know?" I repeat sharply, raising my voice higher than I intended to, my body tensing while I try to control my shallow breaths.

"Yes."

Wow. "Was Judith's position offered to you? Is that why they transferred you so quickly?"

He's shaking his head. "Are you fucking kidding me right now?" He pauses and I can see the wheels turning behind his green eyes. I can't help but wonder if he's coming up with a story.

Unexpectedly, my chin wobbles and I fight back tears and the sobs trapped in my throat.

"It wasn't offered to me but it was mentioned as something that would become available eventually." He pauses. "You know what? To be honest, I don't give a shit. I moved back because I wanted to come home and be with my family. You know this. Right now, I couldn't care less about Judith or being director."

His words from lunch months ago come slamming back to me. "What about campus domination and a hostile takeover? I thought you were kidding!" He doesn't answer and my stomach twists. "Wow. Everything I've worked for— does it really matter? Does anything matter? I mean... You know what, never mind. I don't care. This is bullshit."

"Honestly? Who gives a shit what my last name is?" he says running a hand through his hair.

"It's not about your last name, it's the lie." When he doesn't answer, I go back to pacing back and forth. He takes a step toward me and I stop.

"Olivia..." He's so close, I can feel the tension bouncing off of him and while my body wants nothing more than to hug him and tell him we can work this out, my brain cannot comprehend how this went south so fast.

A tap on the door interrupts us and we both turn towards it. Somebody in a suit opens the door and tells us he has a meeting and needs the room. Tom tells him to give us a minute and turns to me. "Please, let me explain."

"You know what, Thomas, I think I've said everything I needed to say." Even though he looks as miserable as I feel, I walk away before he protests. I sneak back to the meeting room as people settle in. From the corner of my eye, I see him take his seat and for the next four hours, we pretend we're not trying to look at each other. At last, the meeting finishes and I tell Sandra and Ralph I have a previous commitment and we exit the room quickly.

This meeting sucked.

Olivia

I feel like an idiot for having feelings for somebody I now realize I barely know. I know the sex is great, but we haven't been on a date... which is depressing now that I think about it. After my last relationship ended in disaster, I didn't realize I could feel this way about somebody so soon, or at all. The truth is, I've built a wall, carefully constructed around my heart. It keeps me warm and safe. Tom has rammed into the wall and cracks have formed. Now what do I do? Do I keep the wall, patch it up, or let Tom knock it down?

To top it off, the weather sucks. It's been raining all weekend, which is ironic because I feel gloomy and gray. I'm sad, confused and angry. I turn off the phone and park my car in the garage. In Miami nobody uses their garages; with a bit of luck, nobody will bother me. All I want is to be left alone.

This weekend has been a disaster. I wake up in the morning with Tom in my head then tell myself, "I should stop thinking about him. He probably doesn't care for me and I shouldn't either," which leads me to more thinking. Sunday is a repetition of Saturday. I debate this whole thing in my head repeatedly.

What the fuck was I thinking, getting involved with a co-worker? At this point, I don't know what's worse; that he lied or that I have feelings for him and now he might become my boss. Actually, I think the absolute *worst* thing is everybody in the office will think I'm either a loser or a gold digger. *This is literally the stuff of nightmares.*

After a depressing weekend, involving wine and lots and lots of ice cream, I arrive on campus. I've resigned myself to the fact that everybody's going to talk about it. Not even when I put on a cute outfit, and spend extra time on my hair, do I feel better. I also try to hide my red and puffy eyes under makeup. *Lots and lots of makeup.* I'm trying to look and act normal, at least on the outside.

As I walk through the parking lot it occurs to me that, even though work is the last place I want to be, I know seeing my students will get my mind off things. I am a professional and I have a job to do. Besides, department directors must be tough sometimes. This is just a minor setback. I will focus on the students and everything will be fine. I just have to keep telling myself that. *Everything will be fine. Everything will be fine.*

Except as I approach our office, I notice a group of advisors and student assistants huddled together. *Shit. Shit. Shit.*

My resolve shatters and I start having heart palpitations. I shouldn't have had breakfast. I take a deep breath and focus on staying Zen. To die of a heart attack in front of my coworkers is not part of the itinerary. *At least not today.*

At that second, I realize Tom's in the group and everyone is looking at him. When he notices me, he stops talking, and they all turn and stare at me. *Deep breath.* I say good morning to the group and he returns it, as do most of them. I walk straight past them in what seems slow motion and head straight for my office. *That went* okay, *now all I have to do is stay at my desk all day and completely avoid everybody. Piece of cake.* Too bad that will not happen because a few minutes later he's at my door with a soft knock. "Hi, can we talk?" he asks with a low voice.

"I am *super* busy. Maybe another time."

Ignoring me, he comes in, closes the door, and grips the back of the chair that sits front of my desk. "You didn't give me time to explain. Please hear me out."

"You don't have to explain. Don't worry about it, it's fine. You're entitled to your privacy and to decide how much of your private life to share with strangers. It's a secret fling, remember? No harm done." I try to focus on the computer through moist eyes and even manage to open an email.

"Come on. We're not strangers."

"Thomas, it's fine."

"It's not fine. Please call me Tom."

He's not going to make it easy. Is he? "Can you please leave?" I blurt.

"Olivia, I'm about to lose my shit. I'm hanging on by a thread. Can you please look at me for one second?" He sounds desperate and I want to look at him but avoid it.

"I can't. Do you have any idea how difficult this is? It took everything in me to come to work and I cannot do this right now." Once again, my eyes sting and it takes all my willpower to not burst into tears. When I finally look at him, our eyes lock.

For the first time I notice his dark eyes and gloomy expression and despite myself wonder if *he's* okay. After a couple of seconds and what appears to be an internal battle, he bows his head and says, "Okay," before he walks out. After Tom leaves, I take a few minutes to compose myself and will myself to go pick up my first student.

I don't think many of us in the office realized the connection between Tom and his parents. We know who they are, obviously, but our team is relatively young and most of us have not worked with his parents or on the downtown campus. *Except for Judith.*

I walk to the front and notice advisors going in and out of each others' offices. Office environments tend to be loud and ours is no exception. Have I mentioned this is Miami? Loud advisors in offices and cubicles, holding in-person conversations and even louder phone conversations. Phones that never stop ringing. Student assistants answering phone questions and chatting among themselves in cubicles. People talking and holding conversations in English, Spanish *and* Spanglish. Students and non-students in and out, all day, every day, all normal, except today the phones are barely ringing and people are quiet.

What are the odds that they're all talking and investigating?

I greet Erick at the front counter. He's handsome as always and as polite as ever and greets me warmly. "Hi, Miss Olivia," he says as we walk towards my office. "How's your semester going?" He pauses as we reach my door because it only takes him a second to read me. His eyebrows dip and he glances around uneasily. "Are you okay?"

I force myself to go through the motions. I can't share with my student that my heart is broken, so I keep it together and smile. "I'm good. So, how are your classes?"

He says nothing until he clears his throat, "I'm doing great. So far, I have As in all of my classes. I wanted to talk to you about my major. I've decided to keep my major in Finance with a double minor in Creative Writing and Theater. I thought about it and like math a tiny bit more."

"Do you think you'll have the time to do all three?"

"Yeah, I think so. I mean, if you help me plan it, I can do it," he says. *Wow.* I can't believe he made up his mind. He continues. "Before I met you, I didn't think it was possible to combine that many things but now I feel like I'm leaving here with so much more than I had anticipated. Like I'm thinking about internships in theaters, both backstage and front stage and I'm excited to see what turns up."

I want to do a happy dance like Snoopy. It's like I showed him the map and he picked the road. It's an amazing feeling. "I'm so happy for you. It's going to work out so great," I tell him. We talk about the classes he should take and plan for his last two semesters, then I clear his hold and walk him out. At the last minute, he turns and gives me a quick hug.

All morning I repeat the process with other students. For some students this might be their last appointment with me, as many of them will graduate in the spring. Several make comments about how excited they are to graduate and thank me for helping them these last years. It's heartwarming but it's also bittersweet as I know I'm not going to see some of them again.

Although I'm not hungry at all, during lunchtime, I try to leave as quickly as I can. I go through a side door and try to avoid as many people as possible while en route to lunch with my friends. Bianca offers to drive and I'm thankful I don't have to. When we finally make it to an off-campus restaurant, it only takes a nanosecond before the conversation turns to Tom Williams, aka Thomas Whiteford. Rich, handsome, higher ed royalty. Everybody at the campus has heard, my friends included.

"Are you okay?" Nicole asks, her eyebrows dipping in the middle. "We called you several times this weekend."

"Yeah, I'm okay. Except for the fact I'm a loser, I'm great," I moan.

"You are *not* a loser," she says tenderly and touches my forearm.

I place my hand on top of hers. I can't help but look at all of them. "I am. First with Brandon, we bought a house. *A house.* I thought we were good, but instead, I got dumped and cheated on. On my *birthday.* Who gets *that* for their birthday? Now I'm older, still single, still broke, *not* wiser nor married. Aren't we supposed to be better off as we get older?"

"What's with the defeatist attitude? What happened to positive thinking?" Bianca responds, looking at me and frowning. "Come on, have faith. It's all going to work out." She pauses for a moment. "And you are not a loser. You have a career and a job that you're really good at and hundreds of students that love you and appreciate you. Not to mention a beautiful home. So what if you have debt? Tons of people do, plus now you have a roommate. When Leyla moves in, you'll be much better off," she adds.

They make it sound so simple. "You know, I was thinking. I know I'm the same person whether or not I have a boyfriend, but I feel defeated. Now that I think about it, maybe the problem is men are not compatible with me."

"Are you crazy?"

"Look at Brandon *and* Tom. How is that for compatibility?"

"You can't compare the two. Tom's a gentleman... Bran, I mean, he's not a bad guy, but he was an idiot for cheating on you while you guys were living together. If he didn't want to be with you, he should have said something before you bought a house. But that has nothing to do with compatibility."

Speaking for the first time, Valentina narrows her eyes and jumps into the conversation. "Wait, a gentleman who *lies?*" I shoot her a glance. *Not helping.*

"So much for a secret fling. What are people saying? That I'm clueless or that I'm a loser?"

"Nobody's saying that. I'm sure a few of the oldies knew and while it did surprise others, I think it's mostly because he managed to keep it quiet all this time. Honestly, nobody cares." Bianca offers.

"My family already thinks I'm a loser because I'm not married with kids. What's a few thousands more?"

Bianca whips her head to me. "Will you please stop that?"

"Have you spoken to him at all?" Nicole asks as she takes a bite.

"No, not really. He left me alone over the weekend but today he tried talking to me, said he wanted to explain."

"There's nothing to explain, he's a liar. *Un mentiroso,.*" Valentina states.

"You're not helping," Bianca says, shooting her a look.

Valentina doesn't seem convinced and keeps going. "Regardless of the reasons, it doesn't matter. Why would you want to be with somebody that lies about who he is?"

"Valentina, we don't know his reasons. Don't you think people deserve second chances?"

"Why would you give him a second chance? So that he can do it again?!" Val asks, narrowing her eyes at Bianca.

"Why not? Do you want to be alone for the rest of your life and never give people a chance?"

Great. While I'm breaking down these two go back and forth with a moral debate.

Nicole glances at me, then turns at them as they go at it, "Stop. Stop. *Enough!*" She says the last word more forcefully and louder, and because she never raises her voice, both Bianca and Valentina stop and stare at her. As do several patrons around us. "You know what? It doesn't matter. They are not the same person. Olivia, you should hear him out. Regardless, you're not a loser. And who cares what his last name is if you guys love each other?"

I know she's right, but I'm heartbroken and I can't help but feel defeated, "I don't know if we love each other. We haven't even been on a first date and the worst thing is, we were having a secret fling and now because of who he is, everybody on all three campuses and the greater Miami area will hear about it and probably think I'm a gold digger. *Ugh.*"

"I'm sorry to break it to you but your secret romance is no longer secret," Valentina announces as I bury my hands in my face and shake my head groaning. "A bunch of people saw you two holding hands at the workshop, and then you disappeared into a room? Or something?"

A room? I raise my head and look at her through my fingers, "For the record, it was a meeting room, not *a room.*" After a few seconds, I lower my hands. "I can't believe this is happening. That's just what I need. My private life on public display. How long do you think before HR gets involved?" I ask Nicole as she takes a sip of her drink.

"I don't know... maybe nobody will say anything."

I wish I could believe that. "Come on, this is gossip central. Somebody will say something, HR will hear and they'll fire me. Give it a week."

"Maybe. Or maybe, nobody will say anything because they want to be on Tom's good side," Nicole replies, always the logical one. "Look, if they throw you under the bus, they'll throw him under the bus too." She pauses. "But just in case, you need to talk to HR. The sooner the better."

Valentina looks thoughtful, then adds, "On that note, how many women will learn who his parents are and try to seduce him?"

What?! Oh God. My lunch threatens to come out and acid fills my mouth.

"Oh my God. What is wrong with you? Why would you say that?" Bianca gasps, throwing a napkin her way.

The napkin flies back towards Bianca while Valentina shrugs and makes a face. "What? I'm just saying."

At this I can't help but feel double sucker-punched. "You know what? It's fine. He's single. He can do whatever he wants." I'm trying to sound casual, but the reality is I'm nauseated at the thought of Tom being with someone else.

An hour later I'm back in the office. I settle in and start advising, the one thing I *can* control. "Hi Lidia, how are you?" I ask to the student in front of me. "How's the semester going?"

"I'm good and you?"

"I'm okay," I reply as I input her student number in our system. "How's the teaching class? Do you like it?" I ask keenly. She wants to be a teacher; I really hope she liked the class.

"Can I be honest?"

Or maybe not. Here we go. "Yeah. Of course."

"I hate it. I'm in it right now, and we have to do hours in a nearby school and I don't think I can be a teacher. Too many responsibilities. The kids are brats and the parents are annoying."

"Sooo, what do you want to do now?"

"I don't know. I thought I wanted to be a teacher, but now I know that's not for me."

"Well, at least you found out now and not after graduation–Hey, you work in a hotel, right?" She nods. My wheels are turning, I vaguely remember her mentioning that in one of our meetings, so I follow that line of thought. "Do you want to try the Intro to Hospitality class? If you like it, you could major in Hospitality instead."

I can see *her* wheels turning; she's nodding and her smile spreads, which is always a good sign. "I actually like that idea." We talk about the classes a few minutes more and I send her off to do her meticulous professor' research and register. Before she leaves she gives me a hug, and even though my love life is a disaster, at least I can take comfort in the fact that I am good at my job and my students still like me.

Olivia

_M_y phone won't stop beeping, ringing or vibrating. *So much for a secret fling.*

Several people from the conference saw us leave *the room* and now everybody on the campus wants to talk to me. How did they all find my number? I'm going to murder whoever shared it. *The next person to ask if Tom and I are dating is also going to get shot.*

Where are people getting information from? I can't picture Tom having heart-to-hearts with random coworkers. This gossiping is not good for my future job opportunities. I make a mental note to ask one of my friends to investigate who is spreading information. *Actually, Andrea's a great detective.*

Next, find a way to *somehow* control the gossip. Also, find out if I need a publicist and how much they cost.

It occurs to me that, I started the year great, with a boyfriend and a new house... then I got cheated on and dumped on my birthday. At this rate, it looks like I'll be ending the year depressed and homeless. I hope it's not a sign of how next year's going to go. There should be a limit to the number of horrible years you can have consecutively.

I managed to avoid Tom for a week and thankfully, he didn't push it but I have a feeling today he wants to get into it. This is the worst time ever to try to have a conversation. It's the first week of registration and the office has gone wild. Students at the college level have sort of a herd mentality. They all show up on the same day, at the same time to get advisement so they can all register together. Don't ask me how that happens, but every semester it does. The wait to see an advisor is two hours. Students are upset, computers are slow, and all hell is breaking loose.

Tom walks by my office a few times through the morning, and I keep ignoring him to the point *I'm* starting to feel bad. *Today out of all days he wants to talk?* Luckily, my office has been full of students the whole morning. I'm so busy that I don't have time to eat lunch and with my sugar running low, I'm about to explode. *Side note, find out if I'm hypoglycemic or diabetic.*

I'm at the copy machine, printing a student's ten-page appeal form, and have a fifteen-minute break before the next student. *Enough time to make a run for the vending machines.* Food is the only thing on my mind when Jackson, one of the student assistants, tells me Leo's back. I start to protest because I can't deal with Leo either. Thankfully, he tells me he'll take care of it.

I see Tom walking towards me and will the machine to print faster. When we lock eyes, I swiftly turn back to my office and avoid him... *again*. Too bad once I'm back at my office, my stomach growls. *Ack. I need food.*

After I sign the forms and the student leaves, I try again to make a run for the vending machines.

I'm only a few feet away from a side door when Tom appears and unexpectedly grabs me by the elbow and leads me *away* from the door. "What are you doing?! Let me go!" I whisper manically as marches me down the hallway towards the back of the office. I try getting out of his hold, but he switches hands and grips my waist *and* my elbow. *Crap.* I don't want to make a scene at work, but at the same time I can't help myself because I literally want to kill him. "What the hell are you doing?!" I hiss. He's exuding calm and confidence; it's pissing me off more.

"I'm saving you from yourself. You need to eat."

"How do you even know that?" I ask quickly.

"I've been watching you."

I turn to him and gasp. "Watching me or stalking me?"

"Do you really want to know?" I narrow my eyes but when I don't answer he keeps going. "I had to jump in before you said something stupid to a student or one of the student assistants and damaged them for life." Most advisors are too busy to notice us, but others are raising their heads as we walk by their offices. *Shit.*

"Damage them for life? What are they, five? I'm sure they can take it," I say indignantly as we walk.

"I'm sure they can, but you're not usually like this. They'll be hurt because they really like you."

I glance at him. "This is so typical of a guy, taking over the situation. Saving the damsel in distress. I'm not in distress. It's annoying."

"I think you mean *charming.*"

I can't help but scoff. "No. I definitely mean annoying." His lips turn up as we walk and I want to smack the smile off his lips.

"I don't think Judith would agree with you. Didn't we just have a training about customer service?"

I roll my eyes. "Whatever."

"I'll take care of Leo. You will eat something then we'll talk."

"Hey, you're not my boss... *yet.* Don't tell me what to do." I shake my head at him. *The nerve!*

He ignores me and keeps talking. "Lucy cleared you half an hour so that you can eat and avoid going to jail for murder."

"Eat what exactly? I forgot my food and I now don't have any time to go anywhere. *Thank you very much.* Have you seen the line?" I say heatedly while I point back with my hand.

"Don't worry about it, I'm taking care of it."

"Why do you keep doing that? We're not together. I didn't ask you to jump in and rescue me. This is not a relationship. The ship left." As we arrive at the breakroom, he finally lets me go. When we stand by the door, I cross my arms and glare at him.

Tom pauses and looks at me. "The ship?" then he sighs. He is dead set on ignoring my verbal jabs. "Olivia, I'm not trying to rescue you. You're capable of rescuing yourself. I'm trying to keep you from going to jail...or worse, fired."

Ack. Damn those eyes.

While I think about what to say he opens the door to the breakroom. Since I don't move, he takes a step towards me and pauses, never leaving eye contact. "You're not going to make this easy, are you?" he almost whispers. Our faces are inches away from each other. I glance at his mouth and he glances at mine.

We're so close, and he smells so good and my determination's disintegrating faster than I can say *determination*. His hand moves to the small of my back and he nuzzles me inside and closes the door behind us. That's when I notice a bag on the table.

Hand on my back, he leads me to a chair. I sit down and cross my arms while he picks up the bag and plastic cutlery, pushing them in front of me. When I don't grab the cutlery or move from my spot, he empties the containers out. "Fine. Here's some pasta, there's bread and a Tiramisu *and* a cheese-cake *and* a drink." He looks at me and pauses, "Start eating."

Why did that sound like an order? Gah! Fuck his orders. Be mad, very mad.

Against my will, my face softens. He notices and tries to hold a grin, then he bends down and puts his face so close to mine I can feel his breath. I focus hard on his eyes and try not to look at his mouth again as he speaks in his sexy-humming voice. "You can thank me later, now start eating, *please.*" He walks away and closes the door behind him.

Twenty minutes later, I feel much, much better. *Thank God for carbs.*

Tom's returns after giving me a chance to become human again. He has a water bottle in hand and pulls a nearby chair. He straddles it and smiles at me, "How were the tiramisu and the cheesecake?"

That smug face. It's both infuriating and charming. "How did you know I would eat both?"

"I pay attention. Plus, you were hungry." He winks while taking a slug of water.

"Conceited much?"

His smile forms slowly and he shakes his head. "You're mad. I get it, but we have less than ten minutes to work this out." He reminds me of an attorney who's going to offer a plea bargain.

"Here we go. What exactly are we working out?" I'm both pissed off and semi-intrigued while I interlock my fingers and put my hands on my lap.

"The terms of your surrender," he announces.

I can't help but roll my eyes. "Ha. *My* surrender? Sure, whatever you say, Mr. Hyde." I pause. "Tom, I'm sorry to break this to you, but you're a control freak."

"O-kay." He pauses. "It's interesting that *you're* saying that, because ever since I've met you I actually feel that I have no control over anything. Do you have any idea what that feels like?"

The comment makes me pause, but I press on. "Did you honestly think I wouldn't find out?"

"I figured you would at some point, but *I* wanted to be the one to tell you."

"Right. How's that working out for you?" Tom closes his eyes. "Next time, instead of going trying to control everything, try the opposite of that, go with the flow, or even better, maybe try being honest."

"Yeah. I don't think so. The *flow*, is a PR disaster waiting to happen and media camping outside of your parents' house because everybody knows who your family is and where to find them. Or maybe picture this, your parents being VPs of a university and every decision, good or bad, potentially a PR disaster waiting to happen, causing media to camp outside of your house... *again*." He sighs. "Look, I know you're mad at me, and I'm sorry. I didn't mean for you to find out like that, but technically, I didn't lie about my last name. I just wasn't about to advertise who my parents are. They are recently semi-retired. They finally have peace. I honestly thought it was going to come out my first week here or something, and when it didn't, I liked the anonymity. Besides, it's higher ed. Everybody and their grandmother has an idea for a program. Nobody ever wonders who will pay for it." He pauses. "I know I should have been honest from the beginning, but I didn't tell you because I didn't want to screw it up. It was *just* a misunderstanding."

"Wow. The big reveal. And now every single girl on campus wants to date you because you're a handsome, *wealthy*, higher ed prince with green eyes," I say before I can stop myself.

"Hey, be nice. Let's be honest, nobody would expect me, or even you, to start a new job and spill your entire life to people you've just met. That's just not normal or professional. I've known you for months, and you *still* have walls up." Emerald eyes stare at me.

"Okay, fine. I take it back." Deep breath. "First of all, I'm sorry about your dad. I heard that he died in a car accident. I guess I assumed your stepdad was your dad."

I grab his hand and squeeze gently for a few silent seconds. Then I let go.

"Thank you, Olivia. It was a long time ago." There's sadness in his voice and he pauses for a second. "I barely remember my dad. At the same time, we got lucky. My stepdad raised us like his own and he always had my back. He's awesome."

"Look, Tom, to be honest, I don't care what your last name is. I'm more concerned about you lying to me. That's not how a relationship is supposed to work. Not to mention, how is this whole thing it's going to affect *my* career and my reputation?" I am also worried that our relationship is not a relationship, but I need not share that right now. *One thing at a time.*

As if reading my mind he says, "I wasn't lying. My last name is Williams. I don't think you should be worried. Have you met my parents? I've worked hard to prove myself and by no means are jobs handed to me or guaranteed in any way just because they're related to me," he sighs and when he looks at me, he says, "Come on, meet me halfway. How about a truce? I think you're pretty cool and I like you. I'd like to work on the ship," he says with a curved smile.

Are we talking friend-*ship* or relation-*ship*? *Hmmm.*

"Fine. Let's work on the ship." He extends a hand, which I take with trepidation. As my hand slides into his warm fingers, a smile forms on his lips and I fight the urge to smile back. "Friends?" When I say this, his mouth opens but he doesn't say anything.

He never lets go of my hand and the connection does weird things to me. I can feel the sparks between us.

After a few silent moments, he lets me go. We clean up and head back to the offices. "Let's talk about Leo," he says as we walk.

"What about him?" I glance at him. I'm surprised by the sudden turn in conversation.

"I just met with him, but he wanted to know if *you* were available. I offered suggestions on what to take next spring. I encouraged him to try registering on his own, but he said he would come back to see you. He said he needed a letter of recommendation for a job. I went through your notes and in the last five months, he's been here seven times. That's more than once a month, including one for a recommendation for an internship… while on summer break? Don't you think that's excessive?"

I glance at him and my eyebrows raise on their own. "Are we seriously having this conversation?"

"Yeah. This is Academic Advisement, not Student Life. Students only come because they *have to.* They need to be cleared to register, don't know what to register for or have a major issue with a class or a professor," he says, pointing out at each with his fingers, "Otherwise, none would come. I think you know this."

"So, he's a little needy lately. As his advisor it's my job to support him—."

He doesn't let me finish. When he stops walking, I pause in the middle of the hallway. "A little needy? You need to have a serious talk with him."

"Fine. I'll talk to him again." I almost want to roll my eyes, but I don't. Instead, I start walking away and he follows.

"If you want, we'll do it together. I think a male advisor would be better for him. You might need to cut him loose."

When we arrive at my office, I raise up a hand. "Wait, wait, cut him loose? Hang on, just because we're on speaking terms doesn't give you the right to tell me how to do my job."

"I'm not telling you how to do your job. As your *friend*, I'm pointing something out you might have missed. I know you want to help every student and see them succeed, but you've lost perspective."

"What?! Tom, I don't remember asking for your advice and—."

He stops me by raising his hand and shoving an open palm in front of me. "We're not getting anywhere by arguing, and we've seen how you get when you're mad," and renders me speechless with the intensity of his eyes. He lowers his voice a whisper and addresses me. "Will you at least promise you will look through *your* notes, you will *try* to be objective, *then* talk to him?"

I take a deep breath and nod. "Okay." Seemingly pleased with my answer, he shoots me a sexy grin that makes my heart go wild, then slowly backs away and out of my office.

As I settle back on my desk, I think about a new resolution: stay away from him and focus on my career. Actually, that's my old resolution, but still, this will never workout. I will go back to my original plan of Zen and keep calm as a cucumber, ignore him and control my physical impulses. I know what you're thinking, it's too late for that, but if I want to be the director, I must keep my distance and keep it one-hundred percent professional.

Olivia

A few days later, the lines are finally going down, students are registering and classes are filling up. Tom and I are *sort* of speaking and things are looking up. Positive thinking, right?

It's the end of November and there's a storm. *First a hurricane and now a storm?* Whoever thinks climate change is a hoax should have a lobotomy. Since I'm not in the habit of carrying an umbrella in winter aka *dry season*, I get soaked. Thanks to my wet dog episode, I wake up sneezing.

It's mid-morning by the time we all start arriving at the conference room for a staff meeting. Even though I took cold *and* allergy medicine, for some reason I can't stop sneezing.

Damn, I should have Googled *ways to stop sneezing* before the meeting started. *I wonder if there's an app for that.*

General discussions are being shared on office issues, advising, and registration numbers. Staffing updates are followed by the great debate: appointments or walk-ins?

Why does it seem like we talk about this every month? Some advisors rather see students, *by appointments only*, as this gives them complete control of their schedule. Other advisors like *walk-ins*, and others a combination of both. At the end of the day, we're here to help whoever needs us but I will say, there's something magical about a college student walking into your office and you have nooo idea what their problem will be or what will fly out of their mouth. It's both exhilarating and terrifying.

Unfortunately, Judith keeps looking at me as I keep going "aaa-choo." *Every. Second.* I know it's very distracting, but I can't stop it. From time to time, I glance over at Tom across the table. His gaze is fixed on me too. When it's my turn to give details on a form we've updated and implemented and share students' opinion on said form, I try to hold a sneeze. Instead of going "aaa-choo" it sounds more like "aaa-chi-choo," like I have a squeaky toy in my throat. It's both mortifying and hilarious and a few of my coworkers giggle and chuckle.

Tom keeps looking at me with brows furrowed.

To wrap up the meeting, Judith gives us an update on our assistant director. "As you guys know, Grace has been forced to take maternity leave sooner than we thought due to medical issues. She's doing okay but because of this, we need a couple of volunteers to take over the Academic Success Fair she was working on."

Ummm, if I want to be the director I should take the lead, right? Show initiative?

I raise up a hand and Judith smiles. "Thanks, Olivia." A second later Tom also raises a hand. After the meeting's over Judith hands us a folder with information about the Academic Success Fair. Grace had selected a date and location for March. She had also compiled a list of departments and companies that have been involved in the past. All we have to do is fill it up with students. Well not all, but mostly.

Afterward, Tom follows me to my office. He has a mug of hot tea and without asking, places it on my desk. "Here. This will help," he says. After I've thanked him, I take a sip. The warm liquid helps my throat, and I've never been more grateful to anybody for bringing me tea. After a few seconds, he leaves.

I see only *one* student. When he looked at me like I had the plague, or at the very least a huge mole on my face, I figured it was time to go home. I skip lunch and go straight to bed.

It's early evening when hunger wakes me up. My clothes are wrinkled, my hair is a mess and my face has a line right through my cheek, but honestly, I'm too congested to care. I stand in the kitchen and look at leftovers in the fridge, then glance at my microwave. *What are the chances of the microwave exploding?* A knock on my door distracts me from imagining the scenarios.

I walk over to the door. *Tom.* He's dressed in jeans and a fitted long-sleeve gray t-shirt and looks handsome and fresh. He's also holding a Styrofoam container.

"What are you doing here?" I ask. *Ummm, my voice sounds like a monster.*

He raises an eyebrow, and I pinch my lips. "I was in the neighborhood. You sound funny. Are you feeling okay?" he asks.

"Ugh." I can't help but roll my eyes, then move away from the door and he follows me in. "What do you have there?" I ask as I plop on my couch and hug a pillow.

"I got you chicken soup." He carries the container to the kitchen and after opening a couple of cabinets at random, finds a bowl, then a spoon.

"You came to bring me soup?"

"Yep." He sits next to me, then carefully places the bowl on the coffee table.

"Why? And when did you have time? Are you sure you have time for me?"

I go back and forth between glancing at him and at the bowl as he slowly moves the spoon in circles inside of it, in an attempt to cool down the soup. He glances at me. "Are you always sarcastic when you're sick? I'll have to remember that for future reference."

My brain's a little fuzzy and my head hurts when I talk, but I push through it. "You won't get to see me like this again. From now on, this is a strictly professional relationship. No more funny business outside of work. We cannot do this. I'm jumping ship," I say.

"What happened to the secret fling that we have going on? At the very least, I thought we were friends."

"Both are up for debate."

"I'm your neighbor," he states.

"No, you're not."

"Yes, I am. I live on the same block." He pauses. "Are you mad at me or something?"

"Maybe."

"What did I do now?"

"Do you think there's a way, just for one day, you can be less handsome?"

He smiles, bows, and shakes his head before looking at me, "You think I'm handsome yet you're mad at me?"

"NO! I don't think you're handsome." I pause. "Maybe. Your eyes are. I don't know."

His arm raises and he presses the middle of my forehead with his index finger. "Stop thinking."

"I can't."

"Try." He lowers his arm and turns back to the bowl. "Let's start again. Olivia, my brief attention span has been directed toward a single person who I'm trying, very unsuccessfully I might add, to convince to have a relationship with me."

"What are you doing?" I ask as he balances the soup bowl in front of him.

"Feeding you. You're sick."

"Why are you being nice to me?"

"Come on. Isn't it obvious by now? I'm crazy about you and you're hot for me too." He grins at me.

"Sure I am."

"At the very least, you can't deny the sex's pretty good." He winks.

"Oh, my God. Conceited much?" I ask, then take the hot bowl carefully from him. "I'll feed myself. Thanks."

At this, he laughs out loud. "See that right there? Where else am I going to find somebody that doesn't care about my feelings?"

"I care about your feelings... most of the time."

"I know you do."

"I'm sick."

"I know you are."

After a few more spoonfuls, I ask, "Why did you volunteer for the fair today? Are you trying to make a play for director?"

He shakes his head. "Not really. I wanted to be with you and help you."

"Help me or spy on me?"

"You've been avoiding me lately, how else I'm I going to spend time with you?"

"I don't know how to respond to that."

"Then don't, you don't have to." After I finish the soup and put it on a nearby table, he offers a hand. "Come on, grumpy."

"I'm not grumpy," I answer as I stand and he grins. He stops and wraps his arms around me and my head rests on his chest. I hug him back and take a deep breath. My head finds his neck and I instantly relax and breathe him in. "Mmm, this is nice."

"I agree. It's nice for me too." After we embrace for a few minutes, I take a step back and look up at him. He holds my chin and we lock eyes. "I like you, Olivia. Please don't shut me out." The sincerity in his eyes renders me speechless and all I can do is nod. "I'm going to give you space, but I'm not giving up. I want to give this a try. I'm trying to go with the flow because I think we have something special. Okay?" I nod again and he grabs my hand and leads me to my room. "Come on, let's get you out of those clothes. You're about to break a record for most wrinkles in an outfit."

"Didn't I just say no funny business?"

"Who said anything about funny business?" Once in my room, he helps me undress. He's a gentleman and tucks me in, then walks out of the room. He returns with a glass of water, a bottle of aspirin and cold medicine and puts them on the nightstand. "I have to make a few calls, but I'll be right outside. I'll come back and check on you later. Okay?" he says, squatting beside me.

I nod. After a few seconds, he rests his forehead on mine and then gives me a kiss on it. I sigh and watch him leave. My heart melts, right before everything goes black.

I sleep deeply and only the need to go to the bathroom wakes me up. I walk to the kitchen and find him stretched out on my sofa. He's still wearing the same clothes, but his shoes are off. I throw a blanket over him and go back to bed. When I wake up again, he's gone.

A few days later, while sitting in my office talking to Tom about the Academic Success Fair, my phone rings. *Brandon.* I tell him I can't talk and before he has a chance to say anything else, I hang up on him. *Again.* I clear my throat and keep my voice even. "Sorry. Where were we?"

Tom looks at me, but his face gives nothing away. "Was that your ex?" he asks.

"Yeah, we're having a few disagreements. He's dead-set on making me sell my house."

"And why does he think you're going to do that?"

"Because we bought it while we were together but when it came time to sign documents, we agreed it would be best if it was under my name for tax purposes because he already owned a house and I didn't. We also got a better loan because my credit was better. Besides, I ended up giving most of the down payment, but then he cheated and we broke up."

"So technically, it's your house."

"Yes, but he has proof of payment for things he bought for the remodeling. He's also claiming the realtor will be his witness and vouch for him. Basically, he wants to use those things to force me to court. He wants to sue me for *unjust enrichment.*"

"Do you need a lawyer? My roommate Keith's a lawyer," he says.

"I do need one. Thank you." He nods.

We talk a little more about the fair and when he leaves, I walk to the front and call Kevin, my flirty student. I really hope he's come to his senses and *finally* auditions for the music program. I'm pretty sure he'll get in *if* he auditions. Today, however, I'm prepared to convince him.

"Hi, Miss Olivia, how are you?" he asks as we walk to my office. As he sits in front of me, he gives me a bright smile and I can see the charm being turned on. Not a second later, "You look great today, as always." *Here we go.*

"Thank you, Kevin," I reply, trying to sound casual. Less than a minute later, Valentina knocks on my door. This is my idea of an academic intervention. "This is my friend Valentina. She's the music department's coordinator and advisor. She was a music major herself and I thought it would be a good idea if you two talked and got to know each other." He cocks his head and has a perplexed look.

Annnd cue awkward silence and the crickets.

"Sooo I'm going to leave you here... with her... and I'll be back." He says nothing as I walk out, but before I close the door, I turn to see Valentina sitting in my chair. *She's got this.*

I head to the front counter where I chat with the student assistants and let them educate me on college life. While there I answer random questions from students that approach our counter. After a while, I head to the break room for coffee. Finally, on my way back to my office, I run into Tom. He stops in the middle of the hallway and addresses me. "Hi."

"Hi."

"So, here's a question I have a student who was recently hospitalized and for the past few weeks has not been going to class. Obviously, he's about to bomb the entire semester. He doesn't want the bad grades in his record and wants a partial refund. What do you think financial aid will say?" he asks.

"We're more than halfway through the semester and he wants a partial refund? At this point in the semester, it's unlikely he'll receive a refund, partial or otherwise. The best he can hope for is a complete withdrawal from classes. If he disagrees, he's welcome to take it up with the dean." *Why do I get the weird feeling Tom knows this?* I'm about to ask him when Valentina shows up and stands quietly next to us. "Tom, this is Valentina, my friend and the music department advisor. She came to help me with a student."

"Hi, I remember you from the restaurant. It's nice to see you again," he says, offering a hand.

She takes his hand. "Yeah. I remember you too. I've heard a lot about you lately."

"I'm sure you have." He glances at me, "Good things I hope."

"Some good things, others are debatable." I fight the urge to tackle Val to the floor to prevent her from talking. I imagine myself doing so while Tom stares at us, amused. *Or maybe not.*

Catching her eye, he says, "We all make mistakes. Don't you think?"

"The trick is not to repeat them," she replies evenly.

My eye twitches.

"Agreed," he replies.

Are we code talking now? I clear my throat loudly and stare at Valentina. When she looks at me, I make my eyes huge.

"Okay. Now that we've cleared that up, Olivia, he's ready to switch to music. He's going to sign up for the next audition."

I can't help but squeal in delight while Tom grins at me. "Oh my God! I can't believe you did it!"

"Well, we speak the same language. Come on." She puts her arm through my arm and pulls me away.

I hear Tom say, "Bye, friend," and I can't help but wonder if he's talking to me or her. When I look at Val, we both burst into laughter.

Olivia

The first couple of weeks in December are fairly busy on campus. Christmas decorations are up, and the campus is buzzing with holiday energy. Students are busy studying for finals, completing projects and... shopping, *I think*.

We have traffic in our office as some students are getting registered for last-minute classes before they leave for holiday break. After the semester ends, in mid-December, the students will leave and office activity will go down to a grinding-slow-depressing-halt.

Before we go on vacation, we close the office for two hours and enjoy a family lunch. It's another opportunity to talk and get *more* personal with the people we work with every day. *As if we don't know enough about each other's lives.*

Ralph being Ralph is wearing an ugly sweater. It's really ugly. At this point, I don't know which is worse, the Hawaiian shirts or the ugly Christmas sweater. I take pictures of him and send a few to Gabby. She replies with falling down laughing emojis and GIFs, because she probably finds him hilarious. I smile. They're perfect for each other.

After a few words of wisdom from our leader, we all dig in. From the corner of my eye, I see Tom in line not too far behind me, serving himself and talking to Ralph. I serve myself a plate, put it down next to an empty chair, and return to the food table where I fill yet another plate. This one is full of sugary sweets. By the time I come back with a drink, Tom's sitting in the chair next to mine. "Hi," I hear him say as I sit.

"Hi," I reply, not missing the fact that he looks relaxed and that his eyes are only directed at me. I almost feel like we're the only two people here. To be honest, the effect he has on me is alarming.

The magic only lasts until Ralph makes a joke from another table and we all burst into laughter. A fresh wave of conversation fills the space within seconds. "What are you doing for vacation?" he asks in a lower, richer, baritone voice. *That voice.* Our elbows touch, our shoulders are a centimeter apart from each other and my body perks up in attention.

Gah! Body, calm the heck down. What is wrong with you?

Regrettably, my body flat-out ignores me. I clear my throat. "I'm going to go down to the Florida Keys with my friends for a few days. I'm also going to help my sister-in-law with the kids and spend quality time with family."

"Do you like the Keys?" he asks.

"I love the Keys."

"Okay. Good to know."

I can't resist but ask, "What are you doing with your days off?"

He looks at me and his lips turn up. "You mean besides cycling?"

I can't help but grin at him. "Yeah, besides that."

"I'm going to spend quality time with my own family."

"Are you going to see the Red Shoe drop from Key West?" he asks.

The Red Shoe drop, is a tradition in Key West. A local drag queen, inside a huge red high heel, is lowered into the crowd right before midnight. Tens of thousands of people watch it drop. It's a fun and crazy time. Plus, it's warm, dry weather. Full days of sun next to the ocean are very desirable in winter. "I don't think so. We're going to the upper Keys."

"Ah, got it," he says just before Sandra pulls me away into a conversation. For the next two hours, I get no more free time with Tom. We barely talk. *Bummer.* We'll leave right after this lunch and I probably won't see him again until January. *Double bummer.*

I return to my office and start packing up. As I turn off my computer, I look up to see Tom. "Hi," he says from my door. "So, I was thinking, maybe during our break we could get together and talk about the ship?" he says as he approaches me.

"Yeah, I'd like that." He closes the distance between us and gives me a kiss on the cheek. He lingers for a tiny second and I hold my breath. After we break apart, still facing me, he takes a few steps back. "Bye, Olivia—" he says from the door.

"Bye, Tom."

It's the New Year and we're back! *Thank God.* Vacation was great and I love my family, but I was getting bored at home and to be honest, I missed my students. Not to mention, January is my birthday month.

Our office is open for business and classes start in a week, and just like that, we have lines again. It's like the internal alarm of my students switched to *vacation mode* in December. After Jan 2nd, it switched back to *class mode.* Instead of hitting the snooze button, they hit the panic button because they remember they have classes...*or worse,* they don't. After a busy morning, I grab my lunch and find a quiet place. I start eating and look up at the sound of leaves crunching.

He's here. Eeekk!!!

Raising a hand, he says *hi* as he approaches and sits next to me, straddling the backless bench. My heart wants to leap out of my chest at the sight of him. "Tom. Hi, how are you?" I answer, trying to stay cool and sound casual.

"Olivia. I'm good. Good. How are you? How was your vacation?"

"It was nice. Spent a few days at the Keys with my friends, I saw my friend Gabby get engaged to Ralph, and had some family time." I glance at him, then face forward and take another bite and chew slowly. I haven't seen or heard from Tom since December, and I don't want to miss anything he says.

His elbow and forearm rest on the table as he speaks. His other hand comes up on top of his thigh and after a few seconds, his arm slides forward and his thumb gently rubs against my lower back. My heart speeds up immediately.

"I spent a lot of time with my family too. Annoyed the hell out of me, to be honest," he says but he's smiling. I return his smile. "I'm kidding. I'm kidding. I love my family, but you know what I mean."

"Yeah, I know. I feel the same." I turn my head and look at him. I can't help but notice his green eyes and the gold specks in them. "Did you cycle?"

"I did. It was awesome."

"That's great."

"Olivia, I wanted to apologize for not reaching out. I was busy with stuff and then you weren't in town, then I was busy again."

I take a deep breath, put my fork down and turn slightly towards him. "It's fine. You don't have to apologize." I don't know what else to say without it sounding awkward.

He scans my face and stops at my mouth. After a few seconds of silence, he starts again. "I shouldn't have let all that time go by."

Before I can say anything, he raises his hand and touches my cheek with his thumb. I hold my breath. Our faces are centimeters away from each other and my eyes close on their own accord right before he kisses me passionately.

"*Wow*. You really like me, huh?" I say, grinning and looking up at him.

He doesn't smile. He's serious as he says, "You know what, I want us to be on the same page. I don't want any misunderstandings. In case there's any doubt in your mind, let me clear it out. Yeah, I like you a lot. It's time to work on the ship."

Ohmygod! Ohmygod! Eeekk!

"Got it. Very clear." I wrap my arm around his shoulder and his back. His hand hugs my waist and pulls me closer to him as he crashes down on my mouth again. When he finally lets me go, I ask, "Do you have a plan this time around or are we winging it?"

"My plan? For now, preferably in no more than..." he pauses to look at his watch. "In no more than six hours, is to go to your house, get you naked it and get you in bed. After that, yes, I have a plan."

"Wow, that's wildly specific." This time a slow smile forms on his lips before kissing me again. His fingers move from my waist to my back and he rubs. After a few seconds, he gently pulls me closer and kisses my temple. I bury my head in his neck. He wraps his arms around me, hugs me long and hard and takes a deep breath. I lose track of time. This is the moment I realize I've fallen in love with my co-worker.

Let's just say my birthday consisted of two *big* events. A public one and a private one.

The rest of January is a blur.

Olivia

This week is Valentine's Day and I'm at work. I've been thinking that Valentines should be a paid national holiday. If you have a person, you can spend all day with your person and if you don't, you can stay at home all day and avoid everybody that has a person.

I'm alone in my office, answering emails when Tom appears at my door, "Good morning." He's smiling and his eyes are bright. He looks gorgeous with black pants and a white shirt and my stomach somersaults.

"Good morning." His smile is infections.

He walks in and closes the door halfway. "Soo, do you have plans for Valentine's Day?" he asks. *Is he going to ask me out? On Valentine's Day? Eeekk!*

"No. I don't have plans yet, why?"

"I was wondering, do you want to hang out?"

Hangout?

Before I answer, Jackson, our student assistant, sticks his head around my door and tells Tom his next appointment is here. He turns back with an "Okay," then returns his attention to me. "Hold that thought. I'll be back. This conversation is not over."

Except it is. Sigh.

Since I technically don't have a boyfriend on Valentine's Day and my secret lover hasn't shared any concrete plans for said holiday, I decide I'll celebrate with my friends and I'll spend as much time as I can with them.

To start the week, we go to a restaurant near the university. After we order, we all attack the bread. I pick up a warm piece and can't help but hum at how good it is. *Why is it that carbs always make everything better?*

I take a deep breath and look at my friends. "I got an invoice from Brandon today."

They pause to look at me. "An invoice? For what?" Bianca asks.

"Not an invoice, per se, more like a detailed Excel document breaking down what *he* spent."

"How much was it?" she asks, then keeps chewing bread.

"According to him? Thirty thousand dollars." Hearing the sum, causes Valentina to sputter her drink. Her eyes water, and she starts a coughing fit.

"Oh my God," I blurt. I gently tap her back as she dabs her eyes and takes a deep breath, "Are you okay?"

"Yeah. Yeah. I'm good. I'm good," she coughs. "Let me ask you, did he lose his mind along with the money? He wants you to give him that much? Please tell me that's a joke."

"I don't think so. At the same time, I put most of the down payment and bought most of the materials for the remodel. I'm guessing thirty thousand dollars was the total spent on everything, not what *he* spent. He probably put in ten of that."

"What are you going to do?"

"For now, nothing. Legally the title of the house is under my name, so there's nothing he can do. To be honest, I'm hoping he'll tire of asking or makes money somewhere else. With any luck, he'll forget about my house and leave me alone." When

I say this, I notice Bianca raises her head, then goes back to her food.

"And if he doesn't?" Valentina asks.

"I don't know. I'm more focused on Tom. I couldn't care less what Brandon wants *or* needs."

"How is our friend Tom?" she asks playfully. When I shake my head, we smile at each other.

"He wants to go out on Valentine's Day. We'll see how it goes."

Hmmm. Bianca's been unusually quiet today. Shouldn't she be giving me dating advice or talking about the expiration date of ovaries? "Bianca? Are you okay? Anything on your mind?"

"I'm thinking."

As Valentina sips her Coke, she's looking at Bianca through long eyelashes. After a few seconds, she puts the soda down. "You've been thinking since we got here. You keep doing that weird thing with your breath, like you're a *telenovela* actress. Whatever it is, just say it."

"Maybe I don't want to share it."

"Too late, now you have to."

"Fine. Bran proposed to his girlfriend. They're planning a wedding with two-hundred and fifty people in West Palm."

I feel the wind get knocked out of me. I know that we have nothing anymore but it's barely been a year. Am I that replaceable? Not to mention, he's a cheater. *She wants to marry a cheater? Come on!*

Valentina goes red and has a murderous look on her face, "Oh my God. That son of a b—" but she doesn't finish her sentence because Bianca interrupts her.

"Valentina, no need to insult his mother, who's a kind and thoughtful person."

"Who does that? Who marries a cheater? Is that a thing?" Valentina says starting at Bianca.

Bianca looks pensive as she answers. "I don't know if that's a thing. I don't think it is."

Finally, I regain my speech, "Oh my God, are you serious?"

"You should sue him for emotional distress or something," Valentina says, now focused on me.

"I would if I had a lawyer." I glace at my food then whip my head to back at her, "Wait, can I do that?" *I must research that.* There's no way I'm paying for their wedding.

"Don't give her ideas. What good is that going to do?" Bianca says, alarmed.

Valentina shrugs. "I don't know, but he's a jackass. You should try it. If you win, he'll have to pay *you* and he'll die from shock." She pauses thoughtfully. "Should we go to his house? We could slash a tire or wrap the Spyder with toilet paper."

Bianca's eyes bulge out in a horrified look, as she shakes her head. "Oh my God, what are we, twelve? Olivia, forget Bran. We need to find you a lawyer. This is Miami, everybody and their cousin knows a lawyer. Let's focus on that. Val, don't give her ideas."

"You're no fun."

We continue talking but Bianca's right, as much as I would enjoy my ex's suffering, I need a lawyer. I can't control Brandon. *Priorities.*

It's a gorgeous February afternoon, and the weather is perfect. Winter in Miami is dry season, there's barely any rain, and the sky is usually blue and cloudless. The temperature drops and it's very nice. It's so lovely it's hard to resist being outside. When I arrive home I change, grab a water bottle and head out to walk around the golf course. A walk will help get rid of those few lingering holiday pounds. *Great plan.*

I'm at the end of my second round when I hear a group of cyclists barreling down the path and move out of their way. After the group passes me by, Tom breaks away from the pack and returns to me. "Hi stranger," he says when he's within earshot. While he circles around me, I notice his cycling clothes, then his broad back. His upper arms stretch as he grips the handlebar. *Wow, his biceps are amazing.*

"Hi," I pant. *I'm clearly out of shape.* I should walk more, maybe get a bike.

"Do you know where you want to go for Valentine's Day?" he asks.

"I do not, why?"

"Tell you what, let me plan something. I'll surprise you." He pauses to look at me, his feet planted on the ground, "Go on a date with me," he says with a sideways smile, eyes crinkling and the crow's feet on full display.

Upon hearing this, my feet stop working. "Are you asking me on like a date-date?"

"Yes, a date-date. I'll pick you up, take you to a nice restaurant, we can watch a movie and I'll bring you home at a decent time. I promise to call you the next day. We'll talk every day for a few days, I'll plan a second date, then a third and so on and so forth. Eventually, you'll become my girl and you won't be able to deny we have a relationship."

"Wasn't bike day a date?" I ask.

"No. Bike Day was really just bike day. With Keith. Ew. This is a date-date."

I try not to laugh. "Are you sure this is a good idea? First dates are not my jam."

"Positive. Besides, this might be your last first date."

Ohmygod! Ohmygod! Eeekk!

He pulls me by my shirt and gives me a quick kiss. I can't help but smile; I can feel his smile too. After a few seconds, he lets me go.

"Have you thought this through? What if I say no or make other plans? What will you do?" I ask. I cock my head sideways and try not to laugh.

"I *know* you'll say yes. We'll have a great time." He says and winks at me.

"Wow, that's very pretentious, even for you," I say as I start walking.

He swings his legs off the bike and starts walking next to me, then holds my hand and interlocks our fingers. "I have a healthy dose of self-confidence."

"You're very humble too."

"Don't forget handsome." After a second, he tilts his head back and laughs. It's a full-on laugh and I shake my head. I can't help my smile. "Come on, you know you want to," he says before he bounces our shoulders playfully. We walk for a few more minutes but he abruptly halts our momentum when he pulls me by the waist to him. A deeper kiss this time and I wrap my arms around his shoulders. I can feel his heart beating but when he looks at me, it's the fire in his eyes that makes me shiver. "Go on a date with me, please," he whispers.

I take a deep breath. "Can we skip the first date and go to the second?"

"We're not skipping our first date. Trust me. I'm going to blow your mind."

"Ha. Are you now?"

"Oh yeah." He kisses me again. I nod. When he lets me go, we continue down the path.

As my house comes into view, I notice a car in my driveway. On closer inspection, I notice Brandon sitting in my rocking chair. When he finally sees us, he puts away his cell phone and stands up. "Olivia," he says when we're within range.

"Hi, Brandon. Do you remember Tom?" I ask while Tom parks flips down the kickstand on his bike then stands next to me.

"Yes, I do. Hey man." While they shake hands, I can't help but comment on his car.

"New car? What happened to the Spyder?"

"Sold it. Can we talk in private? Are you not getting my messages? Or are you just ignoring me?" He crosses his arms and changes his stance.

"I have, but I've been swamped with students." *Would now be a good time to congratulate him on getting engaged?*

"When are we selling the house?"

He's obsessed with this. Is he ever going to leave me alone? "Sell the house? How many times do I have to tell you, I'm not selling *my* home?"

"Olivia, you're wasting my time. Time's up. You need to decide. Give me the money now or tell me if I have to wait for you to sell it and *then* give me money. I don't have time for games."

I remember our last encounter and alarm bells go off. I instinctively take a step back. "Brandon, *I am not selling it.*"

I glance at Tom and see his chest rise in controlled anger. His jaw tics a couple of times. His eyebrows are low and he's focused on my ex. "Hey, you need to chill. The house is under her name. I don't think you have any claims to this property. She already told you she's not selling it. You need to back the fuck down and leave her alone."

Brandon's focus changes from me to Tom. "Look man, I don't know what's going on between you two and frankly, I don't care, but this is between me and her," he says while pointing at me.

Tom reacts by taking a step closer to him, putting them less than a foot from each other. He has a fierce look in his eyes.

For the first time, I take in Brandon. He usually looks great, sometimes not even a hair is out of place, but today he doesn't look as put together. To start, he's wearing sweatpants and a t-shirt. *I didn't even know he owned a pair.* His face is unshaven, his hair looks messy, and his eyes have dark circles under them. They look darker than usual and flicker with anger. They're almost threatening in a way I've never seen before. The realization gives me an unsettling feeling that chills me. For the first time I realize he's *really* not kidding when he says he wants me to give him money.

"O-kay, let's bring it down a notch." I try to step in between the two because I have enough drama at work, and the last thing I need is a scene at my house. Tom takes a step back and places a hand on my hip. "Brandon, I'm sorry but for the fiftieth time, I'm not selling my home. Send me your lawyer's info and I'll have my lawyer reach out." I don't have a lawyer, but I bluff.

"Fine. If this is how you want it, see you in court." He glares at me, looks back at Tom, and storms off.

Tom and I back onto the lawn as Brandon jumps in his much cheaper car and peels out of the driveway, narrowly missing *my* car. His hand's still on me and he pulls me close. I rest my head on his chest and take a deep breath, "Crap. I need to find a lawyer."

"How many times has he come by? Is he calling you a lot?"

I turn and face him, but it takes me a moment to answer. "He's only been here twice, but I lost count of the number of calls."

"He seems intense, is he always like this?" Tom asks, as he glances back at the street.

"No, he wasn't. It looks like he's having some financial issues."

He focuses on me and his eyebrows dip. "Financial issues. What type of financial issues? What's his last name?"

"Bianca told me he used the term financial issues but I don't know what exactly. He hasn't told me." Tom grabs his cell from a hidden pocket on his shirt while asking me again what his name is. "Brandon Lloyd."

A second later whomever he called picks up. "Hey man, I need a favor. Can you ask Dan or Kyle to check somebody out? Yeah, also, what do you know about real estate law?"

"Who are you calling?" I mouth.

"My best friend Keith, the lawyer. His brother Kyle is a detective at MDPD and we know this guy, Daniel, who has a personal security and investigation company... Yeah... Brandon Lloyd."

"Lawyer, a cop, and a PI? Do you just call people at random and they do whatever you tell them to do?"

"Not always but something like that."

"Tom, wait, wait, there's no need. I appreciate the help, but I'm sure it's not a big deal."

"Yes, it is, he seems desperate. I want to make sure he's not going to do anything stupid."

"It's fine."

"If he keeps calling you and coming by, it's clearly not fine." His eyes fix on me while answering. "Keith, give me a second–"

"Tom–"

"Can you please let me help you? He can't show up in your house wherever he feels like it and disrespect you. I can't allow that, and you shouldn't allow it either. As a matter of fact, next time I see him, I might have to kick his ass."

"How old are you? Fifteen?"

"Twelve."

I cross my arms. "Tom, I appreciate it, but I can take care of myself and if he crosses the line, I can always call one of my brothers."

He looks at me with warm eyes. "I know you can, but I want to help. Besides Valentine's Day is coming and if you're not available, I might have to go out with somebody that actually wants to go out with me."

"I think you could manage a date..."

"I'm sure I can manage but come on, are you really going to turn me down on Valentine's Day? Seriously? You're killing me here." His lips slowly turn up a smile and he grabs my arms and gently untangles them.

"So much ego. It's amazing."

He lets out a laugh while he puts the phone back to his ear. "I'm a confident guy and for the record, I'm not letting you off that easily. Yeah, I'm here... sorry to keep you waiting." He says the last part looking at me and motions for me to open my door. Once inside, he finishes the call with Keith and kisses me passionately, his five-o'clock shadow marking me possessively. I feel electrified. My knees shake and my heartbeat skyrockets. *Wow.*

He tells me to get ready because he'll be back and after he leaves, I quickly shower and change.

An hour later, Tom and Keith show up at my house with Keith's friend Max, who works in real estate law. I give them details of what happened, we talk about how much I spent and I answer what feels like one hundred questions from the three of them. Thankfully, when I bought the house I saved all of my receipts, paperwork and statements. I was hoping to use them for tax purposes, and it's easy to find them. Max asks me to make copies of everything I have and I agree to follow up with him in a few days.

By the time they're ready to leave, I feel much better. I ask Max how much he would charge me but he tells me not to worry about it as he doesn't know if he'll be able to help me. I have no idea what his fee is or how I will pay for it, but I'm thankful. When I walk them to the door, I realize there are three cars in my driveway. After Tom walks his friends out, he comes back inside with me, "Thank you for calling them. I owe you. I really needed a lawyer," I say as he closes the door and grabs my hand.

"It was my pleasure. Besides, I figured it would score me a few brownie points before our date." His eyes focus on me while he pulls me close.

My hands go to his waist. I move my head back and look up at him. I can't help teasing him. "I don't remember agreeing to a date."

"You actually did." His voice lowers a few octaves and my knees go weak. "If not, then I guess I'll have to convince you."

Before I can protest any further, he pulls me closer and kisses me senseless. *Yep. I'm definitely convinced.*

Olivia

Today is the big day and so far, so good. After another fun Valentine's Day lunch with my friends, whom I truly love, I return to my office. Thankfully, there are no major issues. As a matter of fact, it's a very slow day at the office. Nobody wants to see an advisor on Valentine's Day. Our office is empty as a lot of advisors either took a day off or called in sick at the last minute.

Today I have seen little of Tom, but when one p.m. rolls around, I grab my things and head out. I too requested half the day off. Before our date, I have a waxing appointment *and* a hair appointment.

First off is the local esthetician school for wax. They are significantly cheaper than going to a professional wax salon. Besides, I work with college students. I enjoy being there and getting to know them. I usually request my appointments with somebody who's graduating and who's pretty much "salon-ready" and so far, I've had no issues.

I arrive at the check-in counter and listen to the receptionist. "I'm sorry, but she's not here. She called in sick today," she says apologetically, "I can reschedule you."

It's my first date with Tom and it's a special occasion. I need *trimming*, if you get my drift, so I ask, "Do you have another senior student available?"

"We do, but they're all swamped right now. I can squeeze you in to see someone in about two hours if you want to wait."

"I can't. I have a hair appointment later. Do you have anyone available now? Anybody at all?"

"Ummm. Give me a second." Less than five minutes later, she's back. She leads me to a room where a girl who looks like she belongs in a high school classroom greets me. After proper intros and chit-chat, the student positions me on the table, then she slowly lays the hot wax on one side of my thigh. A few minutes later she pulls on it and it's not *too* bad, she's a little jumpy but manages to compose herself.

Next, she applies the wax to the other side. Except for the fact that she's coming *freakishly* close to my girly parts, she's doing okay. When she tells me to, I take a deep breath and... Oh mother... Her eyes grow huge in her panic-stricken face and she wrinkles her nose. I go semi-blind from moist eyes and realize then that this is probably her first time doing this by herself. *Crap. I should have asked.*

I take small comfort in the fact that the worst part is over.

Except it is not.

I stand up and it's only then, as I'm dressing, that I notice a blob of wax has dried up and my va-jay-jay is sealed shut. *Oh. My. God!* This is a disaster. How can I have sex on my first date with Tom if my privates are impenetrable? Freaking out, I call Bianca on the way to my car and she tells me baby oil will remove it.

Based on this information, I run to the closest pharmacy searching for baby oil AND moisturizing cream. After a humiliating penguin walk through the store, I finally find them. I pay and duck into the bathroom where, thankfully, I discover Bianca was right and baby oil does the trick and opens m y...*privates*. I also apply a generous amount of moisturizing cream and head out for my hair appointment.

I know what you're thinking, she's crazy for going to another student, but what are the odds of having two crazy experiences in one day? Statistically, it's impossible. I'm sure it'll be fine. *Positive thinking.*

I arrive at the beauty school for a hair appointment and my regular stylist, a senior student, greets me at the counter. I breathe a sigh of relief because she's in today. We catch up on life and it's all normal and nice. *See, nothing to worry about.* She's applying my usual color. She *cannot* mess it up. While we wait for the color to set, I read a book, send texts and answer personal emails. After she washes the color out, we go back to her station and the towel comes down.

I look up from my phone at the same time she does; I'm caught off guard when she yelps. Her hand covers her mouth and her eyebrows shoot up. *Wait. Let's rewind. Did she just yelp?* It takes me a second to process the image in the mirror. What the freak! My hair's orange! *Oh, Jesus.* I may need a valium after this because I somehow have burnt-orange hair. She finds her professor/manager and they determine the coloring bottle was mislabeled and profusely apologize. They offer to squeeze me in, to fix it, in a couple of days... except my date is today and I have a carrot top. *I literally have a carrot top.* My hair has a faint chemical smell and I decide it's best not to push it. Instead, I contemplate if I should go on my date wearing a wig *or a head-wrap*.

Thankfully, in the end, she does an outstanding job with the blow-dry and style.

With an hour to spare, I finally make it home. No wig and no hat. I run to the bathroom and take a shower, put on matching underwear, and try at least twenty outfits. *What was I thinking?* I should have called one of my friends to help me pick something. After all that, I finally decide on a simple black dress.It's sleeveless with a round neckline which means the girls are covered, and it has a flirty skirt, almost knee-length.Now I need accessories...*piece of cake.*

If only.

After trying on twenty different accessories, I end up with a teal and silver necklace and earrings, wide silver bracelets, black shoes and a black clutch. I put my hair up in a messy bun and start working on my makeup. *I'm finally ready.* When my doorbell rings, I take a deep breath and open it. *Be Zen, you've got this.*

Tom. He's wearing a black bomber jacket, white shirt, and jeans with casual black shoes. He takes my breath away and piercing green eyes look me over before he gives me a dazzling smile.

I think I'm going to melt.

"Hi," he says simply, grinning while his eyes linger on me.

I try to control my face from freezing up because I can't stop smiling. "Hi. Come in," I say as I move to the side. After he takes a step in, he embraces me in a light hug. One of his hands moves to my hips and he gives me a brief but electrifying kiss.

"You look amazing," he says, pulling back. His voice turns huskier while he looks at me with lustful eyes. "Ready? Let's go before I change my mind." He gives me a wolfish smile and all I can do is nod as he grabs my hand and leads me to the car. As we approach it, I ask where are going. "Dinner," he says cryptically and winks at me.

We drive east towards downtown Miami and enter Key Biscayne. There are a ton of hotels and restaurants on the island, many with exceptional downtown and bay views. Any restaurant he picks is going to be amazing.

Except after we cross the causeway, he slows down next to the water. Is this right? *This is a date, right?* "Ummm, Tom?"

Tom's too busy parking then looking for something in the glove compartment to notice me. "Yeah?"

"Where are we going?"

"We're going to dinner."

"I know, but you're on the wrong side of the island. You have a few more miles to go." *Is he lost? He can't get lost on a one-way bridge. I mean... can he?*

"Nope. Come on." When he comes around the car and opens the door, he finally notices me. "Hey, are you alright? You look pale. Wait, are you afraid of heights? Shit... I should've asked." His eyebrows dip in the middle, but he offers a hand and helps me out of the car.

"Afraid of heights?"That's when I notice a small seaplane on the water. We're parked next to a pickup truck and there's a guy inside on a cell.

"Are you?"

"A little, I guess. Why?"

"Because we're taking this seaplane and we're going to Isla Morada to have dinner on a beach," he explains pointing at it.

My eyebrows shoot up of their own accord. "Oh."

"A little bird told me you like the Keys... plus we're having a secret fling, remember? Nobody knows us in the Keys." When he notices I'm not laughing, he looks unsure and his smile disappears. "I'm kidding, I'm kidding," he blurts, shaking his head, "Look, I don't care about any of that. We're taking a seaplane to have dinner in the Keys because it's our first date."

I can't help but look at to him and grin as he takes a step closer to me. "Are you trying to impress me or something?"

"Or something. Is it working?" he asks, then grabs my hand and laces our fingers together.

The guy in the pickup finally gets out of the truck and approaches us. "Hi guys, I'm Enrique, your pilot. Are you ready?"

"Yeah, we are," Tom responds, turning to face him and shaking his hand. After last-minute details are covered, he leads us to the plane on the water's edge.

Once inside the plane, he gives us headphones to drown out the sounds of the engines. Our plane is taking us south and we're traveling next to the sunset. The 40-minute plane ride to Isla Morada is amazing. The views of the city and the water are spectacular. I also enjoy the quiet moments looking at the ocean and the city lights under the glow of the sunset, holding Tom's hand. He's beaming at me. My heart is whole and about to burst and I sigh content. It'll be difficult to top this as a first date. We finally *land* on the water and walk towards the beach.

As we walk, I spot a lone table in the sand not too far from us and the pilot directs us to it, then disappears into a nearby building. The table is covered by white floor-length tablecloth. It's surrounded by torches at each corner, candles, and votives on top. A couple of waiters materialize out of nowhere and tell us about the menu. After the wine arrives, we get into a conversation about the flight and the views. *It's absolutely perfect.*

He sits back in his chair and looks at me. "So, this is our first date. Tell me about yourself? What do you do?" he asks when our meals arrive, pretending to turn serious.

"I work with college students." I reply, trying to match his *serious* tone.

His eyebrows go up in mock surprise. "Really?"

"Yeah, what about you? What do *you* do for a living?"

He takes a sip of wine, then smiles. "Funny you should ask, I work with college students too."

"Is that right?"

"Yeah. I've never seen you around the campus, though. I would have remembered your dimples." He leans closer and continues with a smooth voice, "You're sexy as hell and I love your hair. Believe me, I would have noticed you standing in a line." When my lips turn up, he winks.

I roll my eyes at him but smile. "You crazy man. You did notice me in a line."

"See, I noticed you. You're gorgeous."

"I noticed you too. By the way, this's a great first date. Thank you."

He reaches for my hand and his thumbs rub against my knuckles a few times before he kisses them. The butterflies wake up. "You're welcome. What do you think that'll get me?"

"On a first date? A kiss. Open mouth, for sure."

"Now we're getting somewhere." We grin at each other. The hours are flying by on this beautiful beach. We could talk forever and it wouldn't be enough. There's something in his eyes, in the way he looks at me, that's different from all the first dates I've ever been on. The only thing left to do is embrace the strong connection between us and go with it.

Several hours later we're back at my door. I open it then turn to address him. "Thank you. I had a great time,"

"You're welcome. Can I call you tomorrow?" When I nod, he keeps going. "I would love to take you out on a second date." He takes a step towards me.

"Yeah? I'd like that." I look up at him and can't stop myself from touching him. My palm touches his cheek, then moves to his shoulder, while his hands land on my hip. He pulls me close and kisses me, sending a wave of excitement through my body.

After a few minutes of making out in my doorway, he stops. "Are you going to invite me in? Can I keep you company?" he asks casually.

"It's our first date. I don't sleep with anybody on a first date."

"Is that so?" he smirks. I nod. "Well, lucky for me, it's going to be midnight soon, so technically it's a new day."

"Hmm. How convenient."

"Very." I open the door; he follows me inside. When I close the door, he runs his hands through my hair, liberating it. "Instead of a Key Lime pie we should have asked for a carrot cake," he jokes.

"A what?"

"A carrot cake to match your hair." My eyebrows dip and he tries to suppress a laugh. "Did something happen to your hair?"

"You noticed, huh?"

"It's hard not to notice your carrot top."

"Oh my God, that's so mean."

"I'm sorry. I'm kidding, you know I'm kidding. What happened?" He grabs my hand, leading me to my room.

"There was a mix-up with the bottles." I pause. "Not only that, but I had another accident *before* the hair appointment."

"An accident?" He looks at me.

"At the wax place."

"At the... wax place? O-kay. Do I even want to know?"

"I think you do." I wait a few seconds. His eyebrows release in understanding. "I need help to moisturize my—" before I can say anything else, his lips are on mine voraciously and he swings me into his arms.

Best. Valentine's Day. Ever.

Olivia

After the holiday, we start making plans to get our friends together, *after* our second date or third date. *I cannot believe we're going to have a second date! Eeekk!*

After a full day spent interacting with eager college students, including an advising session with a sophomore student that has changed majors eight times since freshman year, one that emailed five advisors asking all of us the exact same question and a phone advising session with a freshman student who *only* asked the questions that his mom fed him, my day is finally over. *I wonder, didn't the kid realize I was hearing everything?*

As I walk into the almost-empty staff parking lot, I notice Brandon leaning on my car. "Hi," he says with an awkward wave as soon as I'm within earshot. "Can we talk?" I notice that he's wearing jeans and a light gray long-sleeve sweater that looks loose on him and once again, I wonder what's going on with him.

I nod as he walks in my direction. He meets me halfway and I wait for him to start. "Look, I know things have been tense between us and I'm sorry, but I need you to help me."

"Help you how?" I ask. I stand a few feet away from him, put my hands in my pockets and hope for the best. As he talks, I balance on my heels.

"I need you to sell the house or maybe... maybe you don't have to sell it. You can take a loan." He's wide-eyed and has bags under his eyes but I can see the wheels turning. *Did he just come up with this idea?*

I pause. I honestly have no intention of giving him money but I have a feeling he's not going to like my answer. "Brandon, I know that you need money and I'm sorry, but I'm not selling my house. Call me in a few months or maybe a year to see if anything has changed."

"I can't wait a few months, Olivia." He motions with his hands for emphasis. *Did he lose a few neurons along with the money?*

For some reason, he's not getting the fact I won't sell my home. I stop moving and give him my full attention. "Brandon. I. Can't. Help. You."

"Then we're going to have to go to court."

I have a sudden need to punch his stomach, knock him over, and put a booted foot on top of his chest like an action movie hero. Laura Croft comes to mind. Which I control by reminding myself to do something like that is probably illegal, and most likely will land me a free trip to jail for assault. *Not to mention, I don't have boots on right now.* "What the hell's wrong with you, Brandon? Do you want to drag us into a legal battle? Why would you do that now? Do you want to get married that badly?"

"Who told you about that? It has nothing to do with that! I don't want to drag us into a legal battle. That's why I agreed to put the house under your name in the first place, so I could walk away and not do this shit."

On hearing this comment, I pause. "What are you talking about?"

"Right before we bought the house, I was thinking we weren't right for each other. I felt our lives were going in different directions and we wanted different things."

"What direction did you expect to move in when we're buying a house together to move *into*?"

He sighs and looks at the floor, then addresses me again. "Look, I know it's not what you want to hear, but we're not compatible."

My blood boils. *Fuck.* "Not compatible? Are you serious right now? You fucking cheated!"

"I didn't want to!"

"Oh, my God!" I hold on to my purse. For a few seconds, I considered swinging it at him like an old lady in a cartoon.

"Olivia, I didn't want to hurt you but then I realized I wanted to be with somebody else and I couldn't help it."

"You couldn't help it?! Is that an excuse?!"

He massages his temples for a few seconds, then looks at me. "Look, we can't change the past, right now what I need is for you to help me and sell this house."

"I'm not selling it. I shouldn't have to sell my home because *you're* in trouble and by the way, I have a lawyer."

His face flushes and I notice the throbbing veins in his neck, "Have you not been listening?! I can't keep wasting time going back and forth with you!" he roars, taking quick steps in my direction, before suddenly putting his hands on me and squeezing my upper arms tightly. *Ohhh fuck.*

My stomach feels rock hard, and my heart is pounding in my chest. I try to move but I'm pinned in place and I can't escape his grip, "What the hell is wrong with you? Let me go, you son of a..." Almost on instinct, I grab his shirt for balance and lift my knee to his privates with as much force as I can, causing him to fall to the ground twisting in pain. I'm not a violent person, but I grew up with two brothers. My adrenaline shoots up and I try to control my rapid breathing while my heart's in my throat. I grab my phone, intent on calling security or the police when I hear running steps and turn back to see Tom running towards us.

"You bastard," Tom thunders as he approaches us, and I'm forced to get in front of him. He takes his backpack off and tries going around me, his fist clenched at his sides.

I grab onto Tom's shirt *and* his waist and try to hold him in place. *Trying* being the operative word. "Tom! Tom!" He focuses on me for just a brief second and I can see the murderous look on his face.

He's breathing fast and quickly scans me from top to bottom. "Are you okay —Did he hurt you?"

"I'm fine. I'm okay. Let's just go."

Brandon has regained his balance and looks at us, nostrils flaring. His eyes are wide and dark, and protruding from their sockets. "Olivia, what the fuck is wrong with you?" He holds on to his privates as he leans on my car.

"If you ever touch her again, I will fucking destroy you," Tom says, pointing at Brandon.

"Come and get me. I'm right here, you ass..." Brandon's still talking when Tom takes a few steps in his direction. I'm forced to hold on to him with everything in me.

"Tom! Don't listen to him. Look at me. Look at me, we're on campus." After a few seconds, his furrowed brows relax in understanding as the realization that *we are* on campus hits him. He takes a few deep breaths and forces himself to calm down.

His jaw's set tight, and I can feel he's only seconds away from losing it. "Stay the fuck away from her," he growls at Brandon, then he grabs his discarded backpack, and my hand and leads me away.

Brandon scoffs. "You can't tell me what to do. This is not your problem. I'll talk to her whenever I want to and there's nothing you can do, you piece of..."

At this provocation, Tom turns towards Brandon.

I hold on to Tom's hand and look at Bran. "Brandon shut up! Tom, don't listen to him. Let's walk away. Walk away Tom."

Tom takes another deep breath and keeps walking until finally, we're secure in his car.

Let me tell you, I'm no damsel in distress, but that freaked me out. My heart's pumping erratically and my hands are shaking. For the first time in a long time, I wonder if I should call my brothers and have them *talk* to Brandon. I look to my side when I hear Tom calling Keith on his cell. I grab my phone and call security, then call my own friends.

As we drive away, I take deep breaths and try to calm down, but I can't stop shaking. When he notices, he parks the car in another lot and unbuckles both our seatbelts.

In one swift movement, he lifts me up towards him and wraps his arms around me. I'm sitting sideways on his lap, facing the passenger window. I take deep breaths and let my head rest on his shoulder.

He gently guides my face up. "Hey, look at me. It's going to be fine." He soothingly rubs my back and after a few minutes asks, "Are you okay?" His hand cradles my neck and all I can do is nod. He says nothing else and he rests his forehead on mine and holds me. For a few minutes, his embrace insulates me from the world. It's an oddly satisfying sensation of warmth and contentment. Like nothing can get to me because he's holding me.

When we've both calmed down and I'm back on my seat properly, he drives us away.

By the time we arrive at my house, Keith is waiting outside. "Hey," he says, standing up from the rocking chair as we approach. "Are you guys okay?"

"Yeah," we reply as I open the door. A few minutes later, Bianca and Valentina also show up. They immediately embrace me. When I see my friends, my eyes fill up with moisture but I take a deep breath and hold it in.

Tom stands next to me while I talk to my friends. I make the proper introductions and after I make coffee, we all sit down in my living room. "Can we put a restraining order against him?" Tom asks Keith. Our fingers interlace and his thumb is making imaginary circles on my skin.

"I can try, but it's a toss-up depending on the judge. He or she could take Olivia's side. He did just put his hands on you and now we have Tom as a witness or they could say that all Brando was doing is asking for action and she's ignoring him. Which she is. No offense, Olivia. You have every right to ignore him."

"None taken. Can he really sue me for unjust enrichment?"

"Technically, he can. I know that you have receipts, but he could have some too and it's his right. He can sue to get the money he *believes* he put into the house. Can he prove it in court? I don't know."

With my luck? "*Shit.*"

"Maybe we should get a security guard or an alarm system," Tom says next to me.

"A security guard? That's a little too much. I draw the line at a random guy standing watch over my house."

"There is no line. He knows where you live, where you work. I'm not taking any chances," his eyes are tight and worried.

Valentina clears her throat and says, "I'm tempted to go by his house. Maybe I'll talk to him."

"Bad idea, please don't do that. Let us handle it," Keith responds, looking at her through dark eyelashes.

She cocks her head and lifts her chin. "Why? Because *you're* the man?" she says pointing at him and his eyebrows shoot up. "Who are you again?"

"I'm the lawyer."

"Right. Got it. Counselor."

Next to me Bianca asks, "I don't understand, why is he so desperate?"

"Yeah... about that. After he showed up here the last time, we had somebody dig into it." Keith explains glancing at Tom, who stays quiet.

Do I even want to know? Actually, I do. "And? What did they say?" I ask.

"He's being accused of embezzlement. He did some shady transactions and his employer traced them back to him. He needs money for his defense."

"That sucks but what does that have to do with me?"

"My guess is he thinks he can convince you to sell the house, give him half and it's easy money to help him get out of a bind."

Hmmm. These guys seem to have connections. Can they find a hitman? Gah. I'm a horrible human being for thinking this.

Tom takes a deep breath and massages his temple. "Keith, let's call Max. See what he can do to get ahead of it. Considering that Lloyd says he has proof of payments or receipts, and a *witness*, I want to know what are the chances of him being able to sue or make her sell. You're the lawyer, I'm sure you can find something."

"First, I do corporate law. We need Max to look at all the paperwork. The other thing is, real estate lawyers rarely litigate. We might have to find another attorney, but I'll let you guys know. Second, I don't think the realtor can take sides. He can be a witness but there's no taking sides, and third, I think it would be a good idea if you're not alone with him. Olivia, if he bothers you again, let us know and we'll deal with it."

"How *exactly are* you going to deal with it? Should I be worried? You won't kill him, right?" I look at Tom, then at Keith, then back at Tom, but neither of them says anything.

"You have nothing to worry about. *I* won't kill him, but if it comes down to it we'll hire somebody," Tom says nonchalantly and shrugs.

"Tom, that's not funny. Keith, you're a lawyer. You won't let Tom do something stupid, right?" Tom pulls me by the waist and kisses the side of my head; I can feel his smile. "Tom?"

"What do you want me to say? Talk to my lawyer."

Keith tilts his head sideways and purses his lips in amusement. "Don't look at me. I'm a law-abiding citizen. I will not be hiring anybody to do anything illegal."

As Keith is talking, I glance at Valentina. She's awfully quiet and has been staring at him. He's wearing a white shirt and black slacks; his tie is loose around his neck. To be honest, he's good-looking in a handsome TV lawyer kind of way.

Tom continues talking and I focus on him. "Tell you what, we won't hire anybody. I might need help to hide the body, though."

"Tell me when and where," Keith says with a tinge of amusement in his voice.

"Can you not encourage him? You two are not funny. *This* is not funny." As soon as I say this, they both burst into laughter.

Valentina glances at me, "Are these two always like this?"

I'm about to answer when Keith jumps in. "Like how?" He gives her firm eye contact, sits a little straighter, and crosses one ankle atop the opposite knee.

Her cheeks pink, but she recovers and holds his eyes. "Two knuckleheads?" One eyebrow is raised.

"Oh, my God. Did you just call me a knucklehead?" Keith says with sparkling eyes that never leave hers.

"Yes. Why? Are you shocked?"

"I am, actually. You met me five minutes ago."

"Let me guess, people don't usually do that." When he doesn't respond she continues. "Oh well. You'll get used to it."

"If these two keep at it, I guess I'll have to. Talking about which, what's the status with you two?" Keith changes the subject, finally leaving Valentina's eyes and moving his index fingers back and forth between me and Tom.

I'm caught off guard and wait for Tom. When he doesn't say anything, I hedge, "I have no comments. Tom?"

"Yeah, Tom, what are your intentions?" Valentina asks point blank.

Tom throws a pillow at his friend then looks at her. "That's none of your business. Keith, you're fired."

"What?! You can't fire me."

Valentina rolls her eyes, "Should we get ready for the shenanigans with you two?"

Keith gives her a flirty smile. "Are you always this blunt?"

Bianca and I say, "Yes," in unison, while she says, "No."

She squints her eyes and gives me a look. "*Traidora.*" *Traitor*, she mouths, while I suppress the urge to laugh.

Keith uncrosses his legs and loosens his tie. "Bad Latin temper?"

"Latin? Are you seriously typecasting me now? Right now? Based on *one* word?"

While I debate if I should jump in, Tom does it for me. "Okay kids, break it up. We're done... everybody out. Meeting's over."

Keith's eyeing Valentina. "Oh, come on. We're just getting started," Valentina rolls her eyes at him then stands up.

Bianca asks if I want to stay with her and as I'm about to accept, Tom answers for me. "It's okay. I got it. She's coming with us."

"Tom, it's fine. I can go to Bianca's for a couple of days."

"It's not fine. Tomorrow we'll get somebody to install a security system here. In the meantime, please grab some clothes."

"I can't afford a security system."

"Don't worry about it. I'll take care of it."

"Tom, here's a word... despotism. Here's another one... control. Do you just decide shit on your own and people just do what you tell them to do?" I pause. "I hate to break it to you, but you can't tell me what to do."

"Olivia, *please* don't argue with me. I'm trying to protect you. Please pack a bag and let's go."

"Olivia, you'll be safe with us," Keith says in a comforting voice.

Half of me wants to debate this recent dictatorship, but at the same time, I have to admit, it's nice that he wants to protect me and keep me safe. I can't argue with him about that. I take a deep breath and do as I'm told.

While I get a bag ready, I think about Brandon. That was a complete shit show. First cheating and now this? While half of me feels angry, a small part of me feels relieved that we broke up. Never in my wildest dreams did I think that our relationship would end like that.

Olivia

I wake up alone and disoriented. After remembering I'm at *the boys'* home, I go in search of Tom.

Last night, after we left my house, we drove around the block. It surprised me to discover how close Keith's house is. *We really are neighbors.*

Sniff... coffee.

I get up and find Tom in the kitchen. He's facing the counter and doesn't notice me. "Good morning," I yawn.

He looks back at me and gives me half a smile before turning back to the counter. "Good morning, beautiful. Do you want some coffee?" After a few seconds, he turns around completely. He's holding a cup and stirring the liquid before I can even reply.

"Sure. Coffee would be great." I reach him and take the cup he's offering. After I take a few sips, I ask, "What are you doing? How long have you been up?"

"I'm researching."

I notice the laptop on top of the counter. "Researching? At six am?" When he shrugs, I keep going. "Where's Keith?"

"He had to see a client in downtown. He wanted to beat traffic."

"I see." I can't help but take him in. He's not wearing a shirt or shoes. The top buttons of his jeans are undone and his morning hair's super sexy.

While I take a few more sips of coffee, I look around the house. "Nice house you guys have here," I comment.

"Thank you. You seem surprised. What were you expecting? Socks hanging from the ceiling?" he says, one eyebrow raising in amusement over the rim of his cup, a ghost of a smile on his lips.

"I don't know. Not socks, but maybe panties."

He lowers the cup and upon hearing this, he snickers. "Yeah, I don't think so."

"Actually, I was picturing a bachelor pad, all black and chrome, super modern, with a killer boom system, with these huuuge speakers that you bring out every time you throw a party, and the windows shake and colored lights that come out of –"

"Ha. Have I told you lately that you have a great imagination? Your brain amazes me."

"Thank you." I take a few steps farther away from him. I look at the giant flatscreen TV in the family room surrounded by two bookcases. It sits across from a huge brown leather sofa. The entire house is masculine but not intimidating. The bookcase is full of books, but it also has pictures. I can't help but quickly glance at some photos of Keith, Tom, and their families. I also check out a few book spines. After a few minutes, I walk back to him. "There's a lot of wood here. It's nice, warm, I like it,"

"I'll tell Keith you like it."

With my free hand, I hold his waist. His hand lands on my waist and he pulls me in front of him, then kisses me good morning. When I bury my face in his neck, he breathes in the scent of my hair. Still holding on to him, I take a step back. "Are you okay?"

"Yeah. I'm okay."

"Are we going to work?" I ask.

"I'm calling in sick, but I'll drop you off. You can come home in your car. I'm going to need a copy of your house keys or a spare set if you have one."

After he says this, I remember that my car's on campus. "Are you doing the alarm system?"

"That's the plan *if* I can find someone to return my call."

"Tom, you don't have to do this today. It's okay if we do it another day."

"We're doing this today."

"Fine. But do you realize it's not seven a.m. yet? Maybe you should wait an hour." *Or two.*

He claps his hands behind his neck and draws a heavy sigh and briefly closes his eyes. "You're right. Let's get ready or you'll be late. Come on."

When he offers a hand, I take it and let him lead me. "Okay, neighbor."

He glances back at me. "Oh... so it's neighbor now?"

"Am I expected to bring baked goods now?" I joke.

"Baked goods? No, not really. You can bring yourself here anytime you want, though."

"Where are you taking me?"

"You need a shower, *neighbor.*" His eyes go from sleepy to focused to hot. *Okay, then.*

Tom

After I drop her off and we check on her car, I drive back home. I spend an hour calling even more security companies. Those I called before eight this morning are now calling back and my phone is ringing non-stop. Unfortunately, everybody's saying it's too short notice. Oh, for God's sake. All I need are a few cameras. How difficult is it to install a few cameras around a house? My jaw hurts and it's getting worse as the hours go by.

It's mid-morning when Keith calls me and tells me one of our cycling buddies is the owner of a security company and has a crew available. I immediately make plans to meet up with them.

These guys are fast and efficient, and in less than two hours they're done. Feeling much better now that that's taken care of, I head over to downtown Miami and meet up with Keith for lunch. We need a plan.

"What's going on? Did you talk to Max?" I ask as soon as the waiter takes our order.

"Yeah."

"And?"

"We're working on it. We're doing research, trying to find a legal way to stop him from suing her. *Legal* being the operative word. In this country, anybody can sue anybody. I think we'll have something soon. What about security?"

"The alarm system's up. It's top-notch. No expenses spared. Windows and door sensors, security cameras outside. Completely digital and with the option of security monitoring."

"Nice." He nods appreciatively.

Too bad a security system will not stop the dick from coming to her house, but at least it's progress. "Unfortunately, she doesn't want a security guard outside her house. Even though my preference would have been a personal bodyguard, she vetoed that idea too. Sooo, new plan, we'll follow him. I don't want him anywhere near her."

"A little extreme, even for you, but I'll allow it for now. I'll call Dan."

I knew Keith would be *mostly* okay with this idea. He's always had my back. "So, what are we doing?" I ask, moving my hand between us.

"We are doing nothing. We are waiting for him to make a move. He's either going to find a lawyer or do something stupid."

"That is not a plan. He already did something stupid. We're going to sit here and wait? That's your plan?" I'm forced to pause and let the server deposit our drinks and salads on the table.

Keith thanks him and waits a bit for him to leave. When the server finally walks away, he addresses me again. "Yeah, pretty much. We can't go around harassing people. Let's hope he gets a lawyer. If he does, the lawyer will probably advise him to stay away from her. I know that's not what you want to hear, but let's try and avoid trouble if we can. For now, I'll call Dan and we'll have one of his guys follow him. Just sit tight."

I can't help but stab the salad with the fork and Keith raises an eyebrow. "I'm not particularly happy with the options." I hump and leave it at that, because I don't want to explain to my best friend that I literally want to kill that guy just for touching her. I'm feeling irrationally and illogically possessive of her.

"You're going to have to trust me."

"I trust you. I just don't trust him. We'll try it your way and if it doesn't work, we'll pivot and try it my way."

"My way will work. Besides, what's the deal with you two? You're overly protective of this girl," he asks between bites.

"I like her. We'll see how it goes."

He glances at me. "You like her? You're going through an awful lot of trouble for somebody that you *like*." When I say nothing else, he raises his eyebrows. "That's it? That's all you're saying?"

"For now, yes. And while we're having this sharing moment, what the hell was that with her friend last night?"

He pauses, his fork midair. After a few seconds, he sighs. "Dude, I have no idea. I don't know what the hell came over me. I couldn't stop myself."

"I noticed." His eyes drift away, as he shakes his head and I can't help but tease him. "Dude, you're so screwed." He mouths *fuck you* and I laugh. "By the way, that's Olivia's best friend. Please don't do anything stupid."

"Stupid? Like what, exactly?"

"Start something with her friend."

"Okay, Mom. I'll take that into consideration. *Not.*"

"Keith, I'm serious. Don't start anything unless you're sure. I don't want Olivia to have to choose between her friend and us."

"If I decide to do something, you'll be the first to know. Deal?"

"Deal."

Olivia

Two days later, and with a brand-new state-of-the-art security system installed, I return home. It's unsettling to know my ex is after me because of money. This rarely happens to poor people unless they're into shady business. *Ummm,* it almost sounds like the plot to a bad *telenovela.*

Since that episode in the parking lot, I haven't heard from Brandon at all. Half of me is in knots and waiting to be served by a judge or a lawyer... *or a hit-man,* but as the days go by, we don't hear from him and I relax.

Then it happens.

I receive a letter from Brandon's lawyer and my heart drops. Tom and Keith show up, full cycling gear, and go into attack mode. Keith tells me this is good news because now he'll have to stay away until this gets resolved. Moving forward, all communication will be done lawyer to lawyer.

While at work, thinking about my predicament, I have a vision of Brandon chasing me around Miami while I scream, *"You can't have my house, you can't have my house." I seriously need therapy.*

I'm about to call a student when Janine tells me human resources needs to see me and sends me to their office.

I walk across campus with my heart in my throat, running just about every scenario I can think of, each worse than the next, and feeling slightly nauseated. It occurs to me I haven't discussed this with Tom. Lately, we've been preoccupied with Brandon and the whole will-I-won't-I-be-sued predicament, to the point we haven't had our second date yet. When I finally make it to the human resources office and walk in, I see Tom in the waiting area. I don't have time to ask him what's going on because as soon as I sit down, a very nicely dressed woman asks us to follow her.

We are ushered into a conference room and as we walk in, the lone person in the room stands up to greet us. "Ms. Campbell, we haven't met but I'm Jorge, the Human Resources director." *Director?* He stretches a hand and I shake it, then sit. "I'm sure you're wondering why you're here," he begins as he sits.

Yes. "I am," I reply calmly.

"Thomas sent me an email stating he wanted to meet and discuss a *potential* relationship between you guys. I felt that you needed to be part of this conversation. As a rule, all relationships have to be reported. If my office finds out, from someone other than the parties involved, the employees are immediately terminated." *Is this where he tells me you're fired? Like a bad TV show?*

I glance at Tom, who seems oddly calm, and focus on my Zen. "Employees always think we won't find out. You guys did the right thing..."

Wait, does that mean...

"... One of you is going to have to switch departments. We'll work with you to find you a similar job or you can apply to a different *higher* position in another department. I trust that while you transition, that you will continue to be professionals and serve our students to the best of your abilities."

I release the breath I didn't realize I was holding as we both answer, "Yes."

"I'm glad we're on the same page. That'll be all." Tom and I sneak a look at each other. After a few seconds, Tom and Jorge, shake hands. I follow suit then we quietly slip out.

That's it? If I would have known it was that easy, I would have said something earlier. *I feel so stupid.*

As soon as we're out of the office, Tom turns to me. "I would have given you the heads up, but I didn't know he was going to call you in too."

I take a deep breath as we step onto an outside path, my hand on my chest. "Oh. My. God."

He glances at me as we walk. "You were white as a ghost. I thought you were going to faint or something."

"I thought I was going to puke."

"Yeah, he would have definitely fired us both if you did." I look at him and twist my mouth, then we both burst into laughter. We both stop when he smiles and pulls me close. I wrap my hand around his back. After a quick hug, we start our walk back to the office.

I can't believe that was so easy. I feel like an immense weight has been lifted off my shoulders. For now, at least, I don't have to worry about getting fired just for being with him. We can take our time getting to know each other and see where this leads. When he asks what I'm thinking, I reply honestly. "I just can't believe it was so easy."

"Me neither. On that note, doesn't that make you my girl-friend?"

I stop mid-stride and look at him. I check to see if there's anybody around us, but the students must be in class because there's nobody in the vicinity. "Girlfriend? Me?"

"Yes, you." He pauses. "What do you think, neighbor?"

"I think... Yes!"

He wraps his hands around my shoulders and gives me a brief kiss. When a student nears, he lets me go and we resume our walk. "See how easy that was? Next step is date number two. Then you won't be able to deny we have a relationship." When he winks at me, I can't help but grin.

"I guess I won't," I say. A thought hits me and I glance at him. "Are you going to leave? Should I start looking for a new position?"

"I have an idea. Do you trust me?" I nod. I really hope his idea works.

A couple of days later, I'm in the kitchen making dinner with Tom when there's a loud knock on the door. We're not expecting anybody and for a second, I think it might be Brandon. Tom looks at me and shakes his head. *Only way to find out.* A few seconds later, I open the door to my brothers. "Olivia." they say in unison, and I pause.

"Hi? I mean, hi, how are you guys?" I take a step back and allow them entrance to my home. After I close the door, I embrace each one. My oldest brother William holds me just a second longer. It occurs to me, after the events of these last few weeks, I really, really need this and I hold on too. He hugs me a bit tighter. After a few more seconds, I take a deep breath and let go.

"Anything you want to tell us?" Will asks, taking a step back.

Oh fuck. I wrack my brain. I wonder which of my last shenanigans did they hear about. "Not... really?"

"Brandon called us." Wills says and waits for a response. *Crap.*

"It's fine. It's handled. I'm handling it," I answer and stand a tad straighter.

"Are you? You have a funny way of handling it if he's calling me for money, but we'll come back to that in a second. Who's

Tom?" he asks. I glance at Mike, who shrugs and mouths *what?*

Appearing behind them from the kitchen, Tom says, "I'm Tom. Thomas Williams if we want to get technical." He stretches out a hand to Will. "Nice to see you again, Mike," then shakes his hand too. I wait as Tom stands next to me.

"Anything I should know, Tom?" Will asks without preamble.

"I like your sister. She likes me. We work together but we talked with HR. She hates ships, but I'm working on it. Her ex is about to sue her and I hope you know he's a dick." He glances at me. "I think that about sums it up."

I freeze for a second. *Oh my God.* Did he just say that? Will has an amused expression on his face. Mike is grinning.

I groan, then turn and drop my head on Tom's shoulder. He smells great and I rest my forehead for a few seconds.

"I like you. We're going to get along great," Mike says to Tom.

I hear Will comment, "Okay then."

I raise my head up and look at my big brother. "Brandon called us. Told us that you owe him money and that he's suing you. Olivia, I know that we give you a hard time, but you should have told us."

"I know. I'm sorry."

"Did he do anything to you? Do I need to go and beat him up?" he asks, clenching his jaw.

"Besides this? No. There's no need to beat anybody up," I say at the same time that Tom says, "Get in line." I give him some side eye.

I glance at the group. "Are you three serious right now? We're not in high school!" They all stare at me like I'm crazy. I shake my head. "You guys are not beating anybody up. I forbid you. We're civilized people."

Mike's eyebrows go up when he says, "Relax, we're not going to beat him up, but we could." I honestly want to smack him.

"Do you realize that you guys have not gotten into a fight since high school?"

"Whatever. How much do you owe that idiot?" Mike asks.

"We have a lawyer. He's trying to find out exactly. I can give you his information," I say.

"Great," Mike says. "I smell food. Are you going to feed us?"

When I nod, he grabs my hand and pulls me towards the kitchen. He's always thinking about food. I can't help but shake my head at him.

I look back at Tom and Will grinning at me and once again, I'm grateful that my brothers like him.

Olivia

After a busy week where everybody on campus wanted to know if we were actually for real *dating* this time, the chatter is *finally* dying down. We're finally going on our second date and life is good. *Talk about perspective.*

It's almost the end of the day when Lucy knocks on my door and pulls me out of my thoughts. Her eyes are darting all over the place and she's biting her lip. I'm hesitant to ask what's wrong. "What's up?" I ask.

"It's Leo. He's outside, and he wants to see you. I think he's drunk."

And cue the record scratch.

I knew everything was too perfect to be true. This is the universe's way of telling me... actually, I don't know what the universe's trying to tell me. *I need more clues... maybe an email.*

"He's drunk? Did everybody leave?" I ask.

"You, Sandra, Andrea, and Tom are the only advisors left, plus the student assistants. Everybody else is gone."

"Okay. Don't tell Tom and don't tell Andrea, either. She'll come out and argue with him. Let me see what is going on outside." The last thing I need is to prove Tom was right regarding his issues with Leo.

As I walk to the front counter, my heart races. Why would a student show up drunk? Shouldn't he be studying or romancing a girl? Getting laid? I know that sounds cliché, but isn't that what college students do? Believe it or not, this is a first for me. I run through scenarios in my head, but none makes sense. Is he coming for advice on a class? To vent about a problem? A girl?

I approach the counter and nod to the three student assistants behind the counter. Angela's holding her stomach. Lucy's is biting her own lips so hard, she's about to break through the skin, while Jackson's cracking his knuckles. When he spots me, he nods outside. At first glance, I see Leo pacing in front of our double glass doors. "He's being super rude to the girls and he cannot do that. He's drunk and I'm about to jump over the counter and punch him." *Calm those hormones down, sheesh.*

Looking at him, I say exactly that. "Please calm down. That would be bad for him *and* you." I take a few steps towards the door while I simultaneously pray the dean doesn't walk by and witness the scene I'm sure is about to happen.

Too bad Jackson's clearly not happy with my diplomatic efforts. "Olivia, I know he's your student, but we should call security," he says.

I give him a pleading look. "Can you give me a few minutes to talk to him *before* you call security, *please?*" When he nods, I keep walking.

I'm a professional... keep it professional. *If there was ever a time where I needed to channel my Zen, my inner goddess and any other statey of being, this is it.*

"Hi Leo, what's going on?" I ask in my softest voice.

"Hi. I'm drunk," he admits right off the bat with a weird laugh.

Oookay. My entire life's flashing before my eyes right now.

"I can see that, but why are you here?"

"I came to talk to you," he slurs a bit. When he stops, I notice he's swaying slightly. After a few seconds, he goes back to pacing.

I interlace my fingers, put my hands in front of me, and watch him pace. What did you want to talk about?"

"I was wondering if you were single and if you'd like to go out with me." He stops, gives me a sloppy grin, then goes back to marching.

Is he serious?! I really want to slap *his* forehead.

I press my lips together and force myself to stay quiet. How would I explain that to Dean Lozano? He'll probably fire me. No, he'll *definitely* fire me. I'll really have to sell my house... maybe move in with my mom and her new husband. *Oh, God no.*

"Your opinion of me matters more than anyone else's, even my mom's," my student is saying. "I compare every girl I meet to you because college girls are so juvenile now that I've met you. And you're so sooo nice."

I release the grip on my hands and move them as I speak. "Leo, it's my job to advise you and help you navigate college life. I literally get paid to do this." I pause. "I'm very flattered, but I cannot go out with you."

"Why not?" he asks, cocking his head with a weird high vocal pitch.

I try to keep it together, but I wonder if he can tell I'm struggling. "Look, you're a great guy, but to start, you are my student and I.... I could be fired. Also, I have a boyfriend." For a second, other thoughts enter my brain. Leo is at least six-two and towers over me. There is no way I can move him or restrain him in any way, shape, or form.

He's talking and listing reasons why I *should* go out with him and why, in his mind, it *would* work out. I'm trying to not freak out while he seems to get more restless.

I look back at Jackson, who looks ready to jump over the counter. I nod slowly and mouth "no," and hope he does nothing stupid; the last thing I need is two students fighting on my watch.

I glance back at Leo. He has stopped pacing. He looks at me and holds my gaze, then clumsily stalks towards me. *Oh, shit... this might be my cue to run... or hide.*

Out of nowhere, Tom steps between us and stands in front of me protectively.

Oh. My. God. I touch his back with open palms and sigh, relieved. I didn't realize I had stopped breathing until that very moment.

"Hey Leo, what's going on, man?" Tom says.

"Nothing. Do you mind? I'm talking with my advisor," Leo slurs through the word "advisor" and tries to go around Tom.

"I do mind. The girls are a little freaked out. They're about to call security and I don't want you to get in trouble."

"Oh," Leo says, his eyebrows raising slowly. He glances at the counter, then back at us. "I didn't mean to scare them, I just wanted to talk to her," he says, pointing at me.

"I know, she's beautiful, *and* nice, *but* how about if you and I take a walk?"

Leo looks at me and seems to consider this.

Out of the corner of my eye, I see security coming our way. I also see a couple of younger guys jogging towards us. They all reach us at about the same time. The young guys stand protectively in front and next to Leo. I recognize one of them as his friend when he tries to pull Leo away.

The security guys are standing behind me and Tom. In this weird circle dance, with Tom and me in the middle, there's so much testosterone it attacks my senses. Voices are getting louder and I can feel Tom getting tense. I have to fight the panic rising in me from taking over because being in the middle of a brawl is not how I expected to end the day. Except, that's when I notice a small crowd of students is assembling around us. This just keeps getting better. *Wait until the dean hears about this one.*

Tom addresses all of them, trying to defuse the situation. "*Everybody.* Calm. Down. Let's all calm down." The security people don't look convinced, and Tom addresses them directly. "Come on guys, he hasn't done anything wrong, he just wanted to talk to his advisor. No harm done." He turns to Leo's friends. "Guys?" When they back off a few steps, the security guys do the same. After a few tense seconds, Tom grabs my hand and pulls me out of the group and towards the door, and rushes back to the middle of the group. I quietly stand behind the counter with Sandra, Andrea, and the student assistants around me.

After what seems like an eternity, Leo's finally sitting in the waiting area outside our office, a bottle of water in hand. Every few minutes, however, he looks at me.

Tom is standing not too far from him, with folded arms. He's talking with people, but he's also glancing my way. Ultimately, Tom cover over and asks me to go back to my office. I hesitate, as I don't want to leave without knowing what's going to happen with Leo, but when Tom doesn't back down, I relent.

It's less than an hour later when Tom finally enters my office. I can hear an exasperated sigh as he closes the door. "Didn't I tell you to cut him loose?" he says without preamble, pacing in front of me.

"You did tell me, but at the time, I didn't agree with you."

"Why do you think I suggested that?" He stops pacing and stares at me.

"Because you thought..." I raise an eyebrow and wait.

"Because I could see right through him. I knew he liked you."

"Oh right, so here I am thinking maybe there's something wrong with him. That he needs help because he's sad or depressed or lonely or God knows what, when all this time you're relying on your male intuition for a *student?* How was I supposed to guess? You could have told me and saved me the embarrassment!"

He's been pacing again, but stops and groans. "That is not fair. Either way, I look like a jealous creep. If I tell you, I'm getting too involved. If I don't tell you, then I'm putting you out there to be embarrassed. Either way, I'm the bad guy? What the fuck do you want from me?" He stands in front of me, hands on his hips, and waits.

I'm angry and in the heat of the moment, lash out at him. "I don't want anything from you!"

He freezes and immediately I regret my words. I'm about to apologize when he says, "You know what, I don't have time for this. We have bigger things to worry about. Soon the dean is going to receive an incident report from security. Since we don't know what they'll write, we have to jump ahead of it."

I'm mad at him and want to ask, why do I keep being humiliated because of him? But he's right, the dean will hear about this soon and we can't waste time arguing. *Fix this problem first, argue with Tom later.*

"Write your report and send it to me. I'll write mine and we'll compare so that our statements match," he says authoritatively. To be honest, I don't think I like his heavy-handedness.

"Fine!" I say as he storms out.

A while later, I've typed my report. I try to keep it light and factual, then I send it to Tom and read his and they sort of match. *His is excellent, actually.* He makes a few suggestions to mine and when it's done, it is much better and I'm grateful to have his input. I send it to Dean Lozano and pray it all works out.

I sit in my office and as the adrenaline leaves me, I start to panic. *Shit. I cannot lose my job.* After everybody's gone, I don't know what to do or who to talk to, so I walk over to Tom's office.

He is in front of the computer. He keeps his eyes on the screen as I tell him I've sent my report to the dean. I hate that he's mad at me, that I got him involved and now we could both be fired. I fight back tears, but unexpectedly the waterworks come, and I bring my hands to my face to cover my mortification. *This is not Zen.*

He quickly stands up and wraps his arms around me while I cry semi-hysterically. and he rubs my back. I take a step back and look up to him, "I'm so stupid, I'm the wort advisor ever. Now the dean will probably fire me. I am so sorry I got you involved. You were right, I should have said something to him earlier," I hiccup, as tears fall down my face.

He sighs and looks remorseful. "I'm not right and you are not the worst advisor ever. You're a great advisor. Your students love you. The dean knows this. He's not going to fire you. Just because one went rogue doesn't mean anything. There are a ton of students who are grateful that you helped them," he says reassuringly.

"I'm such a loser. What am I going to do if I get fired?" Fresh tears roll down, and he holds my chin up and with his thumb gently wipes the new tears away.

"Will you stop it? you've done nothing wrong. You are not going to be fired. I won't allow it to happen, I promise," he whispers. His eyes are soft and thoughtful. After a few seconds, he pulls me gently towards him with his arm and cradles me against his chest while he holds me. My face rests in the crook of his neck, and I feel safe and comforted. I close my eyes, then wrap my arms around his waist and surrender to his hug and to the emotions. "It's going to be okay, Olivia," he whispers in my ear.

When I finally look up at him, his forehead rests on mine. I can feel his anger dissipating.

After a few more seconds, I take a step back and finally let him go. "I am so sorry, I didn't mean for you to be involved, but thank you for your help, you saved me today," I go back into my office, pick up my things and head for the parking lot.

After I text him good night, his response is brief. Even though part of me is concerned, the other half is too worried about my possible lack of job and income.

Olivia

The next day I walk into the department quietly and try, unsuccessfully, to avoid pretty much... everybody, but they're all saying hello and asking if I'm okay.

When I finally arrive at my office, the first thing I see in my in-box is an email from Dean Lozano stating he wants to see me and Tom first thing this morning. *Here we go.*

I don't even have my coffee yet when Tom's at my door comparing our schedules for the next few hours. He offers to contact the dean's secretary and get on his agenda for the morning. While I wait for confirmation, several advisors come into my office and ask about the *incident*. Everybody's talking about it. *This is gossip central, of course, they are.*

Less than two hours later, we're sitting in front of the dean. We explain what happened, stick to the facts and keep it light. We don't want Leo to get in trouble or worse, expelled for drinking on campus and causing a scene. Thankfully, the dean agrees to let him slide only with re-taking the drug and alcohol program we offer on campus for freshman students and an agreement that a male advisor will see him until he graduates.

When we're done, Tom follows me back to my office and closes the door.

Although he's wearing a dark business suit and looks great, his jaw is clenching and his eyes look dark and drained. "That went well. Nobody got fired," I blurt out. He gives me a thin smile but says nothing. Why do I have this huge void in the pit of my stomach? "*Tom?*"

"Look, I was up all-night thinking... I'm just going to say it... I'm quitting."

I don't want to panic, but what the hell... "Why would you do that?" I ask calmly.

"Because I think it's going to be better for us and our careers," he says with a tightness in his voice that I don't like. "Also, the assistant dean position on the downtown campus is open," he says with a set jaw.

"I didn't know it was available."

"That's because it hasn't been announced yet. I just... know it's available."

"Did you just wake up today and decided to switch campuses? How did you manage so fast? *Wait.* How long have you known?"

"For a few weeks."

A few weeks? When I hear that my heart drops. "So, you get a new job, and that's it? Problem solved?" He says nothing else for a few seconds and I press on. "Tom? Didn't we have a conversation about honesty? What is going on?"

"After we met with HR, we knew one of us was going to have to leave, so I spoke with my parents. Right now, though, the best play is for me to leave."

I stand up from my desk and look at him. "The best *play*? Wow."

"You don't understand. Yesterday, the first thing that I thought about was *you*. Making sure *you* were okay. Making sure *you* were safe. When I saw him, I wanted to punch the guy. *My* job is to take care of students, not to want to punch them. My priority should have been helping *him* not worrying about you."

"Let's pause right there. I appreciate that you worry about me, but if you would have at least mentioned that you thought he might like me, I would've been more prepared and maybe we could have avoided this."

He sighs and his head drops for a second, then he looks at me again. "Are we back to this one? What did you want me to say? 'Hey, I think your student likes you? Stay away from him?' Would you have done that?"

"I don't know, maybe."

"I don't think you would have. You know what, let's forget about it. The best thing is for me to leave."

"You're just going to leave?!" Now I'm shouting. "Seriously?!"

"I don't know what else to do."

"*Wow*. I never pegged you for the running type."

He gives me an icy state, and his eyes narrow. "The running type? You don't even want to have a relationship with me. I'm not the running away type, but this isn't a game. I have to think about my career. My family is my top priority. I cannot let a crazy infatuation tarnish my family's legacy."

"An infatuation?" On hearing that, I can't help but feel like a loser for misreading the situation and thinking it was more than that. *An infatuation?*

"That came out wrong. That's not what I meant," he blurts.

"You know what? It's fine. Good luck with your career." I stand from my desk, intent on walking out of the office, but he grabs my hand as I walk in front of him.

"Olivia, wait, let me explain."

"I think you explained enough. Besides you don't owe an explanation for your infatuation." *Hmmm, that rhymed. Ugh, I'm pathetic.*

"Olivia."

"Tom, there's nothing to explain. The fact is you keep giving me half-truths, making *plays* behind my back and I keep getting humiliated. It's not fair."

"I know it's not fair, but what do you want me to do?"

"I don't want you to do anything. That's exactly the problem. You keep jumping in, trying to help me and fix every single fucking thing. I don't need you to do that. I can take care of myself. All I want is for you to be honest, and you can't seem to be able to do that."

He looks at me and lowers his voice. "I've never lied. Regardless of what it looked like, I've been honest."

"You know what? Maybe it is better if you go. I can't work with you if I don't trust you, let alone be in a relationship with you."

"Yeah. That's debatable. I don't think you want a relationship." He pauses and takes a deep breath. "Olivia, one of us has to leave, and you were here first," he says calmly.

I feel my blood boiling and without intending to, my voice goes up again, "Oh my freaking god. Why do you have to justify everything or try to fix it? I understand why you want to leave, but at the very least, you should have talked to me. That's how relationships work. You can't just jump in whenever *you* feel you need to fix the situation or when it's convenient for you!"

"How is this convenient for me?" Tom says, matching my voice.

"I want a partnership! You should have trusted me. You've known about the position for weeks! Does it ever occur to you to include me in your plans?"

There is a knock on the door and Janine steps in. "Guys, it's getting loud in here. This is an office. You two need to keep it down or move this conversation elsewhere." She glares at both of us like she's scolding us and I have a vision of her dressed in a nun's robes habit coming in with old-fashioned paddles. For a second, I'm afraid of her and close my mouth.

"Cool it down. This is not the place for this," she hisses and closes the door.

I sigh but lower my voice. "We're going around in circles. Maybe you're right, for the sake of our careers, it's better if you leave." Before he answers, Janine interrupts our conversation again and tells me Judith wants to see me.

"See Judith and we'll talk later." I follow him out of my office.

I make it to Judith's office and pause at the open door. "Close the door, please. Have a seat," she says with a stern look. I take a chair that's in front of her desk. While my mind is reeling from that conversation with Tom, I try to keep my cool. I take a deep breath and try to channel my Zen.

"I've had meetings all morning, and I just came in. Imagine my surprise when I read last night's emails. I got copied on an email from Tom to the dean. Then I got to read an email from security to the dean. Both talking regarding you and a situation with one of *your* students. I was expecting an email from you, but I got nothing," she says.

Shiiiit! I forgot to copy her in my emails.

"I'm sorry. I should have told you we had a problem with a student. To be honest, I didn't think it was a problem and—"

"I would have thought you would have been the first one to tell me if something was wrong. Instead, I received yet another email from the dean this morning." I'm speechless as she goes on. "If my staff has a meeting with my boss, at the very least I expect to be notified."

"You're right, I'm—"

"I'd like to say I'm somewhat disappointed." She finally pauses and looks at me.

She's disappointed. Hearing her say it out loud is heart-breaking, painful and upsetting all mixed into one, and I feel awful. *Shit.* There goes my promotion. "What is going on, Olivia?" she asks with a concerned look. When I don't answer, she shakes her head.

"I've had some personal issues. My ex is trying to make me sell my home because he needs money and I have other things going on, but that's no excuse. I am so sorry I disappointed you. I promise it won't happen again."

"What's going on with you and Tom? I heard you guys arguing. The entire office heard you," she says sardonically while gesturing to the door.

"We had a disagreement and we're trying to resolve it."

"It's obviously your personal business, but you need to get a handle on it before it affects your careers."

I take a deep breath. "We're trying to work something out."

"What do you think is going to happen when HR finds out?"

"We've already met with HR and they are aware of our relationship."

"Something else *I* wasn't aware of."

"I'm sorry I didn't tell you, but I didn't know if HR was going to tell you or if I was supposed to. I'm so sorry."

"Regardless, half the office is talking about it. The whole campus is talking about it. I don't want to hear any more about you and Tom. Whatever's happening between you guys, please keep it outside of my office. That is all." She turns her chair and goes back to the computer. *Crap. She's pissed.*

I stand. I'm about to leave, but I address her again from her door. "Can I ask you something?"

"Yes."

"Did you know Tom before you hired him?"

"Yes. He asked me to judge him on his resume and his experience, not on his last name, and I did. I felt he was the most qualified person for the job, and I hired him." Judith sighs and looks kindly at me. "Moving forward, can I expect you two to get along and keep your personal issues outside this office?" she says in a gentler voice.

"Yes." The rest of the day, I stay in my office and keep the lowest possible profile.

I'm mad at Tom and tell him so via text. Tom's upset too. He tells me that until he transfers out, there'll be no contact between us. Of course, he did. He's apparently the fixer-in-chief. *Fuck.*

The day of the Academic Resource Fair *finally* arrives. I've barely seen or talked with Tom these past few weeks, and I don't know what to expect. We've mostly communicated about work and even then, most of our correspondence has been about the event and via email or text. On the other hand, today is the day of the fair and I don't have time to psychoanalyze this.

I arrive at the arena, and it doesn't take long before our entire team is there. Tom included. We have breakfast together, review our plans, then divide and conquer. Tom and I give directions to the rest of the staff, and by the grace of God, nobody complains. As a bonus, we have a full house and students are happy. Besides a few occasional fires, we pull off an amazing event. Both Judith and the dean congratulate us. When the event wraps up, I can finally breathe.

After the event's over, Tom and I go back to the office with several boxes of left-over supplies. We work quietly putting them away and we're almost done when he finally addresses me. "I got the job. The assistant dean job at the central campus," he says as we close the storage room door. "I wanted you to hear it from me before Judith makes the official announcement tomorrow. I'll be gone in three weeks."

I freeze. *Wow.* I can't believe this is happening. I know he's not perfect and I'm definitely not either, but a part of me thought we were good together and complement each other. His intensity against my humor and optimism. I really thought we would somehow work it out.

"Congratulations," is all I can think to say.

As I look at him, it occurs to me that he looks miserable. "Thank you." he replies quietly.

Finally, we're done. "I have to go," he says. "Goodbye, Olivia." I struggle with what to say next. Before I say anything at all he walks away. No explanation. No conversation and I want to scream. *Seriously? Nothing?* I take a deep breath and let it go. Somehow it'll work out. *It has too.*

The announcement and shock of Tom's departure last only a day or two as the posting of the Advising Director's job opening eclipses it.

The next three weeks go by agonizingly slow. Seeing him every day is complete and utter torture. On top of it, interviews start. They are annoyingly slow, exasperating, and cumbersome, all rolled into one excruciatingly sluggish bureaucratic process.

I alternate between at least five emotions over the next fifteen days. I'm excited about the position and the endless professional possibilities. I panic, thinking that I'm not prepared enough to lead the team. I doubt myself because I don't have enough experience as a manager, but then I get excited again because I love students and I love my team.

When it comes to Tom, I feel mostly sadness and frustration. Sadness at what could have been and frustration that for now, I can't do anything about this. Once he leaves, maybe we can talk. Maybe there's hope for us.

In the end, Grace, our department's assistant director, is selected to lead us and Judith recommends me for assistant director. The truth is, by the time the whole process is finished, I'm over it. I don't even care.

Tom comes into my office on his last day and says goodbye. Half of me wants to scream. I want to follow him and demand an explanation, a goodbye, something. How can somebody just walk away like this? Without a fight? I need closure, or at least a reaction out of this man, but there's none. This is über professional Tom, *Office-Tom*, and he's not engaging in anything personal. I'm forced to face the fact that this, whatever's left between us, might be over.

Olivia

I work with college students. This means helping them figure out their educational and career moves, sharing their "aha" moments when they've found their passion, are excited about graduation, or landing their first real job. Being excited for them and with them, for their accomplishments.

The flip side is being brutally honest and calling them on their bullshit when I know their chosen major is not where they need to be.

Sometimes that means being the *bad guy*, and telling my students they can't change their major if they want to graduate on time or when I *know* they won't get into a program. Other times, it means playing referee between them and their parents and, on rare occasions, their significant others. Keeping calm as they completely fail a class, then come back to tell you it was your fault for letting them register for such class, even though they went against your advice. It's a balancing act and you learn to be patient, develop a thick skin, and always keep a cool head amid the drama some students have. Then we do it again. Over and over and over, day in and day out. Some days are so repetitive, you feel your life is stuck in an endless loop where every day is a duplication of the previous day. *Like Groundhog Day.*

I never hear back from Tom and after a week contemplating every existential dilemma known to man. I decide it's time to give up and let it go. *Like a Disney song.*

I have a sudden vision of walking out of the office to the 80s song "It Must Have Been Love," by Roxette playing in the background along with a montage of our relationship. I can't help but laugh at my own crazy imagination.

The truth is, I need to worry more about my house. Thankfully, Max and his team have been fighting Brandon over his greed. After I call him to get an update, we agree to meet in his office in downtown Miami.

"Hi, I'm Olivia Campbell," I politely introduce myself to a young receptionist. "Is Max Rodriguez available? He's expecting me."

"Let me find out. Please, have a seat." She gestures with her hand behind me. I turn around and for the first time, notice the elegant office chairs. These are not typical steel chairs; these are traditional arm chairs. The seats have nice cushions on the back and the bottom that feel like sponge. The brown wood looks solid and the black leather feels real. Even the padded armrest feels nice. "Would you like some coffee or tea?" A different girl asks. I nod and thank her, then watch as she too disappears.

I look around the elegant room. The room is stylishly designed and decorated. One wall has expansive views of downtown Miami. Everything just exudes professionalism and high-end. I pause for a second. *Shit.* How am I going to tell my brothers that I seem to have hired the most expensive lawyers in all of Miami? The bill will probably be twice as much as what I have to pay Brandon if we lose. I'll be indebted to them for life.

"Miss?" the young receptionist asks. "I apologize, but Max had an emergency and had to go. He told me you were coming and told me that you just needed to sign the agreement. Please, follow me."

I follow her and a few minutes later find myself in a conference room with floor to ceiling views of the city. Like in the waiting room there are nice chairs, shiny brass and spotless chrome. The views are amazing, and the room is both beautiful and intimidating in its grandiosity.

"Just out of curiosity, why am I signing an agreement? Did we go to court?" I ask as she's walking out. I'm not familiar with the court system and I know I've been preoccupied with my disintegrating love life *and* my job and the interviews, *but* somebody would have told me if we were going to trial. Right? Right.

When she says, "I'm sorry, I'm not at liberty to say. Please wait here, okay?" The knot in the pit of my stomach grows. I really, really don't want to go to jail. She walks away and returns a few minutes later with an older lady.

"Hello, I'm Mrs. Gonzalez. How are you?" I nod. "So, we've settled out of court. The other party agreed to take twenty-thousand dollars. We'll pay all of his lawyers and court fees and in exchange, he promised to leave you alone. This nightmare is over and now you can move on," she says casually and smiles at me politely.

This is great! I mean, it is, except for the humongous bill that I know is coming, but this is great. Finally, I sigh with relief. When she gives me a pen, I sign the forms where indicated, and wait.

"Alright, we'll get you copies of everything. Your brothers also requested copies of the paperwork. Would that be okay?" I nod. "Great," she says, then hands the stack of papers to the young receptionist, who takes them and walks off.

"Are you going to send me a copy of the...bill?" I hold my breath and try not to wince.

"The bill has been taken care of. Would you like a copy?" she asks. "Do you want us to share it with your brothers?"

"Oh, didn't my brothers pay for it?"

"I'm sorry. I'm not at liberty to say." She says nothing else while we wait and I can't help wondering, if not my brothers, then who would have paid for it.

Finally, the younger woman returns and hands her two stacks of paper. "Here's a copy of everything for your records." She hands me a stack and holds on to the other. "Come on, I'll walk you out," Mrs. Gonzalez invites.

She leads the way and while I walk next to her, I debate if I should let it go or demand to see a manager or a lawyer, someone who can tell me who paid this bill. Ultimately, I decide against it. After she bids me goodbye, instead of going home, I follow a hunch and drive to the downtown campus.

I make it to the dean of students' office, only to lose my nerve at the front door. As I walk away, Alan's walking by. *Shiiiit!* "Hey, Olivia," he greets casually.

"Hi Alan," I reply with an awkward wave.

"Are you here to see Tom?" *Of course, he would ask that.* Why else would I be here? Now *everybody* and their cousins will know I was here.

"I... I umm..." *Ack!*

"Come, I'll take you to his office." Without waiting for an answer, he opens the door for me.

"Thank you." As we enter, I'm trying to come up with an excuse for this impromptu visit. I mean, he's the one who left. He made it clear he doesn't want to see me or have anything to do with me. He needed to get away from me before I screwed up his life and his family legacy, or whatever it is he's worried about, and now I show up here. This was such a bad idea. *What was I thinking?*

As his office comes into view, I notice he's standing up behind his desk and on the phone. He sees us and motions for us to come in. He's wearing a light green shirt and tie, and his emerald eyes focus on me while he speaks. I haven't seen him in a few weeks and I'm reminded of how handsome he is. A few times during these past weeks I've thought about what I would say to him if I saw him again, but at the sight of him, it all goes out the window. My heart starts hammering against my chest.

I barely hear Alan say goodbye and close the door behind me while Tom hangs up the phone. He says nothing for a few seconds. Finally, he does. "Hi."

"Hi, I'm sorry, I didn't mean to bother you. I'm sure you must be swamped." My eyebrows itch and I can't stop myself from scratching. *Be Zen. Relax.*

"It's fine. How are you?" He asks, wide-eyed.

"I'm okay. I'm good. How are you?" *This is so awkward!*

"Glad to hear that. I'm okay." He pauses, "Congratulations on getting the assistant director position. You deserve it."

"Thank you."

After another pause, he asks, "Is there anything you need or anything I can help you with?" he rolls his chair to the other side, seeming needing something to do with his hands.

"Ummm, I just left Max's office. Apparently, we settled out of court. Brandon agreed to settle, which my brothers had offered to pay." I pause. "Something weird happened, though. The bill was already paid and the firm didn't want to tell me who paid it. Would you know anything about that?"

His eyes widen, but he says nothing for a few seconds. He moves his chair to the original position, walks in front of the desk, and leans on it. "It was me. Keith and Max mentioned he was demanding money. Given his current situation and what we know about him, we didn't feel he would back down. Your house is worth much more than that. We spoke with your brothers. We didn't want you to deal with him or go through a long litigation, so we took care of it."

At least he's being honest, but half of me wants to scream and ask him why does he keep jumping in and trying to fix things without asking me, except the *one* thing I want him to fix.

Instead, I take a deep breath and decide I will not be angry. I will be Zen and move on. "I don't know what to say. You didn't need to do that."

"You don't have to say anything, and I expect nothing. I needed to know you were going to be safe, and now you are. Besides, you're the assistant director. We'll work something out later." I know this is Office-Tom, but still, his dryness is startling. Instead of being happy that I don't have to worry about Brandon or that I'll lose my home, my chin barely holds on as I blink away the tears that are threatening to come. I manage a fake smile before a tap on the door interrupts us.

I turn and an older woman nods to me, then directs her attention to him. "The dean's on the phone."

"Okay, thanks," he replies before looking back at me. "It's my boss. I have to take this. Would you like to have coffee? Can you hang around and talk?"

"You know what? I don't want to take any more of your time."

His lips purse, but he doesn't argue. "Okay. It was nice to see you," he says with a heavy sigh before he picks up the phone. I look at him one last time and walk away. Half of me hopes he'll change his mind and run after me.

But he doesn't.

My heart shatters in tiny little pieces, the grim realization that he doesn't care hitting me like a ton of bricks.

On my way out, several people stop me to say hello or goodbye, and I barely make it to my car before I break down crying. After I calm down enough to at least see the road, I get in my car and drive aimlessly home.

Olivia

After the ugly realization that I'll die old and alone and surrounded by cats, actually, let's imagine dogs in this mental scenario... that I'll die old and alone surrounded by *dogs*, I tell Grace I'm sick and stop going to work.

To be honest, I feel like someone's squeezing my heart. *Like an orange.* It's both physically and mentally exhausting.

At this point, the only thing that could be worse is someone breaking into my house. Which my front door opening signals as a real possibility. For a second, my heart stops. I see shadows near my door and look around for a weapon. I have none. If the intruders don't kill me, a heart attack will definitely do the trick.

Then I hear them talking.

"Are you guys breaking and entering now?"

"It's not breaking and entering if you have a key," my brother William states as they walk in and he shows me the shiny item.

I look at them and flop back on the bed. "Whatever."

"Hi sis," my brother Michael calls out.

"Hey, stranger. Well, at least we know she's alive," Will says as he lays down next to me, face up. "Are you alright?" He turns his head and looks at me.

"Yep. I'm great."

The bed bounces as Mike lays down on my other side. "Yeah, *clearly* you're great. Is that why you're ignoring us?"

"I'm not ignoring you. I just don't want to talk to anybody."

"Bianca and Valentina are worried about you. You're not answering their calls," Will says in a softer voice.

When he mentions my friends, my heart breaks. They called my family, which means they're concerned, and I feel ten times worse for ignoring them. "I'll call them later."

"How's Tom?" Will asks.

Wow. Straight for the jugular.

I really, really don't want to talk to anybody, but I'm trapped between the two of them. I take a deep breath and answer honestly. "I think he's okay."

"You think? Did you guys have a fight? Should we go and beat him up?"

And we're back to this one. "No! There'll be no beating up. If you want to beat somebody up, join a boxing class. Leave me out of it."

Will's eyebrow's turn down in the middle.

"Mom's worried about you. We all are. When was the last time you were at work?" Mike says in a softer voice.

"I took a few days off. Everything's fine." I glance at them. They both stare at me, and I can't help but groan. "I really don't want to have this conversation right now. I'm fine. Everything's fine."

"You keep saying that. Yet, you don't look fine. Olivia, what happened with Tom?" Will asks again, this time firmer.

"Oh, my God. I don't want to talk about it. Besides, who cares if I'm dating? Why would I want to get a boyfriend, then get married only to end up in divorce?"

"Are you serious right now?" Mike asks, his brow furrowed.

"Olivia," Will starts, "you can't think about it like that. Yes, it's true, divorce sucks and it's probably one of life's most excruciatingly painful and disappointing experiences somebody could have, but you can't give up."

"Wow, so you agree divorce is excruciatingly painful, and yet you want *me* to go through that? I don't think so."

"You can't avoid marriage because you're afraid you might end in divorce. Now you're taking it to the extreme, you're afraid of getting married and *maybe* ending in divorce, so you're just not getting married at all?"

Pretty much?

"Ummm, not necessarily. I'll keep dating and we'll see what happens." I pause. "You know what, only the hopeless romantic always think that this time it's *for real*," I make air quotes, "or that this time they've met *the one*. It's a never-ending vicious circle. You're constantly looking for *the one* except everybody you meet is *completely* useless. Yet we keep doing it in hopes we meet *the one* who may or may not be willing to put up with us because he's also not sure we are *the one* for *him* and, to be honest, it's extremely exhausting. It's all bullshit."

Will looks at me. "Are you done ranting?"

"NO! It's all bull."

"You already said that. Except you don't actually believe all that." Mike says, pointing at me. "Maybe you're overthinking this."

I lift my head to I look at him, then flop back on the bed. "You're single too! Ugh."

I try to get up from the bed and William blocks me. "Hey, look at me. I'm happily married. You can't ignore the chance to find love because of your past experiences or based on other people's experiences, like mom. At least she keeps trying."

"I'm single and broke with a house I love but can barely afford and a mountain of debt. What do you want from me?"

My eyes sting. I want to bury my face in my pillow and let it out.

"I want you to stop moping long enough to look in front of you and see if maybe you have the *right* guy this time."

"We're not saying run out the door and marry the guy tomorrow. But it's nice to go home and have somebody to love and share things with. We know you want that."

"You guys are so stupid."

"I know we are, but we met him and from what Bianca's told us, do you think maybe there's a chance you found somebody worthwhile?"

"I don't know. Maybe."

"Okay, then start there. Talk to him. Tell him how you feel. Olivia, you have to try again. Come on, try one more time."

"I'm not Mom."

"You're not. If it was her, she would try, try, try, try again." After a beat, we all laugh. He's right, she would. At the same time, I'm not her. Maybe I'm too jaded. When we stop laughing, he's looking at the ceiling when he says, "I know you still think about Dad leaving us." On hearing this, both Michael and I freeze. "I did too, but that's in the past, we can't change it. Now I've built a life with Julie and we're happy. You guys can do that too. You just have to put yourself out there."

He gives me a kiss on the side temple then stands up and offers a hand. "Come on, Julie sent you a few things. Food, wine, and ice cream." I take his hand and get off the bed. He lets go so that we can go through the door.

"Have I told you lately my sister-in-law is very smart?" I say.

"Why do you think I married her? Also, you need to take a shower. You stink."

"No, I don't."

"You do, and it looks like a hair ball grew up on top of your head."

"No, it doesn't," I say as we walk into the living room, and my brother bumps my shoulder.

As I sit on a stool, it occurs to me they're right. *Ugh. I hate that they are.* I have to stop this ridiculousness and talk to Tom.

It's decided. No more sulking. I will take charge of my love life and go back to work. My students need me. I make a mental note, go back to work ASAP and... actually no more mental notes. I should buy an agenda or a cute diary, like Bridget Jones, and start writing things down. *Good plan.*

Since it's April and the spring semester is winding down, my students are making appointments with me and looking for advice for summer and fall classes. Things are busy and moving along.

My last student of the day is John. The drug-dealer/kingpin wanna'—be.

"Hi, John, how's everything? How are classes?" I ask.

"Good. Business's great. Classes are good."

Business? As in the drug selling business? I should ask Keith regarding complicity laws, "Greeeeat, how's your wife?"

Upon hearing this, he grins. His smile lighting him up from within. "She's fantastic. She's happy because I'm in college."

"That's great. How did you guys meet?" I ask absentmindedly as I search for classes on the computer, glancing his way every couple of seconds.

"We had a class together in ninth grade. She was so beautiful. I sat in the back because I was a troublemaker, then one day the teacher moved me to the front, next to her, and she was nice to me. We started hanging out and I asked her to go out with me. After she graduated from college, I snatched her."

Snatched her? Does that mean asked her to marry him? I need to work on my slang.

"... she's legit, and she believes in me. She understands me and doesn't judge me. It's like she can see inside of me," he says, pointing to his chest with his hand.

After a few minutes of hearing him talk about her, it strikes me this clueless-drug-selling man is truly in love with his wife. To be honest, I can't help but feel a tiny bit jealous. "What about you? Do you have somebody?" he asks unexpectedly. Coming from him, the question surprises me.

"There's someone, we're trying to work things out."

"Are you using your brain or your heart?"

"Excuse me?"

"You seem like a brains kind of person."

"I...do?"

"Yes. Here's the thing, your brain controls everything at an intellectual level. Everything's connected to the brain, *but* if your heart hurts, so does your brain, then your whole body is out of whack. So even if your brain is logically right, it's not, but it doesn't know. You have to follow your heart and tell him how you feel. Like you should really tell him."

Did he just say all that? Coming from him, the comment throws me off. I can't help but think his wife might be onto something. "Thank you, John." I say it and I really mean it, "I cleared your hold, you should be able to log into the system and register."

After a brief conversation about the classes he should take, he stands from the chair. "Don't worry, I'll ask my wife to help me register. She's very smart. I'm sure she knows how to do all that." He pulls his phone out of his pocket and I immediately know he's going to call or text his wife. He smiles at me and when he leaves there's a bounce in his step and a sense of awareness that I know comes from the fact that he knows his wife loves him as much as he loves her.

Tom

I started my new job as assistant dean. I keep meeting with students, parents, my colleagues, and they're all starting to sound exactly the same. It's all background noise. I keep thinking, how the hell did it all go so wrong? *Maybe. Maybe. Maybe.* It's all a sea of maybes.

I start my new job, and I assist. I go home and go back to work and assist some more. I assist people, advisors, students and student employees, parents, the deans, and associate deans in an endless loop, assisting everything and everybody around me... *except myself.*

Weeks go by and I go through the motions, but it gets harder and harder because all I can think about is her. I finally have a job that I want, I'm making my family proud, I'm back home, yet it's meaningless. I keep thinking about her; her smiles and the dimples. It's like a movie that keeps repeating itself in my head non-stop, over and over and over, and I can't find the pause button because I'm stuck on a loop.

I've never met a woman as joyful as her, and if I had I just never noticed. Not like I noticed Olivia the first time she crashed into me. Before I knew who she was or that we worked together, when there were no preconceptions or expectations, from that exact moment on, I was smitten. I was hers.

I'm always amazed by her generosity and kindness with people. Not to mention, she's the most optimistic person I know. With her, there's just never a dull moment. I don't know that I have experienced that kind of spiritedness in a romantic partner before and I really want it back. I can't stop thinking about how she laughs and smirks. I love the way she looks at me.

Obviously, I knew it wasn't going to be easy, but this is madness. This is all-consuming and I don't know where to go from here. *Drinking seems like a good idea.*

I'm at home on a Friday night nursing a drink when Keith arrives from a week-long conference. There are no lights on and the house is a mess, but frankly, I don't really give a shit. "Hey man," he says, walking through the door. His carry-on hits the floor, and he pauses momentarily.

"Hey," I say, but don't bother looking up.

"Dude, what the fuck? Who died? What did you do to my house?" he shouts as he takes in the darkness, the empty boxes of pizza, and the several bottles of alcohol consumed on the floor. How do I explain to my best friend that I trashed his house because I'm heartbroken?

"Relax. Nobody died."

"Have you been to work?" He approaches me and looks at me with concern.

"Yes. Kind of. I called in sick yesterday and today."

"Were you planning on spending the weekend drinking?"

The truth is that was exactly my plan. Drink and drown the pain of missing her. No point in denying it. "Yep. Something like that."

"Tom, you look like shit. What the fuck is going on?" he says as he goes to the kitchen and grabs a beer.

"Nothing's going on."

"Right. What happened with Olivia?" he asks.

"Nothing."

"What the hell did you do?"

"Nothing."

"Did you try to talk to her? Did you tell her you love her? Did you apologize?" he demands after he opens the bottle, then takes a sip of beer.

"No. No, and no." I grab my whiskey and take a long pull. My throat burns and I wait for the feeling to pass.

"Are you still in denial?"

"I'm not in love with her."

"Okay, genius. That's not what I asked but keep telling yourself that." When I don't answer he keeps going. "Oh my God. You know what? I can't deal with this. This is bullshit. It's been a long week and I'm exhausted. Clean my house. Tomorrow we're going cycling and then you can explain to me why you're sitting here alone, trashing my house, instead of with her." He goes to his room and slams the door.

He's right, I should be with her. I look at the ceiling. Desperation creeps over me. Fear that I've somehow screwed it all up and that I *am* in love with her.

It's early Saturday morning and we're joining a small group for a ride. We start our warm-up, a few laps around the golf course by ourselves. I take a deep breath. My stomach is uneasy, but I will it into submission because this is what I need right now. I need fresh air, the wind in my face and the soft purr of the bikes to relax and center me.

Keith is next to me. I woke up early and cleaned his house and got back to his good graces. "What's going on with Olivia? Have you spoken to her?" he asks.

"Not really."

"At all?" he glances my way and his eyebrows go up.

"Actually, she came by my new office, and we spoke for a few minutes. She found out about the settlement and wanted to know if we had something to do with it."

"What did you tell her?"

"The truth, that we took care of it so that he left her alone. Then I had a phone call from the dean. I wanted to ask her to have coffee with me, but she left. She didn't want to talk to me."

"You let her leave? Did you reach out to her after?"

"Not really."

"Tom, explain to me why the fuck haven't you called her?"

"Why the fuck would I call her? It's over, it's done."

"Oh, I don't know, maybe because you love her, and you can't stop thinking about her?"

"It doesn't matter. I'm not sure she wants a relationship with me or with anybody else, for that matter. On top of it, she feels I lied to her about my last name, which is technically not true. We also had a problem with a student. I had a feeling he liked her, but I didn't say anything. And the cherry on top? I don't think she appreciates me meddling in her life. I don't know, maybe we need some distance from each other."

"Distance? Are you serious right now? So, you're just going to let her walk away without a fight?"

When he says it aloud, it dawns on me. I *am* letting her go without a fight. "*Fuck.* I see your point, but she hates the stupidity that flies out of my mouth. I implied my family or the family name was more important than her."

"I agree with that. You do say a lot of stupid shit."

"Yeah, yeah," I say, followed by a finger flip and he laughs but continues.

"I don't think she hates you. Yes, she was pissed at you, but this is a solvable situation. Talk to her or, better yet, grovel. Send her a bunch of flowers and apologize. I don't know, but fucking do *something*."

"It's complicated," I murmur.

"No, it's not. Do you like her?"

"Of course, I like her. I love that she never gives up. She's funny, she doesn't take my shit. She's gorgeous *and* she has a great attitude. I love that she's smart, that I can talk to her about anything and she gets it, but—"

"Dude, you like her and she likes you. What else do you need to know?"

"When you put it like that..."

"Tom, you know I'm right. You have been my friend for a long time. I think we can agree, she's the girl we would bring over to meet our moms. I honestly don't know what the fuck you're waiting for. You need to go get her." I notice the group and we speed up to join them. "So, what's the plan?" he huffs with exertion next to me.

"Plan?"

"Yeah, what's the plan to win her back?"

"I have no idea."

A couple of hours later, my muscles are hurting. Deep, confused, frustrated, angry thoughts turn into liquid and vanish thanks to furious pedaling. We're cooling off and it's our last turn.

As we approach her house, I debate if I should stop and talk to her while simultaneously wondering what I would say to her and how fuck am I going to fix it.

"Hey, are you hungry?" I hear Keith ask. At my blank stare he repeats, "Do you want food?"

Food. Then it hits me. I know how to fix this.

Olivia

I have decided to put a new plan in motion. *Operation Woo The Cyclist.* Before I changed my mind, I went to Walmart last night and bought a bike. Not to mention, I wanted to know what all the fuss with cycling is about.

Today is Saturday and I'm cooking lunch for my friends. I need a few things from the supermarket and since it's a beautiful day, I take my brand-new bike. Besides, biking's great for the environment *and* I'm saving money on gas. It's a win-win all around. I put on shorts, thick elbow pads and knee pads, a bike helmet, and grab my trusty fanny pack. I look ridiculous, but I don't care. My goal is to master this contraption and impress Tom.

I take a quick trip to a nearby supermarket, buy a box of pasta, pasta sauce and a couple of bags of pre-cut salad. I'm on the bike path and I'm less than two minutes away from my home when an idling car to my left speeds up suddenly, with me less than a foot behind it. Badly startled by the fear of a car crushing me, I lose control and swerve. I try to overcompensate, which causes the handlebars to shake and sends me on a collision path with the asphalt. Lucky for me, I fall on top of the two supermarket bags, one of which has the two salad bags and they help cushion the fall.

If falling is not humiliating enough, now imagine a lettuce explosion. Lettuce flies everywhere and all around me. *Of course, that would happen to me.*

On the bright side, I'm still on the bike path. I hear the whoosh of cars passing by and manage to sit and extricate myself from the bike. As I take off the helmet, stabbing pain directs my attention to my leg and I see it covered in bright red. When I frantically swipe away at the liquid, I see the gash on my leg. The wound is not big, and the red is mostly pasta goo. The mixture of sauce, dirt, and lettuce is unsettling, but at least I won't bleed to death on the side of the road. *Positive thinking.*

I'm contemplating my next move when, out of the corner of my eye, I see a flock of ducks running my way; some are flying my way. I have a sudden vision of ducks eating me alive. *That would suck.*

I know I shouldn't be so dramatic, but ducks in Miami have been known to attack people. My fear is not unfounded. Luckily, ducks prefer to eat salad and not people. I take comfort in the fact that they don't want to eat me, at least not while there's salad on the ground. However, within a few seconds, I'm surrounded by ducks. I try to stand, but the ducks are too close to me.

These ducks are *loud. Is there such a thing as zombie ducks?*

A group of cyclists zoom past and through white and black feathers, I see Tom and Keith jump off of their bikes and run in my direction. In a matter of seconds, Tom's by my side. Without waiting, he grabs my underarms and lifts me effortlessly while Keith tries to scare the ducks away from us. "Jesus Christ. Are you okay?!" Deep green eyes quickly scan me. His eyes immediately go to the huge red splotch on my leg. "Oh my God."

"I'm okay. It's just red pasta sauce."

"Are you sure?"

"Positive." I take pieces of lettuce off my arms and body, and nod at him. "I'm fine, Tom." To be honest, my palm hurts and my leg hurts. I'm in pain, freaked out, and barely holding in tears. Not to mention, I probably look like a crazy person. No, I *definitely* look like a crazy person.

"Are you sure? Did you break anything?" He's breathing heavily, but he's tenderly touching my arms. Electricity shoots through me and I wonder if it is static. Then I remember this is what it feels like when he's around me. When he touches me and my skin electrifies and hums. My skin begs to be touched by him.

Tom kneels in front of me to examine the gash on my leg. His face is very close to my... *privates. Lord have mercy.* After a few seconds, I gently pull him up. "Tom, I'm fine. I don't think I did any real damage. The lettuce broke my fall."

"What are you doing?" he asks once he's at eye level with me.

"I went to the supermarket."

"On a bike? Why are you even on a bike?"

"Because you like being on a bike?... And I thought I could join you one day? Maybe?"

He sighs and looks at me. "You could've been hurt. What were you thinking?" he says in a softer voice. He reaches over and starts peeling pieces of lettuce off my body and my hair.

"I wasn't thinking." I hold his hand, effectively stopping the lettuce picking, and look up at him.

He sighs. "We need to talk."

Somebody screams, "Shut-up and kiss her already," and we turn to see Keith grinning at us.

Tom gives him the finger while Keith shakes his head. Tom directs his attention back to me. "Ignore my crazy best friend. Have dinner with me? *Please?*"

I nod, not trusting myself to talk. They walk me home, then leave.

After the lunch fiasco, my friends simply show up with takeout and spend the afternoon discussing the situation with Tom and I on a microscopic level. I feel somewhat better, even though I wish being asked out on our second date didn't occur on what appeared to be the murder scene of a vegetarian. While they help me get ready, we have a few drinks. I relax and try to stay positive. It's all going to be okay. *Somehow*.

I end up wearing a casual, mid-calf sleeveless summer dress. It's red with a white-polka-dot print. I keep my hair loose and my makeup light.

A few hours later, I take a deep breath and knock on Tom's door. When he opens, my heart races and my throat dries up. He's wearing jeans and a white button-down shirt with the sleeves rolled up. He looks amazing. I clear my throat. "Hi," I manage with an awkward wave.

"Hi. *Wow*. You look amazing." I smile at his choice of words. I walk in and he leads me to the kitchen.

As the kitchen comes into view, I pause. The kitchen is a mess. Actually, it looks like a bomb went off. "O-kay. Do I even want to know?"

He stands in front of me with his head hung. "I tried cooking, but I went to take a shower and everything burned. I mean, except for dessert. My mother gave me a family recipe for a *flan* and it's currently cooling in the refrigerator." A smile pulls at the corner of my lips. He looks completely out of his element in the kitchen and it's sweet that he tried.

"But don't worry, we are eating. I mean, I ended up getting takeout from a great restaurant... you're going to love it. It's definitely much better than anything I could have done... I mean, Keith might kill me when he sees his kitchen... I have no idea why I'm rambling on about food."

My smile turns to a grin. He holds my hands and takes a shaky breath. I can see his jaw tic a couple of times before he tries again. "I'm sorry that was an idiot. I completely closed myself off. Please forgive me." He pauses and exhales. "I know I can be high-handed and bossy. Being with you made me possessive. I don't know what came over me. I'm not usually this crazy, but I promise I'll spend the rest of our lives making it up to do you. I'll do whatever it takes to prove myself to you. You're smart and charming and sweet and so fucking funny. You're amazing and perfect for me and if you give me a chance, I would love to have a relationship with you because I've fallen madly, deeply in love with you."

"*Tom.*"

"And I know that you're afraid of relationships, but I promise, a ship always comes to port and you're it for me and I don't even know if you want to have a relationship with me, but I hope you do because –."

I gently cover his mouth with my hands to stop him from talking. "Tom, I would love to have a relationship with you. You were right. I didn't really want to be in a relationship with anybody, because I was afraid to get hurt." I pause. "Every time I went on a date it was a disaster. The truth is, I didn't want anybody... Until I met you."

"Wait, wait, wait, you want to have a relationship?" When I nod, he keeps going. "I better take advantage before you change your mind."

"I won't. I do appreciate everything you do and that you want to take care of me. I love that your family comes first. I was stupid. I've just never met anybody like you before. I'm sorry too."

He gently grabs my hand in his. "You're not stupid. I'm in love with you."

"I love you too. I don't want to be without you. I want to be your anchor, or you can be mine. I don't care. You can be the lighthouse or the lighthouse keeper, whatever..."

"Stop. Olivia, stop throwing ship analogies at me. Did you listen to me? It's too late. I'm already in love with you."

"You are?" I want to laugh. He's so intent on convincing me that he didn't hear me make my declaration.

"Yes. And you're in love with me too."

"Am I now? *Wow*, I forgot how conceited you are." When I say this, a flirty smile spreads over his face.

He takes me in his arms, and I melt into his embrace and we just hold each other for a few seconds. He takes a step back and looks at me. "I'm going to kiss you now." His arm comes up and his thumb gently caresses my cheekbone. When I close my eyes, he kisses me madly and when our lips finally connect, it's magic and I know I'm right where I'm meant to be.

Epilogue

O livia

Today is Memorial Day. It's been a year since we kissed and made up and we're celebrating with a BBQ at my house. All our friends are there and it's turning out to be an amazing day.

Somebody places a hand on the small of my back. I turn to see Tom grinning at me. "Hey, can I talk to you?" he says in my ear. When I agree, he offers a hand and leads me to my room.

"What's up?" I ask as he closes the door and motions for me to sit on the bed.

"So, I found this," he snickers while he hands me a folded sheet of paper.

"What is it?" I ask as I unfold it. When it's open, I immediately start laughing. It's a copy of the cheesy flyer I made when I started looking for a roommate. It seems like a million years ago, "Where did you find this?"

"I know people."

"Sure, you do," I smile, and he grins back at me.

"I heard that Leyla might be moving out. Are you searching for a roommate?"

"Why? Are you interested?"

"Maybe." He cocks his head sideways.

"Do you have a bank account?"

His eyebrows lift but he recovers quickly. "Last time I checked, I did. Why is this relevant?"

"The owner of the house is very particular. You would have to go through an interview. For the record, the owner doesn't care what religion you are, but there will be no changing of furniture and no wall painting. Also, if you want an orthopedic bed, you have to buy it."

"Okaaaay. Thanks for letting me know?"

"Although I wouldn't be opposed to upgrading the patio. Let me ask you, do you like cats or dogs? Because the owner is a dog person. The owner does not care for exotic pets."

"Not a problem, spiders and snakes freak me out. I love dogs. You know, I actually know the owner of the house. Do you think that would at least give me preference among other candidates?"

"That depends. How desperate are you?"

"Very. My roommate is a hardcore cyclist... he insists on cycling every day." He grins and I can't help but snicker and giggle. "Would it help if I told you I was in love with the owner of the house?" He says grabbing my hand and helping me up from the bed.

"Are you now?"

Turning a little more serious, he admits it. "I am."

My heart melts when I look into his loving eyes. "I love you too." I grab his face in my hands and kiss him.

He wraps his arms around me. "Come on, why else would I want to move into this house with you?"

"Because you're homeless and it's a big house next to a golf course you like to cycle around?"

"All valid reasons."

"Or maybe you just want to use me for the sex."

"Oh, I definitely want to use you for that," he replies with a mischievous grin and pulls me closer, until our bodies touch. "Can I use you right now?"

"NO! We have a house full of people. Our friends are out there," I put my hands on his chest and push gently, smiling, "Tell you what, your application for roommate has been pre-approved and moved to the top of the pile."

"Would my application be approved if I was your fiancé?" he asks casually.

Wait. What?

He pulls a ring out of his pocket and looks at me, then kneels down. "Olivia?"

My eyes go from his eyes to the ring and back to his face. My breath is caught in my chest and I'm speechless. "Yes?"

"I'm in love with you. Will you marry me?"

"Yes! Yes!" my automatic reaction is to shriek and start jumping in place like an idiot while he gives me a huge smile. He stands up, but when he struggles to put the ring on, I'm forced to stop. Once the ring is on my finger, we crash into each other. He hugs my waist and I wrap my hands around his neck and kiss him while bouncing. He gives me a huge grin. I can't stop smiling. "Yes! Yes! Yes! You can be my roommate!" At this, he lets out a laugh.

He's beaming, but after a few minutes says, "Come on. Let's go tell our friends." When we come out, everybody's in my living room. There's a collective scream, flashes, and what I think sounds like champagne popping.

Best. Proposal. Ever.

Want more of Olivia and Tom? Join my newsletter and get three deleted scenes!
https://books.bookfunnel.com/idaduquebonus

The End

Read Next

The Melody of Love

Don't miss the next story in Ida Duque's Higher Education series!

Meet Valentina! She's outspoken, loyal and fiercely protective of her friends and her students. When her landlord is found dead and his relatives demand she vacates the property, she realizes she's kind of homeless (actually, no, she's really homeless.)

While she ponders her options: she could move in with her friends (maybe,) she could move in with her Latin parents, (probably not,) the last thing she expects is for her mortal enemy to come to her rescue and offer his home. Soon, she can't decide if she wants to kiss the guy or run him over with a truck.

Being roommate with her enemy is not easy and it's not long before she realizes she could lose not only her sanity but (dare she admit it) her heart.

This enemies-to-lovers romcom is "sweet with heat"—the sex is implied, the swearing is real, and the shenanigans are laugh-out-loud funny.

Coming in 2024!!!

Acknowledgments and Thank You's

It takes a village to write a book. I have so many people to thank for helping me with my debut novel. Here are a few:

To Anthony Denito from Wheel Heroes and Rydel Deed from Miami Bike Scene for helping me with the cycling parts, sharing experiences and giving me honest feedback. Thank you!

To Mary Smith from The Chick Lit Shop: Mary was one of the first people to read this book. In the middle her first time reading it, COVID hit and apparently never left. Mary, thank you for sticking with it, and also for being my unofficial book coach. I really enjoy our conversations. Thank you!

To Shika Tamaklo. I found you on Fiveer and it has been life changing. Thank you for reading this several times over the course of the past couple of years and always giving me honest feedback and perspective.

To Tracie Banister and the ChickLitHQ: This was the first writing group I ever joined. For all of the helpful advice (writing and non-writing), the laughs, the invaluable interactions, the networking and so much more, thank you!

To my first ever critique partners: Lucy Beach, Paula Mills and Audrie, I loved getting to know you guys. Too bad COVID cut it short but one of these days we should try again. Lucy, I really appreciate all of your help, the kind thoughts and the helpful suggestions every time I email you about a story.

To everyone in the 20booksto50k © and SPFs community. My deepest thanks to Craig Martelle & Michael Anderle, and Mark Dawson & James Blatch. For the inspiration, the learning, the amazing communities, the laughs (I can't look at dinosaurs without thinking of you guys LOL.) Thank you for being gentlemen and sharing the information so freely for the benefit of hundreds. People are quick to judge and slow to give thanks or acknowledge others, but you guys are doing incredible work, changing lives and many of us do appreciate it. From me and many others, Thank you!

To the new friends I made at the 20books Conference in Vegas: authors Crystal Ferry, Evelyn Mae, Kelly Brakenhoff, Lori Briley, and a few others. Thank you for the amazing conversations and for so much advice! Huge shoot-out, to my 20books roommate and all-around awesome person, author Kimberly Kennedy.

To Jenna Moreci. Thank you for your free writing advice on YouTube. You're literally teaching thousands of writers how to write better and as an educator, I love that! More than that, thank you for speaking openly about what healthy relationships should look like. I have little girls and this means the world. Thank you!

To Sacha Black and Daniel Willcocks from the Next Level Authors: 2020 sucked. Homeschooling, aka the fifth circle of hell, killed my mojo. Then I found you guys. I write romantic comedy, I respond well to humor and shenanigans, and you guys are so much fun to watch together. Thank you!

To author Annabel Costa: thank you for all the conversations. I really appreciate the words of wisdom! I love that we love our jobs (and our careers) and we love writing. When I talk to you, I know it's possible to have both.

To author Rich Amooi: thanks for brainstorming tittles with. Also, for always taking the time to answer my questions.

To Susan Traynor: my amazing cover designer, who skillfully takes my ideas and random thoughts and makes amazing art with it. I love my covers! Thank you!

To my BETA readers: Mary Smith, Shika Tamaklo, Michael Camarillo: Thank you so much for being so nice and professional and for helping me. Initially, I struggled to find editors but I love working with you guys. Your input and thoughtful comments always make my stories better.

To my developmental editor, Karie Crawford, and my copy editor Mary Yakovets: OMG! I'm so lucky to have found you guys! You guys complete me (LOL) In all seriousness, I feel that you guys "got me" from the beginning and never tried to change me or my voice and for that, I'm eternally grateful. Thank you!

To my mom, thank you for all you do for us. I love you.

To my husband and daughters, I love you guys so much!

Also by Ida

If you haven't yet, check out my other stories!

The Humor of Love, Ralph & Gabby's story, a second chance romance, is the entry point to my series "Sunny Beach University," and it has all of the characters from the upcoming books!
Free if you join my newsletter or you can buy (for .99) in a variety of online retailers: https://books2read.com/u/bOz6RK

The Academy of Love, Olivia & Tom's story, it's my debut office romcom with grumpy/sunshine vibes and book one of the series. You can get it for $2.99 or free with KU! Join my newsletter and check out some deleted scenes!
Book 2 of SBU: The Melody of Love, Valentina & Keith's story, is an enemies-to-lovers, close-proximity romantic comedy and Book 3 of SBU: The Balance of Love. a friends-to-lovers romcom are coming in 2024! Stay tuned for the pre-order links!

The "Sunny Beach Bed and Breakfast" series is complete! Check out the seven complete novellas. These are all under 28,000 words and can be read in about two hours:

A Christmas Love for the Dean, about the dean of Sunny Beach University, Carlos, and his love Leyla (Olivia's room-mate!)

Inn Close Proximity. It's the story of Julie & Alex.

Inn Love with the Latin Nerd, is about Christy and Jason.

Inn Love and Money, is Alma & Luca's story.

Inn for the Moment, features Maria and Santiago.

Inn the Wildthe last story in the series, is about Liliana and Leo.
Bonus story: Cuffs and Stethoscopes, a second chance romantic comedy featuring Kate, Alex's sister, and her love Nick. Get it for FREE if you join my newsletter.
If you like second chance romance, check out the Sunny Beach University Second Chance Romance Set. It has three second-chance stories/novellas: The Humor of Love, Christmas with the Dean and Cuffs & Stethoscopes. You can find it in all of your favorite retailers in both eBook and paperback formats!

About Author

Ida Duque writes sweary, sweet with heat, romantic comedies with a Miami flair. Actually, if she's being honest, it's more like loud, crazy Miami-infused romcom. Her books feature smart sassy women who love life, family and each other and are hoping to find true love. Also, there's kissing...lots of kissing!

Ida is a Higher Education professional writing romantic comedy under a pen name, mostly because college students are not impressed by "kissing books." She loves her students and working on campus and there's nothing else in the world she'd rather do. but she also loves writing stories and entertaining. A pen name seemed like a good compromise.

A native of a beautiful island in the Caribbean, these days Ida lives in South Florida with her husband and two kids, one of whose future plans include becoming "the boss of Miami." Seriously. Ida's loving every minute of raising her but will welcome parenting tips on dealing with aspiring dictators. There are currently no playgroups in their area organized for fiercely independent kids also interested in political machinations and autocracy.

Sign up to my newsletter and stay up to date on all new releases and bonus content! Here's where to find me:

Facebook –
https://www.facebook.com/idaduquewriter

Instagram –
http://instagram.com/idaduquewrites

Twitter –
https://twitter.com/DuqueWriter/

My website –
https://www.idaduque.com/

Join my Newsletter –

https://books.bookfunnel.com/idaduquebonus
Email me at:
idaduquewriter@gmail.com or ida@idaduque.com